Yourself
at Home

Ciara Geraghty lives in Dublin with one husband, three children and an adopted dog. *Make Yourself at Home* is her eighth novel. You can find out more about Ciara's books on Facebook and Instagram @CiaraGeraghtyBooks, or Twitter @ciarageraghty.

Acclaim for Ciara Geraghty:

'Tender, emotional and uplifting . . . I loved it'
Lucy Diamond, bestselling author of *The Promise*

'*Rules of the Road* had me laughing and crying on the same page . . . such a talented writer'
Patricia Scanlan,
bestselling author of *A Family Reunion*

'Tender, funny, and heartbreaking . . . Ciara Geraghty is a wonderful writer'
Hazel Gaynor,
bestselling author of *The Bird in the Bamboo Cage*

'Very funny, very moving'　　　　　　　　　　*Irish Times*

'A genuine feel-good hit . . . Geraghty's tightly wound adventure is as touching as it is entertaining'　　　*Irish Independent*

Also by Ciara Geraghty

Saving Grace
Becoming Scarlett
Finding Mr Flood
Lifesaving for Beginners
Now That I've Found You
This is Now
Rules of the Road

Make Yourself at Home

Ciara Geraghty

HarperCollinsPublishers

HarperCollins*Publishers* Ltd
1 London Bridge Street,
London SE1 9GF

www.harpercollins.co.uk

HarperCollins*Publishers*
1st Floor, Watermarque Building, Ringsend Road
Dublin 4, Ireland

First published by HarperCollins*Publishers* 2021
1

Rita's Recipes courtesy of Niamh Geraghty

A catalogue record for this book is available from the British Library

ISBN: 978-0-00-832073-7

Typeset in Birka by
Palimpsest Book Production Ltd, Falkirk, Stirlingshire

Printed and bound in the UK by CPI Group (UK) Ltd, Croydon CR0 4YY

This b

For

For Grace, who makes this house a home every day

Chapter 1

Optimistic people might say that the good thing about hitting rock bottom is that there is nowhere to go but up. Marianne Cross was not one of those people.

Marianne, an accountant in both profession and nature, was a numbers person.

You knew where you were with numbers.

Take the number 435821, for instance. That was the number of the District Court case.

Another number was 84: the number of times Marianne had shoplifted.

Then there was the number of times Marianne had got caught shoplifting: 1. The age Marianne was when she began her shoplifting career: 13. A prime number. Then there was 35. A composite number and the age Marianne was when she married Brian.

The number of years Marianne had managed to remain married: 4. The number of children Marianne wanted: 0.

Which, incidentally, was the same number of children Brian had said he wanted, too.

The number of children Brian was now expecting with his new partner, Helen: 2.

These and other numbers scrolled through Marianne's head that morning when she arrived back at her childhood home.

The circulation figure of the national newspaper where Marianne's crime had been reported in the 'Court News' column: 79,254. The times Marianne's boss apologised during her 'You're fired' speech: 8. The amount of euros by which Marianne was in arrears when the bank repossessed her home: 150,000.

Marianne opened the passenger door and stepped out of her mother's ancient Jeep. She straightened, looked at the house. Another number came to mind. This one was 15. Her age when she had left this place.

She had resolved never to come back and yet here she was.

That's what rock bottom really meant.

No place else to go.

Chapter 2

The house was called Ancaire, named for a granite rock on the beach below, with the curved top of an anchor. Marianne always thought it an appropriate name.

Already she could feel the weight of it, bearing her down. She stamped her feet against the soggy earth to encourage some blood into her toes, wrapped her arms around her body in an attempt to ward off the worst of the bitter easterly wind that tore in from the sea, burdened with the salt water that went to work on her hair, transforming it from barely manageable to frizzy briars, dripping and dense.

'Are you all right, darling?' Marianne opened her eyes. She had almost forgotten about her mother. Which was not something many people could be accused of. Rita's dress sense alone prevented that.

Marianne wondered, not for the first time, why her mother's rig-outs – for there was no other word for them – never paid the slightest attention to the prevailing weather.

Nothing about her headscarf – a bright snatch of orange silk arranged in a turban around her head – or the sleeveless pink summer dress underneath a blood-red bolero jacket suggested insulation or warmth. And the dullness of the day made her enormous sunglasses foolishly redundant. Rita launched herself in Marianne's direction, stopping in front of her with barely an inch between them, reaching up to settle her hands on Marianne's shoulders. Marianne could smell cigarettes and coffee and the herbal perfume Rita insisted on spraying not only on herself but also on innocent by-standers. She smelled like the sap of the dock leaves Marianne used to rub on Flo's nettle stings when they were children.

'Are you going to park?' Marianne asked, stepping away so that Rita's arms hung, suspended in the air for a moment. She lowered them, smoothing the material of her dress down the generous curve of her hips. She turned her head towards the Jeep, which had an abandoned look about it, strewn as it was across the grass, its ridged wheels sinking into the muck. It was an old army vehicle, the tarpaulin at the back torn and billowing in the wind like wings so that the leaking, rusting contraption looked as if it might take flight at any moment. Unlike the enormous rooster, now perched heavily on the roof.

'I am parked,' said Rita, setting the rooster on the ground. 'I told you not to go up there, Declan,' she told him. 'You fell off last time, remember?' The rooster scanned Rita with beady black eyes. 'Go and find Gerard. That old goat will let anyone perch on him.' Rita's fingers tickled the bright comb of feathers sprouting from the rooster's head. Marianne lifted her two suitcases out of the Jeep.

'You're travelling light,' said Rita.

For one horrible moment, Marianne thought she would cry. Cry in front of her mother like she was still a baby who didn't know any better. She set the suitcases down and pretended to cough instead. Rita whacked her on the back and Marianne stumbled forward. Her mother was stronger than she looked. She'd forgotten that.

She turned and took in the house.

It hadn't changed. Still the same crumbling quality, the suggestion that it was only a matter of time before it succumbed to the lure of the cliff edge. The tall, grey façade was mostly covered now by the ivy that her late father, William, had occasionally tried to tame. At least the riotous greenery hid some of the decay of the ancient sash windows. Marianne could hear the panes of glass rattle in their tall frames in protest at the cutting wind that slashed across this exposed hilltop. And behind the house, the roar of the sea battering the coastline, dragging it away, piece by piece, year after year. One day, Marianne would arrive at this place and there would be nothing left.

She shivered, tightened the coil of her arms around herself and squeezed her eyes shut. But even then, in the sudden darkness, she could see the house: the steep pitch of the roof, the bald patches where some of the slate tiles had come away, the precarious slant of the chimney pots. The heavy slab of the wood-panelled front door, its paint peeling and the brass of the lion's-roar door knocker faded with the passing of the years and the gripping of hands.

When Marianne opened her eyes. Rita was kneeling at the front door, her hand buried in the soil of a chipped terracotta planter out of which nothing but weeds grew.

'Here it is,' she said, drawing a large silver key out from beneath the clay. She banged it on the side of the planter to get the muck off it, then used it to open the door. Already, Marianne could smell the house. A damp smell, reaching for her like hands. Something of a greenhouse about it. Organic, like the house was alive in some way. Breathing.

Rita held the door open. Marianne picked up the suitcases. The handles dug into the tender skin of her long, bony hands and she refused to think about the fact that everything she now owned could be accommodated within them. She negotiated her way inside, careful not to come into contact with either Rita or the door, like a child avoiding cracks on a pavement. Perhaps she thought that if she managed not to touch anything, she could somehow make it back home. Back to her house on Carling Road. It had been a new build in Drumcondra when she and Brian had bought it for an outrageous amount of money at the height of the boom. Still, even with the starkness of the repayments she entered into her household accounts spreadsheet, it had been worth it. The house paid homage to all the things that Marianne valued. Things like insulation. And security. Central heating that responded to the touch of a button instead of having to be coaxed and enticed and whacked betimes with one of Rita's rolled up copies of *Vanity Fair*.

Marianne walked down the hallway, concentrating on the black and white tiles on the floor, arranged in diamonds. The dado rail. The wallpaper, the pattern of which was long forgotten with the many coats of paint it had endured over the years.

Rita followed her. Now, as well as the damp, Marianne

could smell the fake tan on Rita's legs, which did little to conceal the clumps of swollen blue veins that bulged at the back of her knees.

The door into what her grandparents had called the drawing room, and where Marianne's parents had once hosted their frequent and elaborate dinner parties, was closed.

From behind the door, a cacophony of voices.

'What's that?' asked Marianne warily.

'The Get-Well-Sooners,' said Rita, smiling.

The voices were chanting now.

Get Well Soon.
How?
Don't drink and sing this tune.
When?
Every day, starting today, you'll
Get. Well. Soon.

'That seems fairly . . . straightforward,' Marianne said.

Rita did not rise to her dismissive tone. Instead, she said, 'I left them here while I went to collect you.'

'On their own?'

'They're fully grown adults, Marnie,' said Rita.

'My name is Marianne.'

Get Well Soon™ was what Rita called her programme. She insisted on the ™ even though Marianne was pretty sure she had never actually registered it as a trademark. She had been running the programme since she got sober and realised that AA wasn't a good fit for her, the acknowledgement of a 'Higher Power' not being within her gift. She also disliked the perpetual aspect of AA, the idea that alcoholism was a disease from which you could never recover. Her Get Well Soon™ philosophy was more upbeat, Rita felt, with its use of the word 'soon' and its presumption of recuperation.

Membership was largely informal and word-of-mouth based. There was no hard-and-fast rule about how long you could stay. As long as it took, was Rita's rule of thumb.

'Besides,' went on Rita, 'Patrick was with them earlier. Teaching them how to whittle.'

'Where is he now?' said Marianne. 'Putting out the fires in the Amazon, I suppose?' Her tone was caustic. When she was within a certain circumference of Rita, she couldn't seem to help reverting to a version of herself that was both childish and churlish.

'He's putting solar panels in the roof,' Rita said. 'The power of the sun is an amazing thing. And free to all. Patrick says—'

'What room should I put my cases in?' Marianne cut in. Couldn't her mother wait until she took her anorak off before she started waxing lyrical about bloody Patrick? She supposed he could be described as . . . what? Her foster brother, maybe? He was eleven when he came to live with Rita that winter. Marianne was fifteen and had persuaded her mother to let her leave the local day school and enrol in a boarding school on the other side of the country. William left that summer, too, shortly after Rita stopped drinking. Those two events were not unrelated.

Patrick was one of a long line of children Rita began fostering after she got sober and William left and Marianne left. Most of the foster kids stayed for a matter of days or weeks, but Patrick never left. On his eighteenth birthday, Rita had given him a half-acre at the north-eastern edge of Ancaire on which he had built a carpentry workshop with an apartment above it, and cultivated a kitchen garden that was, of course, rude with abundant growth, no matter what the season. He insisted on paying a mortgage on the property but Rita just squirrelled the money away for him. She had given Marianne the details of the account, for safekeeping. 'You're good with money,' she had said.

That had been true once.

Patrick was as much a fixture at Ancaire as Rita and Aunt Pearl, who was not really Marianne's aunt but Rita's father's cousin. When Rita inherited Ancaire from her parents, she had also inherited Aunt Pearl.

'Put the suitcases in your bedroom, of course,' said Rita. She glanced at the clock. 'The Get-Well-Sooners are finishing up now,' she said, beaming. 'They're dying to meet you.'

'I don't want to meet them.'

'Of course you do. They're darlings.'

Rita opened the door and strode into the drawing room, clapping her hands for attention. 'Everybody, this is Marnie. Marnie, everybody.'

Marianne stood at the door, the outsider looking in. It was a familiar condition but no less awkward for that. The room seemed crammed although there were only four people inside. Two women, two men. One was a young woman, maybe twenty-five, who studied Marianne with long, navy eyes like she was a foreign film with no subtitles. In the weak January sun struggling through the windows, the rings in the woman's nose, chin and along her ears glinted, as did the silver studs across the shoulders of her black leather jacket. It was difficult to tell what colour her hair was, since her head was shaved clean. Her maroon leather skirt struggled to cover the gusset of her tights, the legs of which ended in a pair of white wedge-heel trainers, with laces the same shade of red as her lipstick.

'You don't look like a Marnie,' the young woman said. She had a hoarse voice and her tone was one of deep suspicion.

'I'm not,' said Marianne. 'I'm a . . . Marianne.' Everyone smiled as if Marianne had said something amusing.

'Well, I'm a Shirley,' she said, snapping a wad of chewing gum around her mouth. 'I'm getting evicted too.'

'I wasn't evic—'

'Eviction, repossession, same shit, different class,' said Shirley, shrugging.

'How do you do?' The other woman, a diminutive elderly lady, buried beneath layers of cardigans, shuffled towards Marianne in an enormous pair of woollen slipper-boots. She stretched out an ancient, arthritic hand and slipped it into Marianne's. It felt like a small bundle of twigs. Marianne held it rather than shook it.

'Ethel Abelforth,' the woman said. 'Delighted to make your acquaintance.' She smiled a sweet, little old lady smile. She looked a most unlikely addict with her blue rinse, freshly set in stiff curls. Rita would not approve of such thinking, insisting that addiction was an equal opportunities condition.

'I'm sorry to hear about your young man,' Ethel went on, her brown eyes enormous behind thick spectacles and concern plaguing her features.

Marianne withdrew her hand and glared at Rita. 'Is there anything you haven't told them?' she snapped.

One of the men stepped forward and examined Marianne's face. 'She failed to impress upon us how beautiful you are.' He splayed a set of short, fat fingers across his cheeks. 'Why, in this light, you're like a young Katharine Hepburn.'

'Hashtag, objectification,' piped up Shirley.

'Hashtag, can't a man compliment a woman anymore?' he said. He was immaculately turned out in a three-piece suit, the buttons of his waistcoat straining against his stomach, across which a thick gold watch chain stretched. His hair was dyed black and was slick with gel at the sides, while the top was arranged in a buoyant quiff. He lifted one of Marianne's hands and bowed his head. 'Bartholomew Sebastian Doyle the third, recovering alcoholic, at your service,' the man said. Then, without warning, he pulled her into an all-encompassing hug that left her stinking of Paco Rabanne. Marianne coughed and extricated herself from his embrace.

'You might be an alcoholic but, as I have said repeatedly, I only occasionally drink problematically.' This came from the other man, a twitchy specimen, wearing a limp brown corduroy jacket with leather patches at the elbows.

'I hear the Nile is beautiful this time of year,' said Bartholomew, catching Marianne's eye so he could wink at her.

The stick man, long and narrow, with watery grey eyes and thinning grey hair, pushed his wire-framed glasses with small round lenses up the bony ridge of his nose and studied the ceiling. He mouthed counting to ten, which, as someone who often had to resort to such measures,

Marianne could relate to. 'Freddy Montgomery,' he said then, nodding briskly at her. 'I'm a local businessman so let me know when you're ready to start job-hunting and I may have some contacts for you.'

'Ha,' shouted Bartholomew, but Rita put her hand on the shoulder of his suit jacket and he fell silent.

'That won't be necessary,' said Marianne. 'I won't be staying long.'

'You can stay as long as you like, Marnie,' said Rita.

'Once I get myself sorted, I'll be on my way'

'Well,' said Freddy, 'all the same, let me know if you need—'

'I won't need anything,' Marianne said. She picked up her cases and marched out of the room. She closed the door behind her, stood in the cavernous chill of the hallway. From inside the room, there was silence. They might be whispering. They were probably whispering. She didn't care. About any of them. She couldn't even remember their names. She had been tired when she arrived and now she was exhausted. The kind of exhaustion that feels damp and cold. As if Ancaire was already seeping under her skin.

Chapter 3

The bedroom hadn't changed much. Two narrow single beds on opposite sides with matching candlewick bedspreads, the buttery yellow faded now to a porridge grey. Marianne moved automatically to her bed, taking care not to step over the line she had drawn down the middle of the room in indelible marker years before.

Old habits are the hardest ones to kill.

The bookshelf at the end of Marianne's bed housed her collection of Encyclopaedia Britannica. She had asked for one from 'Santa' every Christmas, although she couldn't remember a time when she actually believed. The racket Rita and William used to make, fumbling about the bottom of the beds with the stockings, while Marianne pretended to be asleep.

The owl posters, at the foot and head of the other bed, were faded by years of daylight, curling at the corners, their eyes fixed on Marianne, as if they were waiting for an answer to a question that she had long forgotten asking.

Even the curtains were the same. Blue and yellow Paddington Bear ones. The sticker on Paddington's suit-case: 'If lost, please return to Darkest Peru.' For years, Marianne had thought that Darkest Peru was a person. Someone exotic.

She set down her cases on either side of the door. She had taken no keepsakes from her house but one of the cases contained a small porcelain owl. She had wrapped it in tissue paper, pushed it inside a sock, then a slipper, which she had wrapped in a towel. And an Aran cardigan.

She hoped that had been enough to protect it from Rita's unorthodox driving style and the lack of any semblance of suspension in her ancient Jeep.

Through the bedroom window, the garden. Although it wasn't so much a garden as a vast field, the end of which dropped suddenly and treacherously to the sea, some fifty metres below. The rooster was now perched on top of a threadbare donkey with inexplicably perky ears. Chickens pecked in the dirt beneath the canopy of a homemade run beside a luxurious-looking coop. At the far end of the field was Patrick's apartment, with his workshop below, the double doors flung open as usual, as if it wasn't winter and he wasn't teetering on the edge of a sodden, wind-swept cliff. In front of the workshop was his kitchen garden, infuriatingly neat and robust, around which a long-horned goat performed jerky little jumps that seemed involuntary, like a nervous tic.

Beyond the garden, it was difficult to tell where the sea ended and the sky – leaden and low – began. When people found out where Marianne grew up, they always seemed delighted about the proximity of the sea, the prospect of living on a bluff, which must seem, they felt, like being marooned on your very own island.

Marooned was an apt word, Marianne thought.

No matter how precarious the purchase of the house to the edge of the bluff looked, it clung on. It was a bit like Rita, Marianne thought. Indestructible. It had been built by an American – a pork belly trader called Ron Stark – in the spring of 1930 for the love of his life, Julia. Ron had fancied himself the romantic type, and a brooding house flanked by nothing but raging water and hard rock and rich earth and huge sky might have seemed in keeping with this notion of himself.

A year later, he had boarded up the house and fled back to Vermont. He did not put it up for sale, so certain was he that no one in their right minds would purchase such a monstrosity.

He was wrong.

That summer, the summer of 1931, Rita's parents bought the house. They had made an accidental fortune by writing and illustrating a series of 'How to . . .' books. Their subjects were random – *How to Sketch Toes and Other Peripherals*, *How to Comfortably Live Beyond Your Means*, *How to Sleep, Perchance To Dream* – but what made the books sell like hot cakes were Archibald and Ruby themselves. While they wrote and drew pictures relating to, for example, edible seaweed, they also – wittingly or otherwise – revealed themselves to their readers, who couldn't get enough of them.

Their most popular edition was entitled *How to Raise a Good Girl*, written during the first few tender months of Rita's life. In later years, they had to concede – privately, at least – that their only child could not be relied on to prove the thesis of their book.

Some of the books were still in print although their continued success was mostly down to an ironic sense of nostalgia. Still, the modest book sales were enough to sustain Rita in her current incarnation, the material demands of which, Marianne had to concede, were minimal. This dribble of income was also the reason why Rita – an artist – could refuse to sell any of her paintings on the grounds that her work would be contaminated and compromised by such a gross act of commercialism. As would she.

Marianne sat on the edge of the bed and thought about unpacking. And she should probably have a shower. Change her clothes. Had she brushed her teeth this morning? She must have. She couldn't remember. There was a sour taste in her mouth. She should brush her teeth. Drink some water. Instead, she allowed her body to sag sideways until her head was on the pillow, then she pulled her legs onto the bed. She was too tired to unlace her runners so she let them hang over the edge.

She shouldn't be tired. She hadn't done anything today. Or any other day. Only sit and wait for the axe to fall, which it had been doing, bit by bit, since Brian left her twelve months ago.

Sometimes, she still couldn't believe it. How thoroughly everything had fallen apart in the end. How quickly. They'd mapped everything out, her and Brian. Their lives. Just the two of them. That would be enough. For both of them. That's what they'd agreed. Marianne had even worked out when they would die. Not in a morbid sense. More of an actuarial equation that provided an estimate – loose, granted – based on variables such as diet, exercise, environment, genetics, etc., notwithstanding external factors such as an apocalyptic event or something more ordinary but none the less catastrophic, such as a road traffic accident or being mauled to death by a pit bull.

Even when Brian left, Marianne had managed. She had managed to keep the house on Carling Road. It seemed imperative to keep the house. She used all her savings, buying Brian's share. It hadn't been enough so she'd remortgaged. Which was tight but manageable, with her salary. She was sure she would have kept on managing if she hadn't been caught shoplifting. She hadn't planned on doing it that day. She thought it had something to do with Brian's news. About Helen. Expecting the babies. The twins.

And then the shoplifting. She had done it almost without noticing. But the security guard had noticed.

'It's just . . . it looks bad,' Marianne's boss had said, after she was convicted. 'I mean, if you'd done something else, like, I don't know, stalking or something, it wouldn't look so bad. You know? But an accountant who steals. It's too hard a sell, Marianne. For our clients. I hope you understand?'

'Of course I understand,' snapped Marianne.

No salary. No savings. It was only a matter of time before the bank started asking questions. At first, they wrote to her. Polite but firm letters, which Marianne ignored. Then the phone calls, which she didn't answer, her voicemail box crammed with messages she didn't listen to. She just sat in her house and waited for the axe to fall.

She felt there should be some sense of relief, now that

it had finally fallen. She had imagined that waiting for the worst to happen might be the worst bit.

But now that the worst had happened, she realised – too late – that the waiting hadn't been that bad. With hindsight, the waiting had been almost pleasant. Because she had waited in the comfort of her own house.

Her home.

She must have dozed off because the dinner gong, when it sounded, caused Marianne to jerk awake and bite her tongue, the sharp pain of which brought her back to the present moment, which in turn brought her back to the realisation that the worst had happened.

Rita stood at the door of the dining room, pounding on the lid of a biscuit tin with a wooden spoon. Her sunglasses were perched on top of her turban, which was bright pink now. She had changed for dinner, Marianne noticed, and was wearing a ballet-length emerald-green satin dress, with a sweetheart bodice, out of which her breasts spilled, like they were jostling for position. Marianne felt cold just looking at her.

'There you are, Marnie,' Rita shouted over the noise, beaming.

'Can you stop banging that thing?' said Marianne.

'What did you say, darling?'

'Can you stop it!' Marianne raised her voice just as Rita stopped whacking the tin.

'There's no need to shout,' said Rita. She set the tin on top of a stack of self-help books on the hall table and tossed the wooden spoon inside it. 'Now come along, everyone's waiting for you.'

'Everyone?' Marianne's gut twisted at the word. Even

before Brian left her, they had eaten their dinner on trays balanced on their knees while watching the news. Or *Nationwide*, during tax return season, when they sometimes had to work later than usual. They had never formally introduced a conversation embargo during mealtimes. There had been no need.

The dining room was still the draughtiest room in the house. This was largely due to the enormity of the tiled fireplace, out of which gushed the wind, freshly arrived from the Arctic, it seemed. It was a big room and had been elegant in its day with its high ceiling framed by an ornate margin of coving, a wide bay window across which the heavy, velvet curtains had been pulled, and the chandelier still lording it over the table, albeit grimier than Marianne remembered and missing some crystal pendants.

'You finally decided to grace us with your presence.' Aunt Pearl's tone was as pointed as the collar of her blouse. Marianne didn't have to look to know that she was wearing a tweed A-line skirt, thick flesh-coloured tights and sturdy brown leather lace-ups. She had been wearing only very slight variations on that outfit for as long as Marianne could remember and, when she walked, she emitted a strong smell of camphor.

'Now sit down so we can eat.' Despite the thin quality of Pearl's voice, it had a remarkable capacity for disapproval. Even when she was just asking someone to pass the milk jug down the table. Marianne thought it had something to do with her mouth; the set, bloodless line of it.

Pearl was a collection of rigid bones that poked through the pale blue film of her skin. Her hair, coarse and grey, was restrained in its usual bun at the nape of her neck.

Six-year-old Marianne had asked her, one Halloween, if she was a witch and Aunt Pearl had never forgiven her for it.

'Hello, Aunt Pearl,' Marianne said. 'It's . . . nice to see you.'

'Don't be ridiculous, Marianne,' snapped Aunt Pearl. 'Nobody thinks it is nice to see me. Why on earth would they? Yet here I am, all the same. Now, can we please eat?' She glared at Rita, who beamed as if Pearl had complimented her dress.

'Certainly,' Rita said, moving towards the door. 'I'll serve up now.' She disappeared out of the room, towards the kitchen.

'Hello, Marianne.' She looked around and there was Patrick, standing and pulling a chair out for her before resuming his place beside Aunt Pearl, his bulky frame making the old woman seem even frailer. 'It's nice to see you,' he said.

Pearl glared at him, then at Marianne as if perhaps she had missed something on her initial inspection. She shook her head, then busied herself with her serviette, tucking it into the high-collared neckline of her blouse.

'Hello, Patrick,' said Marianne, sitting down. She reached for the jug of water but Patrick was already lifting it, filling her glass. Typical. He reminded Marianne of a pit bull terrier, bald and stocky, hard lengths of muscle barely contained beneath his Metallica T-shirt. Along his arms and up his neck were tattoos of animals – snakes, leopards and sharks mostly. When he spoke – which he did as seldom as possible – his voice was so soft and faint, people strained to hear him.

Marianne met Patrick when she returned from boarding

school at mid-term break. She shrugged as she always did when her mother introduced her to the children she fostered. Perhaps because she associated them with her mother's sobriety, which seemed to Marianne, back then, fragile and transient.

Patrick was one of those kids who had been in many foster homes, always for brief periods before being returned, like faulty goods, to State care. There were reasons, of course. There are always reasons. An addict mother, who overdosed when Patrick was seven. A drug-dealing father, who got sent to prison when Patrick was nine.

Patrick's social worker whispered to Rita that he was convinced the boy was a psychopath. Or a sociopath. 'Which is the one who's not charming?' he wondered.

Rita ignored him.

Marianne didn't see Patrick until the third day of that long mid-term, when she had completed the holiday work her teachers had set for her and was mooching about, trying simultaneously to avoid Rita and find something of interest to engage her. Instead she found Patrick, small and scrawny back then, straddling the branch of an oak tree with a slingshot and a collection of vicious stones, his eyes trained on a bird's nest perched at the end of a slender branch above his head.

'Don't you dare,' Marianne hissed up at him. Patrick shifted his position and stared at her. He picked up one of the stones and slotted it into the elastic band, which he pulled taut, aiming it right between her eyes. Marianne didn't flinch. She glared at him with her hands on her hips. It was Rita, in the end, who saved them. Inadvertently, of course.

She rang the gong for lunch. That was also new. The gong. And regular mealtimes. The worst of it was Rita's newfound penchant for cooking. Which wouldn't have been so bad if she wasn't so awful at it that first year. Everything was either soggy or hard as nails. There was no middle ground. Not with Rita.

Now, twenty-five years later, Patrick was still here, still hanging on to Rita's every word, grateful as a pound puppy who finds his 'forever home'.

And Rita encouraging him. Telling him all her secrets. Seeking his counsel on every tiny thought that passed through her head.

It drove Marianne crazy, the way the two of them went on. Like one couldn't do without the other.

Rita pushed a silver trolley on sputtering wheels into the dining room. 'Everybody hungry?' she said as she wafted her way around the table, taking the long way and unleashing her scent as she went. A cloying mix of figs and roses, Marianne thought, burying her nose in her napkin. Patrick lifted the heavy silver soup tureen from the trolley onto the table.

'Thank you, my boy,' said Rita, patting his arm. She lifted the lid of the tureen. The smell was immediate and delicious, in spite of its alarmingly bright green colour. 'Garden peas and mint soup,' Rita said by way of explanation, when she clocked the distrust on Marianne's face. She dished up and sat down.

'Eat up, everyone,' she said, sitting down. 'It'll get cold.'

For a few moments, nobody spoke, not even Rita. The silence wasn't awkward as such. And even if it was, Marianne was disinclined to do anything about it, given how much energy she was expending simply by sitting upright on a chair in a room with people other than herself in it.

There was just the scrape of spoons against bowls, the pat-pat-pat of Pearl's napkin against her mouth, the rattle of Rita's bangles as she reached for a slice of rye bread. Even Patrick's silence made a sound, a low thrumming, like a generator.

Marianne mostly stirred the soup round the bowl with her spoon, dipped pieces of bread into it and watched as the soup stained it green.

After a while, Rita put down her spoon and raised her glass of water and beamed at Marianne. 'I would just like to say . . .' she began.

'Please don't make a speech,' said Marianne.

'I'm not making a speech,' said Rita. 'I merely want to say welcome home.'

Marianne could feel something twist in her gut at the word. Home.

'And I also . . .' Rita went on.

'I thought you weren't going to make a speech?' said Aunt Pearl.

'Okay, fine,' sighed Rita, lowering her glass.

Patrick lifted his. 'Welcome home, Marianne,' he said with a small smile.

Marianne focused on the table. It was a monstrous slab of mahogany, as pockmarked as her teenage acne-riddled face had been. Rita had softened its imperfections by lighting long, slender candles down the middle of it, their flames swaying in the draught, casting yellow light in shaky circles.

'Those things are a fire hazard,' said Aunt Pearl, nodding at the candles and wrapping her shawl tighter around her thin frame. 'I'm a stickler for health and safety but your mother takes no notice.' She shook her head and Marianne fancied she could hear the bones in her neck chafing against each other. The list of things that Aunt Pearl was a stickler for would fill one of Marianne's encyclopaedias but Marianne didn't say that. She didn't say anything.

'How long are you staying?' Aunt Pearl barked then.

'Not long,' said Marianne. 'I'll be leaving as soon as I . . . as soon as I sort things out.'

'So you have a plan then?' said Aunt Pearl, sitting even straighter in her chair.

Patrick picked up his glass and, in her peripheral vision, Marianne could see the sharp angle of his Adam's apple scrape along the taut skin of his throat.

'Give her a chance, Pearl,' said Rita, reaching across the table to collect the empty bowls. 'She only just got here.'

There was a clatter of hoofs, and the long-haired goat Marianne had spotted earlier in the garden ran into the room, doing a lap of the table, stopping beside Rita, sniffing hopefully at the trolley.

'Who let that animal in again?' asked Aunt Pearl icily.

'He must have smelled the peas,' said Rita, bending to pull gently at the goat's long coarse beard. 'You love peas, don't you, Gerard?'

'It's unhygienic,' said Aunt Pearl. 'Animals in a dining room.'

'Gerard keeps himself very well,' said Rita. She stood up and pushed the trolley towards the door, breathing hard as she navigated it over the hump of the saddle board. Gerard trotted after her. With the rattle of the trolley, Rita's high heels and the sharp clip-clip-clip of Gerard's hoofs, Marianne fought an urge to clamp her hands over her ears.

Patrick distributed plates around the table. The same blue and white dinner plates with repeating patterns of ships and anchors and waves. When she was a child, Marianne had had to stand on a kitchen chair to reach them. She'd fry an egg, arrange beans like spokes around it. 'Guess what it is,' she'd say.

'The sun,' Flo would reply.

'Are you all right, Marianne?' Rita asked when she returned, scattering bowls of vegetables around the table. 'Do you not like the couscous? Don't worry, I have mash as well so—'

'I'm fine,' said Marianne. Rita handed her a plate with chunks of turnip and carrot and mushrooms in a dark red sauce dotted with chickpeas and butterbeans and whole cloves of garlic and sprigs of rosemary. Marianne couldn't remember the last time she'd eaten. Had she had breakfast? She often didn't eat before she went to work, but then the cart would come round at eleven and her colleagues would form an orderly queue in front of it and Marianne would be reminded to eat. With the absence of a workplace and the snack cart and her colleagues it hadn't been all that easy to remember, these past months.

She pushed the vegetables around the plate with the fork.

Rita was talking. She had been talking for ages, as far as Marianne could tell.

'. . . so I suggested to Shirley that we . . .'

'Your dinner will get cold,' Marianne said.

'It always does,' said Aunt Pearl.

Rita ploughed on as if nobody had said anything.

'. . . just five minutes in a room with that nasty man and—'

'Most men are nasty,' cut in Pearl. 'You'll have to be more specific.'

'Shirley's landlord. Have you not been listening to a word I've been saying?' Rita shook her head. 'He's ordered Shirley out of her home by the end of April.'

'Is Shirley the single mother?' Aunt Pearl's mouth curled around the words.

'She's the mother of two adorable boys,' Rita said briskly.

'I'm afraid I have met Sheldon and his brother, Harrison,' said Aunt Pearl. 'And adorable is not the adjective that sprang to mind.'

'And,' Rita went on, 'Shirley doesn't even have the benefit of a lease agreement to protect her. Or any help from the PRTB because, of course, that article never registered with them.' She stabbed a chunk of tomato with her fork and waved it about. 'All he cares about is . . .' She looked at Marianne. 'What do you call it?' she asked. 'It's some type of line. People who are obsessed with money are always talking about it.'

'The bottom line,' said Marianne.

Rita beamed. 'That's it,' she said. 'My clever girl.'

Patrick gathered the dinner plates and the tureen and placed them on the trolley. He pushed it out of the room, lifted it over the saddle board like it was a bag of feathers. Rita trailed him. Marianne heard Patrick say something and then Rita's high trill of a laugh, dribbling away as they moved down the corridor, towards the kitchen.

Pearl made a *tsk* noise with her tongue but exactly what

element of the evening she was *tsking* at was unclear. Marianne took off her glasses and worried at them with the edge of her napkin.

'I think they're clean now,' said Aunt Pearl.

Ever since she had started wearing glasses – aged fifteen, during the first week of boarding school, when her maths teacher realised that Marianne was using complicated guesswork to make out the equations on the blackboard – she had taken to them. She favoured heavy, solid frames so there could be no mistaking them, even from a distance. They felt like a shield. They protected her. They announced her. People made assumptions. Serious. Quiet. No nonsense. And even though those assumptions might not be true for everybody, Marianne knew they were true for her.

Marianne slid her glasses back on and Aunt Pearl came into sharp focus. Her silver-blue eyes were undimmed by her many – might she be ninety? – years. Still as clear and glinting as a block of knives. 'Really, Marianne,' said Aunt Pearl, patting her bun to make sure it hadn't budged, which it hadn't because it wouldn't dare to, 'stealing. I really don't—'

'Dessert,' roared Rita, sprinting into the room. Aunt Pearl, who resented her sweet tooth, broke off to inspect the trolley. 'Is that a roulade?' she asked.

'Made from our very own raspberries,' declared Rita.

'Raspberries are not in season,' Pearl sniffed.

'Patrick froze a few batches of them last September,' said Rita, smiling at Patrick, who arrived with a pot of coffee and a jug of cream. The coffee smelled dense and earthy. Marianne never drank caffeine after 4 p.m., but she accepted a cup so she could wrap her cold fingers around it, hold her face over the mug and let the steam fold into her skin, warming it.

'So, what is this Shirley woman going to do?' asked Aunt Pearl, accepting the plate that Rita handed her and guiding it to the table, as gently and carefully as if it were a baby bird that might take flight at any moment.

Marianne said, 'No thank you,' when Rita offered her dessert. She did not have a sweet tooth but even she had to admit that there was something almost beautiful about the curve of raspberries, curling through the circle of thick, wobbly meringue, staining it with their dark pink juice.

'Well,' said Rita, spooning roulade into her mouth and then speaking long before she had swallowed it, 'we're going to stage a sit-in at Shirley's house before the actual day of the eviction.'

'When is the eviction date?' Patrick asked.

Marianne noticed how people sort of froze when Patrick spoke, as if they were afraid that his quiet words might burst like bubbles if they so much as blinked. Aunt Pearl's napkin, held at the corner of her mouth, Marianne's hand reaching for the water jug.

Rita, who had been burrowing for a raspberry that had fallen down the deep valley of her cleavage, recovered first.

'Sometime in April,' she said, bending to lift a bulging diary out of her handbag. She leafed through it. 'Of course, the landlord might have changed his mind by then. If not, we'll throw everything we've got at it. Even Aunt Pearl, if we have to.' She winked at Pearl, who grimaced. 'I can't find it,' she said then, tossing the diary on the table. 'The light in here is too poor.'

'You might be able to see better if you wore the glasses the optician prescribed for you,' sniffed Pearl.

'I don't need glasses, I just need a second opinion,' said Rita, running the pad of her finger around her plate to collect the last of the cream and raspberry juice, licking it noisily.

The diary lay on the table, open on the last week of April. Marianne glanced at it and saw a red X with several exclamation marks and a rudimentary drawing of a matchstick house with matchstick people across the front of it, holding up matchstick placards, each containing a single letter that, together, spelled S.H.I.R.L.E.Y. with love hearts – crayon red – on the placards at either end.

The eviction date, she presumed.

She leaned closer.

It was scheduled for the thirtieth of April.

Marianne retreated in her chair until she reached the back of it, felt the hard lines of wood dig into her shoulders and down her back, concentrated on that sensation, the press of her skin against the chair.

'Marianne?' Rita looked at her. 'You're as white as a sheet.'

'I'm . . . fine,' said Marianne. 'I . . .'

An image of five-year-old Flo bloomed in her mind, as sudden and vivid as a pinprick of blood on the tip of a finger. Flo's first day at school. Marianne letting go of her hand at the school gates. Flo handing Bruno's lead to Marianne, bending to kiss the dog's nose no matter how many times Marianne told her it was unhygienic. Flo's black patent shoes that used to be Marianne's, which she had polished so that they shone like new.

'Aren't you scared?' asked ten-year-old Marianne.

'Of what?' Flo said, her blue eyes wide with curiosity.

'Of going to school,' said Marianne.

When Flo shook her head, her pigtails flew about her head like chair-o-planes.

Marianne stood up, the legs of her chair scraping against the flagstones on the floor, making a grating, shuddering sound. Everybody looked up. Their faces seemed small. Far away. Like Marianne was peering at them through the wrong end of a pair of binoculars.

'I'm not feeling well,' said Marianne. She turned, moved towards the door. It, too, seemed far away, like a door in a dream.

'Do you want me to come with you?' Rita called after her.

Marianne shook her head. The door wouldn't open. Marianne yanked the handle up and down.

'You should take a spoon of cod-liver oil every morning,' declared Aunt Pearl. 'A cure-all.'

Patrick appeared beside Marianne. He performed a complicated, counterintuitive manoeuvre with the handle and pushed at the door which, of course, opened without even a creak of hinge.

'Sometimes it can be difficult,' he said.

Marianne swept past him, into the corridor and up the hall. She took the stairs two at a time, ran the length of the landing, didn't stop until she was safely inside the bedroom, leaning against the closed door.

The room seemed to mock her. As childish as she was, it seemed to suggest, with its unchanged landscape, Flo's bed on the other side of the line, the pillow plump and smooth, the sheets and blankets beneath the counterpane neatly turned and tucked. Marianne knew they were because she had turned and tucked them herself. Every morning. Just as she had turned and tucked her own. She hadn't minded. She had loved the order of the made beds, everything in its place, just as she had left it. It had been the only room in the house that she could count on. Where everything was just so.

Now look at it. The sheets and blankets of Marianne's unmade bed in a tangled clump on the floor. Marianne looked through the window. All she could see was the sea. It looked the same as it always did, the constant movement of the grey water, the curl of the waves closer to shore, their tops frothy and white, the thump of the water against the dark sand, against the sharp rocks, against the base of the cliffs. It had looked the same on the thirtieth of April, twenty-five years ago. It had sounded the same. To Marianne, standing at the window with her face pressed against the glass, it seemed like everything was the same. Nothing had changed.

Not even Flo, who would always be ten. Who had been ten for the past twenty-five years.

Chapter 4

Marianne got into bed in a pair of tracksuit bottoms, one of Brian's old T-shirts, a fleece and a pair of slipper socks. Essentially, her clothes.

In spite of this, Marianne was cold, and the cold, coupled with the rock-bottom condition of her situation, made for a fitful night's sleep. Whenever she woke up, which she seemed to do at intervals, the mean time of which came in at thirty-seven minutes, according to Marianne's calculations, she spent the first few minutes trying to work out where she was. When she remembered, she felt a fresh gush of grief, surprised by the strength of it every time. The way it took her breath away like a punch to the solar plexus. She calmed herself by thinking about a piece of furniture in her home.

Like the splendour of the matching Vienna vases on either side of the hearth in the sitting room, filled with identical artificial flowers. All you had to do was shake the dust off them every few days and they were as good as new.

Not one visitor had noticed that the flowers weren't real. Not that there had been many visitors, Marianne conceded. Mostly Brian's sister, Linda, on her twice-yearly visits from Guernsey. Linda, who had raised Brian after their parents died when he was twelve and she was eighteen, was a taciturn woman. She had never mentioned the artificial flowers although Marianne suspected that had more to do with her disinclination to speak in general.

Marianne had never been keen on inviting people into her home. Ancaire, by contrast, had always been full of strangers. Rita told her daughter that there was no such thing as strangers; just friends who hadn't met.

Brian didn't take any of the furnishings when he left. He said it was only fair, since Marianne had chosen most of them. And gone to such trouble to do so. As if spending a Sunday afternoon in a furniture outlet in Kildare sourcing the perfect coat stand was trouble.

Before she met Brian, she had long since accepted her status as a 'singleton'. Not that she would have classified herself thus. The word implied youth and sinew and suppleness and a future that was not yet squandered. In fact, she embraced it. She lived alone. She slept alone. In her divan bed, so solid that even the most strenuous of tossing and turning would not produce so much as a peep or a creak out of it.

She worked alone. From the spare room in her apartment that she had converted into an office.

She had gone to boarding school alone. Then the scholarship to Queen's University. Her accommodation was tiny and basic. She shared a bathroom with six older girls. The water was never hot when it was her turn for the shower.

The accountancy course was gruelling, with a high drop-out rate. Marianne didn't speak to any of her fellow students and, after a while, they stopped speaking to her.

She graduated top of her year and was offered her pick of jobs. She chose one that allowed her to work from the tiny flat in the apartment block she rented at the top of Griffith Avenue. Marianne liked how secure it felt. And how bright it was, with double-glazed windows looking out over the Tolka river. The back garden was so untamed, none of the other residents ever went out there so it felt like it was all hers and there were nights in the summer when she lay there, hidden by the tall grasses and watched the stars bloom like flowers across the darkening sky.

If company policy hadn't changed, requiring the home-workers to move into the head office in the IFSC, none of this would have happened because she wouldn't have met Brian in the kitchenette on the fifth floor.

At 4.37 a.m., there was a scraping sound which, at first, she ignored. It was probably the branches of the silver birch, laid bare by winter, bent by the wind tap-tap-tapping against the windowpane. After a while she realised the sound was coming, not from the window but the door, and she concluded that it was mice scurrying behind the wain-scoting.

At 4.46 a.m., with the scraping sound growing in intensity, Marianne flung the bedcovers back and quailed against the immediate onslaught of cold that the action produced. She marched to the door, for it was clear now that the sound was coming from the other side of it, and flung it open.

There, his paw cocked in mid-scrape, was a dog. He was

neither young nor old. He was a middle-aged dog. A tall, thin, middle-aged dog, with coarse fur the colour of water left in a sink. A stagnant grey. His eyes fixed on Marianne and he cocked his head to one side, his ears like antennae on his head, upright and quivering.

Marianne shut the door and got back into bed.

Despite the menagerie of animals that Rita facilitated, she had never got another dog after Bruno.

The dog on the other side of the door continued scraping at the door with his nails, which, from the quality of the sound they produced, needed to be cut.

Marianne pushed her head under the pillow, gripping it around her ears, the better to drown out the sound.

The dog continued to scrape but also to whimper, and it was this whimpering sound – aching and forlorn – that felled Marianne in the end.

She wrenched open the door and glared at him. 'What?'

The dog responded by licking at a patch of skin above Marianne's ankle, in the space where her tracksuit bottom ended and the slipper sock began. 'Stop it,' she said, stepping back. The dog walked into the room. He circled the space on the floor beneath Marianne's bed before settling himself there. He glanced at Marianne, who stood at the door. 'Shoo,' she said, pointing out to the landing. The dog blinked slowly, once, twice, then stretched his front paws out in front of him like the slats of a bed, arranged his head there, and fell asleep.

In the end, Marianne, frozen with the cold, had no choice but to get back under the covers. She came at the bed from the bottom to avoid the dog, crawled to the top, wormed her way back inside.

She woke at 5.30 a.m., roused by the dog's snores, each of which was so loud and long, it caused her grandmother's collection of glass in the dresser below to vibrate against the shelves.

When Brian snored, Marianne took to the spare room. She did the same when either of them had a cold. Or a cough. When she had her period. When one or the other of them had to get up earlier than the other the next morning.

All things considered, she had slept in the spare room more often than not.

Now she felt hot. Febrile. She turned onto her side and threw her arm out from the covers to prompt a drop in her temperature. Her hand landed on the dog's coarse, scratchy fur. She snatched it away but the dog, perhaps thinking that she had patted him, stood up and placed his fore-paws on Marianne's bed. She felt the current of his hot, damp breath against her face and drew back. He was not the sort of dog who benefited from close-ups. His thick, matted eyebrows formed an awning over his rheumy amber eyes and spools of drool hung from the corners of his mouth. 'Get down,' Marianne hissed at him. He licked her face. She pushed his paws off the bed and turned towards the wall, pulling the covers over her head so she wouldn't have to see or smell him.

She must have fallen asleep eventually because she dreamed about Brian and Helen, which she sometimes did when her defences were low.

In her dream, Helen was in bed but awake. Perhaps the baby had been kicking and woke her.

No.

Babies.

Two of them.

Twins.

Brian hadn't wanted a baby. Or babies. Neither had Marianne. This communal and fervently held pronouncement formed much of the foundation of their relationship. It was a done deal, as far as Marianne was concerned. Set like cement.

'People change, Marianne,' Brian had said, his tone soft and beseeching.

'I haven't,' she said.

Chapter 5

'Oh, I see you've met George,' said Rita, barging into Marianne's bedroom the next morning and yanking the curtains open.

Daylight flooded the room. It flung itself against Marianne's face, charged into her eyes so that her pupils constricted, leaving her technically blind for a good minute.

Rita bent to pet the dog, who rolled onto his back with his paws splayed so she could rub his belly.

Marianne reached for the beaker of filtered water she kept on her bedside locker before remembering that there was no longer a beaker, there was no longer a bedside locker. She also remembered that she hadn't brushed her teeth last night. She'd been too cold. She fancied she could feel the roots of a tooth loosening in her gum. She could hardly bear the thick, fetid smell of her own breath. She tried and failed to run her hands through her hair. In the absence of the taming product it required – or, indeed, even the benefit of warm water and shampoo – her hair had become matted and dense, like the forest that grew around the castle where Sleeping Beauty had slept for a hundred years.

'You should eat something,' said Rita.

'I'm not hungry.'

'Something nutritious,' Rita went on. 'I'll make chia seed pudding. That'll give you a bit of a lift.' Her face was set with determined optimism as well as a thick layer of pan stick. Today, her turban was white, so bright that Marianne felt it might be dangerous to look directly at it. Rita held her vape pen between two short, fleshy fingers. The vapour smelled of Polo mints and brought to mind the chocolate mint ice cream that Marianne and Brian treated themselves to every Saturday night as they settled down to watch a nature documentary.

'Or I could whip you up a smoothie. I've got avocados and blueberries. You look like you could do with—'

'It's hard to believe you used to count the olives and lemons in your vodka-tonics as two of your five a day,' snapped Marianne.

'That was a long time ago,' said Rita, evenly.

One would almost be nostalgic for the old Rita. The drunken, brawling one. At least you knew where you stood with her. With both of them. Her and William's epic fights, which might start off in the bathroom over the misappropriation of one of their tubes of lip balm and end up in the garden, their drama softened by moonlight, one chasing, the other catching, then vice versa until they seemed to Marianne, with her nose pressed against the bedroom window, like beautifully choreographed blurs of colour, as fascinating and unknowable as shooting stars.

'The hens have been busy this morning,' said Rita, 'if you'd prefer eggs.'

'I thought you were a vegan now,' said Marianne.

'I am,' said Rita. 'Except for eggs. Free-range ones, obviously. And cheese occasionally. But I never drink milk.'

'You hate milk.'

'Come on, darling, get up. You need to bring George for a walk.'

'Why on earth do I need to bring George for a walk?' said Marianne.

Rita pointed at George, who had scrambled onto all fours and was standing at Marianne's bedside, gazing at her.

'Because he's picked you,' said Rita. 'It's about time he picked somebody.'

'You said you'd never get another dog after you got rid of Bruno,' said Marianne. If Rita heard the jagged edge of Marianne's tone, she did not comment on it.

'I wasn't going to,' she said. 'But then George showed up about a month ago, half starved and one paw bleed—'

'I don't need to hear his tragic back story.'

'We fixed him up fine,' continued Rita. 'But up till now, he hadn't picked anyone to be his pack leader. It's like he was waiting for you to arrive.' Rita looked delighted at this turn of events. Marianne did not.

She struggled into a sitting position. Rita took the opportunity to snatch her pillow and punch a bit of life into it. Her collection of bangles jangled against each other and made Marianne want to clamp her hands over her ears. Rita drew the pillow behind her back.

'It's time to get up, Marianne,' she said, and something

about her tone – a hint of authority in it – made Marianne look at her mother. The two women studied each other, perhaps noticing for the first time that they had the exact same eye colour. Not just that their eyes were blue but that they were the same shade of blue, which is to say a gunmetal blue. Nobody would ever recommend that a living room be painted that colour. It must be awful for a mother to look into the face of her middle-aged daughter, Marianne thought. Especially one who is fully dressed, in bed, unemployed and, no doubt, unemployable, alone, homeless. Marianne could go on but thought it wise to stop there. The bottomless capacity of her self-pity remained a surprise to her.

It was only when Rita left that Marianne noticed her mother hadn't stepped across the line in the middle of the room.

Marianne lay back down, idly wondering what Rita had done with the pillow. Her thoughts were like the emails and the phone calls and the instant messages she used to receive in work: they just kept coming.

She missed her job with a savageness she did not know she was capable of. She remembered the T-shirt Brian wore the first time she met him, on one of those awful casual-clothes Fridays. A pale blue cotton T-shirt with navy writing across the front that said, 'Numbers add up. People don't.'

Marianne couldn't have agreed more.

George's head appeared beside hers, regarding her with his curious amber eyes, as if he was waiting for her to say something. To do something.

'What are you plans?' Aunt Pearl had asked.

Marianne didn't have any.

George barked and looked as if he was set to bark some more.

'Okay, fine,' Marianne snapped at him. She kicked off the covers and swung her feet onto the floor. The shock of the cold, even through her thick socks, was like a shot of adrenalin.

'Why are you here?' she hissed at the dog, who now sat on one of her feet, his chest up tight against her legs. He licked her hand and padded to the door, scraped it with his paw. The noise made the fillings in Marianne's mouth vibrate.

'I said fine,' she snapped. The idea of taking off her clothes and subjecting herself to an onslaught of water was exhausting. Instead, Marianne left on the clothes she had worn to bed, adding the scratchy wool cardigan lying on the floor where she had thrown it last night. She thought about the wall of built-in wardrobes in her bedroom in her house. The house that used to be hers. Every boot, shoe, scarf, blouse – everything – had its own particular spot. And now look at her. She tucked the ends of her tracksuit bottoms into her socks, zipped herself into her anorak and clamped a woolly hat on her head.

In the cavernous bathroom, Marianne sat on the edge of the claw-footed bath, its copper long tarnished and stained by the damp of years. The toothpaste fizzed against her gruel-grey tongue, which she scrubbed as vigorously as her teeth. She avoided her face in the mirror but she couldn't help catching a glimpse of it as she stood to turn the water off, the bulging stump of the copper tap requiring two hands to persuade it to yield. Her face had a baggy, creased look about it, like a bag emptied long ago and forgotten at the back of a wardrobe.

In the back kitchen, there was an entire cupboard dedicated to wellington boots. Marianne waded through it until she found a pair in size seven. She pulled these on and opened the back door, ushered George outside. Whereupon he ran. Much faster than Marianne would have given him credit for. A blur of fur, his long ears flying behind him, like they were trying to keep up.

She hadn't thought about a leash.

'George!' Marianne shouted. 'Come back.' George ran to the bottom of the garden and disappeared.

'Oh, bloody hell,' said Marianne. She ran after him. She hated running. She never ran. She didn't understand why anyone would do it voluntarily. All that heaving and gasping and sweating. Now here she was, heaving and gasping and sweating. Because of a dog. Marianne didn't care if she never saw him again but she imagined Rita would not take the news of George's disappearance well.

She set off after George, towards the rickety wooden gate at the bottom of the garden. She reefed it open and it creaked loudly in protest. She slammed the gate behind her, so hard that the gate post, already crooked, listed with a groan until it reached the ground and lay there, as if spent. The wood – splintered and swollen with sea and rain – lay against the hard, bare ground, like some abandoned, useless thing. Was there nothing in this godforsaken place that wasn't falling apart?

From here there were steps to the beach, steep and treacherous, covered with a slick layer of moss.

'George?' she called. From below, a single bark, faint, like an echo of a bark.

'Get back here this instant,' she called. The wind, salty

and stinging, whipped her words away and she had no choice but to navigate the treacherous moss-slick steps.

On the beach, George ran into the water, barking at the waves, turning tail as they crested, barking again when they crashed along the shore before wading back in to begin the process anew. He paid not the slightest attention to Marianne's roared commands to 'Heel, boy'. She faced into the wind and trudged along the beach, her hands bunched into fists and stuffed deep inside her pockets. She tried not to think about anything but she couldn't manage it. She thought about a plan and the fact that she didn't have one, and that thought went round and round her head until it was a blur.

Marianne studied her feet and concentrated on walking, borne along by the elements that always seemed more dramatic here than anywhere else. Thick clouds obscured the sun as it struggled over the horizon, rendering the difference between night and day small and miserable.

When she reached George, he abandoned his post at the water's edge and fell in behind her, silent as a ghost. When she got to the end of the beach and leaned against the rock that was shaped like an anchor, he pawed at a stone near her foot, stood in front of her, expectant.

'I'm not throwing that stone,' Marianne said.

George regarded her with his amber eyes. After a while, he nudged the stone with his nose.

'No,' said Marianne, refusing to look at him. She could feel his breath, warm against her frozen fingers, as if he was thawing them out.

'Okay, fine, I'll throw it once and then that's it, understood?'

George cocked his head to one side. Marianne picked up the stone and hurled it into the sea. The dog launched himself into the water as if it were not dark and cold and January and hopeless. When he returned he dropped the stone at her feet and shook himself. Marianne ran down the beach to avoid the freezing water arcing from his fur, but George followed her, dropped the stone at her feet again.

'No,' said Marianne. 'I mean it.' The wool of her hat was heavy with sea spray and she felt sodden with self-pity.

George barked and Marianne picked up the stone and hurled it again. George chased it, retrieved it, returned it to her.

No matter how far she threw it, the dog found it.

Marianne threw it again.

And again.

Chapter 6

The kitchen was empty when Marianne returned. Rita was probably out rescuing some cat stuck up a tree and Aunt Pearl was likely at mass imploring St Jude – the patron saint of lost causes – to work some sort of miracle for Marianne. Patrick was no doubt in his workshop, fashioning something both useful and beautiful from the gnarled stump of a tree. Or in his apartment, coming up with a grand plan to halt climate change. Or maybe Agnes had stayed over last night and he was making her an egg-white omelette, flavouring it with the herbs he grew in the kitchen garden.

Marianne's nostrils flared. Even Patrick had managed to sustain a relationship. She'd met Agnes a few times. A girlish type of woman, just as quiet as Patrick. She was a librarian, as far as Marianne knew. She had seen them once walking the cliff path. Not talking, just walking, their bare arms sometimes glancing against each other. They seemed happy. Looking at them, you could be fooled into thinking relationships were easy. Effortless.

Marianne wandered through the house, up the stairs, towards the bedroom, George following her no matter how many times she told him not to.

Having no place to be and no tasks to do felt so much more vast, here at Ancaire. She sat on her bed and George sat beside her, resting his head on her knees. She shifted her legs but he just stretched his neck to slot his head back on her knees. She moved down the bed but all he did was shuffle along the floor until he reached her again.

The wardrobe was where it had always been, along the wall at the end of Marianne's bed. It was a monstrosity of a thing, dark with mahogany. The stout, curved legs had long ago settled into the floorboards, the hollow of the dents they had made there smooth and almost ornamental. Marianne put her fingers on the handle.

'If you can't find me, don't worry,' Flo had said, opening the wardrobe door and lifting Bruno inside, before crawling in after him, settling herself beside him against the back of the wardrobe. 'I'll be in Narnia.'

Marianne squeezed her eyes shut. Shook her head to dislodge the memory. But Ancaire was like the past itself, reaching through the years to grip her with both hands, to pull her back.

The wardrobe door released a sigh when Marianne opened it. She winced at the smell: a damp, musty smell, laced with dust and wood.

Empty clothes hangers hung from the rail and moved against each other in the draught, creating an eerie noise, hushed and insistent. On the floor, one white sock. An ankle sock with a yellow rose embroidered on the side. A lacy frill around the top. Marianne's hands gripped the edge of the wardrobe door. She thought briefly about pulling it off its hinges.

Instead, she closed the door, leaned her head against the hard wood. Rage was exhausting, Marianne thought. She favoured quieter emotions, if she had to endure any at all.

But the anger was there all the same. It was in her breath and the ragged way it poured from her mouth. It was in the pounding of her heart in her chest and her ears and at the base of her throat. All that blood, racing and pushing and pulsing about her body and no way to contain it. At least, that's how it seemed to Marianne.

She strode out of the bedroom, ran down the hallway. 'Rita,' she shouted at the top of the stairs. When there was no answer, she shouted again. 'RITA.'

'What on earth is all the racket about?' Aunt Pearl's bedroom door opened and she glared at Marianne, her bony hands clamped on her bony hips.

'I'm looking for Rita.' Marianne's voice sounded hot and strangled. There was spit on her chin. She wiped it away with the back of her hand.

'I managed to work that much out all by myself,' said Aunt Pearl. 'I also worked out that she does not appear to be in the house. I am hoping that you have arrived at a similar conclusion?' She arched her eyebrows into stiff peaks near the top of her forehead.

'Rita has gotten rid of . . .' Marianne began, then stopped. She pointed towards her bedroom. 'The wardrobe is empty,' she said.

'Of course it is. It's been twenty-fi—'

'Rita should have told me she was emptying it.'

Aunt Pearl sighed and the sigh robbed her face of

some of its severity. She looked tired. And old. 'She did tell you. She asked me if she should and I said, yes, of course she should, and then she spent an eternity wondering if she should write to you. Or telephone you. Or pop into your house. You know how she thinks nothing of popping into people's houses without giving them due, or indeed any, warning?'

Marianne nodded. Her head felt heavy.

'She phoned you. Do you not remember?'

Marianne shook her head this time.

'And you said, fine. You insisted you didn't want anything out of the wardrobe.' Aunt Pearl craned her neck towards Marianne and peered at her.

Marianne shook her head again. 'I don't remember,' she said.

'Well, she did,' said Pearl, straightening with sudden briskness. 'Now, come along.'

'What?'

'Don't say what, say pardon.' Aunt Pearl trotted out the well-worn line. 'I need help.'

She swivelled and vanished into her room. Marianne entertained a fleeting notion of not following her. Of shutting herself in her bedroom with the empty wardrobe and carrying on.

Aunt Pearl's bedroom was a vast mausoleum of a room containing the same five pieces of furniture that had been here since Marianne was a child. A single bed with legs as skinny as Pearl's. At the foot of the bed, a wooden tea chest, locked with an enormous, rusty padlock. Marianne and Flo had once tried to open the chest using one of Pearl's long, rigid hairpins during the one and only time their aunt had left the house for a protracted period of time. She'd gone to hospital to have a heart bypass. Marianne remembered being surprised. That Pearl had a heart to bypass.

A bookcase containing the various copies of 'How to . . .' books on the top shelf, the other shelves filled with Mills and Boon books, in alphabetical order by title. *Affairs of the Soul. Be Still My Heart. Call the Doctor. Dreaming of You. Every Beat of My Heart* . . .

A dressing table with tweezers, a pot of Pond's face cream and a metal comb with one lone grey hair hanging from it.

A straight-backed Queen Anne armchair.

A gigantic stuffed panda bear, one eye missing, stuffing sprouting from various tears and rips along ancient seams, the fur hardened by the trudge of years. The bear had been won at a fairground in the summer of 1966, after Pearl's fiancé correctly guessed the number of marbles in a glass jar.

One hundred and sixty-three.

That's how many marbles had been in the jar.

He was married to someone else by the following summer.

'Now,' said Aunt Pearl, when Marianne closed the door behind her, 'I want to move the bookcase over beside the armchair.'

'Would it not make more sense to move the armchair over to the bookcase?' Marianne enquired.

When Pearl shook her head, Marianne could hear the bones in her neck creak. She examined the bookcase, which was a sturdy oak affair. 'It looks fairly heavy,' she said. 'I don't think we can . . .'

'We shall remove the books,' said Pearl.

'But we might get them mixed up,' said Marianne. 'It wouldn't do to have *The Keeper of My Heart* before *Last Lover in Lagos*, would it?'

Aunt Pearl pinned Marianne to the spot with the icy blast of her stare. 'Are you mocking me, Marianne?' she asked.

Marianne straightened her face. 'No.'

'Good.' Pearl began taking the books off the shelf. 'I've decided to rearrange them anyway. In order of publication date.'

The job, while tedious, was curiously relaxing, even allowing for Pearl's thorny presence. It required much concentration and a good working memory, which both women possessed. There was one terrifying moment when Marianne saw herself in forty years' time, doing the same thing with her collection of natural history encyclopaedias. In her bedroom at Ancaire. She expelled the thought from her head by bearing down on the title of the book she was holding – *Passion in Paradise* – and making as many words as she could from the letters.

Dire. Sad. Rip. Noise. Raid. Despair.

Pearl glanced at her. 'If the wind changes direction, your face will stay like that, you know,' she said.

'Like what?'

'Dour,' said Pearl.

Marianne struggled to think of an uglier word.

Dour.

Aunt Pearl set the pile of books she had been sorting on the floor and looked at Marianne. 'You know,' she said, 'it wasn't easy for Rita. Clearing out the wardr—'

'I can't find the publication date for this one,' said Marianne, pushing a well-thumbed copy of *Return to Love Island* into her hands.

'October 1994,' Pearl said, barely glancing at the book. She looked instead at Marianne, her eyes like drills boring into her face. When Marianne did not look at her, Pearl reached over and poked her arm.

Marianne looked up.

'You want to end up like me?' Pearl said.

Marianne considered this to be a trick question. It would be rude to say no. But it would also be rude to say yes. In the end, she said nothing, concentrating instead on the pile of books in front of her. After a while, Aunt Pearl did the same. They worked in silence. It was neither companionable nor awkward. It was just there.

Like the two of them.

'If you ask me,' said Pearl, after a while, even though no one had asked her anything, 'it's nonsensical. Rita and Patrick, swimming in these conditions.' She nodded towards the window where the bare branches of a horse chestnut tree flailed in the gusting wind, their tips scratching at the window like skeletal fingers.

'Is that where Rita is?'

'It's full tide,' said Pearl, 'so I presume so.'

Marianne looked out of the window. The waves crested high and grey, like prison walls, before crashing onto the shore. 'Dangerous,' she said because some word seemed to be expected of her.

'If that boy gets pneumonia again, he'd better not come crying to me,' said Pearl.

Marianne picked up another book – *Seduction by*

Numbers, a story of a secretary who starts to temp at the accountancy firm of a powerful man with a tragic past, according to the blurb on the back – and opened it to examine the publication date. 'I don't remember Patrick having pneumonia,' she said.

'You had left for boarding school by then,' said Aunt Pearl, fondly inspecting the creased cover of *Doctor's Orders*, which featured a chiselled-jawed man with lavish hair and intense eyes, pressing a tiny but perfectly formed nurse against his immaculate surgical scrubs. 'Patrick had been here for four long months. Couldn't get a word out of him all day and then, oh my goodness, the racket he made at night. Shouting and roaring in his sleep. And Rita insisting they go swimming every day. With no thought to the dangers. Even when the winter started in earnest. No wonder the child got sick. And not a pick on him, no matter how much food Rita made for him.'

'I'm surprised he didn't get food poisoning,' said Marianne. 'As well as pneumonia.'

'That's not a very Christian thing to say,' said Aunt Pearl. She inspected her watch. 'I have to leave now if I'm to be on time for mass.' She stood up and smoothed her skirt with her hands, which were, Marianne noticed, similar to her own. The same long nail beds with the nails themselves cut short and square; the same long, bony fingers.

'Your mother will probably pick up her motley crew of undesirables after her swim so you'll have to wait until she gets back if you want to berate her.'

'I don't want to berate her.' Marianne's earlier anger had drained away. She didn't have the energy to sustain it. To sustain anything. 'I mostly just want to avoid her.'

'Business as usual then,' said Aunt Pearl, buttoning herself into a gaberdine mac. 'Well, there are plenty of places in the house to hide,' she added, crossing the room and opening the door. 'At least it's got that going for it.'

Chapter 7

When Aunt Pearl drove away in her old but immaculately maintained Peugeot 106, Marianne wandered the corridors. Ancaire was like an insistent tour guide, pointing out all the wear and tear her memory had managed to plaster over.

There was the dent in the wainscot where Rita and William, waltzing towards the stairs, had tripped over each other's feet and crashed into the wall. They hadn't felt the pain until the next day when twelve-year-old Marianne, bringing the tea and paracetamol they had requested, filled them in. They laughed. Marianne did not.

There was the crack in the windowpane at the end of the landing, a long crooked line stretching from it but not far enough to shatter the glass. 'You could have had my eye out with that,' William had roared at Rita, picking up the lethal stiletto shoe Rita had flung.

'One of your roving eyes,' Rita had roared back.

And there was the faded red damask of the chaise

longue beneath the window. The love-seat, Rita called it. Spent and slumped now, having borne the weight of the two of them down through the years, draped across each other, just before an argument, or just after.

Theirs was an explosion of a relationship. The alcohol lit the fuse. Then Rita sobered up and William didn't and, after a while, he left to pursue his twin hobbies: drinking and women. In both endeavours, he was initially successful, guarding jealously the last vestiges of his rangy swagger, his thick, steel-grey hair and tales of his long-ago travels to India, following which one of his paintings – a watercolour of a be-sandalled pair of dusty feet standing beside a well – was exhibited in the Guggenheim in New York.

'I peaked too early,' he told Marianne once when he arrived at her apartment in the middle of the night, maudlin with drink. She let him sleep on the couch. In the morning, he was gone again.

He dated a string of women, their ages in ascending order. His last girlfriend – Simone, Marianne thought – was a ballroom dance teacher who openly admitted to being fifty-nine, which meant she was anywhere north of sixty-five.

Then William had a stroke. Nothing too serious, but serious enough to ward off any further ability on his part to pursue women. He arrived back at Ancaire and persuaded Rita to take him in. Marianne assumed it didn't take much. She also assumed they'd be a disaster again. Just an older version of the same disaster. The fighting, the yelling, the cheering, the roaring, the rigorous love-making, the flinging, the smashing. Even when they laughed, it was raucous. Like a murder of crows.

But it didn't turn out like that. For starters, William

became non-verbal after the stroke. The doctors couldn't work out if he couldn't speak or just wouldn't.

Either way, he never spoke again.

He kept on drinking, using his left hand instead of his right.

He spent a few months at Ancaire before the second stroke.

It was the second stroke that killed him.

Marianne gripped the brass handrail on one side of the wide, sweeping staircase as she made her way downstairs. She remembered sliding down it as a child, Flo on the other side, the pair of them whooping, and Bruno pounding down the stairs, barking. Marianne always let Flo win. Flo never guessed.

Marianne wasn't hungry but she ended up in the kitchen all the same. It was the smell, she presumed. Rita made sure that the smell of her home baking got into every corner, seeped through every crack in every wall. It was like an assault, the smell, an in-your-face-I-told-you-so sort of smell, smug and superior.

While the kitchen retained some of its period charm, it was definitely more shabby than chic these days. The brass pots and pans that hung from the ceiling near the ancient Aga swayed in the draught above the Belfast sink, chipped and stained from years of service.

On the counter, wrapped in a damp tea towel, the source of the smell. A cake of soda bread, still warm. Beside it, a dish of butter, creamy and soft and made by Rita in the ancient churn in one of the outhouses.

The woman who had preferred drinking to eating turned out to be somebody who made her own butter.

Rita put it down to time. There was so much of it after she stopped drinking. She said she had never realised how long twenty-four hours could feel. How never-ending it could seem.

In the beginning, she burned everything she cooked. Threw it out. Started again. And again. She kept starting again until she managed not to burn everything. And still, she kept going, until eventually, she managed to produce lemon melts that could floor you with their irresistible aroma and their capacity to melt on your tongue and make you weak with gratitude and coerce you into longing for more.

Absentmindedly, Marianne cut a thick slice of soda bread, slathered it in butter and ate it on one of the carver chairs at the kitchen table, propping her childhood copy of *I Capture the Castle* against the milk carton. She enjoyed re-reading novels. She found it comforting, knowing what was going to happen next.

Marianne stopped when she heard the strained effort of Rita's Jeep, struggling up the driveway. She picked up a novena Aunt Pearl had cut out from the newspaper. It would do as a bookmark until Marianne eventually got around to unearthing the beautiful fabric ones in her suitcase. She made sure she was out of the kitchen and up the stairs before the Get-Well-Sooners spilled out of the Jeep and Rita found the key in the planter, scraped the muck off it and worked it into the lock.

Marianne sequestered herself in Rita's studio. It was at the gable end of the house with floor-to-ceiling windows through which she could see nothing but water so that it felt like she was tossing about on the high seas in a precarious rowing boat. The room still contained an easel, a high

stool and a paint-spattered wooden table that accommodated rows and rows of paint tubes, long congealed, and
an old ice-cream carton full of paintbrushes, their bristles
hard and unyielding. Rita's paintings, stacked sometimes
five deep, faced the wall so the paintings themselves could
not be seen. Marianne didn't inspect them. She knew what
they were.

Self-portraits in the main.

Rita.

Over and over again.

The studio was one of the coldest rooms in the house,
the windows single glazed and poorly fitted. However, it
was a room that Rita never used any more – she hadn't
painted since that summer when she stopped drinking – so
Marianne had thought it safe to settle there, far enough
back from the windows so she wouldn't be spotted by any
of the Get-Well-Sooners.

She could hear them below in the drawing room. Their
incessant talking and raucous laughter breached the ancient
floorboards and arrived in a dark cloud around Marianne's
head, no matter how tightly she pressed her hands against
her ears.

Then the singing at the end.

Dear God, the singing.

Get Well Soon.

How?

Don't drink and sing this tune.

When?

Every day, starting today, you'll

Get. Well. Soon.

They had lunch in the kitchen. Marianne knew, because she heard Rita banging on the gong.

After lunch, the stout crunch of Aunt Pearl's walking stick as she set off on her afternoon constitutional, carefully plotted so she would meet nobody and would not be obliged to return a pleasantry.

Later, the cough of Rita's Jeep. It sounded like the cough of a very old person, incessant and feeble. Rita wrestled with it, stamping on the accelerator with her high heel – not for Rita the sense of changing into a shoe suitable for driving – so that the engine roared before cutting out. It took three attempts to catch and when it did, the Get-Well-Sooners cheered loudly.

After that, the soft hiss of Patrick's bicycle as he sailed down the avenue towards the main road, his toolbox strapped onto the back.

And then Ancaire was silent again. Apart from the shuddering of the windowpanes, the gurgling rattle of water struggling through the pipes, and the ragged moan of the radiators, begging to be bled.

By the time the doorbell rang, Marianne was already more than halfway through the book. George, lying on the floor by her feet, lifted his head, his ears twitching. Marianne knew that Pearl, Patrick and Rita had keys to the house. She wasn't expecting anyone else. It was probably some door-to-door salesperson. They would leave eventually.

She read on.

The doorbell rang again, this time with greater insistence.

Marianne looked over the top of her book through the window but from this vantage point, she couldn't see the front door.

She could, however, see a bottle-green Jaguar. Not vintage but old enough to warrant the obvious care and attention its owner lavished upon it, the body polished and buffed to a sharp shine and the seats inside reupholstered in distressed brown leather.

The doorbell rang for a third time.

'Oh, for Christ's sake . . .' Marianne bookmarked her page, set the book aside. She stood up, hesitated.

She hated answering the door unless she knew for a fact who was there.

Even then, she wasn't keen.

George stood up and barked. 'Oh, fine,' said Marianne, marching out of the room and down the landing to the stairs.

She wrenched open the front door.

A man stood on the other side. An enormous man wearing a bright green tartan kilt that did nothing to conceal a pair of knobbly knees and sturdy calves, thick orange ankle socks tucked into a pair of massive Doc Martens. His hair was as orange as his socks and just as thick. It fell to his shoulders with a hint of a kink. Marianne had to take a step backwards to take him in, such was the height and breadth of him.

He grinned at her and his eyes, as garish-green as his kilt, disappeared into slits.

'Yes?' she said.

'Ah, you must be Rita's daughter,' the man said in a Scottish accent as thick as his hair. Thicker. 'Marianne, isn't that right?'

She nodded and he extended a massive hand, and Marianne felt she had no option but to offer hers in response.

She braced herself as he shook it but the handshake didn't have the violent clasp and pump she had anticipated.

'I love what you've done with your hair,' he said when he let go of her hand.

'Are you being facetious?' Marianne asked icily.

The man grinned. 'I am, aye.'

'Well, I hardly think—'

'I'm a hairdresser by trade,' said the man, as if that somehow excused his rudeness. 'Hugh McLeod, by the way.' He rummaged in the leather sporran hanging from a belt around his hips, drew out a business card and thrust it into Marianne's hand. In the middle of the card, centred and bold, was 'Happy Hair' and below it, all italics and exclamation marks: '*You grow it! We do the rest!*'

'Who's "we"?' Marianne asked.

'Just me and my wee apprentice, Shirley,' said Hugh. 'We've a salon in Rush. Well, it's a log cabin in my back garden. Your Patrick built it, as a matter of fact. But "salon" sounds more professional, doesn't it?'

Marianne tried to return the card but Hugh shook his head. 'Keep it,' he said. 'Just in case.'

'In case of what?'

'In case of emergency,' he said, grinning again like he was making fun of her. Marianne waited for his grin to fade. 'Rita's not here. She's dropping off her . . .' Marianne wasn't sure what to call the Get-Well-Sooners so she said, '. . . people'.

Hugh nodded. 'I used to be one of her people, did she tell you?'

Marianne shook her head, hoping to dissuade him from any further revelations.

'Aye,' he went on. 'I'm a graduate, I suppose.' He pushed his hair out of his eyes and grinned at her.

'Yes, well, that's . . . good,' said Marianne stiffly.

'Although your mother deserves a lot of the credit, she really—'

Marianne pulled her cardigan tight around her. 'I don't mean to be rude but . . .'

'Sorry,' said Hugh. 'I'm keeping you from . . . what are you up to?'

'Are you always this nosy?' snapped Marianne.

'I am, aye,' said Hugh, grinning again.

'I see,' said Marianne. And then, when he appeared to be prepared to wait as long as it took for a response, she added, 'I'm reading.'

'I won't disturb you so,' said Hugh, shaking his massive head so that his mane of hair swished around his head. 'I only wanted to give you this.' He handed her a driving licence. 'Rita must have dropped it when she was at mine for dinner the other day.' He waved, then turned and walked towards his car.

'Thank you,' Marianne felt obliged to call after him. Although she wished she hadn't because he stopped and turned.

'What are you reading?' he asked.

What Marianne wanted to say was, 'None of your bloody business.' What she actually said was, '*I Capture the Castle.*'

'I'm the same,' said Hugh, smiling broadly. 'I go back to the old classics when I need a bit of comfort.'

'I didn't say I was in need in comfort,' said Marianne. 'I just . . . I couldn't find anything else to read.'

But Hugh had turned again, waving at her as he manoeuvred himself behind the steering wheel of his car.

Marianne shut the door and leaned against it, closing her eyes and exhaling. She felt exhausted. Too much exposure to people. At least, in the last few months, while she had waited for the bank to come good on their promise of repossession, she had waited alone.

She looked at her mother's driving licence. Rita's photograph – taken at least ten years ago – was a riot of colour: bright yellow hair, streaks of pink along her cheek-bones, a scarlet scarf tied around her neck and a speck of ruby-red lipstick staining one of her front teeth.

A date in the bottom corner.

The expiration date.

The licence was out of date.

It had been out of date since Christmas.

Perhaps this was her old driving licence? Her current one was in her wallet, surely?

But Rita did not own a wallet.

And Marianne would be prepared to bet a sizeable amount, were she a betting person and if she had any money, that there was no current licence.

Marianne ran to the studio and picked her phone out of her handbag, scrolled to Rita's number.

'Hello?'

'Rita?'

'Yes?'

'It's me. Marianne.'

'How lovely of you to ring. How are you?'

'Are you driving?'

'Yes.'

'Well, you shouldn't be on your phone then.'

'But you rang me.'

'Just pull over.'

'Whatever for?'

'So I can talk to you,' said Marianne with as much patience as she could muster, which wasn't much.

'There's no need to shout, darling.'

'Have you pulled over?'

'Oh, fine then. Hang on, there, yes. Yes, I have.'

In the background, Marianne could hear a blare of car horns. She pressed the phone closer to her ear.

'A Scottish man – Hugh Mc-something or other – dropped your driving licence in just now.'

'Darling Hugh,' said Rita. 'He's such a—'

'It's out of date.'

'What is?'

'Your driving licence.'

'Oh.'

'Did you know that?'

'Well, now that you mention it, I think I did know.'

'Well, why didn't you renew it then?'

'I did. Well, I mean I meant to. I got the form from the post office and everything.'

'So why didn't you fill it in?'

'Have you seen the length of those forms? The amount of questions they ask?'

Marianne couldn't think of a suitable response to that.

'Don't be cross, darling,' Rita said. 'I promise I'll send the application off tomorrow. Or definitely by the end of the week.'

'You know it's against the law to drive without a valid driving licence?' said Marianne.

'Oh dear,' said Rita, giggling. 'Two criminals in the family.'

'That's not funny,' said Marianne stiffly. Down the line, she could hear the blare of a police siren and she felt her muscles clench. Rita said something but Marianne couldn't hear her over the din. Gradually the sound petered away.

Marianne did her best to compose herself. 'You're not parked in a bus lane or anywhere else inappropriate, are you?' she asked.

'Am I in a bus lane, darlings?' Rita shouted.

'Any particular number bus, dear?' enquired Ethel earnestly.

'I wouldn't know,' said Bartholomew. 'I never get the bus. I prefer taxis.'

'Which begs the question,' piped up Freddy, 'why you don't take a taxi to Ancaire instead of getting little old ladies to pick you up.'

'Who are you calling a little old lady?' Rita shouted.

'Listen to me,' Marianne cut in urgently. 'You can't drive at the moment. You have to get your licence renewed first.'

'I have to drive, darling,' Rita said. 'How else am I going to get my clients to Ancaire?'

Marianne closed her eyes. Exhaled.

'You are in a bus lane,' shouted Shirley. 'So unless you want to get flattened by the number twenty-seven, I suggest you shut up yapping on the phone and move your arse.'

Marianne could hear Rita say, 'Does anyone know where the hazard lights are?' and then the line was disconnected.

Chapter 8

Marianne didn't see Rita until later, at dusk, when she spotted her and Patrick through the kitchen window. They were laughing, their arms linked. Patrick noticed Marianne first. He nodded at her and gently extricated his arm from Rita's. He moved towards his apartment, melting into the darkening evening.

'Don't worry, Marnie,' shouted Rita as she opened the back door. Immediately the kitchen was filled with icy wind that carried a hint of rain, perhaps even snow. Rita had to use both hands to wrestle the door shut. 'I've come up with a brilliant plan.'

Unlike George, lying on the floor by her feet, Marianne felt her hackles rise.

'If your brilliant idea has anything to do with me driving your . . . people to and from Ancaire, then the answer is no,' said Marianne firmly.

'It wouldn't be for long,' said Rita. 'Just until I got my licence sorted.'

'That will be months,' said Marianne.

'It won't take that long,' said Rita airily.

'It will. You'll need to do a medical. And an eye test.'

'Such a money-making racket,' said Rita, with a theatrical sigh. 'Not to mention ageism. The system is riddled with it.'

Marianne concentrated on scrubbing the mugs, all of which she'd removed from the cupboard since their insides were stained rusty brown from years of tea.

'Besides,' went on Rita, 'it'll be good for you.'

'How do you make that out?'

'Getting out and about,' said Rita. 'Meeting people.'

'I hate meeting people,' said Marianne.

'You just haven't met the right people,' said Rita.

'You could cancel the meetings until you get your licence,' Marianne suggested.

Rita shook her head. 'Out of the question.'

'Why can't they just drive here themselves?'

'It's part of the Get Well Soon recovery programme,' said Rita. 'I don't want my clients to have to think about anything else except getting better.'

'I don't see how any of this is my problem,' said Marianne.

'It isn't,' said Rita.

'But you're making me feel like I'm responsible, all the same,' snapped Marianne. 'Nothing new there, of course.' The bitterness surprised her: how fresh it was, how plentiful. It lodged in the back of her throat, sharp as a fish bone.

'I'm sorry, Marnie,' Rita said, her voice devoid of its usual frivolity. The two women looked at each other and Marianne felt the silence between them like a weight, bowed down with all the things they had never said to each other.

Marianne pulled the plug and watched the water circling the drain, powerless against the suck and pull of it. 'Look,' she said, turning on the tap and rinsing the suds off the mugs. 'I can't help you with this. I don't drive.'

'You passed your test, didn't you?'

'Yes. But that was years ago. I haven't driven since then. I hate driving.'

'What do you hate about it?'

'Other drivers,' said Marianne, raising her voice over the noise of the water coming in sporadic spurts from the tap.

'But you can drive?'

'Technically,' Marianne allowed. She had taken driving lessons when she got her first job after university. She thought that's what adults did. She had passed her test first time and thereafter travelled wherever she needed to go on buses, trains and trams. She wore comfortable shoes, in the event of a strike or mechanical breakdown or terrorist threat, whereupon she walked.

'Why does Patrick not drive?' Marianne snapped, turning round to look at Rita again.

'I did try to teach him a few times,' said Rita, shaking her head.

'Anyway,' said Marianne, rounding on a flaw in the plan, 'I'm not insured on the Jeep.'

'It's open insurance,' said Rita. She bent to pick up her swimming togs from the floor where she'd thrown them earlier and wrung them out over a gigantic yucca plant in the corner. 'It's like riding a bicycle, apparently,' she went on. 'You never forget.'

'I said no,' said Marianne, turning off the tap and folding the dishcloth neatly over it.

'Is that a hard no?' asked Rita.

Marianne nodded.

'Okay, darling,' said Rita. 'I understand.'

Marianne should have been suspicious, given the speed at which her mother capitulated. Instead, she gave it insufficient thought and took to her bed, citing a headache and clamping the pillow over her face when Rita sounded the gong for dinner.

By the time Marianne struggled – late – out of bed the following morning and returned from the beach, having succumbed again to George's persistent pleading, Rita was ushering the Get-Well-Sooners into the drawing room.

She beamed when she saw Marianne. 'Good morning, darling. How's your head?'

'How did they get here?' asked Marianne, pointing into the room. Rita shrugged. 'Same way as usual,' she said.

'So you blatantly broke the law?' said Marianne.

'Well,' said Rita, tilting her head to one side, 'is it not more of a recommendation than a law? A best-practice idea? It's not like I've suddenly lost my ability to drive, is it? It's just a minor administrative issue.'

'No,' said Marianne. 'It's an actual law.'

'Well, don't worry, Hugh has offered to pick them up after today's meeting.'

'But what about tomorrow?' demanded Marianne.

'I find it best not to worry about tomorrow until tomorrow, Marnie,' Rita said. She stepped closer to Marianne and lowered her voice. 'Besides, I have another, more pressing, issue.'

'Another one?' said Marianne, trying to push George away. He had an annoying tendency to lean against her legs when she stood still for any length of time, as if he was intent on propping her up.

'This one wasn't my fault. It's Gerard, he—'

'The rooster?'

'No, silly,' said Rita, smiling indulgently. 'Gerard's our goat. Anyway, I think Donal— Oh, have you meet Donal yet?'

'Is he a threadbare donkey, by any chance?'

'Threadbare is a little strong,' said Rita. 'He has the sweetest nature but can be somewhat greedy, I'm afraid. I think he ate Gerard's breakfast again so Gerard ate all the teabags and now I've none left for our mid-morning snack.'

'Goats don't eat teabags.'

'Gerard does.'

'Is everything all right, Rita?' enquired a man's voice from inside the drawing room.

'Fine, darling,' said Rita, planting an enormous smile across her bright red mouth. She turned back to Marianne. 'Can you tell Patrick,' she stage-whispered. 'He'll know what to do.'

'What? Buy teabags?' said Marianne testily.

Rita shook her head impatiently. 'It's more complicated than that, Marnie,' she said. 'Ethel likes peppermint tea in a muslin teabag with a string attached so she can pop it back into the cup if she wants a refill. Freddy and Bartholomew are strict PG Tippers, even though they hate the fact that they have something in common, and Shirley insists on Lyons tea leaves. If you go near her with a Barry's she'll call you a "Blueshirt". Even if it's their Classic Blend.' Rita was breathless after all the stage whispering.

'That is complicated,' Marianne had to concede.

'I'd say Patrick keeps an emergency stash in his house for this kind of eventuality.' Rita clasped her hands together in a sort of begging gesture. 'Would you go and ask him?' she said.

'Bloody hell,' said Marianne.

'Pretty please with a *petit four* on top?'

'Oh, fine.'

Marianne made her way to Patrick's workshop. He was sanding an ancient cabinet when she arrived. It was worse for wear, the wood faded and splintering in places, one of the doors hanging off and some of the handles missing.

'Hardly worth the bother,' Marianne said.

Patrick ran his hand down the side of the unit. 'The structure is still sound,' he said.

Marianne pushed her hands into the pockets of her anorak to protect them from the worst of the biting wind. Patrick returned to his sanding. Marianne cleared her throat. 'So,' she said. He stopped sanding again and looked at her. 'Aren't you going to ask me why I'm here?' Marianne said.

'I presumed you'd let me know when you were ready,' he said, and it sounded reasonable, the way he said it.

'I'm ready now,' said Marianne.

Patrick set the sandpaper down and looked at her.

'Well,' began Marianne, 'it's about teabags, which I know is—'

'Did Gerard eat them again?'

'Eh, actually, yes,' said Marianne. 'He did.'

Patrick rose from his stool. He opened a door at the back of the workshop where stairs led to his apartment. Marianne looked around while he was gone. Yellow sawdust covered the cement floor and tools hung on rows of nails along each of the walls, in an orderly and efficient way, she had to acknowledge. Logs of wood stacked in a corner smelled sweet and dense. Patrick returned with what looked like a toolbox. He handed it to Marianne. Inside, she was unsurprised to find different brands of tea, in sealed Cellophane bags. PG Tips, peppermint tea in muslin, Lyons tea leaves and one containing the weeds Rita used for her own brand of herbal tea, complete with mucky roots.

'Rita can always rely on you,' said Marianne, snapping the box shut.

'I relied on her for a long time,' said Patrick.

'Lucky you,' said Marianne. She hated how harsh and sour her voice sounded. Patrick's face flooded with colour and he lowered his head as if she had shouted at him.

Marianne picked up the box. Moved towards the door. She stopped there. 'Sorry,' she said in a quieter voice. 'It's this place, it's like liquorice: it doesn't agree with me.' She laughed as if she had told a joke.

Patrick did not laugh. Instead, he said, 'No need to be sorry,' and something about his voice, so gentle, so careful, caused a lump to form at the base of Marianne's throat and she bowed her head, swallowed, hard, a couple of times before she was absolutely certain that she would not cry.

What the hell was happening to her?

She hated Patrick being there, a witness to her struggle, but when she looked up, he had returned to his workbench and was measuring a slat of wood.

In the kitchen, there was no sign of Rita, although she had put the kettle on and set a selection of mugs on a tray. A delicate china cup and saucer with floral print. That was for the elderly lady, Marianne guessed. Ethel, was it? A sturdy black mug with '#mefuckingtoo' emblazoned along the middle in gold lettering. The angry young woman, Marianne presumed. Shirley, wasn't it? And her children must be in there too, since there were two smaller mugs – *Star Wars* ones – already filled with hot chocolate, the surface foaming with frothy pink bubbles.

The *Gilda* mug with a black-and-white photograph of Rita Hayworth printed on it was most definitely Rita's. Which meant that the last two – a dainty Mr Neat cup and a massive, bright pink Chippendales mug – belonged to the PG Tips drinkers, Freddy and Bartholomew.

It took Marianne an age to make all the different varieties of tea and carry them into the drawing room.

It was a bright, airy room with an enormous bay window, which, like most of the windows at Ancaire, framed the restless, grey sea. A fire burned in the grate and, while it did little to penetrate the sharp chill, the long orange flames dancing up the soot-thick walls of the chimney introduced a small degree of cheer into the room, Marianne had to admit. However, it also prompted a concern about the chimney itself and she wondered when it had last been swept.

The group was sitting on chairs in the centre of the room, arranged in a circle. They were either meditating or had dozed off. Either way, they didn't notice Marianne's arrival.

On the other side of the fireplace, Rita had set up what could pass for a play area. A carton of Lego. A stack of papers – mostly bills – to draw on the back of, and an old beer tankard, crammed with colouring pencils. Two large cardboard boxes bulged and shifted, leading Marianne to conclude that they contained children. This turned out to be accurate as a crashing noise, like a localised tropical storm, erupted from the boxes before they burst open, revealing two boys, maybe six and eight. They clambered out and stood in front of Marianne. They were largely made up of white, skinny legs and arms, both clad in matching football shorts and socks. They had the same long navy eyes as the angry young woman, Shirley. Each had a collection of bright orange freckles smattered across the bridge of his nose.

'Is that our hot chocolate?' said the smaller one, standing on his toes to peer over the edge of the tray.

'Introduce yourselves before you start tormenting her,' the angry young woman shouted at them, her eyes still closed.

'Sheldon,' the taller one said, pointing to his chest. 'Eight. He/him. Second class. He's Harrison. Five. He's only in Senior Infants.'

'I can say my own name,' said Harrison, hotly.

'Yes, this is your hot chocolate,' said Marianne, lowering the tray before Harrison, who had formed a tiny fist with his hand, could land a punch on his brother's skinny arm. The boys lifted their mugs and sat cross-legged on the floor, pulling their boxes over their heads.

'Ah, Marianne, lovely to see you again,' boomed Bartholomew, approaching her with his arms outstretched. Marianne grabbed the Chippendales mug and thrust it at him. 'You already know my mug,' he said, beaming.

'Is there any semi-skimmed milk?' enquired the skin-and-bone man with the worried face. He pushed his wire-framed glasses up his nose and peered at Marianne through small, round lenses. Freddy, Marianne remembered.

'I'll fetch some,' Rita said.

'And some cake?' Bartholomew asked hopefully. 'That meditation has given me an appetite.'

'Applying lip gloss gives you an appetite,' said Shirley, grabbing the #mefuckingtoo mug off the tray. 'No offence.'

'There should be cake,' said Rita as she trotted out the door. 'Gerard is gluten-intolerant so I don't think he ate much of the lemon drizzle I made.'

'Aren't you having a cuppa, dear?' asked the little old lady, lifting the china cup and saucer from the tray and smiling at Marianne.

'No,' she said, taking a step back and standing on Shirley's foot. Shirley glared at her.

'Sorry,' mumbled Marianne.

'You look like someone who understands theorems,' Shirley said. 'No offence.'

'Eh . . .' began Marianne. 'None taken.'

'Rita said you're an accountant,' said Shirley.

'I used to be.'

'So can you explain what that prick Pythagoras was on about?' said Shirley.

'Do you mean now?' said Marianne. She felt vaguely foolish.

'I'm doing the leaving cert in June so sometime before then would be handy,' said Shirley.

'I'm helping her with French,' said Bartholomew proudly, rushing to occupy the seat closest to the fire.

'Yes,' said Freddy. 'He knows the French for entrepreneur and cul-de-sac, I believe. Oh, and bureau de change.'

'And I also know the French for imbecile,' retorted Bartholomew.

'Are you staying for the meeting?' Shirley barked at Marianne as she strode over to Bartholomew. 'That's my chair,' she told him.

'Could we not take turns?' asked Bartholomew, more in hope than expectation.

'No,' said Shirley. He got up and Shirley sat down, crossed her legs so her short skirt rode even further up her legs, revealing a large rip in her fishnet tights. She glared at Marianne. 'Well? Are you?'

'No,' Marianne said, and her voice was louder than she'd intended. More like a shout. A wail.

'You'd be more than welcome,' said Freddy. 'It might be beneficial for those bona fide addicts in the group to hear from someone who is not an alcoholic but who has been affected by alcoholism.' He gestured at Bartholomew, Ethel and Shirley.

'You actually said something that makes sense, Frederick,' boomed Bartholomew, who appeared to have recovered himself after his abrupt eviction from Shirley's chair. 'And your capacity for self-delusion is exemplary, may I say.'

'I take exception to—' began Freddy, reddening.

'The more the merrier,' cut in Ethel, smiling.

'Hardly merry,' fumed Shirley. 'Given how fucken sober we all are.'

'Sobriety is a—' began Bartholomew.

Freddy stood up. 'I swear, if you say "Sobriety is a gift that keeps on giving", I will have no choice but to box your ears.'

'Ooh, Frederick, I'm quaking over here,' said Bartholomew, bravely standing behind Ethel.

'Boys, please,' said Ethel. 'What will Sheldon and Harrison think?'

But the two boys were too engrossed in making a Lego housing estate to pay any attention to the grown-ups. Marianne put 'grown-ups' in inverted commas in her head.

'That better be a social housing estate,' Shirley barked at them.

'Yes, Mam,' said the boys in unison, not looking up from their efforts.

Shirley's harsh expression softened like butter on a pan. 'Look at my boys,' she said, almost to herself. 'They're fucken deadly, so they are.'

Everybody gazed at them and smiled. Beside the boys, sitting in a row and staring with glassy eyes, was a selection of soft toys that had once belonged to Marianne and Flo. Marianne bent to collect the boys' now empty mugs and picked up the owl. It was smaller than she remembered, with stuffing oozing through the seams in places. The wings, once soft and golden, were rough to the touch now, and faded to a dull beige. Marianne hardly recognised her face in the owl's brown eyes. She looked like a fainter version of herself; pale and wary.

'I hate owls,' declared Harrison, beside her all of a sudden with his little hands on his hips.

'Why?' Marianne couldn't help asking. He seemed so adamant.

'They eat mice, so they do,' said Harrison grimly.

'He loves mice,' said Sheldon, bursting out the top of

one of the boxes. He shook his head and rolled his eyes and looked alarmingly like his mother.

'Just as well,' said Shirley. 'Since the kip we live in is inundated with them.'

Marianne put the mugs on the tray and stuffed the owl into the pocket of her anorak.

Rita returned with most of a lemon drizzle cake. Distributing it appeared to be a dangerous and thankless job.

'Why is his slice bigger than mine?' Freddy demanded, pointing at Bartholomew's plate.

'It is most certainly not,' said Bartholomew, quickly taking an enormous bite of his portion of cake.

'So, we'll see you in the morning then, dear?' said Ethel, reaching up to set her cup and saucer on the tray.

'Why?' said Marianne.

Ethel smiled. 'You're very kind to agree to drive us while Rita is unable to.'

'No,' began Marianne, glaring at Rita. 'I never—'

'You don't want me to break the law, surely?' said Rita.

'No, of course not,' snapped Marianne.

'It'll just be until I get my licence renewed,' said Rita in a bright tone.

'Only a matter of weeks, I'd say,' said Bartholomew. 'A month, tops.'

'A month?' The cups on the tray slid to one side and Marianne struggled to straighten it.

'It'll be good for you to have something to do,' said Freddy.

'I have things to do,' said Marianne hotly.

'Feeling sorry for yourself doesn't count,' said Shirley.

'No offence,' she added hurriedly as Marianne's face contorted.

'Let's discuss the finer details later,' said Rita, draining her cup and setting it on the tray.

'There's nothing to discuss.'

'Oh, and, just so you know, I'll need a lift to Hugh's salon after the Tuesday and Thursday meetings,' Shirley told Marianne. 'I'm his apprentice,' she added, unable to conceal a faint touch of pride.

'She could probably give your hair a bit of a trim,' said Freddy. 'Only if you thought you needed one,' he added hastily.

Marianne could see her hair in the reflection of Freddy's small, round lenses. It was like a foreign land, the dark, tangled shores of which had never felt the weight of a human foot.

Shirley looked dubious. 'I'd say I'd need more training.'

Marianne was suddenly exhausted, the fight all drained out of her. How did these people manage to meet like this every day? How did they ever expect to Get Well Soon in this place? All anyone would achieve in this environment was a headache. And an addiction to caffeine and sugar.

Chapter 9

Marianne hated to admit it but Rita was right. Driving was like riding a bicycle. An ancient, buckled bicycle with a flat tyre and a rusted chain. 'The engine just needs to warm up,' Rita shouted from behind an enormous hydrangea bush that would prove scant protection if the Jeep were to make a lunge at it.

She had insisted on coming out of the house the next morning to see Marianne off, dressed in a purple kimono that clashed horribly with her orange turban. She'd acted pleasantly surprised at breakfast when Marianne told her she'd drive the Jeep, but she was fooling no one.

They had both known Marianne would do it.

Rita inserted a cigarette into a long, slim holder and lit it.

'Give it a bit more poke,' she roared.

'What do you mean?' Marianne screeched out the window, which had to be kept open to prevent the windscreen from misting over.

'Accelerate,' Rita yelled, smoke pouring out of her mouth and nose.

'Why didn't you just say that in the first place?' shouted Marianne.

She increased the pressure of her foot against the accelerator and the Jeep coughed and spluttered in protest, then seemed to accept its fate, moving in the direction dictated by Marianne's steering of the wheel, more or less.

Patrick walked out of his workshop, tucking a chisel into the tool belt slung low around his hips. He smiled at Marianne as he passed the hydrangea bush where Rita was now whooping and punching the air with her fist. Marianne noticed a modest sensation of achievement passing unchecked through her system.

She was driving.

It felt good to be in charge of something. To press a button here or push a pedal there and for that action to cause a reaction, however much it made the whole contraption shudder. Even the sight of George, sitting upright in the front passenger seat, his head leaning out the window so that the wind caught his ears and tossed them behind his head, like schoolgirl pigtails, did not irk her as much as it had every right to. He had followed Marianne into the Jeep and refused to get out. In the end, Marianne had no choice but to wrestle the seat belt around him.

After some warm-up laps of the house, Marianne manoeuvred the Jeep down the avenue. The road was empty as far as the eye could see in both directions and she drove out the peeling wrought-iron gates and down the road.

Marianne always held her breath when she passed the spot. There was a small wooden cross there, often with flowers propped against it. Marianne tried not to look but even so, she saw them on the periphery of her vision. On the grass verge at the side of the road.

Today, the flowers were pink lilies. Marianne held her breath, accelerated past them.

George barked. A brief, solitary bark.

'Be quiet, George,' Marianne said. He responded by stretching his head towards her and flicking his long, pink tongue along her hand, gripping the steering wheel.

'Stop that,' said Marianne, wiping the back of her hand on the leg of her tracksuit. George ignored her, leaned out the window, anxious not to miss anything.

Ethel's house was a semi-D in a housing estate on the outskirts of Skerries. The estate was called The Cedars, but there were no cedars as far as Marianne could see. In fact, there was no foliage of any kind. Number thirty-nine was crammed along a row of identical houses, each with a tiny square of grass in front, separated from the garden next door by a low line of box hedge.

Marianne walked up the narrow driveway and rang the doorbell. It played an out-of-tune version of 'God Save the Queen'. A door at the end of the hallway opened, spilling light along the linoleum floor and through the small square of glass in the front door, Marianne saw the slow-moving form of Ethel Abelforth. She removed a collection of keys on a ring from a deep pocket in an oversized cardigan, then spent an age selecting this key, then that one, turning them in various locks, then sliding bolts, following which the front door opened a slit before it was brought to a halt by the door chain. Ethel's face appeared around the edge of the door.

'Yes?' said Ethel.

'Hello, Ethel,' said Marianne.

'Hello,' said Ethel, in a small, wary voice.

'It's Marianne Cross.' Marianne did her best not to sound impatient. It was difficult at the best of times. 'Rita's daughter.'

'Oh, yes, so you are,' said Ethel, a smile widening across her face. 'Sorry, dear. It's just, I was hoodwinked recently and the nice policeman told me I should be careful, answering the door.'

Marianne was aghast to feel the prick of tears behind her eyes. The kind that would fall if she blinked. She thought it might have something to do with Ethel's use of the word 'hoodwinked'. She was careful not to blink.

'You'll have to sit in the back,' said Marianne as they walked towards the Jeep. 'I can't seem to persuade George out of the front seat.'

'Dear George,' said Ethel, opening the door to pull gently at his ears. 'He's much more settled since you arrived.'

'He's very needy,' said Marianne, sighing.

'Aren't we all?' said Ethel, using the headrest of the back seat to pull herself inside the Jeep.

Marianne drove down the road, stopped at the end, looked left and right, then pulled away.

'Are you all right, dear?' Ethel asked, leaning forward.

'Yes,' said Marianne.

'It's just, you seem a little – and I hope you won't mind my saying so – anxious?'

Marianne tightened her hands around the wheel. 'I haven't done much driving.'

'Well, you seem very competent to me,' Ethel said. 'Although what do I know? I haven't driven in five years.'

Marianne didn't respond.

'You're probably wondering why?' Ethel said.

'No, I—'

'I had an accident, you see,' said Ethel. 'It was my dear Stanley's anniversary and I'm sorry to say that I marked it by getting rather intoxicated. We'll be married fifty years this year.' She paused there and Marianne was unsure if she was expected to say 'Congratulations'. She didn't say anything.

'The driver of the other car will be in a wheelchair for the rest of his life. The judge was lenient and gave me a fine and a lifetime driving ban.'

Marianne could feel Ethel looking at her through the rearview mirror. She concentrated on the road. 'That's how I met Rita, you see,' Ethel went on. 'She was giving an art class to some patients in the hospital and I arrived to visit Gavin. That's his name, dear. Gavin Enright. Do you know him?'

'Should I?' said Marianne.

'It's just everybody in Ireland seems to know everybody else, I find,' said Ethel. 'Anyway,' she continued, 'his family were furious when they saw me. I had a bunch of grapes, of all things. Can you imagine? Rita heard the commotion and she rescued me, took me to Ancaire.'

'Did you . . . ever get to speak to Gavin?' asked Marianne.

Ethel brightened. 'Oh, yes, dear. Rita takes me to his house to visit once a month. We only go when he's not expecting any of his family. Gavin has forgiven me, bless him, but they haven't and I don't blame them.' Ethel looked out the window. 'Take this next left for Balbriggan,' she said. 'We'll pick Bartholomew up next. All right, dear?'

Up ahead, the traffic lights changed from green to amber. Marianne slowed down.

'We always go to the church dinner-dance to celebrate our anniversary, Stanley and I,' Ethel announced.

'I thought Stanley was . . .'

'The dear man sends me a sign,' said Ethel, beaming. 'Every year, without fail.'

'A sign?'

'From the other side, dear,' said Ethel, patiently.

'Oh,' said Marianne.

'I expect you're missing your young man?' Ethel said then, settling her head against the back seat.

Marianne yanked on the handbrake. 'I don't think Brian was ever young,' she said. 'He by-passed childhood and went straight to adulthood.'

'That's a shame,' said Ethel.

'I think that's what I liked about him.' This admission surprised Marianne – not just the fact that she told Ethel when she'd had no intention of telling Ethel anything, but the truth of it. She had never really known why she had decided to let Brian in when she had already resigned herself to being alone.

'He made you feel safe,' Ethel murmured from the back seat.

Marianne glanced in the rear-view mirror. Ethel's eyes were closed. Perhaps she had nodded off. Marianne squirted water onto the windscreen, turned on the wipers to clear it.

The lights went green and Marianne drove on.

Bartholomew was waiting outside a terraced house, on a quiet road just off Balbriggan's main street. The house presented in a shabby, run-down kind of way, the wood of the window frames rotting in places and the net curtains, hanging limply across them, yellowed and thin. Even to Marianne's unfamiliar eye, Bartholomew seemed less than his exuberant self when Marianne pulled up. It might have been his suspiciously black quiff, which did not seem as buoyant as yesterday. Or the shirt – the same pale blue as his eyes – tucked into the trousers of his three-piece suit, the tail of which had escaped and hung, like a flag on a windless day, below his jacket.

'Thank you for picking me up,' he said, opening the passenger door, trying and failing to persuade George out of the front seat. He sighed and looked at Marianne. 'And just so you know, this place is merely a stop-gap. Until I get myself sorted out.' He lowered his voice to a stage whisper. 'I'm between lovers and jobs right now. A bit like yourself.'

He climbed into the back seat and wrestled the seat belt around his bulk. He sighed again and waited for someone to ask him what the matter was.

Marianne indicated and pulled out.

'What's the matter, dear?' asked Ethel, obligingly.

'I applied for that usher job at the theatre,' said Bartholomew, 'just as you all insisted I should.'

'Go on, dear,' said Ethel when it became clear that Bartholomew was awaiting a cue.

'And I've heard nothing,' he said. 'Not. One. Word.'

'You only sent the letter a few days ago,' Ethel reminded him. 'They probably haven't had time to process all the applications yet.'

Bartholomew groaned. 'There'll be thousands, won't there? What chance do I have?'

'The theatre will be very lucky to get you, dear,' Ethel insisted, rubbing his back.

'There're holes in my CV as big as . . . as . . . as Donegal . . .' He paused there and poked his head around Marianne's seat. 'Donegal is big, isn't it?'

Marianne nodded, not taking her eyes off the road.

'As big as Donegal on my CV,' Bartholomew went on. 'I could hardly put toy-boy alcoholic in there, could I?' Since Bartholomew was somewhere north of fifty, Marianne didn't think he quite qualified for the title of 'toy-boy'.

'And any actual proper job I ever had,' continued Bartholomew, 'like on the Caribbean cruise ship, and window dressing in London, and the cocktail bars in Manhattan, I got fired because of my drinking.'

'You don't drink any more,' Ethel told him soothingly.

'But I haven't worked in nearly a year,' Bartholomew said, his voice high with panic. 'Rita said I should concentrate on my sobriety, and I did, but I can hardly tell them about that at the interview, can I? And that's if they call me at all, which, let's face it, they won't, will they? Once they read my CV.'

'You'll make a great usher,' said Ethel, patting his arm. 'And Rita can do her breathing exercises with you before the interview. You'll be magnificent.'

Bartholomew shook his head. 'They're looking for someone calm. And experienced. And bubbly.'

'You're bubbly,' said Ethel, after a while. Bartholomew slumped in his seat. Ethel reached across the seat and slipped her tiny hand into his meaty fist. Marianne drove on, towards Rush, where Freddy lived.

'Just here, dear,' Ethel called out as Marianne drove down the main street in Rush. She pointed a crooked finger at a small shopfront, meticulously maintained, squashed between a closed-down Chinese takeaway and a shabby bookies. The sign above the door spelled 'Razzle Dazzle' in gleaming sequins with the words 'Costume Hire' in neat lettering below. In the window, a mannequin dressed as Dorothy in a blue and white checked pinafore with white lace trim and sparkling red ruby slippers. Beside her, the Scarecrow: an imaginatively put together series of hessian sacks, tied with twine and spilling straw, held upright by a wooden stake, over which a patchwork smock and panta-loons had been assembled. The Tin Man was a suit of armour, so brightly polished his chest could be used as a shaving mirror.

Of the Cowardly Lion, there was no sign.

Marianne was pulling up the handbrake when a long, thin face, a lot of it concealed behind a pair of enormous sunglasses, appeared at her window. She jumped and acci-dentally pressed down on the horn. The man jumped too.

They eyed each other warily.

'That's just Freddy, dear,' said Ethel from the back.

'Yes, I'm afraid it is,' added Bartholomew, sourly.

The man removed the sunglasses, underneath which perched another pair of glasses. A wire-rimmed pair with small round lenses. Now Marianne recognised him as the tall, narrow man of indeterminate age and watery grey eyes she had met at Ancaire. Freddy.

Marianne rolled down the window. Freddy straightened

and stepped away from the Jeep. He was dressed in a long, thin cardigan, the same gruel grey as his thinning hair, over a faded *Hairspray* T-shirt and a pair of brown slacks, shiny from years of laundering. On his feet, a fashion faux pas the likes of which even Marianne could not countenance: white socks and brown leather sandals.

'Sorry for blaring the horn,' Marianne said. 'I didn't notice you coming.'

'He gets that a lot,' boomed Bartholomew from the back. Freddy leaned in through the window and glared at him. 'I'm sorry I can't say the same about you, you great lump of goose fat.'

'I'll have you know I lost two pounds at Slimming World this week,' said Bartholomew.

'Not off your behind, that's for sure,' declared Freddy.

He turned to smile at Marianne. 'Pardon my French,' he said. He opened the back door and stepped delicately past Ethel, folding himself in the cramped space between her and Bartholomew.

'Aren't you going to wave goodbye to your mummy?' said Bartholomew, pointing at the door of Razzle Dazzle where a tall, thin elderly woman stood erect, with long, fine white hair hanging like a mantilla around her head. She wore a severe black suit, a severely starched white blouse, thick black tights and black court shoes. She stared at them with very little expression on her face.

'You'd better wave, Freddy dear,' said Ethel. 'You know she won't go in until you do.' Freddy waved. The woman, who did not wave back, stepped backwards and disappeared into the shop.

Once settled, Freddy petted George's head, then presented

his cheek to Ethel, who kissed him obligingly. He ignored Bartholomew in a blatant and, Marianne suspected, routine way but, when Bartholomew did not rise to this bait, Freddy examined his face and said, in a not unkind tone, 'Who's eaten your sticky toffee pudding?'

Bartholomew shrugged so it was left to Ethel to explain about the job application.

'Well,' said Freddy, 'if it helps, you certainly look like an usher so—'

'What's that supposed to mean?' thundered Bartholomew.

'I just meant, you look . . . smart,' said Freddy, flushing.

'Oh,' said Bartholomew, trying not to look pleased.

A gap appeared in the traffic and Marianne wrestled the Jeep into first gear and moved off.

'How many days now?' asked Ethel.

'Twenty-five,' said Freddy in a flat voice.

'That's marvellous,' Ethel told him, patting his arm.

'It's just further proof that I don't need to be in Rita's Get Well Soon programme,' said Freddy 'I can quite clearly take it or leave it.'

Nobody responded to that.

'Shirley's in Swords,' Ethel told Marianne.

'I can give you directions, if you like,' piped up Bartholomew.

'Ethel is perfectly capable of giving directions,' said Freddy, primly. 'There's no need for you to mansplain.'

Bartholomew flushed. 'I was merely—'

'Turn right here, dear,' said Ethel, delicately.

Marianne tried not to dwell on the fact that Brian lived in Swords now, too. With Helen. She gripped the wheel tighter, her skin clammy against it.

Shirley's house was a two-storey pebble-dashed terrace, in the middle of a row, with long weeds growing out of the guttering and up through the cracks in the narrow driveway. The garden was a miserable, uninspiring affair, a square of patchy grass, flattened and muddy.

The front door was wrenched open and Shirley appeared, wearing ripped jeans and a black T-shirt with a woman's hand on the front, her middle finger raised, the nail painted a bright pink. She scowled at them, then spat a wad of chewed up gum out of her mouth into the drain.

'There she is,' said Ethel, beaming.

'The little dote,' said Freddy, waving.

'Hello, sweetheart,' called Bartholomew, rolling down the window and blowing a kiss.

Shirley opened her mouth and roared, 'SHELDON. HARRISON,' and the two boys barrelled out the door. They skidded to a halt beside the Jeep.

There mustn't be school, Marianne thought. Or maybe it was the weekend? Yes, it was. Saturday, she thought. No. Sunday.

Shirley, who looked more like the boys ferocious older sister, strode to the jeep, unfurled her fists and placed a hand on each of their heads, careful not to disturb their matching blond mohawks.

'Oh, look,' the smaller boy – Harrison, Marianne thought – said. 'It's George. Can we pet him?' He addressed this question to Marianne, who felt an unexpected lurch of protectiveness towards the dog. 'Only very gently,' she found herself saying.

They ran to the other side of the Jeep, but not before

inspecting the road, looking left, then right, then left again. They flung the passenger door open and hauled themselves inside. George moved over to accommodate them, licked their faces. The boys shrieked with delight, which made Ethel, Bartholomew and Freddy laugh out loud, which made Shirley shake her head and glare at Marianne, which prompted Marianne to say, 'Don't worry, George doesn't bite.'

'Unlike me,' said Shirley, hitching the strap of a schoolbag onto her shoulder. She ordered the boys into the very back seat of the Jeep, behind Ethel, Bartholomew and Freddy, glared at them until they had secured seat belts around their skinny bodies, then marched to the front passenger seat and pointed at George. 'Out,' she told him and, without so much as a whimper, the dog vacated his seat and inserted himself between the boys. Sheldon pulled a seat belt around George, and Harrison slung as much of his arm as he could reach around the dog's neck, stuck his thumb in his mouth and leaned his head against George's unkempt fur.

Shirley arranged herself into the passenger seat, snapped on her belt and pulled down the visor to examine her face in the mirror. She found a spot on her chin and squeezed it between two bitten fingernails until it burst. Marianne did her best not to notice. She concentrated on driving.

'You're off the hook this week, by the way,' Shirley said, pushing the visor back into place and leaning back against her seat. 'I'm concentrating on Irish poetry at the moment.'

'Sorry?' said Marianne, when some response appeared to be anticipated.

Shirley studied Marianne's face. 'My leaving cert,' she said. 'You promised to help me with maths, remember?'

'Did I?' Marianne struggled to recall.

'So,' went on Shirley, 'I'm just letting you know that I won't need your help till next week 'cos I'm working on Irish paper one at the moment.'

'I see,' said Marianne.

Shirley continued to look at Marianne. 'You're not an alcho, are you?' she asked.

'Shirley!' said Freddy. 'You can't just ask a question like that.'

'Why not?' demanded Shirley.

'Children of alcoholics either follow suit or become strict teetotallers,' said Bartholomew with authority.

'Where'd you get that little gem?' said Shirley. 'From an issue of *Take a Break?*'

Bartholomew ignored Shirley's sarcastic tone. He held up a vast fleshy hand. 'Let's take a punt on it.'

'You're not supposed to be gambling,' Shirley told him. 'Next thing you know, you'll be face down in a ditch, without the arse in your trousers. No offence.'

'It's only gambling if there's money involved,' Bartholomew said. 'Rita said—'

'I say teetotal,' offered Freddy.

'So do I,' said Bartholomew, scowling at Freddy to demonstrate his displeasure at agreeing with him.

'Me, too,' added Shirley.

They looked at Ethel, who flushed. 'I really don't like to make assumpt—'

'You have to say,' Shirley told her.

'Teetotal,' said Ethel in a small voice as two small pink circles appeared on her cheeks.

'What's a teetotal?' called Harrison from the back.

'It's someone who totally likes tea,' said Sheldon with authority. 'Isn't it, Mam?'

'Something like that,' said Shirley.

They all looked at Marianne. She could see them, despite her concentration on the road. When it became apparent that they weren't going to stop staring until a response was forthcoming, she nodded and said, 'Yes. Teetotal.'

'Knew it,' said Bartholomew smugly.

'Know it all,' said Freddy.

'Good for you, dear,' said Ethel.

'I've never met a teetotaller before,' said Shirley. When she smiled, she looked very young and very pretty. Marianne was sure Shirley wouldn't be thrilled to hear either of those things so she said nothing.

Chapter 10

Marianne felt weak with exhaustion and relief as she drove up the avenue at Ancaire with everybody intact.

The Get-Well-Sooners made their way into the drawing room, but of Rita there was no sign.

Patrick stood at the sink in the kitchen, rinsing a bunch of mucky carrots. He wore his uniform of tight leather trousers and sleeveless T-shirt sporting the name of some death metal band or other. He turned when Marianne entered, smiled his gentle smile.

'Shouldn't you be at work?' she snapped at him.

'I am,' said Patrick, nodding towards the carrots. 'These are for dinner tonight.'

'I meant . . . whatever it is you do in your workshop.'

'I make things,' said Patrick. He made everything sound so simple. When nothing was simple. Not one bloody thing. The anger Marianne had felt two days ago, when she opened the wardrobe, hadn't gone away, she realised. It was like a storm at sea, at times coiled and waiting, then whipping her thoughts into a frenzy, showing no sign of blowing itself out.

'Where's Rita?' she asked.

'She's not here,' said Patrick. He lay the carrots in the wicker vegetable basket, as one might a sleeping infant.

'Well, her clients are,' said Marianne, making sure Patrick saw her putting the word, 'clients' in inverted commas with her fingers.

'Rita has set up the drawing room for them,' said Patrick, wiping his wet hands on his T-shirt. 'They're painting today.' Patrick moved towards the door, anxious to be gone. Marianne couldn't blame him.

'Rita never said she was going anywhere,' she said, hanging the keys of the Jeep on the hook by the door. 'Where is she?'

Patrick stopped at the door and shrugged. 'She said she'd be back later,' he said.

Marianne felt exhausted. As if she hadn't slept at all, with Ancaire like a solid presence all around her so she had to struggle to negotiate her way through it.

The Get-Well-Sooners took the news of Rita's absence well, perhaps sensing that Marianne had reached the very outer perimeter of her patience. They arranged themselves behind the easels that Rita had set up for them and set to work.

Marianne marched with purpose to the door, as if she had someplace to go. She stopped when she reached it, turned round. 'Will you be okay?' she asked them. The anger was tamer now. Perhaps she simply lacked the energy to sustain it. Or maybe it was the sight of Freddy and

Bartholomew sitting side by side on stools, painting the still life Rita had left for them – a knot of seaweed, a tarnished silver fork, a roll of toilet paper, half a mango and a corset – the tips of their tongues trapped between their front teeth in twin concentration. The silence between them was almost companionable.

'Harrison could do better with his left hand,' said Shirley, standing behind her easel and slashing at the canvas with her brush.

'Oh, it's not that bad,' said Freddy, peering over the rim of his glasses at Shirley's painting.

'I was talking about yours and Bartholomew's,' said Shirley.

'I'm leaving the room now,' said Marianne.

'I wonder if Rita left any treats?' Bartholomew wanted to know. 'I only ask because Ethel's blood sugar levels could be low by teatime.'

'This little piggy stuffed his face with cream buns,' said Freddy.

'Don't make me go over there, Frederick,' hissed Bartholomew.

'What are you going to do? Sit on me and squash me to death?'

Ethel smiled at Marianne. 'Don't worry, my dear. I have everything in hand.' She gestured around the room and her hand hit off the edge of her easel, which collapsed as easily as a house of cards.

Shirley picked it up, rearranged it in front of Ethel. 'Go on,' she said to Marianne. 'I'll sort them out.'

Marianne made it as far as the landing. 'Could you summon a taxi for me, Marianne?' Aunt Pearl called from her bedroom as Marianne walked past her door. 'I need to go and buy spark plugs for my car.'

Marianne bristled. She was turning into some sort of a Girl Friday here at Ancaire. Where fully formed adults sat around painting half-eaten pieces of fruit and rolls of toilet paper. Or washing mucky carrots. As if things like stable employment and tax returns and refuse collections didn't exist. And why couldn't Aunt Pearl summon a bloody taxi herself? And who the hell said 'summon' anyway?

'I don't believe in the telephone,' added Aunt Pearl, as if she could read Marianne's mind and see all the ugly thoughts therein.

Marianne wouldn't be surprised if she could.

Pearl's face appeared around the bedroom door. 'I prefer eyeballing people when I speak to them,' she said.

Marianne marched back down the stairs. Hanging on the back of the kitchen door was a cork board. Scribbled on a scrap of paper and pinned to it was the number of the local taxi company, Tried and Tested Taxicabs. Marianne rang the number. It rang and rang. To pass the time, Marianne counted down from a thousand in multiples of fifty-nine and a quarter.

'Hello, hello, hello,' said a jovial voice with a thick Scottish accent.

'Hello?' said Marianne tentatively.

'Hello,' said the man.

Marianne wasn't sure what to say next.

'Now it's your turn to speak,' said the man.

'Is that, eh, Tried and Tested Taxicabs?' said Marianne.

'It is indeed.'

'Why didn't you say that, when you answered the phone?'

'Didn't I?'

'No, you didn't,' said Marianne. 'You said, "Hello, hello, hello."'

'Sometimes you fancy a change, d'you know what I mean?'

'It's confusing,' said Marianne. 'For your customers.'

'Fair point,' the man said. 'Let's start again, shall we? Just press redial when I hang up.'

'No, wait, I—'

The line went dead.

'Hello?' said Marianne. 'Hel . . .? Oh, for Christ's sake.' She pressed redial. This time, there was no need to count down from a thousand in multiples of fifty-nine and a quarter. The phone was answered on the first ring.

'Tried and Tested Taxicabs, good afternoon, Hugh McLeod speaking. How can I be of assistance?'

'Hugh McLeod?'

'At your service,' he said. Marianne could tell he was smiling. Also that he had put on a telephone voice.

'You said you were a hairdresser,' said Marianne stiffly.

'I like to keep busy,' he said. 'Is that *I Capture the Castle*?'

'It's Marianne Cross,' said Marianne.

'Which bit are you at?'

'Sorry?'

'My favourite bit is when they swim in the moat at night.'

That was Marianne's favourite bit too, but she wasn't going to admit that. 'I need a taxi,' she said.

'Well, you've come to the right place,' the man replied, ignoring Marianne's nettled tone. 'Is it for yourself?'

'No.'

Hugh waited.

'It's for Pearl.'

'Ah, how is Miss Havisham?'

'That's a bit rude,' said Marianne, who was glad she was not 'eyeballing' Hugh, which would allow him to see the grin that had forced its way onto her face.

'She knows I call her that,' said Hugh.

'You call her Miss Havisham to her face?'

'Pearl agrees with me that Miss Havisham is undoubtedly one of Dickens's finest literary achievements,' said Hugh.

'I suppose what you call your clients is your own business,' said Marianne.

She cleared her throat.

'When can the taxi be here? Pearl is going to Swords.'

'Halfords?'

'Yes.' Marianne wondered how he knew but didn't ask, not wanting to encourage him.

'That woman really knows her way around an engine,' said Hugh.

'Are you impressed just because she's a woman?' said Marianne huffily.

'I'm just impressed in general,' said Hugh. 'She helps out with the cabs sometimes, you know. No one does a pre-NCT inspection as thoroughly as Pearl.'

'So,' said Marianne, determined to steer the conversation back to a more businesslike footing. 'What time did you say you'll be here?'

'Will five minutes do?'

'I suppose it will have to.'

She hung up.

Chapter 11

By the time Marianne had dropped the Get-Well-Sooners home, there was still most of the afternoon to go. Even after she'd lost her job, she'd maintained something of a routine, keeping the house in order, re-reading her collection of *Accounting Weekly* and updating the spreadsheet she used to keep abreast of her finances. A fairly redundant exercise in the end, she had to concede. Still, it filled the space.

Here, at Ancaire, she felt the length of the afternoon hours stretch out before her, empty and endless.

Rita had not returned from wherever she was and, from the sporadic and random words coming from the sitting room, Marianne deduced that Pearl was in there, watching *The Chase*, which she denied being addicted to.

There was no sound other than the erratic spluttering of the grandfather clock in the hall. Even the kitchen seemed cavernous and echoey, without the mess Rita generated when she cooked and baked, using all the surfaces and most of the bowls and cutlery in the process.

Through the windows, the usual roil of the sea and rattle of wind against the glass panes, interspersed with the occasional braying of Donal, the threadbare donkey, whenever Declan perched on his back or Gerard sheltered between his legs.

Everything was so alien yet it felt horribly familiar. She had been gone for twenty-five years but here, at Ancaire, she was fifteen years old all over again, suspended somewhere between the past and the future.

She had to get out. Marianne pulled on her anorak and clamped a woollen hat on her head, doing her best to get as much of her hair inside it as she could manage. She opened the door of the back kitchen and was assailed by the sharp tang of the sea and the nearly sweet smell of various animal droppings and pelts. She stuffed her hands into her pockets as she passed the animals. If she let her arms swing, they often formed the – false – impression that she had brought something for them. A mint, perhaps. Or a carrot stick. She did not make eye contact with any of them, giving them a wide berth as she picked her way through the long grass at the top of the kitchen garden. Through the glasshouse, she could see Patrick's workshop, the doors wide open as usual, and Patrick sawing through a sheet of wood.

Instead of taking the steps down to the beach, Marianne struggled through the small but dense forest at the edge of Ancaire on the other side of which was a trail that led along the coast towards Rush. She was nearly warm when she stumbled out of the forest. When she took her hat off, the wind lifted her hair away from her face and she could see for miles; the trail winding its way along the crooked coastline and the sea below, always moving, stretching out to the horizon where she could make out the outline of boats. One was a ferry, she thought. It was too far away for her to tell if it was coming or going.

She hadn't meant to walk as far as the graveyard. She hadn't realised that's where she was until she arrived, as if the wind had borne her there like a dandelion seed. It was a mostly overgrown and forgotten affair now, crouched behind the ruin of an ancient church.

The latch on the gate made a clicking sound as Marianne opened it. She hadn't been here since the funeral, which she barely remembered. She had no idea where the grave was. It wasn't beside her grandparents' one, which was near the entrance, their names barely visible under clumps of lichen that had spread across the stone over the years. Maybe it wasn't here at all? Maybe it was in a different graveyard? But something about the sycamore tree at the stile snagged on a memory in her head. The tree was bigger now. Taller. Twenty-five years will do that to a tree. Twenty-five years on the thirtieth of April. Rita's careless, childish drawing in her diary, marking Shirley's eviction. As if she didn't remember it was Flo's anniversary. Or as if she did. And didn't give a damn.

Usually Marianne marked the day on her own. Did something she thought Flo might have liked. Ate a banana split at an ice-cream parlour in town. Went to see a Disney film in the cinema. Traipsed around the zoo. She hated the smell of the zoo and the weather could be harsh at that time of the year but she mostly had the zoo to herself, the last time she had gone there, so that had made it more bearable.

Now, this year, she would be here.

At Ancaire.

Because she had nowhere else to go.

She leaned against the trunk of the sycamore, letting her eyes travel from one side of the graveyard to the other. When she saw it, she wondered how she hadn't seen it before. A slab of sandstone, with William's name at the top and below it, Flo.

Flo Cross
1982–1992

In front of the stone, a rectangle of grass and, around the edges, rose bushes, thorny and bare. No weeds strangled the bushes and the grass was a vibrant, lush affair. In a glass vase at the base of the stone, fresh-cut pansies.

The overall effect was one of colour: the brownish-red of the sandstone, the soft green of the grass, the purple and yellow of the petals.

The overall effect was one of care: the patch of ground was tended by somebody.

Marianne suspected Patrick. It would be typical of him. To take such an interest in something that had nothing to do with him. She crouched down and put her hand on the stone – on the F of Flo – and waited to feel something.

She felt foolish.

And cold.

She didn't know why she had come. She didn't feel close to Flo. She felt the same way she always felt. Guilty. Anxious.

And yes, she was ashamed to say, sorry for herself. For what she had done without, all these years. For what had become of her. Flo had looked up to her. Marianne had taken it for granted. And now look at the state of her.

She wiped her face with her hands, wiped her hands in the grass. It was icy cold, the ground. Marianne snatched her hand away. More than anything, she wanted to unfeel it. To have never touched it. The hard cold of the ground.

She rubbed her hand up and down the leg of her track-suit, trying to warm it. Behind her, a clicking sound. It was the sound of the latch on the gate. Marianne turned and saw Rita, turning to close the gate behind her, bending to pick up a canvas bag from the ground, arranging the straps over her shoulder. Marianne bent low and ran to the next grave, then the one after that, using the headstones to conceal her. The thought of speaking to Rita, here, was impossible. Because what else would they talk about but Flo? And they had never talked about Flo afterwards.

Marianne hid behind the grave of someone called Thomas Dunne, who had died in 1876.

Rita made her way through the graveyard, her cerise-pink trench coat unbuttoned and billowing behind her, revealing her dress, which was a more subdued shade of pink. The canvas bag hung off her shoulder now, clanking against her body as she walked. When she got to Flo's grave, she sat down as if the ground wasn't cold. And hard. From the bag, she lifted a fresh bunch of flowers. Marianne craned her neck but couldn't make out what type they were. Bright orange ones. She removed the pansies from the vase and replaced them with the fresh ones. Marianne could hear her talking out loud. Then laughing. Her comic book laugh.

Hee hee hee. Now she seemed to be cutting the grass with a . . . Marianne squinted . . . was that a pair of nail scissors?

Marianne's back ached now from the bending and crouching. She needed to get out of there. She peered again round the edge of Thomas Dunne's grave just as her phone rang. Rita stopped talking and looked around. Marianne ducked behind the stone and dug in the pocket of her anorak for her phone, stabbing furiously at the button to disconnect the call but not before she saw that the caller was Brian.

She slumped against the stone, trying to get her breath under control, straining to hear Rita. She could hear her high heels, clip-clop-clipping against the cobbled path. She could hear the chime of Rita's earrings – slender lengths of bamboo – tapping against each other, and her mother's voice, frailer than usual, not as sure of itself as it normally was, struggling to be heard over the wind. 'Hello? Is anybody there?'

Marianne shut her eyes tight. She knew she should stand up. Reveal herself. Put her mother's mind at ease.

Instead, she set off on her hands and knees towards the gate, concentrating on the pain of sharp pebbles cutting into her skin. It distracted her from thinking about Brian. Imagining that he could see her now. Crawling through a graveyard. Trying not to be seen or heard by her mother.

Maybe he wouldn't be surprised.

She crawled on until she got to the gate. She opened it and scrambled to her feet, bent low as she ran through the gate, not stopping to close it. She kept going, not knowing if Rita was looking her way, if she could see her, running away like some sort of thief in the night.

Hugh's car was parked on the road. At first it looked empty but, as Marianne approached, she saw him, reclined in the driver's seat, a beanie pulled down over his eyes and a copy of *I Capture the Castle* open across his chest.

Marianne was backing away when he sat up, pushed his hat off his face and grinned at her, his eyes disappearing into slits with the intensity of it. He rolled down the window.

'Hello, Marnie.'

'It's Marianne,' she said stiffly.

'I was close,' he said. He picked up the book, put a gigantic dog-ear on the page he'd been on and tossed it onto the passenger seat. He saw Marianne looking at it. 'You reminded me of that book the other day,' he said. 'I thought I'd re-read it. It's a cracking story.'

'Do you not have a bookmark?' she said.

'Would you be more kindly disposed towards me if I did?' He leaned out the window and regarded her with a tilt of his head that prompted his hair to fall across one side of his face. In the failing wintry light, it was the colour of conkers, shiny and in shockingly good condition. Marianne pulled her hat out of her pocket and wrestled it onto her head.

'No,' she said, frostily.

'I'll get one anyway,' he said, 'just in case.'

'Are you waiting for Rita?' asked Marianne then.

'Aye,' he said. 'I told her not to come today on account of her not feeling the best, but she insists every day, rain or shine. You know what she's like.'

Marianne didn't know what her mother was like. Nor did she know Rita wasn't feeling the best. She didn't know anything.

'I would be obliged if you didn't tell Rita that I was here.'

'No bother,' said Hugh.

'Do you promise?' Marianne couldn't help adding.

Hugh drew a cross on his heart with his forefinger. 'Cross my heart and hope to die,' he said. 'That do you?'

'I suppose it will have to,' said Marianne, straightening.

'You're welcome,' said Hugh.

'Oh. Thank you,' said Marianne, hurrying away.

Chapter 12

Marianne was acutely aware of the weight of the phone in her pocket. It beeped as she walked away from Hugh's taxi, which meant that Brian had left a message.

She would not listen to it.

But she found it impossible to stop thinking about it.

About the message.

What he might have said.

She hadn't spoken to him since the day he left. He had emailed her in work that day.

Marianne,
    Are you available for a meeting in the house tonight at six thirty?
Regards,
    Brian

While the wording of the email was pretty standard, Marianne noted Brian's reference to 'the house' instead of the more usual 'home'.

Alarm bells sounded.

She stopped in Arnotts on the way home and stole a tube of moisturiser. On Liffey Street, she handed the cream to a woman sitting in a doorway on a sleeping bag, shaking a worn-out paper cup at passers-by.

'What's that for?' the woman asked suspiciously.

Marianne examined the box. 'It says it locks in moisture, plumps your skin, and wards off the appearance of fine lines.'

'Do you think there's something wrong with my face?' The woman glared at Marianne.

'Do you want it or not?' said Marianne.

'It's Crème de la Mer,' the woman said. 'Of course I want it.'

At home, Marianne put on a blue T-shirt that Brian had once admired. 'It's the same colour as your eyes,' he had said.

Afterwards, when she revisited the scene in her brain, she would flinch at her preparations. Inspecting her teeth in the bathroom mirror. Pouring serum into her hair. As if finally succeeding in calming it would make him leave her less.

Because, from the moment she read his email, that's what she'd assumed.

Expect the worse.

'You look lovely,' Brian said, when he arrived. It was almost an accusation, the way he said it. Like she had taken some unfair advantage. She shouldn't have used so much of the bloody serum.

'Do you want a cup of tea?' she asked. 'Before we start?'

Brian sat down suddenly as if the muscles in his legs had given way. Put his hands flat on the table, like he was bracing himself. The breath he took then. The deep, long breath. Deep enough and long enough to say all the things he had to say. She knew what he was going to say before he said it. Was that love? Or just familiarity?

Either way, it was over.

'Aren't you going to say anything?' he asked, when he had finished.

She couldn't think of a thing.

Brian dragged his hands down his face. He looked tired. It was true that he hadn't been sleeping well lately. Marianne had put it down to work. An upcoming audit of one of Brian's major clients. There wasn't an accountant in the world who slept well before an audit.

'You've got to admit, Marianne, this is more like a business arrangement than a relationship.'

Marianne was stung with the unfairness of the statement.

'We agreed,' she finally said. 'No drama. An ordinary, quiet life. That's what you said you wanted, too.'

Brian shook his head. 'I'm sorry, Marianne,' he finally managed.

Since then, he had emailed her twice. Once with his new address and the name of his new girlfriend. Although he didn't use that word. 'Girlfriend'. He called Helen his 'partner', which sounded more ominous.

The second time, he wrote with the news that 'they' were expecting a baby.

Two babies, in fact.

Twins.

When she read that email, Marianne could not detect anything other than a huge sense of relief. That Brian had not managed to change Marianne's mind in this regard. That the burden of responsibility for these babies was his alone. His and Helen's. She remembered being horrified at the idea of Flo's fontanelle. Aunt Pearl had explained it to five-year-old Marianne in lurid detail. Marianne imagined a gaping hole in her sister's skull through which Flo's small baby brain could be seen, pulsing like a jellyfish.

She remembered thinking that Brian now had two fontanelles to worry about.

He went on to express his uncertainty, emailing her. He imagined that she had long ago moved on with her life. But he didn't want her to hear it from anybody else.

In her head, Marianne drafted many responses. In the end, she deleted the drafts and left his email unanswered.

Now, here he was on her voicemail. Back at Ancaire, she decided the easiest thing to do would be to destroy her phone. She went into the garden shed and hunted about for a suitable tool. Because the shed was mostly Patrick's domain, it was meticulously neat. Drawers had labels telling you what they contained. Seeds and bulbs in the main. Items like shears and rakes and trowels hung from a line of hooks, and a dustsheet had been arranged over the lawnmower, defunct now since the arrival of Gerard the goat.

Marianne had to concede that Patrick's system allowed her to find a hammer quickly. She picked it up, felt the heft of it in her hand, placed her phone on the ground and knelt down, raised the hammer. What gave her pause was the thought that this bore all the hallmarks of something Rita would do. It would make a noise, create a mess and, yes, while it would solve her immediate dilemma of Brian's message, it would also mean that she would no longer get text alerts from CPA Ireland, keeping her abreast of all things accounting. Or from her bank if there was unusual activity on her credit or ATM card.

Not that there had been any activity on either, unusual or otherwise.

Rita would insist on calling that a 'positive'. Marianne clenched the hammer tighter, lifted it higher.

The door swung open and there was Rita.

'Marnie!' she said, and she sounded delighted, like Marianne was exactly the person she had been hoping to see.

She had changed her clothes and now wore a sheer white ballet-length strapless dress with a bright green sash around the middle, the same colour as her turban – but, beneath her make-up, Marianne thought her mother looked tired.

She lowered the hammer. 'What are you doing here?'

'Oh,' said Rita, casting about the shed. Her eyes lit on a screwdriver. 'I was looking for a screwdriver,' she said, pointing at it.

'No you weren't.'

'What are you doing?' said Rita, nodding towards the hammer clutched in Marianne's hand.

'I asked you first.'

'Okay, fine,' said Rita, holding her hands up in surrender. 'I came in to see what you were doing.'

They were both distracted by an enormous spider, which was making a valiant effort to crawl up Rita's dress. Rita bent and scooped the spider into the curve of her palm, set it down gently in the corner of the shed furthest from the door.

'So,' she said, turning back towards Marianne. 'Do you need help with anything?'

'No,' said Marianne, hiding the hammer behind her back.

'You were about to demolish your phone, yes?'

'Of course not.'

'You have a voicemail,' said Rita, picking up the phone and pointing at the message on the screen.

'I'm well aware of that,' said Marianne.

Rita nodded then, as if Marianne had explained everything. 'I could listen to it,' she said then. 'If you like.'

'Why?' asked Marianne.

'To see what it says,' said Rita.

'What will you do after you listen to it?' said Marianne.

'What would you like me to do?' asked Rita.

'It depends,' said Marianne.

Rita nodded as if this made perfect sense. She pressed a button on the phone.

'Wait,' shouted Marianne, scrambling to her feet.

Rita paused, looking at Marianne as she waited.

'Aren't you going to ask me what it depends on?' said Marianne.

Rita took a moment to consider this. 'I suppose,' she said after a while, 'if it's a life or death situation I'll tell you?' She looked at Marianne for confirmation.

'What about if he says he—' Marianne began.

Rita interrupted. 'How about I listen to the message, see

what he says, and then I'll synopsise it for you. Or, if you decide you don't want to hear it, I'll just delete the message. Or I could help you smash the phone, if you prefer.' Rita smiled at Marianne. 'Okay?' She lifted her – mostly drawn on – eyebrows as she waited.

Marianne put down the hammer and nodded. Rita pressed a few buttons before raising the phone to her ear. Marianne leaned against the wall and tried not to clench as Rita got into her voicemail and listened to the message. Her face was impassive as she listened. Even at this remove, Marianne could hear the careful monotone of Brian's voice.

Rita hung up.

'Did you delete it?' Marianne asked her.

'Yes.'

'Well?'

Rita took a breath. 'The babies were born.'

'Oh.'

'Are you okay?'

'Why did he ring to tell me that?' said Marianne.

'Maybe he didn't want you finding out from anyone else?'

'Like who?'

'I don't know,' said Rita, shrugging. 'Maybe one of your work pals?'

'I don't have work pals.'

'Did you never go for lunch with anyone?' asked Rita.

'I ate at my desk.'

Neither of them spoke for a bit after that. It had never bothered Marianne; not having work pals, eating alone at her desk. It was just, now, saying it out loud, it sounded a bit, well, pathetic, she supposed.

She cleared her throat, transferred the hammer from one hand to the other.

'Are they all right?' she asked.

'Who?'

'The babies.'

Rita had a think. 'Well, he didn't say they weren't all right so I imagine they're fine,' she said.

'There's something else,' said Marianne, eyeing Rita suspiciously. 'Isn't there?'

Rita glanced at the hammer, still clenched in Marianne's hand, shifted her weight from one foot to the other.

'Tell me,' said Marianne.

Rita expelled air from her mouth in a lengthy breath. 'He mentioned your house,' she said. 'There's a "For Sale" sign outside. And he wondered if you were okay. He hoped you were okay.'

'Which is it? Wondered or hoped?'

'Does it matter?'

'Yes.'

Rita had another think. 'Hoped,' she said.

'Are you sure?'

'One other thing,' said Rita in a surprisingly good imitation of Brian's generic accent. 'I was driving down Carling Road earlier and I noticed your house for sale. I just . . . I'm sure you are but . . . I hoped you were okay.'

'He's sure I am what?' snapped Marianne.

'He's sure you're okay,' said Rita. 'Then there's a sizeable pause at the end before a fairly rushed, "Okay well, I'd better go, bye, bye, bye, bye, bye."'

Marianne couldn't help feeling impressed at Rita's

attention to detail. Five byes. Brian always said five of them in a row like that.

'Could you hear the babies in the background?' she asked.

'No,' said Rita.

'A "For Sale" sign,' said Marianne.

Rita nodded.

'It used to be our house,' Marianne said, almost to herself. She hated the way her mother looked at her then, like she felt sorry for her. She supposed she couldn't blame her.

'You also got a message from Shirley,' said Rita, brisk now. 'She said tomorrow suits her fine.'

'For what?' asked Marianne.

'She didn't say,' said Rita, 'but I think it's something to do with maths. She mentioned looking up calculus in the urban dictionary and the definition is "legalised torture".'

Marianne nodded. There was nothing torturous about calculus. Calculus made a lot more sense than most things.

Rita held the phone towards Marianne. 'Do you want it back?'

Marianne flushed. 'You must think I'm pretty childish.'

Rita shook her head. 'I've never thought that about you,' she said.

Marianne took the phone, slipped it back into her pocket. 'Thank you,' she said.

'You're welcome,' said Rita. She touched Marianne briefly on her arm before opening the shed door and bustling away.

Chapter 13

T he thing was, after Brian left her, nothing much changed in Marianne's life. She went to work, came home in the evenings, made dinner, watched nature programmes on the television and went to bed.

The weekends were spent catching up on housework, doing her weekly shop, restoring a piece of furniture she might have bought at a market and going for brisk walks in the park.

'How are you managing on your own?' asked Rita, during one of their sporadic meetings in a café not in Marianne's catchment area, when Marianne eventually told her that Brian had left.

'Fine,' said Marianne.

'Really?' said Rita.

'Yes,' said Marianne. It was true for the most part. She had papered over the crack that Brian had made in the wall in her life and got on with things. Apart from those few, inoffensive, maintenance-level shoplifting episodes.

And then of course, the one where she hadn't paid as much attention as she should. Not nearly as much attention as the security guard.

The babies arriving did not fell her as much as the house being sold.

Her home.

She supposed she would paper over this crack, too.

The next morning, she was jolted awake by the rooster – Declan, she thought – crowing. It was a broken, ragged sound, more obligation than enthusiasm, as if the rooster's heart wasn't quite in it. She lay in bed, momentarily startled by her surroundings before she remembered that she had returned to Ancaire with no prospects and no plans, and no chance of any of that changing in the near, or indeed far, future.

George stood on his back legs with his front legs on the bed, pawing at whatever bit of Marianne he could reach until she gave up and got up, threw on several layers, comprising T-shirt, tracksuit, and fleece, and took him outside to do his business. George did his disappearing act down the treacherous moss-slick steps as soon as Marianne opened the back door. Marianne had heard people talking in an effusive manner about the benefits of sea air, using words like 'bracing' and 'exhilarating'. One excitable man in the office had gone so far as to call it 'life-affirming'. George, barrelling along the shoreline with his tail a blur of wags, possibly felt the same way. To Marianne, the sea air felt dark and damp, heavy with salt, and full to the brim with January. Loud, too, with the roar of the wind tearing at the manes of the horses on the beach and the strident cry of the herring gulls as they dived at the water, breaking the steely surface with their beaks.

On her return from the beach, Marianne did her best to sneak past the kitchen window, where she could hear Rita clanking and banging and force-feeding anyone she came upon. But, in the stuttering effort of daylight, she was spotted by her mother, who rapped on the window, beckoning her inside.

'Go and pull a brush through your hair if you can, and I'll make you a cheese and tomato toastie before we go and collect my clients,' said Rita.

Rita's cheese and tomato toasties were delicious. She made them in the pan with butter. The bread was crispy and sweet, and the cheese melted all over the circles of vine tomatoes, and the whole lot sort of sang and danced in your mouth in a bonanza of taste that could make you forget about almost everything. Just for a moment.

It occurred to Marianne that her mother felt sorry for her. After yesterday. That scalded

'I'm not hungry,' said Marianne. 'And there's no need for you to come with me,' she added. 'I can pick up the Get-Well-Sooners by myself.'

'I know you can,' said Rita.

Pearl swept into the kitchen, soundless and swift, as if she were on casters, and issued a clipped, 'Good morning' to no one in particular.

Then came Patrick with the eggs, still warm from the weight of the hens. He handed them to Rita, who kissed him on both cheeks, called him 'my darling boy', and steered a wooden spoon of whatever concoction she was stirring in a pot towards his mouth, which he ate obediently. Their effortless domesticity made Marianne want to throw something. Break it. She glared at the coffee pot. 'Would you like me to make you some?' said Patrick, picking up the pot.

'No,' said Marianne, striding towards the door.

'No thank you,' said Aunt Pearl from behind her newspaper, but Marianne had already left the kitchen.

In the bedroom, she could smell Patrick's coffee already and her mouth watered, its dense, earthy scent invading the furthest and dankest corners of the house.

Marianne pushed as much of her hair as she could manage into a scrunchie and ate the banana she had filched from the bowl on the hall table. Above the table, a framed, blown-up photograph of Rita's parents, Ruby and Archibald, standing in front of Ancaire with their arms wrapped around each other and not just smiling at the camera but laughing. There was something so unguarded about their happiness. As if they expected nothing less.

Marianne made sure the keys didn't jangle when she slipped them from their hook in the hall, but Rita heard her anyway.

'Wait for me,' she called, pouring her weed-choked tea into a portable cup. She ran after Marianne, as fast as her snake-print high-heeled ankle boots would allow her towards the Jeep, almost glorious in a full-length cream faux-mink coat with a matching turban wound round her head, and squashed herself into the front passenger seat beside George, who had no choice but to accommodate her. There was nothing else to be done. Not with Rita.

'How are you feeling this morning?' Rita asked, as

Marianne waited for a tractor to pass before pulling out of the avenue, onto the main road.

'Fine,' said Marianne.

'Now, you're supposed to ask me how I'm feeling,' said Rita.

Marianne glanced at her mother, who nodded encouragingly at her.

'How are you feeling?' Marianne asked.

'I'd feel a lot better if you let me smoke in the Jeep.'

'You're not smoking in the Jeep.'

'I know. I just said I'd feel better if I could.' Rita took her vape pen out of her red velvet clutch bag, which did nothing but clash with the bright pink pinafore beneath her coat. She pulled on it with great enthusiasm, inhaling in large, loud gulps before breathing out, creating a vast cloud of vapour that filled the car and smelled of purple Fruit Pastilles.

'Jesus, Rita, I can hardly see where I'm going,' said Marianne.

'You're not going anywhere' said Rita, pointing through the fug at the red light.

'Thanks for reminding me,' said Marianne drily.

The two women glanced at each other. Long enough to notice the similarities between them, perhaps. The small hollow in the middle of their chins, the shape of their mouths, wide and full and a little too big in the pale circles of their faces.

The traffic lights turned green.

Marianne moved off but only got a couple of metres before the Jeep cut out. The driver of the car behind beeped. Marianne put on the hazard lights, turned the key in the ignition, stepped gently on the accelerator. The driver beeped again, leaning on the horn this time so that it blared.

Marianne glared in the rear-view mirror. 'Can he not see I'm having difficulty here?'

'He's being a dick,' said Rita, adjusting the rear-view mirror the better to see the object of her derision.

'Can you put that mirror back to the position you found it?' said Marianne.

'Hang on,' said Rita, handing Marianne her vape pen and pulling down her window.

'What are you doing?' said Marianne, suddenly nervous.

Rita undid her seat belt, kneeled on her seat and leaned out of the window. She waited until she was sure she had the driver's full attention before extending her hand with her middle finger up.

'Will you get in before you get us killed,' Marianne hissed at her. She turned the key again, floored the accelerator. The engine did not turn over. Behind her, the driver was leaning out his window now, shouting obscenities at Rita, who hadn't budged from her blatantly antagonistic position.

'I presume there's no central locking system in the Jeep?' Marianne stabbed at a few buttons, just in case.

The driver was purple with rage by the time he manoeuvred his way past them. He glared at Marianne as he drove by and she bowed her head, although she could see his fist, shaking, in her peripheral vision. Another car drove up behind them and stopped. Marianne tried again to start the Jeep.

'You have to talk nice to it,' Rita said, climbing back inside and resuming her seat beside George. She leaned forward. 'Who's a lovely Jeep then?' she said, patting the dashboard. 'Now try again.'

'I think the engine is flooded,' said Marianne, turning the key in the ignition and stepping cautiously on the accelerator. The engine wheezed and juddered, then turned over.

'See?' said Rita.

Marianne drove on.

She picked up Ethel, then Bartholomew, who was already waiting outside his house when she pulled up. He ran to the Jeep, flung open Marianne's door, then jumped up and down on the spot several times. In one of his hands – both of which he waved above his head, like antennae gone berserk – he clutched a white envelope.

Ethel leaned forward and peered at him. Marianne waited for him to run out of puff, which didn't take long.

'You are not going to believe it,' he panted. He thrust the envelope under Marianne's nose. 'Guess,' he said. 'Go on, you'll never guess.'

'You got called for the interview at the theatre?' said Ethel.

'How did you guess?' he demanded.

'Darling Bartholomew.' Rita clapped her hands. 'I knew you could do it.'

'I can only assume they haven't contacted any of my references yet,' said Bartholomew, deflating like a punctured balloon.

'Could you get in?' said Marianne, gesturing him inside the car. She was, after all, parked on double yellow lines.

Freddy sprinted out of Razzle Dazzle when he heard the Jeep roaring up the road, his long, spindly legs a blur of speed. 'Go, go, go,' he hissed desperately at Marianne as he hurled himself into the back seat and slammed the door. In the rear-view mirror, Marianne could see Freddy's mother, walking at a brisk clip towards the Jeep.

'Whatever's the matter, dear?' asked Ethel.

'Can we just please move?' begged Freddy, adjusting his glasses, which had slipped down his nose in his haste. 'Before she reaches us?'

Marianne pumped the accelerator. Plumes of noxious black smoke billowed out of the exhaust pipe and the Jeep heaved and coughed. 'Come on, come on,' she urged it, thumping the steering wheel. Rita looked pointedly at her.

'Lovely Jeep,' Marianne said, in a less aggressive tone. The Jeep emitted a short groan and then the engine caught and while the Jeep's initial movements were jerky, it cheered up in second gear and she was able to drive away before Mrs Montgomery caught up with them.

'Can everyone smile and wave,' said Freddy fretfully, 'so she doesn't think that we're running away from her?'

'Isn't that what we are doing?' enquired Ethel.

'I'm not running away from anyone,' said Bartholomew.

'Please?' said Freddy, and his voice was so plaintive that they all planted smiles on their faces and waved at Freddy's mother.

Even Bartholomew.

Mrs Montgomery did not wave back.

'What ails her today?' asked Bartholomew. 'Another severe bout of homophobia, perhaps?'

'She's not homophobic,' said Freddy. 'There are just some people she doesn't like who happen to be homosexual.'

'How could anyone not like David Norris?' said Bartholomew, shaking his head.

'Another of your conquests, I assume?' snapped Freddy.

'A gentleman doesn't kiss and tell,' said Bartholomew. 'But I will allow that David and I were very close during his gay rights campaign. You might say I was his muse.'

'So what were you going to say about your mother?' asked Rita, and Marianne, who feared that Freddy might box Bartholomew's ears if he was not sufficiently distracted, was relieved.

'Well,' said Freddy, sighing, 'she has found out that Marianne is separated.'

'What?' snapped Marianne.

'I'm sorry, Marnie,' said Freddy. 'Mother has a way of worming things out of me. And I'm afraid that she has decided that you would make an excellent catch, being a professional. And, you know, available.'

'And a woman,' added Bartholomew, drily.

'I may be separated but I am most certainly not available,' snapped Marianne.

'No, I didn't mean . . .' Freddy said, flushing. 'I'm afraid Mother's right. I always I manage to say the wrong thing.'

'Has she considered taking up motivational speaking?' wondered Bartholomew.

'She means well,' said Freddy. 'She's just wishes I wasn't a loser, like Dad.'

'I'm sure your father isn't a loser,' said Ethel, patting his arm.

Freddy shrugged his shoulders. 'I don't know much about him. Mother says he was an alcoholic but that's about all I know. He left before I was born.'

'To live with a man,' said Bartholomew pointedly.

'They were just good friends,' said Freddy, tensing. He

slumped against the back of his seat. 'Can we not talk for a while?'

Marianne thought that was an excellent idea.

Shirley had Sheldon and Harrison with her again. 'Fucken in-service training day at school,' she said, rolling her eyes. 'Whatever that means.'

'Fucken school,' said Sheldon, grinning. Shirley rounded on him. 'Don't say "fucken".'

'You said it.'

'That's different.'

Shirley glared at Marianne, her jaws working a wad of chewing gum around her mouth. Today she was wearing oversized navy overalls, pinched in at the waist with a wide rainbow-coloured belt and rolled up at the bottoms so that her Doc Martens were on show. Most of her face was covered with a pair of massive sunglasses with white plastic frames and a *Star Wars* schoolbag hung off her shoulder.

'So,' said Shirley, when she had put her seat belt on. She leaned forward and poked Marianne's upper arm. 'Maths lesson today, yeah?'

'Well, I . . .'

'I'll pay,' Shirley said. 'I'm not expecting a hand-out.'

'It's not that, it's . . .'

'Or I can do your eyebrows instead. You decide. But, if I were you, I'd take the eyebrow offer. No offence.'

'I'm going to be a train driver and a referee when I grow up,' shouted Harrison from the back of the Jeep.

'You can't have two jobs,' Sheldon informed him.

'Can so,' said Harrison. 'Can't I, Mam?'

Shirley kissed the tips of her fingers and pasted them

against Harrison's forehead. 'You'll be the best train-driving referee in the world,' she said.

Harrison smirked at Sheldon, who responded by sticking his tongue out.

Marianne deposited them at Ancaire, then went, without being instructed, to the kitchen to make tea.

She supposed she was becoming institutionalised.

She had taken to employing a tape measure to divide up Rita's various wares. Today, it was her shockingly sweet and extremely popular millionaire slices which Rita had re-named socialist slices since confectionary – like everything else – should be for everybody. Freddy and Bartholomew scrutinised the portions Marianne handed them with zealous concentration, the warmth of their fingers prompting the caramel to ooze from the biscuits in long, golden lines, which the men caught – expertly – on their tongues.

It wasn't exactly the routine Marianne might have hoped for but it was a routine of sorts, none the less, and it distracted her from things.

Like Brian and Helen and the babies.

The twins.

It distracted her from thoughts of her home. Its contents, each item hand-picked by Marianne with the sort of care and attention that other people simply didn't understand in this world where everything was replaceable and expendable. Where nothing lasted.

It distracted her from thoughts of strangers being shown around her home, inspecting it with a critical eye, already making plans to change everything that had taken Marianne so long to perfect.

Chapter 14

In the end, Marianne agreed to give Shirley a maths lesson after the Get Well Soon meeting.

Or rather, she failed to come up with an excuse that Shirley would accept.

Besides, Marianne told herself, she loved maths. It would serve as a welcome distraction from everything else.

After she dropped Bartholomew, Ethel and Freddy home, Marianne pulled up outside Shirley's house. Harrison and Sheldon scrambled out of the Jeep. 'You two better not break another of Mrs Hegarty's china dogs, do yiz hear me?' Shirley shouted after them as they ran towards the house next door.

'We only broke two,' said Harrison, holding up five pudgy fingers, then carefully folding down three of them, the tip of his pink tongue sticking out of the corner of his mouth.

'She has millions of them,' said Sheldon.

'Don't even look at them,' said Shirley. 'Don't breathe in their general direction. Is that understood?'

The boys nodded sombrely as the front door swung open and a large, plump lady appeared with her arms outstretched. The boys succumbed to her embrace as she gathered them to her enormous bosom, soft and wide as pillows.

'I'll be back in time to give them their dinner, okay, Mrs Hegarty?' shouted Shirley from the Jeep.

Mrs Hegarty nodded and ushered the boys inside, waved at Shirley and Marianne. Her eyebrows looked out of place, being very full and dark while the rest of her features had a sort of bleached, worn-out appearance.

'Do you pay her in eyebrows?' wondered Marianne aloud.

Shirley nodded. 'Mostly,' she said.

Marianne turned off the engine but Shirley made no move to get out of the Jeep. 'Hugh said we can study in his house,' she said. 'I'm working in the salon later, which is in his back garden.'

'Or we can study in your house and I can drop you to work afterwards,' said Marianne. She imagined Hugh's house to be a place where things like disarray and clutter were not just acceptable but celebrated. Shirley looked at her house and shook her head. 'I used to love that house. That's where I moved when I finally got round to leaving my ex and got my shit together with the drinking. It was always a kip, being honest, but it was my kip, you know? Mine and the boys'.'

Marianne nodded. She got that.

'I hate being in it now, knowing that we'll have to move out soon.'

'You don't know that for sure,' offered Marianne. 'Rita reckons the protest—'

'Come on, Marianne,' said Shirley, 'you look like a clever woman. No offence.'

'Eh, none taken,' said Marianne.

'A handful of recovering addicts shouting a few slogans and holding up their homemade placards? It's hardly going to make front-page news.'

Marianne thought that an accurate summation.

'And the landlord's a developer,' Shirley went on. 'It's not just my house he owns, it's the entire row. He's going to empty them all, one by one, then raze them to the ground and build apartments. He's got his fingers in lots of pies and throws money at whoever he needs to – politicians, big business, same thing really – to get what he wants. That's the T.'

'The tea?'

'The goss, the news, the word on the street,' said Shirley, shaking her head at Marianne's ignorance. 'I hope you have way more patience than me, by the way,' she added.

'Well, I definitely couldn't have less,' said Marianne.

'Are you slagging me?' asked Shirley.

'I'm not sure,' said Marianne.

Shirley shrugged. 'It doesn't matter so long as you're a good teacher.'

'I've never taught calculus to anyone except myself,' Marianne admitted.

'And do you get it?' asked Shirley.

'I love it,' Marianne couldn't help saying.

'Fucks' sake,' was all Shirley could manage after that.

Hugh lived in a small cottage near the end of Sandy Lane in Rush. It looked like a child's drawing of a cottage, with its bright red front door and a small square window on either side, books piled against them so that Marianne wondered how any natural light managed to penetrate inside. The gable wall had a bumpy appearance and, as Marianne pulled up outside, she saw that seashells had been stuck onto the plasterwork. The front garden was an uncultivated affair, long grasses swaying on their slender stems, interspersed with bright pockets of heather, in purples, greens and yellows. An enormous cat sat on a sturdy wooden bench and studied Marianne, then flicked his tail at her before dropping his gaze, as though he had seen enough.

Shirley slid her hand along the narrow ledge on top of the front door and lifted down a key, which she fitted into the lock, turned it. The door swung open.

'It's not exactly Fort Knox, is it?' said Marianne.

'There's nothing to steal in here,' said Shirley, stepping inside. 'Unless you count books.'

Marianne followed her. The door led directly into a sitting room. It was small and square, taken up mostly by an oversized, squashy couch in soft brown leather with a tartan wool blanket draped across the back and cushions scattered across it. A squat, black wood-burning stove had been set into the wall and was lit. Along the gable wall, an enormous bookshelf, crammed with – Marianne paused to look – old classics in the main. In the middle of the room, a beautiful wooden slab of a table – beech, Marianne thought – with benches along either side.

Marianne suspected Patrick's involvement.

'Do you want tea?' Shirley asked.

'Let's get started,' said Marianne, setting her bag on the

table and rummaging through it, pulling out a notebook Aunt Pearl had given her – 'It's just a lend, mind' – and the fountain pen she had bought Brian for their third wedding anniversary. She had thought he'd loved it, the pen. She'd found it on the floor under the sideboard after he'd left.

Marianne took off the cap. Well, she wasn't going to let it go to waste.

She sat down and Shirley sat beside her. Marianne shuffled a bit down the bench. The spine of Aunt Pearl's notebook cracked when she opened it. She cleared her throat and began. 'The reason why calculus is fun is because—'

'Seriously, can you actually hear yourself?' said Shirley. 'Like when you talk out loud, I mean?'

'I . . .'

'Ah, don't mind me,' said Shirley, nudging Marianne's elbow with her own. 'Maybe if I'd thought calculus was fun in school, things might be different.'

'Maybe fun is the wrong word,' said Marianne, moving her elbow away from Shirley's. 'Fascinating is probably better.'

'Right,' said Shirley, who didn't sound convinced.

Marianne tried a different tack. 'All calculus is really about,' she said, 'is change.'

'Change?'

Marianne nodded. 'It's the mathematics of change,' she said. 'And growth. Take your boys, for example.'

'O . . . kay,' said Shirley.

'They're constantly growing, right?'

'Well, with the amount of Cheerios they demolish, they'd want to be.'

'Do you keep a record. A height chart, for example.'

'Of course,' said Shirley picking up her phone, which was never beyond the perimeter of her arms. She jabbed at a few buttons, presented the screen to Marianne.

'Perfect,' said Marianne. 'So, with calculus, we can plot their growth, and the time it took them, on a chart like this, see?' Marianne drew a grid. Shirley looked on with something approaching interest. Marianne began plotting. 'We'll be able to derive all sorts of information about the boys from this chart,' she told Shirley. 'Like which of them is growing at the fastest rate.'

'It's Sheldon, isn't it? He wins everything, that fella.'

'Actually, it's Harrison,' said Marianne.

'There'll be killings,' said Shirley darkly. 'Can it tell me if they'll ever brush their teeth without being threatened with the wooden spoon?'

'Calculus is brilliant but it has limitations,' Marianne had to admit.

They worked for about an hour, after which Marianne set Shirley a problem to solve, working out the dimensions of a designated area for the boys' Lego within the confines of their bedroom. Marianne sat back while Shirley worked it out. All Marianne could hear was the *scratch-scratch-scratch* of Shirley's pencil against the page, the crackle of the logs in the wood-burner and the purring of Hugh's cat, who had taken up residence across Marianne's feet and fallen asleep. She had tried to shift him a couple of times but he paid no attention to her efforts. Also, she had to admit that her feet, which often fell victim to poor circulation, were warm as toast beneath the bulk of his body.

'Ta-dah,' sang Shirley, lifting her head from the page and pushing it towards Marianne. 'Nailed it.'

There was something childishly neat about Shirley's handwriting that made Marianne's heart sort of lurch in an uncomfortable way. Something hopeful and trusting about the arrangement of the letters and numbers, like a declaration of confidence in Marianne's ability to see her through.

Maybe she could? At least in mathematical terms?

'You actually have . . . nailed it,' she told Shirley, who beamed.

Shirley stood up. 'Break time,' she declared.

'I was going to do tangents next,' said Marianne.

'Well, I'm going off on a tangent to make tea,' said Shirley. 'That's a pun, by the way. Shakespeare is only mad about puns; he thinks he's so fucking funny.'

'You don't like Shakespeare?'

'Like, I've read *Hamlet* and I didn't laugh out loud once. Hugh says I have to remember that the humour is "of its time"' – she put the words in inverted commas with a caustic tone and a roll of the eyes – 'but, like, funny is funny, isn't it? No matter what century you're in.'

'So, Hugh likes Shakespeare?'

Shirley nodded. 'He didn't always. When he was in school, he thought Shakespeare was a dickhead too.'

Shirley disappeared into the kitchen and made tea.

'Do you want me to set you some homework?' Marianne called into her.

'That'd be great,' said Shirley.

Marianne was stunned. 'Great' seemed like a furiously optimistic term, coming from Shirley.

Shirley popped her head out of the kitchen, as if she knew that her use of the word required clarification. 'I like having stuff to do when Harrison and Sheldon go to bed. The house gets quiet without that pair bulldozing about the place.' She withdrew into the kitchen again and Marianne heard her opening presses. 'There's a bar of chocolate here. Only dark stuff, with . . . fucks' sake, chillies in it. Do you want some?'

'Eh, won't Hugh mind?' said Marianne.

Shirley poked her head out again, grinning. 'Ah, no,' she said. 'He said I'm the main reason he's not fat. I'm like a dose of colonic irrigation.' She threw a slab of chocolate at Marianne, who caught it in one hand.

'Impressive,' said Shirley. 'Didn't have you down as the sporty type.'

'I was asked to play on the lacrosse first team in school,' admitted Marianne, feeling a degree of pride. 'But I didn't in the end.'

'Why not?'

'I was good at the mechanics of the game, the catching and throwing and all that,' said Marianne 'But I just . . . wasn't great at being on a team, you know?'

Shirley nodded. 'No milk, no sugar, right?' she said, holding up a mug of tea.

'Thanks,' said Marianne.

The back door opened and Hugh barged in, making the room seem immediately smaller. He grinned at Marianne, who did her best to deflate her cheeks, which was difficult given the amount of chocolate she had crammed into her mouth. 'You're both still in one piece,' he said.

'Actually calculus isn't too bad,' said Shirley, settling herself cross-legged on the rug in front of the wood-burner. 'This from the girl who threatened to vandalise the bust of Isaac Newton in the Long Room at Trinity last week?' He said 'gir-del', which Marianne couldn't help finding amusing.

'Are you not cold in that rig-out?' she asked, nodding toward his kilt, which he was wearing without the benefit of socks, his barge-long feet slotted into a pair of pink flip-flops.

She was appalled to hear how like Aunt Pearl she sounded.

'I don't tend to feel the cold,' he said. 'And besides, trousers snag something terrible on the hairs.'

Marianne couldn't help a brief eye-dart to his legs, which were, she observed, as long and sturdy as one would be entitled to expect from a man of his size. They were matted with pale red hair. Strawberry blond, she supposed.

'I told you I'd wax them for you,' said Shirley.

'I believe I declined your kind offer,' said Hugh, backing away from her.

'Big baby,' she said.

'You're not wrong,' he said, tucking a thick strand of hair behind his ear. 'I just came in to let you know that Mrs O'Driscoll has arrived and she's insisting that you do her hair. I offered but she's not for turning.'

'All she wants is her usual bloody blue rinse,' said Shirley, sighing. 'Even Harrison could manage it.'

'We're just finishing up here,' said Marianne, standing up.

'Take your time,' said Hugh, his eyes settling on Marianne's, in a way that made it difficult for her to look away. Maybe because of their green colour. Like cat's eyes. Something hypnotic about them. 'I said I'd make Mrs

O'Driscoll a brew and I've given her a copy of a Royal special of *Hello!* so she's grand for a wee while.'

Now, his eyes had slid to Marianne's mouth. He looked at it. Like he was studying it. Marianne twitched under so much scrutiny. 'Shirley found my stash again, I see,' he said.

'Oh,' said Marianne, scrubbing furiously at the tell-tale chocolate stain on the edge of her mouth.

'It's a delicious combination, isn't it?' he went on. 'Chocolate and chilli?'

'I'll . . . replace it,' said Marianne.

'No need,' said Hugh, turning for the door. 'You can take me for an iced coffee sometime instead.'

'I don't drink cold coffee.'

'We'll ask the waiter to heat yours up,' he said, grinning again before he left the house. The room seemed still and quiet when he'd gone.

'The bang of pheromones in here,' said Shirley, flapping her hands about as if she was clearing the air. She turned to smirk at Marianne. 'Although aren't you people a bit old for that type of thing? No offence.'

'I definitely am,' declared Marianne, hoping that might be an end to it.

'And Hugh certainly is,' Shirley went on. 'He's thirty-eight.' She raised her hefty eyebrows so that they almost managed to reach her hairline.

Marianne ripped a page out of Aunt Pearl's notebook, filled now with her small, neat print. 'Here's your home-work,' she said in a loud, definite voice, holding the page towards Shirley.

'Although,' Shirley went on as if Marianne hadn't tried to change the subject, 'it is true to say that most of our clients are women and they flirt with him non-stop and tip him outrageously. But he shares the tips with me so I try not to object to their blatant objectification.'

'If you have any problems with the calculus question I set you, you can—'

'One of the women – I mean, she must have been thirty-five, easily – asked him out direct. Like, in front of me. Well, I was in the back but I could hear every word.' Shirley shuddered at the memory. 'And Hugh was lovely to her, of course he was, the sap. But it was a hard no, all the same. I assumed he was gay for a while, you know, with the kilt an' all. But no, turns out he just likes reading and learning new things.' Shirley glared at Marianne to make sure she was listening, which she was because she wouldn't dare do otherwise. 'I'm talking poetry and plays and whatnot,' she added. 'For, like, fun.'

Marianne wasn't sure how to respond to this. Shirley seemed genuinely addled. 'Well,' she ended up saying, 'once you get your exams over and done with, you'll probably feel differently about, you know, learning.'

Shirley withered Marianne with a look.

'Why do you want to do the leaving cert anyway?' asked Marianne then, her curiosity getting the better of her fear. 'Since you're training to be a hairdresser.'

Shirley shrugged. 'I want to know that I can, you know? I didn't do a tap in school. Too busy making a tit of myself for the boys. Drinking my head off. What a fucken dope I was.'

'And do you like hairdressing?' asked Marianne.

Shirley nodded. 'I really like it,' she said. 'Plus I'm brilliant with people so . . . you know, makes sense.'

'Right,' said Marianne.

Shirley grinned. 'Wait'll they hear he's asked you out on a date.'

'He didn't ask me out on a date,' said Marianne, nettled now.

'Okay, okay, keep that mop you call your hair on,' said Shirley, arranging her hands in a defensive position in front of her body.

'Besides, I don't go on dates. I never have.'

'What do you mean?' said Shirley. 'I thought you were married?'

'I am married,' Marianne corrected her even though she had no idea why she bothered. Her marriage was as much a relic of the past as her grandparents' 'How to . . .' books.

'And you never went on a date with your husband?' said Shirley.

Marianne shook her head.

'Not even before you got married?'

Marianne shook her head again. 'We talked in work. Sometimes we ate lunch together. Or went for walks.'

'Stop it,' said Shirley. 'This sentimental mush is making me nauseous.'

'It worked,' said Marianne. 'Well, I thought it worked.'

'And here's me thinking that Mills and Boon were dysfunctional,' said Shirley, rolling her eyes.

'Who's Mills and Boon?'

'Freddy and Bartholomew,' said Shirley, picking up her and Marianne's empty mugs and walking to the kitchen.

'Are they a couple?' said Marianne, following her.

Shirley turned on the tap, washed the mugs. 'They sort of were. Only when Freddy was good and drunk mind you,' she said, setting the mugs on the draining board. 'They met when Bartholemew's amateur dramatics group rented costumes from Freddy's shop. They were so cute together, so long as Freddy kept his glass topped up. And then BAM.' Shirley clapped her hands together, making Marianne jump. 'Freddy is drunk as a lord in Razzle Dazzle. one night, smoking his head off, tosses a match on the ground and sets the Cowardly Lion costume on fire.'

'On purpose?' Marianne couldn't help getting sucked into the story.

Shirley rolled her eyes. 'No, you big dope, he would never do that. He's petrified of his mother.'

'Right,' said Marianne, feeling foolish.

'You're lucky, with your mother,' said Shirley then, in a quieter voice. 'Rita's been great with Freddy. With all of us.'

Marianne bristled. 'Lucky is not the word I'd use.'

'Anyway,' Shirley went on, 'Freddy's mother put her foot down after that. Said he had to sort out his drinking or she'd disinherit him. Bartholomew got him into the programme. And sober Freddy can hardly bear to look at him. So we're stuck with the pair of them. Mills and bloody Boon. The bit where they're trying to convince themselves that they hate each other, you know?'

Marianne shook her head. 'I've never read a Mills and Boon,' she said.

'And Hugh calls you a lover of literature,' said Shirley, grinning. She walked to the table, stuffing her maths book and pencil case into the *Star Wars* schoolbag. 'If you'd bothered reading a Mills and Boon, you'd know that you're supposed to go on dates with your fella.' Shirley heaved

the bag on her back, grabbed her coat and opened the front
door. She jangled a set of keys. 'You have to leave now,' she
said.

'Oh,' said Marianne, scrambling to her feet and grabbing her bag. 'So, do you want to do this again? Sometime?'

'Do you promise it'll be as much fun as today?' Shirley
said, making her navy eyes even wider and gazing at
Marianne.

Marianne hesitated before she answered. 'You're making
fun of me, aren't you?' she said.

'Yes,' said Shirley. 'But I would like to do it again. If you
don't mind?'

'No,' said Marianne. 'I don't mind.'

'Cool.' Shirley swung a punch, which landed on
Marianne's upper arm. She now seemed to be waiting for
Marianne to do something so Marianne made a fist of her
hand and punched Shirley's arm.

'Ouch,' shouted Shirley. 'That fucken hurt.'

'Sorry,' said Marianne, mortified 'I . . .' She didn't finish
the sentence because she had no idea what to say. Or do.
She never knew. She was exhausted, trying to work it out.
Trying and failing.

Shirley grinned. 'You better hope my arm's not too sore
to blue-rinse the shit out of Mrs O'Driscoll's hair.' She
nodded at the door Hugh had barged through earlier. 'Do
you want to see the salon? It's just through there, in the
back garden.'

Marianne shook her head. 'I'd better head off.'

Shirley opened the door but before she left, she turned
and said, 'I still hate calculus but I'm not, like, furious with
it any more.'

'Not furious is a great first step,' said Marianne, smiling.

Shirley banged the door behind her, but by now Marianne knew that it was not because she was furious with calculus or with her or with anything really.

It was just the way she closed doors.

Chapter 15

Marianne hadn't opened the wardrobe in the bedroom again.

Instead, she took whatever clothes she needed out of the two suitcases, open on either side of her bedroom door, until one of them was empty and the other held nothing but the little porcelain owl, still wrapped in tissue paper but no longer encased in a sock, slipper, towel and her Aran cardigan. The tissue paper was soft and made a delicate rustling sound between her fingers as she unwrapped it. The owl itself was small. 'Is it a baby owl?' Flo had wanted to know when Marianne presented it to her for her tenth birthday. Marianne said no. She was a fully grown lady owl.

Flo liked the owl being a lady owl. Also being fully grown. Flo was in a hurry to be bigger. To be older. She hated being the baby. She had sometimes accused Marianne of babying her and perhaps she had a little.

Flo had been such a good baby. She had only cried when she absolutely had to, and when she did, Marianne cried too, even though she was six by then. She thought it had something to do with the size of Flo's tears. They seemed much too big for such a small baby.

'What are you going to call her?' asked Marianne, when Flo had unwrapped the owl, the morning of her tenth birthday.

'I don't know yet,' said Flo, holding the owl in front of Bruno's face so he could lick it.

The owl still didn't have a name. Marianne set it on her bedside locker. It seemed to regard her in a vaguely resigned manner. Marianne turned it round.

In the back kitchen, she stuffed her clothes inside the ancient twin tub and threw a scoop of washing powder over them. Then threw in another scoop since her clothes – tracksuits and fleeces, in the main – were riddled with sand and muck and animal hairs and George's drool. They smelled, too. A damp, salty smell. When she turned the machine on, it shuddered and groaned before settling into a begrudging rhythm.

In the kitchen, Rita scattered flour across the table and vigorously kneaded a ball of pastry.

'Good morning, Marnie,' she called out, stopping to pull her vape pen out of her apron pocket and suck noisily on the tip of it. Marianne struggled through the fug and made it to the counter. She opened Aunt Pearl's newspaper on the jobs page and picked up a pen. She didn't know how to do anything except accountancy. Could she be a receptionist for a start-up? No, you needed 'people skills'. She crossed it off. A local café was looking for a waitress. Experience essential. She crossed that off too.

'You don't have time for a job at the moment, Marnie,' said Rita, now scattering flour on an old Powers whiskey bottle. Marianne crossed off a dog-walker job. Walking George was hazardous enough. 'What do you mean?' she said, looking up warily.

'I need your help,' said Rita, panting now as she used the bottle – and her entire body, it seemed – to roll out the pastry.

'I'm already helping,' said Marianne. 'Driving your lot here, there and everywhere. And now Shirley seems to think I'm available for regular maths lessons. Then there's George. Not to mention Pearl, with her persistent furniture rearranging and—'

'I need you to come to the Get Well Soon meetings this week,' said Rita, lifting the circle of pastry off the table and arranging it into a pie dish.

'No,' said Marianne. 'And when I say no, I actually mean, absolutely no way.'

Rita raised her face towards Marianne. 'Could you scratch the end of my nose, darling? My hands are covered in flour.'

'Oh, for Christ's sake,' said Marianne, running the pads of her fingers up and down her mother's nose. This close, she could see the glue Rita used to stick on her eyelashes.

'It's just for a few days,' said Rita briskly. 'We need some help with the preparations for the protest at Shirley's house.'

'No,' said Marianne.

'We're making placards,' Rita went on, as if Marianne

had made some interested enquiry. 'And the Get-Well-Sooners, well, they're the best in the world but their arts and crafts skills are limited.'

'So are mine,' said Marianne.

Rita looked at Marianne. 'But you're so . . . neat.'

'I'm not doing it.' Marianne folded her arms across her chest, so tight her breathing was compromised.

'You're looking for a job,' said Rita, nodding towards the newspaper. 'This is a job.'

'I meant a paying job,' said Marianne.

'Okay, so there's no salary,' admitted Rita. 'But there's also no experience required. And I'm prepared to overlook your criminal conviction.'

'That's not funny,' said Marianne.

'It's a little bit funny,' said Rita.

Marianne sighed.

'So you'll do it?' asked Rita, picking three enormous, misshapen cooking apples from a bowl on the table.

'Do what?' said Aunt Pearl, who was, all of a sudden, at the kitchen counter. Marianne jumped, banging the hard bone of her elbow on the edge of the fridge.

'Marianne's agreed to help out at the Get Well Soon meetings.'

'Just for two days,' Marianne said.

'Or maybe a week,' added Rita.

Marianne was about to correct her mother when Aunt Pearl chimed in with an almost cheerful, 'That's good.' Marianne and Rita stared at her. Aunt Pearl collected herself before she added, 'The devil makes work for idle hands.'

Chapter 16

Rita was right. Marianne was good at making placards. This came as a surprise to Marianne, who had alienated herself from her classmates in primary school by declaring arts and crafts 'boring'. Now here she was, doing a passable job of colouring in between the lines, which was the task Sheldon set for her the following Saturday morning.

Sheldon was the self-appointed placard-printer. He used what he called 'bubble-writing'. Harrison decided what colours should be used; he favoured a different one in each bubble letter, which Marianne felt looked childish. She did not voice this opinion, given that her co-workers were, in fact, children.

Bartholomew was glad of the work as it distracted him from his worries about the impending job interview, about which he seemed increasingly pessimistic.

'Just be yourself, dear,' Ethel instructed him.

Bartholomew looked horrified. 'Why on earth would I do that?' he said.

'Marianne's got experience,' said Rita. 'Interviewing people. Haven't you, darling?'

'I thought you used to be an accountant?' said Shirley suspiciously.

'I still am an accountant,' snapped Marianne.

'How many people have you interviewed?' asked Bartholomew.

'Only two,' Marianne clarified. 'And that was over a twenty-five-year period. I managed to avoid interviewing, in the main.'

'Have you ever fired anyone?' asked Freddy, his watery grey eyes widening behind his glasses.

'Of course she hasn't,' said Ethel, tutting. Marianne wondered how Ethel knew this about her.

'So you could . . . maybe give me some pointers?' asked Bartholomew, stepping gingerly towards her.

Marianne shook her head. 'I'm hardly what you might call a go-to for interpersonal skills, Bartholomew.'

'That is true,' said Bartholomew, 'but you're also the only person I know with any experience so, you know, hit me up!'

Freddy snorted. 'It's so embarrassing when you try to be down with the youth,' he said.

'I suppose we could go through a few things,' said Marianne quickly before Bartholomew could retort. 'Like your previous experience, for example. Any qualifications that might—'

'You don't need qualifications to be an usher,' said Freddy. 'You just need to smile and point.'

'There's a lot more to it than that,' thundered Bartholomew.

'I would be the interface between the theatre, the players, and the audience. It's a crucial role.'

'Here's another crucial role,' said Shirley, handing him sheets of paper and cardboard.

Bartholomew sighed and stood up, removing his suit jacket and arranging it carefully across the back of his chair. He set his cufflinks carefully on the windowsill and folded up his shirt sleeves, applying himself to the task of pasting the sheets of paper onto the cardboard.

The affixing of the handle to the placard was completed by Patrick.

As well as colouring in between the lines, Marianne also had to correct Sheldon's spelling without him realising.

She and Bartholomew developed a system for this particular task. When Sheldon passed Bartholomew a page, complete with a slogan in bubble writing and a typo, Bartholomew turned it upside down and slid it along the floor towards Marianne who slipped it inside her hoodie and excused herself. 'I'm just going to the loo,' she called cheerily.

'Again?' said Sheldon.

'Eh, yes,' said Marianne.

'I'd hate to have to go to the toilet as much as you do,' said Harrison, 'because then I'd have to wash my hands, like, billions of times.'

In the bathroom, Marianne got to work with the Tippex, whiting out the 'shun' of 'evicshun' and waiting for it to dry before – painstakingly – copying Sheldon's bubble writing so he wouldn't suspect a thing.

'Thanks, by the way,' said Shirley the next day when

Marianne drove her home after another maths lesson, this one done in the kitchen at Ancaire, quiet after their meeting and still warm from the oven Rita had used earlier to make a controversial batch of macaroons. The controversy arose since the quantity made was not evenly divisible by the number of interested parties.

Marianne shrugged. 'I like maths.'

'I'm not talking about maths,' said Shirley.

'Oh,' said Marianne.

'I'm talking about the boys. You're lovely to them,' said Shirley, looking out her window so it sounded like she was talking to herself. 'Sheldon's dyslexic and . . . I saw how you were with him yesterday.'

'He's a good kid,' said Marianne, indicating onto Shirley's road.

'Good?' Shirley said, turning to glare at Marianne.

'I mean great,' said Marianne urgently. 'He's a great kid.'

Shirley grinned and nodded.

As soon as Marianne pulled up outside Mrs Hegarty's house, the front door flew open and Sheldon and Harrison appeared, with a worn out Mrs Hegarty behind them. The boys flew down the garden path towards the Jeep, a blur of boyhood in matching football strips, intent on their mother. Shirley looked at Marianne before she opened the door.

'See you tomorrow?' she said.

Marianne nodded. 'Yes,' she said. 'See you tomorrow.'

Shirley got out and braced herself before the boys hurled themselves at her, covered her in limbs. George climbed into the front passenger seat and pawed at the window, which was Marianne's cue to lower it. He leaned his head out and the boys detached themselves from their mother and ran to him, running their small, sticky hands along his head and down his back.

'I'm going to teach him how to shake hands tomorrow,' said Harrison.

'He doesn't have hands, dope,' said Sheldon. 'He has paws.'

'They're the same as hands,' said Harrison, stung. 'Aren't they, Marnie?'

Marianne felt herself stiffen in her seat. In the rear-view mirror, she could see Flo, sitting on the cushion Marianne had filched from one of the Queen Anne chairs in the drawing room, so Flo could see out the window. She was small for her age, Flo. Unlike Marianne, who was often mistaken for somebody older on account of her height. Flo was holding a buttercup in her small hand. Holding it under her chin. 'Do I like butter, Marnie?' she said, lifting her chin so that Marianne could see the soft yellow glow of the petals reflected on her skin.

'Aren't they, Marnie?'

'Marnie?'

'You okay, Marianne?'

Shirley leaned through the window, past George, her hand warm on Marianne's wrist.

Marianne nodded. 'I'm fine.' She looked past Shirley to where the boys stood. 'Yes, they're exactly the same as hands,' she called to Harrison, even though her statement could not be regarded as, strictly speaking, true.

'He's the image of you when he smiles,' Marianne told Shirley.

'God help the little fucker,' said Shirley, moving back from the Jeep.

She blew Marianne a kiss and tucked the boys on either side of her. Marianne waved back. It felt awkward, the wave. And sort of foolish. But she couldn't help feeling sort of pleased too. Like she and Shirley might be friends. She could imagine what Shirley would say if she knew what Marianne was thinking.

'You're a daft cunt,' she would have said. 'No offence.'

Chapter 17

The day of the protest at Shirley's house started out pretty much the same as all the other days had started out since Marianne had returned to Ancaire.

There was a flurry of activity in the kitchen when Marianne and George returned from the beach. The kitchen counters were covered with slices of bread that Rita was buttering in a frenzied manner.

'I'm making a picnic lunch,' she declared, carefully laying circles of hard-boiled egg across a slice of bread, then leaves of lettuce and slices of cheddar cheese. She covered it with another slice of bread, spread with relish, on top of which she placed rings of red onions, peppers and garlic cloves. She topped that with another slice of bread, then squashed the sandwich with her bare hands before cutting it in half, then quarters.

Marianne felt relieved that she and Flo had been spared these monstrosities, since it had been Marianne who made their school lunches.

Rita wiped her hands on the apron she had put on over her clothes. Today, she wore a jade-green boat-neck cashmere jumper with a full skirt that boasted many themes on the colour red. The jumper and skirt met at the waist, which was nipped in with the help of a wide purple belt studded with rhinestones. The whole effect was one of visibility, which Marianne conceded would be beneficial at the protest.

Rita stepped back to admire her work. 'What do you think?' she said.

'Well, if the protest doesn't yield results, you could always pin the landlord down after lunch and breathe on him,' said Marianne.

Patrick arrived then, his arms filled with Tupperware. He spilled the boxes across the kitchen table and began to fill them with Rita's sandwiches. 'I've made flasks of coffee,' he said. 'And I've got fruit and nuts in case we run out of sandwiches.'

'What about dessert?' Rita asked anxiously.

Patrick nodded. 'Don't worry, I've packed the batch of brownies I made yesterday.'

'Do you think we'll have enough?' said Rita, putting more eggs on to hard boil.

Marianne stood up. 'You're going to Swords, not the Arctic Circle.'

'Are you wearing that?' asked Rita when she turned round and saw Marianne.

Marianne looked down at herself. She was wearing a navy anorak with fleece lining, which was as practical as it was comfortable. Her tracksuit bottoms were also navy so they matched the anorak. The ends were tucked into two pairs of thick wool socks, which kept her feet warm while the wellington boots kept them dry.

'Which item of clothing are you referring to?' asked Marianne.

'Well . . . the whole ensemble, really,' said Rita.

'Yes, I'm wearing all of it,' said Marianne, defensive. 'Why?'

'No reason,' Rita said, airily.

Patrick – whose outfit did not warrant any commentary, adverse or otherwise, from Rita – eventually staggered out of the house laden down with the Tupperware tubs. Marianne helped him arrange them inside the Jeep. He walked back towards the house, giving Pearl, who had appeared at the front door, a healthy berth.

'I suppose I'll have to fend for myself, shall I?' she said, her lips thin and bloodless as she surveyed them with even greater disapproval than usual.

'I told you that you're more than welcome to join us, Pearl,' Rita told her. Pearl didn't dignify the suggestion with a response. 'There's a Spanish omelette in the fridge,' Rita added as she opened the Jeep door. 'You just need to heat it up in the range for—'

'I'm perfectly well aware of how long I need to put a tortilla in the range,' Pearl said.

Patrick returned, this time with the placards. He had swaddled them in bubble wrap, like they were works of art.

'Thank you, darling boy,' gushed Rita, catching his face in her hands and kissing his cheek.

Marianne bristled. She felt something butt her thigh. It was George looking at her with his serious golden eyes as if he was wondering what she was thinking.

'Nothing good, George,' she said, absently allowing her hand to drop onto his head. 'No, don't lick my . . . Stop, George, I don't like it, I told you.' She wiped her hand on her tracksuit bottoms and felt vindicated in her decision to wear them. Other fabrics were not so absorbent.

George leaped into the Jeep before she could stop him. 'George, get out,' she shouted at him. 'You can't come today. There's not enough room.'

'Ah, let him come,' said Rita, leaning towards the dog and allowing him to lick her mouth.

'You know he cleans his testicles with that tongue, don't you?' said Marianne.

Rita laughed as if Marianne had said something amusing. 'He can sit on my knee,' she said.

When they were settled inside the Jeep, Marianne drove down the avenue. At the gates, she indicated and looked both ways before turning onto the main road. She held her breath at the spot in the road, accelerated past it. Nobody told her to slow down. Nobody said anything. It was like they were all holding their breath.

Chapter 18

Marianne picked up Ethel, followed by Bartholomew and Freddy. She stopped outside Shirley's house and everyone poured out of the Jeep and stood in a line on the footpath. Shirley walked along the line, like a drill sergeant, inspecting them. She smiled at Ethel, punched Patrick, Bartholomew and Freddy in the arm, patted George, tugged at a lock of Marianne's hair and kissed Rita on the cheek.

'Where are little Sheldon and Harrison today?' Ethel enquired.

'At school, thank fuck,' said Shirley.

'Okay then,' said Marianne, backing towards the Jeep. 'So, I'll come back at . . . what time do you think you'll be finished?'

'Where are you going?' asked Rita.

'Aren't you staying?' said Ethel.

'You can't leave now,' spluttered Bartholomew, resplendent in a bright blue suit, white shirt and polka-dot tie.

'He's right,' said Freddy. Bartholomew smirked as it dawned on Freddy that he'd just openly agreed with him. Even George assumed a sort of beseeching expression.

Marianne looked at them. 'I'm just the driver.'

'But I packed a lunch for you,' said Rita.

'You shouldn't have bothered,' said Marianne.

'You have to stay,' said Shirley. 'You're the only one who looks halfway normal.' She turned to the others, shrugging her shoulders in apology. 'No offence,' she told them.

'I don't go on protests,' Marianne said.

'Oh,' said Ethel, worried. 'I thought it was a sit-in? Look, I bought this.' Out of her shopping-trolley-on-wheels, she pulled a fold-up stool. 'I was worried about getting a chill in my kidneys from sitting on the ground at this time of the year,' she explained. 'Stanley got one once. After a picnic on Hampstead Heath. A terrible bout, he had.'

Rita put her hand on Ethel's thin arm, squeezed it gently. 'We'll be doing a sit-in on the day of the actual eviction,' she explained. She glanced at Shirley. 'On the off chance that today's protest doesn't yield results.'

'Yeah,' said Shirley, drily. 'Just in case.'

'Look, regardless of whether it's a protest or a sit-in, we need you, Marianne,' declared Rita.

'Yes,' said Freddy, 'your fine voice will swell the timbre of the slogans.'

'Oh, yes,' said Bartholomew. 'I meant to ask about the slogans.'

'Well,' said Rita, thinking, 'my favourite one is, "We will not be moved". It works as a chant as well a song.'

'Oh, I've got a song, too,' piped up Freddy, pushing his glasses up to the top of his nose. 'I've written down the words.' He handed out flashcards covered in his neat, methodical print. 'It's called "Power to the People".' He gave one to Marianne with his shy smile. 'Your mother's right,' he whispered to her. 'We need you.'

Marianne shook her head. 'I can't sing.'

'You can't? Or you don't?' Freddy asked.

'Both,' said Marianne.

'There're some really nice harmonies in there,' said Rita, offering Marianne a placard that read, 'There's no place like home'.

'No,' said Marianne resolutely, 'I just . . . I can't.'

'I wouldn't blame you,' said Shirley. 'I wouldn't be seen in public with this lot unless I really had to.' She looked down the line of them. 'No offence,' they roared, in unison.

Ethel stepped forward. 'I'll take a placard, Rita,' she said with great ceremony, her twig-like arm reaching across the space between her and Rita. Marianne watched her grip the handle, her arm shaking with effort.

'Oh, fine, I'll stay,' said Marianne, grabbing the handle before Ethel collapsed under the weight of it. 'Ethel, maybe you could just chant? I'll hold your placard.'

'And sing, don't forget,' added Freddy.

'Give me strength,' said Marianne under her breath.

The day surprised Marianne by being not as awful as she had feared, even though it involved some of the things she hated doing. Speaking in public. Although it was more shouting than speaking. Slogans weren't really effective otherwise.

Then there was the singing. She never sang, not in the shower, not in the car, nowhere. She didn't even hum.

Now here she was, singing at the top of her voice in a front garden in Swords.

It could have been something to do with the song itself – 'Power to the People' – which turned out to be quite catchy.

Rita and Shirley sang each line and this was then echoed by Marianne and the others. They got louder and louder as they progressed through the song so that, by the end, Marianne felt herself surrounded by the sound in a way that was sort of . . . she cringed as she thought of the word she was about to use . . . uplifting.

It was something to do with the collective nature of the sound. Hearing their voices, rise together, louder and louder. All the different sounds they made. Ethel's high, quivering voice. Rita's belter. Patrick's low and melodious one. Shirley's surprising sweet tone. Bartholomew's booming vibrato. Freddy's timid lilt.

Mostly they were ignored. It was a Thursday morning on one of the myriad of back streets beyond Swords village. Occasionally, people passed. Women wheeling buggies in the main, a few joggers, one speed walker, a couple of dogs, cocking their legs at lampposts.

The passers-by looked up when they heard the chanting – *What do we want? Homes for all! When do we want it? NOW* – but most of them bowed their heads when they realised it was a protest and hurried past. Some people stopped. They wanted to know what was going on. Of these, some argued that landlords should be allowed sell their own properties whenever they liked. Weren't they entitled to turn a profit? Hadn't they taken a risk? Marianne tried to stop Rita shouting 'Capitalist Pigs' at them as they marched away.

Some signed the petition that Patrick had typed up and printed out.

Marianne tried to stop Rita kissing and hugging these people.

'I'm just showing my appreciation,' Rita said.

'Try saying "thank you",' said Marianne.

By midday, following a glut of people walking past to collect toddlers from various play schools and Montessoris in the locality, they had nearly a hundred signatures on the petition.

Hugh drove by in his bottle-green Jaguar. He had a customer in the back, a fidgety bald man, more bone than brawn, leafing through a sheaf of notes. Hugh stopped the car outside Shirley's house, rolled down the window and leaned out.

'I promised to bring this fella to a job interview, otherwise I'd be here with you,' he called to them. Today, his hair was gathered in a scrunchie at the back of his head. Maybe it was his work hairstyle, Marianne thought. The absence of its frame around his face served to exaggerate his features; his green eyes seemed greener and his orange freckles brighter, and were there more of them today? Or was that just the way the light fell across his face?

'You have my deepest sympathies,' Bartholomew shouted at the nervous wreck in the back seat, giving him a thumbs-up. The man stared at Bartholomew as if he were a creature from a different planet, then returned to his notes.

'Don't forget your Happy Hair appointments tomorrow,' Hugh told them, releasing the handbrake and indicating. 'I've block booked three hours for you, just after lunch, okay?'

'Do you have the purple dye for me, Hugh?' called Ethel.

'Buckets of it, my love,' said Hugh, smiling at her. 'Stanley will think you're a vision at the dinner dance.'

'Oh, Hugh,' giggled Ethel, blushing.

Hugh looked at Marianne. 'You're welcome to come too,' he said.

'Are you suggesting I need a haircut?' said Marianne stiffly.

'Well,' said Hugh, 'it could benefit from a wee bit of TLC, to be honest.'

'Couldn't we all?' said Bartholomew, batting his eyelashes in Hugh's direction.

Freddy rolled his eyes and shook his head.

'My hair is fine as it is,' said Marianne, pushing her fringe out of her eyes.

'Suit yourself,' said Hugh. 'I'll see the rest of you tomorrow.'

He pulled away from the kerb, waved out the window.

The passenger in the back seat looked relieved to see the back of them.

The rain that had threatened earlier began to fall just as Patrick was unpacking the Tupperware boxes from the picnic basket in the back of the Jeep.

'Yiz can come inside, if you like,' said Shirley.

'We could eat in the Jeep if you prefer not to have us traipsing into your home with our mucky feet,' said Rita.

'Yes, we don't want to intrude, my dear,' said Ethel.

Shirley shook her head. 'It's grand. Be nice to have people in the house who don't pick their noses in plain view, for a change.'

She unlocked the front door and ushered them inside.

The hallway was narrow and dark, and led to a cramped kitchen-cum-living room with a white plastic table and three chairs. The cooker was ancient and the fridge was a portable, stand-alone affair. The walls were a dull beige colour, the paint peeling in places. A dehumidifier plugged in and humming in the corner, made little impact on the damp, the smell of which was sour and dense. On the walls near the ceiling, circles of black mould were spreading.

Shirley had covered the kitchen presses with drawings. An alien slithering out of a spaceship. Three matchstick people holding hands and standing outside a matchstick house under a circle of yellow sun wearing shades. A dog jumping over a hurdle. The artist had drawn a love heart above the dog and inside the heart was the word 'George'.

A picture of the sea – green – the sky – blue – and the sand – yellow – beneath a tall, crooked cliff at the edge of which stood a matchstick house. At the water's edge, jumping the waves, two matchstick boys.

A certificate declaring Sheldon 'Student of the Week' last November. Harrison's spelling test – seven out of ten – tacked to the fridge door. A photograph of Shirley in a photo booth, with the boys on either side of her, their faces pressed together so they could all get in the frame, their eyes squeezed shut and their mouths wide open with the laughing.

'I'll put a brew on,' said Rita, picking up the kettle.

'It's broken,' said Shirley.

'Not to worry,' said Rita, fishing around in her enormous bag. 'I brought flasks.'

Rita's doorstep sandwiches turned out to be just the

thing, Marianne had to admit. Once you got over the smell of so much hard-boiled egg in such a confined space. Once you squashed them into a more manageable height and took several of the cloves of garlic out, they were actually quite edible.

She put it down to hunger being a good sauce.

Unusually for the group, they ate without speaking for the most part. Marianne was glad of the break. She was drained after all the slogan-shouting and the singing. Which was not a sentence she ever expected to hear herself think.

'What's so funny? Rita asked, waving her hand in front of Marianne's face.

'Oh. Nothing,' said Marianne, blinking and looking around. 'I was just . . . thinking it odd. Me, being here. I'm not exactly protest material.'

Rita smiled. 'I really liked that slogan you came up with, the one about the vulture funds.'

'Oh, the "We've a bone to pick with you" one?'

'That was clever,' Rita said.

'I was just trying to mix it up a bit.' Marianne gathered her cup and plate and stood up.

'I'm going to have a cigarette and then we'll resume, okay?' said Rita, picking up her handbag.

'I can't believe lunch is already over and it's not even one o'clock yet,' said Bartholomew, looking worried.

'Activism is hungry work, my dear,' said Ethel, patting her concave stomach.

'Don't worry, everyone,' said Freddy, 'we've still got Patrick's brownies to look forward to.'

Bartholomew stood up and turned, sweeping chocolate crumbs from his face and waistcoat in a fluid, covert move.

'What do you mean, resume?' Marianne wanted to know.

'Keep your hair on, Marnie,' said Shirley through a mouthful of sandwich. 'I've to go and collect the boys from school at two so I need yiz to be gone by the time I get back.'

Marianne looked at her watch. Another hour to go. She thought she could manage that.

Shirley took an enormous gulp of tea, wiped her mouth with her arm. 'It's just, I haven't exactly told them. The boys. That we have to move.'

'You mightn't have to tell them at all,' piped up Ethel, shaking an arthritic finger towards Shirley. 'Where's your fighting spirit, young lady?'

Shirley shrugged. 'I used it all up, getting sober and springing the kids out of care.'

Ethel patted Shirley's arm on her way to visit the 'little old ladies' room'. Patrick left to check the Jeep, which had emitted blacker fumes than usual from its exhaust pipe earlier. Freddy and Bartholomew followed, arguing over which social media platform was best suited to get some traction for the protest.

'I'll wash the dishes,' said Marianne, walking to the sink.

Shirley followed her, glared at her. 'You probably think I'm a terrible mother,' she said. 'Having my kids taken into care.'

Marianne hunted in the press under the sink and found a bottle of washing-up liquid. When she straightened, Shirley was still glaring at her. Marianne shook her head. 'I don't know anything about motherhood,' she said, 'but I'm pretty sure that you're not a terrible mother.'

Shirley opened a drawer, took out a tea towel. 'Rita said you were more of a mother to Flo than she ever was.'

Marianne turned on the tap. 'Do you have a J-cloth?'

'Is that a polite way of telling me to fuck off and mind my own business?' said Shirley, handing Marianne a cloth.

Marianne squirted washing-up liquid into the water in the sink. Swirled it around with her fingers. 'I suppose so,' she said.

'It's the bloody Get-Well-Sooners,' said Shirley. 'They've infected me with all their incessant talking. I'm becoming institutionalised.'

'How did you find out about them?' Marianne asked, turning off the tap.

'I tried to get sober by myself,' Shirley said. 'I lasted two months before I bought a bottle of vodka. I put it on the floor and sat there, looking at it for about two hours. Then I remembered Rita. She was invited to our school once to talk about addiction and all that shite. So I rang her. She came straight away. Poured the vodka down the sink, put me in the Jeep and brought me to Ancaire.'

George poked Marianne's leg with his paw and she fed him a piece of cheese that had fallen out of one of Bartholomew's sandwiches.

'That was a good day,' said Shirley, almost to herself.

They did the dishes. Marianne washed and Shirley dried. The silence was sort of companionable, Marianne felt, until Shirley whacked her leg with the corner of the tea towel.

'Spit it out,' she said.

'What?'

'You've been washing the same plate for ages. What's eating you?'

Marianne shook her head. 'I just wondered,' she began, handing the immaculate plate to Shirley, 'if there is a Plan B.'

In her job, Marianne had been a stickler for Plan Bs. A 'what if' scenario.

What if the protest had no impact?

What if the landlord remained unmoved by Shirley's plight?

What if he went ahead with the eviction?

Judging by the registered letters Shirley received in the post most days, it seemed clear that he fully intended to.

'Well,' said Shirley, opening a drawer and arranging the cutlery she had dried in neat rows inside, 'Rita said me and the boys can move into Ancaire.'

'Oh,' said Marianne.

'Your face,' screamed Shirley, laughing.

'What?'

'Don't worry, I'd look the same if someone threatened to land that pair on me,' said Shirley. 'I swear, their only saving grace some days is the fact that I pushed them out of my own vagina.'

'I . . .' Marianne was not sure how to proceed.

'Anyway,' said Shirley, grinning, 'I'm on the housing list so it's all G.'

'Is G short for good?'

'Something like that,' said Shirley.

Marianne brightened. A housing list. Of course. That sounded like a workable Plan B.

'How long have you been on the list?' she asked.

Shirley creased her forehead in concentration, counted on her fingers, mouthing numbers. 'Three years, five months, two weeks and four days,' she said.

'Oh,' said Marianne.

Shirley shrugged. 'I applied the day after I left the kids' da. He'd only ever started on me before then. But he gave Sheldon a shove that day. Sheldon was only four. His little face, when he looked at me. Like he couldn't believe I'd allowed it to happen.' Shirley's voice was nearly a whisper by then but Marianne could hear every word, each one clear and stark, like Shirley's memory of that day. She wanted to take one of her hands out of the sink, touch Shirley in some way, let her know that she was here, she was listening, whatever good that would do. Shirley tossed her head, smacked her chewing gum between her teeth and grinned. 'We left at the stroke of midnight,' she said. 'Like Cinderella, I was. Except with a pair of kids instead of glass slippers and the handsome prince off his bin in the flat and a dent in his face from the hurl.'

'Jesus, Shirley.'

'I didn't kill him,' Shirley said indignantly.

'No, I didn't think you had.' Marianne was ninety-five per cent certain about that.

'I hate that he'll always be their dad,' said Shirley, then. 'I hate that I did that to the boys. Gave them a shit dad.'

'It wasn't your fault,' said Marianne, pulling the plug and wrapping the chain around the tap.

'Ah, you know how it is: us women always blame ourselves,' said Shirley. She flicked Marianne's leg with a corner of the tea towel again and picked up her placard. 'Come on,' she said.

Back in the front garden, Marianne assumed her earlier position, at the end of the line, beside Bartholomew, who seemed to have taken it upon himself to teach her the ways of the protest. He even demonstrated a way of holding the placard that doubled as a workout for the biceps.

'I used to date a gym manager, you know,' he said. 'He was pretty high profile so I won't divulge his name. Suffice to say, I had a key to his penthouse apartment on Merrion Square, a VIP pass to any of his gyms and I could bench press 120 without even breaking a sweat.' Bartholomew's tone was wistful. 'Then of course I slept with one of his exes and it ended fairly shortly after that. Another epic fail.' He lowered the placard and Marianne was terrified he might cry. She scrounged around for one of Rita's self-helpy mantras. Something about failure being good or . . . what was it? Oh, yes. 'Eh, failure isn't final, you know,' said Marianne.

Bartholomew looked at her, his pale blue eyes damp. 'Do you think I'm a failure?' he whispered.

'No, no, not at all,' said Marianne, wishing she had said nothing.

'I suppose I am,' said Bartholomew mournfully. 'I've made my bed. And half the beds in the city, let's face it.'

'Yes, but . . .' Marianne struggled to come up with something else. Anything to dissuade Bartholomew from crying. 'You've changed the sheets,' she said in a rush.

'What do you mean?' asked Bartholomew.

'Well, you stopped drinking, for starters,' said Marianne. 'And you got called for that interview.'

Bartholomew paused to consider that. When he smiled, he did so with the entirety of his round face. 'I did, didn't I?' he said.

Marianne felt a smile work the muscles of her cheeks. She supposed it was Bartholomew's hopefulness, the infectious nature of it. 'Oh,' she said, fishing around in her handbag. 'I've also written out the most awkward interview questions I could think of for you. So you can, you know, prepare yourself a bit. In case you're asked any of them.' She handed him a page she had torn out of Aunt Pearl's notebook. Bartholomew unfolded the paper, studied it. 'If I was a play, what play would I be?' he read, shaking his head.

'They probably won't ask anything so obscure,' said Marianne, 'but I put it down just in case. It is a theatre position, after all.'

'Something absurd and tragic,' said Bartholomew, sighing. 'Beckett would do the job, I'd say.'

'Maybe pick something a bit more upbeat?' suggested Marianne. 'Also, I see you have put Rita down as one of your referees?'

'All the local theatre people adore Rita,' said Bartholomew. 'She's done a lot of Get Well Soon work with them – it's dipso-central in lala land, as you can imagine – and she often helps out with set design and costumes. That's how we met actually, Rita and I. I fell off the stage during a performance of *The Rocky Horror Picture Show*. I played Eddie.' Bartholomew struck a pose and sang, 'Hot patootie bless my soul I really love that rock 'n' roll' in a loud, Texan accent.

A pedestrian hurried past, looking worried.

'Maybe just add another reference,' suggested Marianne. 'As well as Rita, I mean.'

Bartholomew looked stricken.

'Even just one,' said Marianne. 'Someone who will say you're good in a crisis. Or . . .'

'Oh,' said Bartholomew suddenly. 'I did deliver my boss's baby in the back of a Mercedes van once.'

'That's an effective demonstration of crisis management,' said Marianne.

'She did all the work,' admitted Bartholomew. 'I just knelt beside her bed and did breathing exercises to keep myself calm.'

Bartholomew returned to Marianne's notes. 'What's my greatest achievement?' He looked into the middle distance, stroked his chin. 'Outrunning Panti Bliss is certainly up there. She took umbrage after I hated on the dress she wore when she did the Noble Call at the Abbey. I mean, who wears mauve?'

'You outran Panti Bliss?' Marianne couldn't help saying.

'She was wearing high heels at the time, in fairness.'

'You could talk about your sobriety,' suggested Marianne.

'They'll just think I'm an overweight loser who can't control himself.'

'It shows determination,' said Marianne. 'You identified a problem and dealt with it.'

'Wow,' said Bartholomew, smiling at her. 'I sound great, coming from you.'

'We should probably get on with the chanting now,' said Marianne, although she couldn't help feeling pleased. Bartholomew nodded and she picked up her placard and held it away from her body as Bartholomew had instructed. So, when she spotted him, she was chanting, 'The Minister for Housing's a holy show, The Minister for Housing's got to go.'

He wasn't hard to spot, given the size of the buggy he was wheeling.

A double buggy.

The width of a modest bulldozer. Attached to the handle of the buggy were two dog leashes and at the end of the leashes were matching Bichon Frises, yapping as they pranced along, pulling at their leashes and getting under the feet of the pusher of the buggy who, as a consequence, had to walk in a mincing sort of way, with his head down for the most part.

At first, it was the yapping of the dogs that drew Marianne's attention.

Then, the double buggy. The monstrous size of it. She idly wondered what the father would do if he met oncoming pedestrians. A fellow buggy-pusher, even? One of them would have to go out on the road. How to decide which one? Maybe there was buggy etiquette? A double buggy trumps a single one?

Afterwards, Marianne would wonder at herself, at her train of thoughts as her brain caught up with her vision.

Because the pusher of the buggy was Brian.

Of course it was.

It was too late to dart inside Shirley's house. Or to hide behind the Jeep. As a last resort, Marianne considered ducking behind Bartholomew's back. It was wide enough to shield her, although her height meant she would have to crouch.

But the chanting had attracted Brian's attention, as it was supposed to do, and now he was looking straight at her. Marianne lowered her placard, the muscles in her upper arms throbbing and the blood rushing up her neck, into her face.

After a moment, the others lowered their placards too, the chants dribbling away until a hush fell upon them.

'Marianne?' Brian looked confused, like he used to look when a spreadsheet wasn't adding up.

'Hello, Brian,' said Marianne, her voice high and bright. A nothing-to-see-here sort of voice. A little strangled at the edges. Brian seemed the same as he always did and yet there was something utterly changed about him. His clothes, for one thing. They matched. And they weren't all black or navy. There were colours. Mustard trousers and a yellow and black check shirt with a thick black leather jacket and desert boots. The trousers weren't quite tight-fitting but they were snug all the same.

It was Brian all right. The same fine fair hair, the same narrow nose, the same light blue eyes, watering in the sunlight.

It was just . . . a different version of Brian.

Like he'd had a system update.

It was the strangest sensation.

'What are you doing here?' he asked carefully, his eyes travelling down the line of them as if they might be henchmen, hired by Marianne to do him in.

Marianne cleared her throat. 'I would have thought that was perfectly obvious,' she said, raising her placard and waving it at him.

'Oh. Right. Yes, of course,' said Brian. 'I heard your vulture fund chant as I was coming down the road. Really . . . pithy.'

Marianne nodded stiffly.

'Oh, and there's Rita. Hello, Rita,' he said, his tone nervous. He had never been sure how to handle Rita, although he was not alone in that regard.

Rita, looking unimpressed at best, raised her face in his direction. 'Hello, Brian,' she managed.

'Is that your young man?' piped up Ethel, peering at Brian over the top of her spectacles.

'No,' Marianne hissed, stepping in front of Ethel, who looked like she was about to take a run at him.

'Are they the twins?' Marianne felt duty-bound to ask. The double buggy was like this gigantic exclamation mark over their heads. Bright red and screeching for attention. As elephants in rooms go, this one was too big to ignore.

'Eh, yes,' said Brian, and his smile began, as it always did, at the corners of his mouth, which twitched with the effort of trying not to smile. He couldn't help it in the end. By the time he had lowered the two hoods, he was beaming. 'This is James,' he said, pointing at the one on his left. 'And this is David,' he went on, now pointing at the other one, who looked exactly the same.

'How do you tell them apart?' Marianne asked.

Brian laughed.

Marianne didn't.

When he realised she wasn't joking, he stopped. 'Well, I . . . I just can,' he said. 'I'm used to them, I suppose.'

Marianne wanted to remind him that he used to be used to her. He used to be able to tell her apart. To know what set her apart from everybody else. Which was pretty much everything, she supposed. Maybe if she had been more like everybody else, he would have stayed.

She bent down and peered at the twins. She was glad they were asleep. Babies often cried at the sight of her. She thought it might be something to do with her hair. The untamed amount of it.

'People say they look like me,' Brian said.

Marianne thought they looked like miniature Winston

Churchills. She nodded and said, 'Yes, they do,' which must have been the right thing to say because she could feel him swelling with pride. She straightened. 'What age are they now?'

'Three weeks,' said Brian. 'And five days,' he added, unable to help himself.

Marianne understood this part of him. The accountant part. She knew she should enquire about Helen. The mother. She imagined her waving them off at the front door, her peaches-and-cream complexion, cupping her hand around the babies' tiny heads and kissing Brian on the corner of his mouth, which would already be twitching with the makings of a massive smile. An 'I got everything I ever wanted and more' smile. An 'I broke my promise and got away with it' smile.

She wondered what they called each other. 'Pet', maybe. 'Goodbye, pet,' Helen might have said. 'See you in a little bit, darling,' Brian might have responded even though he was not a terms-of-endearment kind of a fellow. Except now he was, in Marianne's head. He might have waved, a small self-satisfied wave that hinted at more where that came from when he got back with the babies, fast asleep. More terms of endearment. More affection. More love. Lots of love. Plenty to go around. Just not enough for Marianne.

'So,' said Brian, shifting from one foot to the other. 'You got my telephone message?'

'Yes.'

'I hope you didn't mind my calling you,' he said, looking carefully at Marianne. 'It's just . . . I wanted to tell you myself, you know? About the babies. And you probably already knew about For Sale sign but . . . I know how much you loved that house.'

'Not so much after the bank repossessed it, to be honest,' said Marianne.

Brian had the grace to flush.

'I . . . heard about that, all right,' he said in a small voice. 'I'm sorry.'

His pity stung like a swarm of wasps.

'I wasn't surprised that it sold so quickly,' he said then. 'Sold?'

'Yes. Sorry. I thought you . . . I saw it online.'

Marianne cleared her throat. 'Right. Well, I won't keep you. I'm sure you're . . . busy. You and Helen. How is she?' It sounded like she was speaking through gritted teeth. Were her teeth gritted? She wasn't even sure what that meant. Or how to achieve it. Either way, she didn't think they were gritted. Although her jaw ached, she noticed. As if she had been clenching it.

'Oh, Helen's fine. A little tired, of course,' said Brian, doing that small laugh that people do when they roll out tried-and-trusted lines.

'Of course,' said Marianne, who almost always felt exhausted these days and that was while getting a full eight hours' sleep a night with no infant twins or their fontanelles to worry about.

'And she's finding the breastfeeding a little tricky,' confided Brian. 'But not to worry, we'll get there in the end.'

'I'm not sure what your role is in the whole breastfeeding business,' said Rita, appearing beside Marianne like a ship out of the mist.

Brian reddened. 'Oh, you know, a bit of moral support.'

'Good to see you've finally learned how to give some,' said Rita, reaching up in an effort to get her arm around Marianne's neck.

'Well, it was . . . nice to see you,' said Marianne in a rush. She was in an awkward position now, having to bend and twist at the waist to accommodate Rita's arm.

'Oh . . . right . . . yes, I'll . . . see you soon.'

'What do you mean?' Marianne said, alarmed.

'No, I just meant . . . you know . . . goodbye.'

'Oh. Yes,' said Marianne. 'Goodbye.'

It sounded maudlin, the word. Drenched in pathos. Especially since the others stepped forward and said it too. 'Goodbye.'

Brian turned briefly. He lifted his hand when he saw the solemn line of them, staring after him. Waved it.

Goodbye.

Chapter 19

'I must say, Marianne, I'm the tiniest bit confused. A lovely filly like yourself teaming up with that oaf.' Freddy shook his head.

'Filly!' snorted Bartholomew. 'Who do you think you are? Rupert Campbell Black?'

They were in the Jeep and Marianne was driving everybody back to their various houses. She gripped the steering wheel until her knuckles whitened. 'Do you mind if we don't talk about it?' she said.

She glanced in the rear-view mirror and caught Patrick's eye, who nodded briefly.

'Of course, my dear girl, as you wish,' said Bartholomew.

'What are we not supposed to be talking about?' piped up Ethel from the back.

'Marnie's ex,' said Rita. 'The dick.'

'That's not helping,' said Marianne.

She yanked at her indicator all of a sudden and scorched

round a corner, left instead of right, fast enough for the wheels to protest against the road surface.

Everybody jerked.

'Sorry,' said Marianne, accelerating up the road.

'Why are we going this way?' Freddy wanted to know.

'Take it easy, dear,' called out Ethel. 'The undertaker may have his eye on me but I'm not ready to be laid out just yet.' She chuckled at her little joke.

'Several fortunetellers have told me I would die young,' said Bartholomew, with a tragic air.

'Well, they got that wrong, clearly,' said Freddy, smirking.

'But where are we going?' Bartholomew went on, ignoring Freddy.

'I'm certain Marianne has it all in hand,' Ethel piped up.

Marianne, who did not share Ethel's certainty, said nothing.

She drove on, to Carling Road.

She saw it immediately. A 'Sold' sign covering the 'For Sale' on the board.

She slowed down.

Then stopped.

She looked at the house. She hadn't realised until now that she still thought of it as her home. She had harboured some vague idea, tucked in a bottom drawer at the back of her mind, that she would return here someday and everything would get back to the way it used to be. That she would get back to the way she used to be.

As someone who was rarely given to unsubstantiated optimism, Marianne realised this idea – this hope – was out of character.

Also foolish.

Marianne tried not to think about strangers in her house, poking around, turning their noses up. Or even loving it as she had. She drove on. Up the road. Away from the house. She concentrated on the road. On her hands wrapped around the steering wheel. The glint of sunshine on the band of her wedding ring. Technically, she was still married, she had reasoned when she noticed that she hadn't taken it off. Not when Brian told her he was leaving. Not when he left. Not when he never came back.

She jammed on the brakes and wrenched the handbrake up. Everyone was jerked forward, then back.

'Are you all right, Marnie?' asked Rita in the kind of cautious voice one might use on an unpredictable animal. Marianne grabbed the ring on her finger and pulled. She twisted it this way, then that, yanked again. It wouldn't budge. It was stuck. As stuck as she was.

More infuriating was the fact that it was Brian who had wanted to get married. He said it would make the management of their affairs easier, in the event of one of their deaths. He also spoke about the burden of taxation being easier to bear, as a married couple. Marianne was sure he must have said other – nicer – things but she couldn't for the life of her remember any of them now.

They got married in the registry office on Lombard Street. Marianne invited Rita, only because Brian might have thought it strange if she hadn't. After all, he had his sister, Linda, as his guest, and his cousin Bernard as his best man. Marianne said she didn't want a bridesmaid – who would she have asked if she did? – but she supposed it would look strange if she had nobody.

Rita wore a white, floor-length dress. Marianne wore a navy trouser suit with a cream blouse and a pair of Nike runners, new ones, to facilitate the walk from their house to the registry office. Afterwards, Bernard returned to the printing press where he worked and Marianne and Brian took Rita and Linda to dinner in a restaurant in Drumcondra, and after that Linda returned to Guernsey, Rita returned to Ancaire, and Marianne and Brian returned home to Carling Road where they watched a nature programme – a family of polar bears in the Arctic – before going to bed. They read their books as they always did – *Tales of the Unexpected* for Brian and *Watership Down* for Marianne – before they settled themselves on their respective sides of the bed and fell asleep. As far as Marianne remembered, they didn't have sex, which suited her just fine. She had only ever slept with Brian and while she didn't mind sex, she would much rather read. She had never told Brian that. She knew enough to know that some men might take such a preference personally.

She had assumed Brian felt the same way, since he rarely initiated sex and often said, 'No thank you,' when she wondered if he wanted to.

Now she knew that he did want to have sex. Just not with her.

That stung more than she would have imagined.

Sometimes, she imagined them in bed, Brian and Helen. In her imaginings, they were noisy and sweary and sweaty. Helen wore sexy things, like . . . Marianne wasn't sure . . . something lacy and black. Suspenders maybe. High heels. Or those boots that go up to your thighs.

She couldn't imagine Brian in anything other than his boxer shorts, his erection enormous in her imaginings, making a tent of the material at the front. He called Helen 'baby' when he came. 'Oh yeah, baby, oh, that's so good, baby, don't stop, baby.' That kind of thing. Which seemed most unlikely. Brian had never called Marianne anything other than her full name. Why would he call Helen baby? Infantilise her in that way? She was sure he didn't. So why did he do it when she imagined him having sex with Helen?

And why on earth was she imagining such a thing in the first place?

Marianne tugged harder at the ring.

'You need a bit of butter, dear,' said Ethel, leaning forward and patting Marianne's shoulder with one of her long, thin hands.

'I don't have butter.' Marianne's breath was laboured with exertion.

'Stop,' said Rita. 'You'll pull the finger off yourself.'

Marianne's finger was an alarming purple colour now, the knuckle swollen with all the pulling and reefing. Coming up the road behind her, a man in a sharp suit and a Lexus, speaking into a phone. Marianne closed her eyes and heaved with all her might and, bit by bit, the ring relented and she was finally able to persuade it off her finger. She held it aloft and everybody cheered, and there was a moment when Marianne considered doing the same. Instead, she rolled down her window.

'Wait,' said Rita. 'What are you doing?'

'I'm throwing it away,' said Marianne. 'I should have done it ages ago.'

'Give it to me,' said Rita, holding out her hand. 'I'll sell it on eBay and give the money to Focus Ireland, okay?'

Marianne sighed. She handed her wedding ring to her mother and turned the key in the ignition. Nothing happened.

'Move it, will you?' the driver in the Lexus behind shouted out of his window at Marianne. 'Bloody women drivers.'

Rita undid her seat belt.

'Please don't,' said Marianne as her mother turned round and kneeled on her seat.

'I'll just be a tick,' said Rita. She rolled down her window, leaned out until she was sure she had the driver's full attention. Then she extended her arm in his direction, unfurling her middle finger from the circle of her hand as she did. The man's face registered surprise followed quickly by a sort of frustrated fury. He bore down on his horn. Rita beamed at him before arranging herself back inside the Jeep, rolling up the window, putting her seat belt on. She patted the steering wheel. 'Who's a lovely Jeep then?' she said, and nodded at Marianne. 'Now try.'

When Marianne turned the key in the ignition, the engine coughed, then roared.

She drove away.

'At least you're not an alcoholic,' offered Freddy, 'so you can get drunk if you want to without worrying.'

'Yes, but if she wants to get drunk, surely that's a sign that she could be an alcoholic,' said Bartholomew peevishly.

'Wanting to get drunk after meeting your ex hardly makes you an alcoholic,' snapped Freddy, using the fallen hem of his corduroy jacket to wipe the lenses of his glasses.

'That just makes you a common-or-garden Irish person.'

'I don't want to get drunk,' said Marianne.

'What do you want, dear?' asked Ethel, gently.

'I . . . I don't know,' said Marianne. She wished her response didn't sound so feeble. She wished she was the type of person who did get rip-roaring drunk. Who shouted and railed. Someone who could make herself heard.

But that was not her way.

Chapter 20

In fact, Marianne did know what she wanted to do. She wanted to steal something. She managed not to by sequestering herself upstairs in Rita's draughty studio at the gable end of the house, where she sat on the high stool by the windows and watched the tide flooding and draining far below. The movement of the water, rising and falling, swelling and receding seemed relentless. Like life. It just kept going. It wouldn't let her be.

At dinner she endured Aunt Pearl, who was frosty and took more pleasure than usual in dousing the protest in cold, stagnant water.

'So has the decision to evict Shirley been withdrawn? No? Did the landlord respond in any way? I didn't think so. And that councillor you've been flirting with, Rita? He was a no-show? Well, I did tell you not to bother. I hope none of the neighbours complained about noise pollution. So unladylike, screeching in public.'

Rita put down her knife and fork and smiled. 'Ah, Pearl,

if I'd known how much you were going to miss us, I would have dragged you along.' She put her chubby warm hand on Pearl's icy skin-and-bone one.

Pearl yanked her hand away. 'I really can't imagine how you arrived at such a conclusion, Rita,' she said in a strained voice while two bright pink circles bloomed in her cheeks.

After dinner, Marianne further distracted herself by going to bed and reading. She was halfway through *Jane Eyre* now. George insisted on getting on the bed and resting his head in the crook of her elbow, which made turning the pages awkward. She read until she was too tired to read, then turned off the light and tried to sleep. When she couldn't, she sat up, turned the light back on and read again. When she woke up, it was morning, her light was on and the book had fallen across George's face so that all she could see was the damp tip of his nose at the base of the spine. She lifted the book. The skin on her finger was indented with the shape of her wedding ring. Soft and pulpy too, with a deathly pallor as if the blood supply had been cut off years ago.

She wanted to steal something. Something small and inconsequential. She would be careful this time. Professional. She would make sure she had eaten something light but nutritious beforehand. Eggs. She would eat eggs for lunch and then she would steal something.

Some part of her knew that this was not a sensible plan. That rational people did not come up with such schemes as solutions to whatever hurdles they might be facing.

And anyway, she wasn't facing any hurdles. Maybe that was the problem. Her hurdles were behind her, lying where they had fallen. Her marriage, her job, her home. She had knocked them over, each of them in turn.

Seeing Brian wheeling his babies with such pride and love brought all of Marianne's failures into sharp focus. Even when she closed her eyes, she saw them still. There was no getting away from them.

Her plan – however misguided – distracted her. It got her out of bed and dressed. It allowed her to run the gauntlet of the moss-slick steps to the beach, throw a stone for George. And another one. And another.

It propelled her into the Jeep, got her to Skerries, to Balbriggan, to Rush, to Swords, back to Ancaire, where she remembered who took what type of tea and managed to divide Rita's butter shortbread into twelve identical portions.

Afterwards the Get-Well-Sooners were going, *en masse*, to Happy Hair, where Shirley and Hugh would bestow a purple rinse on Ethel, see to Bartholomew's hot-towel shave, and barely trim the ends of Freddy's hair. Rita, her jade-green turban wound tight around her head, said she had only just washed her hair that morning but would come along anyway, if only as an independent observer.

Marianne pulled up on the main street in Rush and the Get-Well-Sooners exploded from the Jeep like shrapnel.

'Miss you already, Marnie,' said Bartholomew, blowing a kiss at her.

'You sure you won't change your mind and come with us?' said Freddy. 'Hugh could easily—'

'Hugh's good but he's no miracle worker,' said Shirley, picking up a strand of Marianne's hair. 'No offence,' she said, grinning at Marianne.

Rita leaned in through the Jeep window, looked at Marianne. 'You okay, Marnie?'

Marianne didn't bother correcting her. She nodded. 'I'm fine,' she said.

Eventually they left, linking arms as they walked away, so that they looked like a scene from the director's cut edition of *The Wizard of Oz*.

Marianne thought about stealing.

In a last-ditch effort to dissuade herself, she pictured Judge Henderson's face, peering at her from her elevated bench at the top of the courtroom. Marianne remembered the sharp flash of her blue eyes, the stiff helmet of wig perched on top of her head and the way she took Marianne in at a glance, summed her up.

The judge had been, quite frankly, judgemental.

And nosy.

'Why do you do it?' she had asked, leaning across the bench and eyeing Marianne as one might a curious animal in a zoo.

'I only do it when I'm stressed,' Marianne had said.

'Next time, you might consider yoga,' Judge Henderson said, straightening before announcing the sentence.

While she had been let off with a fine, Marianne was positive Judge Henderson would not display the same leniency the next time.

So there could not be a next time.

Marianne twitched with want.

She walked down the main street in Rush and stopped outside the newsagent's. The scene of the original crime. She pressed her face against the window. It was a Centra now. Not as dark as it used to be, tubes of fluorescent light running across the ceiling and making things trickier for the likes of her.

She had just turned thirteen, that first time. Tall and gawky, awkward and taciturn. Even after eight years in the local primary school, Marianne's peers continued to find her a source of curiosity and suspicion. She put it down to the contents of her lunchbox, which were often not in keeping with the corned beef and Easi Singles sandwiches of the other girls. There might be a triangle of Camembert in Marianne's lunchbox, already melting and stinking by the time little break came round. Or a handful of gooseberries picked from the garden, which made the girls screech and yell, 'Hairy!' as they gathered to inspect the offending articles in the yard. A mound of couscous, perhaps left over from a party the night before and carefully spooned into Flo and Marianne's lunchboxes the following morning as she scavenged around the kitchen at Ancaire. Once, Marianne had packed miniature bottles of Peach Snapps, which she had mistaken for fruit juice. That had aroused the attention of Miss Spellman, which had resulted in a flamboyant visit of Rita to the school, which in turn had aroused more curiosity, more suspicion.

'What's wrong with your mother?' hissed Clare Hickey that day, a dislikeable child with thin, white pigtails poking out from either side of her head.

Marianne ignored her. From the back of the classroom, she could smell Rita. A brass band of perfume and powder, lipstick and rouge. The salty damp of Ancaire, seeping from the silk of her red dress that was and unlike anything the other mothers wore. And the inevitable vinegary smell of the wine. Marianne could see Miss Spellman's nose wrinkle in distaste, the almost imperceptible step back she took.

Marianne pushed open the door of the Centra, stepped inside. There were no other customers and the woman behind the counter peered into the screen of her phone, scrolling and clicking.

That day, the one when Marianne was thirteen, had been a Wednesday. She waited for Flo outside school as she always did, declining the usual offers of a lift from Clare Hickey's mother, who worried about the lack of a footpath along the road to Ancaire, the hairpin bends. Usually, Flo skipped out of school, tucked her hand into Marianne's and chattered all the way home about Miss Flynn, whom she adored, Aideen O'Reilly, her best friend, a run-down of the game she had played in the yard that day, along with methodology, rules, and stars out of ten. Most games got ten stars out of ten.

That Wednesday, Flo was last in the line, her usual sanguine disposition much depleted. Marianne knew immediately that it was something to do with their mother. Something she had done. Or neglected to do.

William was the subject of much less – if any – scrutiny. Perhaps because, while he too forgot items on his daughters' schedules, he never promised to remember them in the first place.

'She's a little upset,' Miss Flynn whispered at Marianne, who felt that the observation was unnecessary. 'The art class was supposed to . . .'

'My mother is sick today,' said Marianne quickly.

Miss Flynn clapped her hands and beamed as if this was the best news she'd had in ages. 'See?' she said to Flo.

'Mammy is sick. That's why she couldn't come in to paint with us.'

'She isn't sick,' said Flo, who had not yet mastered the art of making reality more palatable for people.

'Come on, Flo,' said Marianne, taking Flo's bag off her shoulders and carrying it. 'Bruno will be waiting for you at home.'

They walked through the village. Marianne wondered why her mother couldn't just keep her big trap shut. Why was she always making grand gestures, then forgetting all about them, and all about the people she had made them to in the first place.

Flo dragged her feet through the village. Outside the newsagent's, she came to a complete stop. 'Mum said she'd buy me a treat.'

'Well, she's not here,' said Marianne. 'Now come on.'

'She said she'd buy me a Loop the Loop.'

'Bloody hell, Flo, I—'

'It's bad to say bloody.'

'It's bad to be demanding.'

'She promised. A promise is a promise.'

Marianne remembered wondering what age she was when she discovered that a promise was not in fact a promise. Younger than Flo, she thought.

'Fine,' said Marianne, opening the shop door. 'You wait here.'

It was easy in the end. To take it. The man behind the counter glanced up as she came in the door but then retreated behind the pages of the *Racing Post*. Marianne pretended to look at the comics. Then, she shuffled down to the freezer, picked out a Loop the Loop, slipped it up the sleeve of her school coat and crept out the door. The man never even looked up.

The Loop the Loop made Flo forget about Rita and her no-show. She sucked it noisily and regaled Marianne with the game of What Time Is It, Mister Wolf she had played in the yard at big break. She gave it ten out of ten.

Marianne pretended to listen and thought about what she had done in the shop and tried to work out how she felt about it. She was surprised to discover that she didn't feel bad, even though she knew it was a really bad thing to do and it was against the law and she could go to gaol.

In spite of the knowledge, she found that she felt sort of good. There was something rushing through her body. At the time, she didn't know what to call it. Later, she identified it as adrenalin. It brought with it a sense of control. A feeling that she was in charge of things. Just for a moment. She found that she liked it.

Marianne could feel it now. The adrenalin. An impression of control. She reached for a packet of thumb tacks.

'Marianne? Marianne Cross?'

Marianne whipped around, her pulse beating a drum in her forehead, her neck, her chest. Along her arms, she could feel goose bumps rise. She shivered.

The sales assistant was a short, stout woman with thin shoulder-length hair, dyed a straw-blond, and thickly painted red fingernails stuck onto the ends of stubby fingers. She was looking at Marianne, her head cocked to one side, with a quizzical sort of a smile on her face.

'It is you, I knew it,' the woman said, her voice progressing in volume and height. 'Marianne Cross!'

While the woman looked familiar, Marianne couldn't place her.

'It's Tessa,' the woman said, almost shrieking now. 'Tessa McCarthy.'

'Oh. Yes. Hello, Tessa.'

Tessa extended her hand so Marianne had no choice but to approach the counter. She held out her hand, which Tessa shook with enthusiasm before pulling Marianne into a tight hug over the counter, during which Marianne struggled to remain calm.

The woman released Marianne, then backed away from her, scanning her from head to toe. 'You haven't changed a day since school,' she declared eventually. 'How've you been?'

'Oh. You know. Fine,' said Marianne. A vague memory was stirring at the back of Marianne's head. A pimply girl with a loud mouth who claimed she could make butter in her stomach by drinking a pint of milk and then jumping up and down for five minutes. She never vomited and the other girls never tired of watching the process.

'And . . . you?' said Marianne, when it became clear that some response was expected of her. 'How have you been?

'Ah, you know yourself.'

Marianne nodded. She had no idea.

'The kids and himself are driving me spare but other than that, all good.' Tessa laughed then and so did Marianne. She was like a lyrebird, imitating the sounds that Tessa made.

Tessa leaned against the counter and folded her arms. 'So,' she said. 'Tell us all.'

'What do you mean?'

'You know, what are you up to? What do you do for a living? I bet you're something serious. Like, I don't know, an astrophysicist or something.'

'I'm unemployed.'

'Really?' said Tessa, her jaw slack with shock and something akin to wonder.

'I was an accountant,' said Marianne when it became clear that Tessa was expecting more words to be issued. 'Until I got fired.'

'No. Way,' said Tessa, draping herself across the counter now, all the better to get the details. 'Married?' she asked.

'Separated.'

'Oh, so sad. It's so hard on the children, isn't it? When a marriage breaks down.'

'I don't have any children.'

'Oh.'

'I think you've produced enough of those to go round, Tessa.' The shop door opened and there stood Rita in the doorway, her hands on her hips and her hibiscus-purple cape flowing around her body, looking for all the world like a super-hero come to the rescue. Or perhaps that's just how Marianne saw her in that moment.

Rita stalked inside. Immediately the shop, which had a jaded deli smell, was filled with her scent, so strong that Marianne could taste it.

'Oh, hello, Mrs Cross,' said Tessa. 'You're looking very . . . dramatic.'

'Thank you,' said Rita. She gripped Marianne's arm. 'Come along, Marnie, you don't want to be late for your hair appointment.'

'I don't have a—'

'Wash and blow-dry, remember? Hugh's expecting you,' Rita insisted, steering Marianne towards the door.

'Did you want to buy those thumbtacks?' Tessa called after her.

Rita took the box out of Marianne's hand, put them on a shelf. 'I already picked some up,' she said, smiling brightly at Tessa before gripping Marianne again, bustling her through the door and down the street, stopping only when they reached the Jeep. Rita leaned on it, out of breath. 'If you're going to steal something,' she panted, 'could you at least take something useful? Like baking powder.'

'I wasn't going to steal anything,' said Marianne haughtily.

'Or chocolate,' Rita went on. 'There was a lovely selection of Lily O'Brien's at the back.'

'Why aren't you at Happy Hair?' said Marianne.

'I . . . needed something in the shops,' said Rita.

'What did you need?'

'Eh, paperclips.'

'You were checking up on me.'

'Well, clearly, it was warranted.'

'I'm going back to Ancaire,' Marianne said. Her tiredness was like the sea, the way it came in waves, submerged her.

'You have an appointment, remember?' said Rita.

'I thought you just made that up to get me out of the shop?'

'Well, technically, yes,' said Rita, reaching up to pull the hood of Marianne's anorak down. 'But, dear Lord, have you seen your hair?'

'No.'

'Take my word for it. It's a demolition derby up there.'

'I'm not going to Happy Hair.' Marianne's tone was bullish.

'It's either that or the police station,' said Rita.

'But I haven't done anything,' said Marianne.

'Attempted robbery is a crime, you know,' said Rita, 'and I promised Judge Henderson that I'd keep an eye on you so you wouldn't reoffend.'

'It was a packet of thumbtacks.'

'And this is just a wash and blow-dry,' said Rita, gripping Marianne's arm again and marching her down the street. 'Think of it as an intervention.'

Chapter 21

Marianne stopped outside Hugh's house. 'I really don't need—' she began.

'It's just in here,' Rita said, opening the side gate and ushering Marianne through.

In the back garden there was the log cabin that Hugh had described. It was more modern than Marianne had envisaged, the timber pale and smooth, the words 'Happy Hair' engraved in jaunty italics along the floor-to-ceiling windows.

Through the glass, Marianne could see Hugh, sweeping hair from the floor, his kilt swaying to the beat of that Proclaimers song, which he sang loudly, as if he were alone in the shower and not in a small makeshift salon. He picked up the debris with a dustpan and brush and disappeared into a storeroom at the back.

Rita propelled Marianne through the door. Bartholomew sat at a mirror, studying the form in a glossy hairstyling magazine. He looked like a much tamer version of himself with his hair, wet and limp, hanging around his face. 'What do you think of this one, Marnie?' he said, turning the magazine round and pointing to a photograph of a middle-aged man with greying hair in a short back and sides style.

'It's . . . neat,' ventured Marianne.

'Exactly.' Bartholomew nodded with enthusiasm. 'I thought, you know, with the interview tomorrow, I should at least look the part.'

'There's no point going as anybody else,' declared Shirley, striding over and whipping the magazine out of Bartholomew's hands. 'Your quiff is quintessential you. Plus it's theatrical. And it gives you a bit of height. Otherwise you're just a short gay man with commitment issues.'

'It must be tiresome, being short,' said Freddy, puffing his narrow chest out. He sat on a chair at the workstation beside Bartholomew. When he looked up from his iPad – he was taking a survey to see if he was an alcoholic, as far as Marianne could make out – he saw her in the mirror and performed a small wave with his hand.

Marianne waved back.

Freddy's neat helmet of pale grey hair appeared unchanged although he must have acquiesced to a trim because Marianne could see occasional snippets of his hair on the floor around his chair.

'It must be tiresome, accommodating your great height in that closet of yours,' said Bartholomew smoothly.

The enormous dome hood of an ancient hairdryer lifted to reveal Ethel, whose hair was very much purple now, although its tone was more raucous than regal. 'I thought it was you,' she said, smiling at Marianne. 'Are you all right, dear? You look a little shook.'

Marianne did her best to rearrange her face.

'What do you think?' Ethel asked, reaching to gingerly pat the elevated hair on the top of her head. 'Is it purple enough?'

'Yes,' said Marianne.

'Oh, good,' said Ethel. 'Do you think Stanley will approve?'

'I . . .' Marianne faltered. Talking to these people was as exhausting as chewing on a piece of Rita's homemade toffee.

'For our wedding anniversary dear,' Ethel explained. 'Remember? The dinner-dance?'

'Yes,' said Marianne. 'I remember.'

'Stanley is such an elegant dancer,' said Ethel, fondly.

'As good as me, Ethel?' said Bartholomew, leaping out of his chair and waltzing about the room, holding an imaginary partner – much too tightly, Marianne thought – in his arms.

'Even better than you, dear Bartholomew,' cried Ethel, clapping her hands in appreciation of Bartholomew's efforts. Ethel patted her hair carefully. 'And I have a nice purple frock to match. Stanley always said it was a regal colour; made me look like a queen.'

'A proper gentleman,' said Rita, bending to kiss Ethel's cheek.

'Precious few of those left,' said Freddy, looking pointedly at Bartholomew.

'You are rocking that colour,' Bartholomew, ignoring Freddy, told Ethel. As far as Marianne could tell, he was being genuine.

Ethel beamed. 'You sure this will hold until Sunday evening, Shirley?' she said.

'You could jitterbug the length of the beach and your hair won't budge,' said Shirley, with a degree of pride. 'Just don't stand near any naked flames.' She lowered the hood of the dryer and set it on 'High'. She leaned down. 'Don't come out of there again until I tell you, okay?' she shouted through the hood. Ethel raised a shaky thumb.

'Ah, you persuaded herself to come,' said Hugh, coming out of the storeroom. He grinned at Marianne as he leaned on the top of a sweeping brush, which looked like it might snap beneath his bulk.

'It looks like you're busy,' said Marianne, edging towards the door.

'Not at all,' said Hugh. 'What are you having done?'

'Bagsy not doing it,' said Shirley. She looked at Marianne's hair. 'I don't think I have the physical endurance to take it on.' She grinned at Marianne. 'No offence,' she added.

Hugh set the brush against a wall and stood behind Freddy. 'Do you have enough physical endurance to rebuild Bartholomew's quiff?' he asked, removing the towel from Freddy's shoulders and brushing stray hairs off his neck with a soft-bristled brush. Freddy giggled. 'That tickles,' he said, gazing at Hugh through the steamed-up lenses of his glasses.

'Affirmative,' said Shirley, appearing suddenly in the mirror in front of Bartholomew's chair. 'You startled me,' he said, placing his hand over his heart. 'For one awful moment, I thought you were Freddy, trying to jump me again.'

'As if,' spluttered Freddy, his face reddening.

Rita positioned herself between them; nodded at Freddy's iPad. 'Have you totted up your score?' she asked him.

Freddy nodded mutinously. 'I'm intermediate level,' he said gloomily.

'You're improving,' said Rita.

'But last week I scored a "low level of alcohol dependence" rating,' said Freddy.

'Exactly,' said Rita, kissing him on both cheeks. 'Now come along with me. There's a new charity shop up the road and I fancy a browse.'

'Fine,' said Freddy, standing up. He knew he was being distracted like a child but could not resist Rita when she subjected him to the brightness of her smile.

'I'll be back in forty minutes,' Rita said to Hugh. 'Will that be enough time?'

'Enough time for what exactly?' said Marianne, feeling panic advancing on her like a tide.

'I'd give it an hour,' said Hugh, eyeing Marianne's hair. 'To be safe.'

It was quiet in the salon once Rita was gone. Hugh went to 'put on a brew' and Shirley frowned in concentration as she swiped at the ends of Bartholomew's hair with a pair of scissors. Beneath the dome, Ethel was snoring. Marianne had no idea if she should sit and, if so, where, and if she should take her anorak off before or after sitting down.

'You can pop yourself here, dear girl,' said Bartholomew, patting the chair beside him, 'now that mummy's boy has finally left.' The seat was still warm, which Marianne usually found uncomfortable but she was cold and glad of the heat in this instance.

Shirley plugged in a hairdryer and began drying Bartholomew's hair with vigour, wrapping pieces of it around a brush, then rolling it out, her tongue trapped between the gap in her front teeth.

'Could you be a little gentler?' Bartholomew suggested, raising his voice to be heard over the drone.

Shirley snapped off the dryer. 'Do you want to look your best at the interview tomorrow?' she said.

'I don't know why I applied for that job,' said Bartholomew, forlorn all of a sudden. 'I don't stand a chance.'

'Not with that attitude you don't,' said Shirley, swivelling his chair round so she could glare at him. She held up the hairdryer, pointed it at him like a gun. 'Now,' she said, 'are you going to stop bellyaching?'

'Fine,' said Bartholomew, perhaps sensing that Shirley's stock of patience was thinning. Marianne was surprised it had lasted so long.

Shirley turned his chair so that he was once again facing the mirror and resumed her machinations.

Hugh appeared with a mug in each hand and a packet of Club Milk trapped under his arm. He looked at Marianne. Then he laughed. Marianne glared at him.

'Sorry,' said Hugh. 'It's just, you look petrified.'

'I am most certainly not petrified,' said Marianne. 'I just . . . it's been a long time since I had a haircut.'

'Really?' said Hugh, smirking.

'That's not very professional,' said Marianne stiffly.

'You're right,' said Hugh, handing her a mug and a Club Milk. 'Can we start again? I'll be as professional as I can.'

Marianne nodded. She was suddenly tired, in the wake of the earlier adrenalin rush in Centra.

'Why don't you take off your anorak?' suggested Hugh. 'I'll pick you a novel to read.'

'Why aren't you offering me a magazine?' said Marianne, gesturing towards the one Bartholomew was engrossed in.

'Do you read magazines?' asked Hugh.

'No.'

Hugh picked a book out of the bookcase. *Little Women*. 'Have you read that one?' he asked.

'Of course,' said Marianne. 'When I was a child.'

'I left school early,' said Hugh. 'So I'm catching up now.'

'Are you one of those hairdressers who keeps up a persistent line of patter?' she asked him as he helped her into a black smock.

Hugh appeared to give the question careful consideration. 'Sometimes,' he said. 'When the situation warrants it.'

'This is not one of those times,' said Marianne.

'I'll be quiet as the day after Hogmanay,' Hugh promised, gesturing to the chair at the wash basin. Marianne sat down and now Hugh was behind her, gathering her hair in his hands, easing her head over the lip of the sink. He was uncomfortably close. Marianne could smell him. He smelled like a hotpress. And something else. Lemongrass, she thought. Possibly a hair product. His hair certainly looked glossy enough. A lock of it slipped from behind his ear and trailed across Marianne's cheek. It was soft and silky. Marianne thought about her coarse hair clogging up the sink.

'Sorry about that,' said Hugh, tucking his hair behind his ear. He trained the shower head on the ends of her hair. 'How's the temperature?' he asked.

'Fine,' said Marianne. Her voice was tight. She felt hot. She tried to remember to breathe. She had heard people in the office talking about how relaxing it was. Having their hair washed. How they'd nearly fallen asleep.

Marianne couldn't remember the last time she'd felt so uncomfortable. She couldn't see Hugh but she could feel him all around.

'You've got good quality hair,' he said as he swept her fringe away from her face. 'Is that chestnut brown your natural colour?'

'Yes.' There was nothing natural about her voice, which came out as a sort of high-pitched squeak. She could feel Hugh's enormous hands through her hair. It felt like he was . . . was he massaging her scalp? No, he was just applying the shampoo, like a normal hairdresser. She had to relax. But the shampoo smelled like rose petals and the water was warm and soft, and his hands in her hair were gentle and careful, and she tried to remember the last time somebody had touched her like that.

'Are you okay?' asked Hugh. 'Water not too hot, is it?'

'No, it's . . . fine,' she managed to say.

He rinsed her hair and she felt relief. It was nearly over. But no, he was off again, shampooing a second time, his fingers now kneading the base of her neck.

'Conditioner,' he said when he had finished the second rinse.

'No,' said Marianne, louder than she'd intended. But he was already working the conditioner through her hair.

'It wasn't a question,' Hugh explained when she opened her eyes to glare up at him. 'I was just letting you know.'

Marianne squeezed her eyes shut. Resigned herself.

'See?' said Hugh. 'I can now get my fingers through the

entire length of your hair without fear of entanglement.'
He sounded pleased with himself.

Marianne tried not to notice the delicate movement of
his fingers along the strands of her hair, slick with conditioner. She tried not to be so aware of him, behind her.
Even over the din of Shirley's hairdryer, she could hear
him breathing, a steady, slow breath that seemed deeper
than it should, as if he were concentrating on a complicated
mathematical equation.

Finally, he turned off the water and wrapped her hair
in a warm towel before leading her to a chair in front of
a Hollywood-style mirror, lined with brutally bright
bulbs.

'I'm knocking off now, Hugh,' said Shirley, whipping the
towel from Bartholomew's shoulders and scrubbing
the back of his neck with it.

Bartholomew shifted this way and that, trying to dodge
her. 'Leave me a few layers of skin, can't you?'

Marianne tried not to look at herself in the mirror.
Under the lights, her face was a harsh white and her mouth
and eyes seemed too big and too loud in its small circle.
Beneath her eyes, the semicircles of skin were a bruised
blue. If Marianne had been the type of person who carried
make-up in her handbag, she might have gone so far as
to apply some.

She couldn't believe how long her hair had grown, past
her shoulders. It had a tendency to curl out rather than
down but, in the weeks since her arrival at Ancaire, it
appeared to have done both.

'Nice work, Shirley,' said Hugh, smiling at Bartholomew,
whose quiff rose from his forehead like the masthead of

a ship, high and full and gleaming. Shirley, a little pink around the edges and breathing hard, nodded briefly but couldn't quash a small smile of pride that stole across her face.

She lifted the dome off Ethel's head and blew gently on her cheek to wake her up. Ethel's hair was an even brighter purple, now that it was dry. When she put on her white wool coat, she looked like a child's blackcurrant lollipop.

'I could sit under that dryer all day,' she sighed. 'So warm.' She took a plastic scarf out of her handbag and arranged it carefully over her hair.

'It's yours whenever you need it, Ethel,' said Hugh, reaching down to tie the scarf under her chin.

'Free gaff, you two,' said Shirley, smirking at Hugh and Marianne as she pulled a beanie over her head and reefed herself into her leather jacket.

'Oh, yes,' said Bartholomew, wagging his finger at them. 'No hanky-panky.'

'Where's the fun in that?' said Ethel, closing the gold clasp of her handbag.

Marianne's face flooded with colour as if she was some awkward teenager with an awkward teenager crush. She acted like she hadn't heard them and concentrated on the blurb at the back of the book.

Jo March and her sisters live in genteel poverty in Massachusetts with their mother.

She read the line over and over until it no longer made any sense, and Shirley, Ethel, and Bartholomew had been shown the door by Hugh.

Now he was behind her again, studying her reflection in the mirror. In her head, Marianne begged him not to make any reference to what the others had said. Not even a jokey one. Especially not a jokey one. She would have no idea what to say or do. She never knew.

Slagging. That's what they called it in the office. Good-humoured slagging. Or joking. Or having a laugh. We're just having a laugh, Marianne. As if she should somehow know how to do that. Or, more often, how to take it.

Perhaps if she said something first. Set the tone. Her mouth was dry when she opened it.

But it was Hugh who spoke first. 'I'm going to brush it first, okay?' he said, holding a rake comb in his hand and looking at her in the mirror.

Marianne nodded, relieved. 'And then what?' she asked.

'And then whatever you like. I can do all sorts: undercuts, overcuts, blunt cuts, slicks, tapers, fades . . .'

'I would have thought purple rinses are more your area of expertise,' said Marianne.

'I do believe you just made a joke,' said Hugh, twirling the handle of his scissors around a finger, like a gunslinger.

Marianne nodded. 'It must be the fumes of the industrial-strength hairspray.'

'So what'll it be?' asked Hugh.

'Um, a trim?'

'Excellent choice,' said Hugh. 'And, because it's your first time here, I will throw in my blow-dry special.'

'What's your blow-dry special?' Marianne couldn't help asking.

'It's pretty much a standard blow dry, but you get a Happy Hair badge at the end,' said Hugh, opening a drawer where there were many Happy Hair badges, in different colours.

Marianne struggled not to smile. 'Okay,' she said gruffly, settling back on the chair.

She opened the novel at the last page. Read the last paragraph. Then to chapter one, which she began to read.

'Do you always do that?' asked Hugh, coaxing the comb through Marianne's hair.

Marianne nodded. 'I don't like surprises,' she said.

For the next fifteen minutes there was no sound other than the snip-snip-snip of Hugh's scissors along Marianne's hair. Even though Marianne did not like surprises, she was surprised none the less to find that she did not overly mind the procedure. Hugh had a solid presence and cut her hair with an attention to detail that Marianne had not expected. On her previous annual visits to hairdressers – she never went to the same one twice – she was always on tenterhooks, anticipating the catch of the teeth of a comb in the fold of her ear or a throwaway remark about the unruliness of her hair or the casual insistence of this product or that product, regular application of which would transform her gnarled thicket into flowing locks.

Hugh was careful with the comb and made no remarks, throwaway or otherwise.

He cut her hair. Marianne read her novel. When she turned a page, she formed the habit of glancing at him over the top of the book, careful not to move her head. Everything about him was big. His hair, his face, his whole head. But there was a curious sort of delicacy along the line of his jaw and across the raspberry pink of his mouth, and while his green eyes clashed noisily with the rash of bright orange freckles across his face, Marianne found her habit of glancing at his face at every page turn sort of reassuring.

Like she was in a safe pair of hands. This surprised her, as did the conversation, when it began. Because it was Marianne who began it.

'How come you picked hairdressing?' she asked, the next time she turned a page and glanced up.

'Well,' said Hugh, straightening and looking at her in the mirror, 'it's easier than clearing drains.' He grinned. 'Smells a hell of a lot nicer, too.'

'Is that what you used to do?' asked Marianne.

Hugh shrugged. 'I mostly did drugs, to be fair. With a few wee jobs in between to pay for them. I once got a job in a spray-tan place, if you can believe that.'

Oddly, Marianne could believe it.

'They even wanted to keep me on. But, Jesus, the smell of the place. Worse than drains.'

Marianne laughed. She couldn't help it. Nor could she blame Hugh, who looked sort of startled. She stopped laughing. 'You didn't answer my question,' she said.

'Did I not?'

'About why you chose hairdressing?'

'I didn't choose it as such,' said Hugh, lifting Marianne's fringe and trapping it between his fingers before snipping at the ends of it with his scissors. 'The judge said it was either rehab and an apprenticeship or he'd send me to the Big Hoose.'

'What's the Big Hoose?'

'Barlinnie prison. All my brothers had been there and gave it a pretty poor rating on TripAdvisor.'

'Oh,' said Marianne.

'So I did the hairdressing. It was the only class available.'

'You must have had a good teacher,' said Marianne stiffly.

'Are you giving me a compliment?' asked Hugh, pausing to look at her in the mirror.

'I am commenting favourably on your professional hair-dressing skills.'

'That's a compliment.'

'And then you decided to move to Ireland?' Marianne asked.

Hugh resumed his careful concentration on her fringe. 'Rita was a guest speaker at the rehab centre. She spoke about her Get Well Soon programme and I knew I wouldn't stay clean in Glasgow. The flats were like a den of addiction. If you weren't using, you were the odd one out. I wasn't using *and* I was a hairdresser.'

He opened a drawer and took out a hairdryer. Marianne wanted to ask him more things. Instead she said, 'Are you going to straighten my hair?' Brian had bought her a straightener one Christmas but Marianne had never been able to achieve the look promised by the model on the box.

Hugh shook his head. 'It'd be a crime to straighten curls like yours.'

He said 'curr-dels'. Marianne's hair sounded delightful, the way he said it. She couldn't help smiling when he finished drying her hair and held a mirror behind her head, so she could see the back of it, the sides of it.

Marianne reached a tentative hand to her head, ran it down her hair. It was soft and bouncy and no longer just a mousy brown but a vibrant, rich, yes, chestnut brown with glints of something like gold in it, as if she had got those things that her colleagues – her ex-colleagues – were always getting. Highlights.

She looked like a woman with highlights in her hair. A woman with highlights in her hair wearing a tracksuit.

But still.

Hugh lifted her hair off her neck and brushed the stray hairs away.

'You going out tonight?' he asked.

'You said you didn't do the patter,' said Marianne.

'I'm not,' said Hugh. 'This is actual conversation.'

'I'm not going out,' said Marianne. 'How much do I owe you?'

'Twenty-five euros,' said Hugh.

'It can't be that little.' Even Marianne, with her limited experience, knew that hairdressers were supposed to charge you exorbitant prices, then tear a rip in the lining of your coat if you didn't leave a hefty tip.

'It is,' said Hugh, handing her a Happy Hair badge.

'Are you charging me that little because my house was repossessed and my husband left me and I lost my job because I got a criminal conviction for stealing?'

'No,' said Hugh. 'That's just the price.' He nodded towards a price list on the wall.

'Oh.'

Hugh pulled her anorak off the hanger and helped her into it. She turned round and nearly laughed with pleasure as her hair lifted and swirled around her head.

'My hair,' she blurted. 'It's . . . nice.'

'It is, aye,' Hugh said, grinning at her. His green eyes had disappeared into their slits with the strength of his smile. He looked like somebody who knew where happiness lived and how to get there. For a moment, she considered asking him.

She was looking at his mouth now. The glistening flush of it. She would need to stand on her toes to reach him.

She stepped back and fumbled with the zip of her anorak. She tried to remember Brian's mouth. When was the last time she had kissed him? She couldn't remember. It was probably a brief peck on the cheek. If she had known it was the last time, maybe she would have taken more notice. Made more of an effort.

She had no idea why she was thinking about such things. She put it down to the heat of the hairdryer. Her face was flushed with it.

'Thank you,' she said. 'That wasn't as . . . awful as I'd imagined.'

'Likewise,' said Hugh.

Chapter 22

'You're looking very pleased with yourself,' said Aunt Pearl when Marianne arrived in the kitchen.

'I got a good night's sleep,' said Marianne, buttering a slice of toast.

'Don't your troubles seem halved?' said Rita, setting a plate of warm scones on the table.

'No,' said Marianne.

'Quartered, though?'

'It's her hair,' said Aunt Pearl, leaning towards Marianne and examining her. 'Did you brush it?'

'Hugh cut it,' Marianne admitted when it became clear that Aunt Pearl was not going to let up without some sort of plausible explanation.

'Ah, Hugh,' said Aunt Pearl, and Marianne waited for the rest of the sentence, which, no doubt, would drip with vitriol and disapproval. But Pearl said nothing further. There was even a trace of a smile across her face.

Bartholomew's interview was at eleven o'clock in the

morning so, after Marianne had picked up the Get-Well-Sooners and dropped them at Ancaire, she drove Bartholomew to the theatre in Rush where the interview would take place. She parked outside the door.

'Oh dear, Marianne,' said Bartholomew, immaculate in a navy herringbone suit with a triangle of handkerchief peeping out of the breast pocket, in the exact same shade as his tie. 'I don't think I can do this.'

'You can,' said Marianne in the voice she used to employ when her clients got jumpy around tax return season.

It seemed to work because Bartholomew looked at her with his damp, pale blue eyes and said, 'Do you really think so?' His tone was plaintive but there was a sliver of hope in there somewhere.

Marianne nodded briskly.

'Perhaps we should do the breathing exercise Rita swears by,' suggested Bartholomew after a while.

'We?' said Marianne.

'It's good to have a bit of company,' said Bartholomew.

They sat in the car and breathed in for five, held it for five, breathed out. Bartholomew insisted on doing it ten times. When Marianne opened her eyes – she hadn't realised she had closed them in the first place – Bartholomew was looking at her and smiling.

'What?' she said, straightening. 'Do I have food on my face?'

'I was just thinking how fabulous your hair is,' said Bartholomew. 'Hugh's got a great pair of hands,' he added, wistfully.

'You should go,' said Marianne, looking at her watch. 'I suppose you want me to wait for you?'

Bartholomew shook his head. 'I'd prefer if you didn't,' he said. 'Just in case it goes balls up.'

'It won't go balls up,' said Marianne.

'You said balls,' said Bartholomew, grinning.

'Go on,' said Marianne. 'You don't want to be late.'

'But if I'm too early, I'll look desperate,' said Bartholomew, widening his eyes so that he did look a bit desperate.

'You'll look enthusiastic,' said Marianne.

Bartholomew, who had been sitting on his hands, plucked one from beneath him and placed it on Marianne's, gripping the wheel. 'You know,' he said. 'I don't think I'd have come if it weren't for you.'

His hand was warm from the recent weight of his backside on it. Marianne surprised herself by not pulling her hand away. In fact, she turned it so she was now holding Bartholomew's hand in hers, her fingers long and white and thin against Bartholomew's short, brown ones. Bartholomew smiled at her, steeled himself and opened the car door.

'Wait,' said Marianne, diving for her handbag and reaching inside. 'Freddy gave me something to give you. I nearly forgot.'

'What is it?' asked Bartholomew.

'This.' Marianne handed him what looked like a shopping trolley token, in the colours of the rainbow.

'Oh, my word.' Bartholomew took it gently from her and placed it in the centre of his palm. He shook his head. 'He kept it,' he said, almost to himself. He looked at Marianne and there were tears in his eyes and she cursed herself for giving it to him at all.

'The night of the marriage referendum,' Bartholomew

said quietly. 'We were so drunk, me and Freddy. I wanted to take a trolley from outside the supermarket and wheel Freddy around in it. Like a triumphant lap, you know? But we didn't have a euro coin to put in the slot and then an old queen gave Freddy this token and away we went, Freddy in the trolley and me pushing and the pair of us singing 'People Get Ready'.

Marianne really regretted giving Bartholomew the token now because, while he no longer looked like he might cry, there was every possibility that he was going to sing.

Which he did. 'People Get Ready'. He closed his eyes and spread his arms while he sang the entire first verse and there was absolutely nothing Marianne could do but wait for him to stop. When he finally did, he slipped the small token into the inside pocket of his suit jacket, patted it there.

'Now,' he said, 'are you sure I look presentable enough?' He pulled down the visor and examined his teeth in the mirror.

'I am,' said Marianne.

'Right then.' Bartholomew hauled himself out of the Jeep, closed the door behind him and Marianne watched him until he disappeared inside the theatre.

When she lifted her hand from the steering wheel to take off the handbrake, it was shaking. She was as nervous as if it was she who was about to be interviewed. Which was ridiculous. Bartholomew was a grown man who could take care of himself. It was just . . . this was so much more than a job interview. It was Bartholomew taking his first, shaky-legged steps into this brave new sober world he had managed to build for himself. Stepping off the carousel of casual hook-ups, crashing hangovers, and lost opportunities. Living alone and independently for maybe the first time in his life. Doing his best not to depend on anyone. Trying not to let anyone down. Having his heart broken by Freddy, who hadn't meant to break it but who broke it all the same.

Marianne had a sudden and terrible urge to run into the theatre and talk to the interviewer. Let them know just how brilliant Bartholomew would be at the job, no matter how chequered his work experience might appear on the two pages of his curriculum vitae.

And then she remembered. She had told him he could do this. She had led him to believe that she believed in him.

She would just have to have a bit of faith.

Chapter 23

Marianne was not needed the next morning. Hugh had driven the Get-Well-Sooners to Ethel's house where the meeting was taking place. It was Ethel and Stanley's wedding anniversary and Ethel was keen to stay close to home until the dinner-dance that evening. 'Just in case dear Stanley sends me a sign earlier than usual,' she had explained to Marianne who managed not to say anything sceptical.

Marianne had thought it would make a welcome change, not having to drive around the country in Rita's unpredictable Jeep, picking her clients up and dropping them off and listening to their bickering and singing and whooping.

The house seemed very quiet.

She thought about Bartholomew, who had phoned her after the interview.

'When did they say they'd let you know?' she asked him.

'Next week sometime,' he said.

'How do you think it went?'

'Do you mind if we don't talk about it?'

Marianne walked through the quiet house, George's nails tap-tap-tapping on the floorboards behind her. Goose bumps erupted onto her skin. It seemed like a betrayal, worrying about Bartholomew and his interview. A lack of confidence in his ability to shine.

Marianne pressed her nose against the window in Rita's studio. Patrick's workshop door was closed. He must have gone to meet a customer. Or get supplies.

The grandfather clock in the hall chimed loudly.

She marched to the kitchen where she filled a bucket with hot, soapy water and carried it out to the glasshouse. She had thought about clearing it out for ages but never appeared to have enough time or energy to follow through.

Now, she seemed to have a surfeit of both.

She scrubbed at the glasshouse, filled Patrick's wheelbarrow several times with the overgrown foliage from inside, refilled some of the now empty pots with fresh compost, pushed some seeds Patrick had given her deep into the soil, watered them.

Again and again, Marianne poured the tepid, dirty brown water out of the bucket, refilled it. She scrubbed at the last traces of moss and algae, kept scrubbing until they relented and let go. She used the hose to rinse the suds off the glass. She stopped for a quick lunch of one of Rita's roasted asparagus and goat's cheese tartlets, eating it on an upturned bucket in the glasshouse, washing it down with a glass of milk.

By the time she finished, in the late afternoon, she was sweating and out of breath. Her hair had reverted to type, back to the tangled, wild version of itself, George having insisted on his morning walk on the beach, unable or unwilling to acknowledge the adverse effect of the salty sea wind on her freshly coiffed do. She pushed as much of it as she could fit behind her ears, stepped away from the glasshouse to get a better view. With the amount of foliage she had cut away inside, she could now see right through the glasshouse, all the way to the sea.

Today the water was a bright green with the slant of the setting sun on the surface, and the waves were gentler, ripples rather than surges.

'You've done a great job.'

Marianne turned round. Rita was standing on the grass with her hands on her hips, smiling. She was even more dressed up than usual, no mean feat, Marianne thought. Although the overall effect was demure rather than her usual exuberance. There was a definite black tie tone to the outfit: a sleeveless black silk gown with a scooped, ruffled neckline, pinched in at the waist, a fishtail skirt ending at her ankles and a pair of high-heeled gold sandals with her toes poking out the top, uniformly painted the same sophisticated gold as her shoes. Even her fingernails matched. A black and gold leopard-print cocktail bag was tucked under her arm. A cropped black jacket hung off her fingers.

The entire effect was one of attention to detail and seemed to suggest a 'less is more' policy that was not in keeping with Rita's usual sense of carnival when it came to dressing.

'You look . . . lovely,' Marianne couldn't help saying.

'Oh, I'm not too conservative?' said Rita, looking down at herself.

'No,' said Marianne, stung.

'Sorry, darling, It's just, I have to go to Ethel's churchy dinner-dance thing and I didn't think they'd let me in if I was in one of my usual rig-outs, as you call them.'

Marianne couldn't help feeling a modicum of shame. It was true that she referred to Rita's outfits as rig-outs. And not in a kind way.

'You don't give a whit what other people think,' said Marianne.

'Well, no, I don't usually, but Ethel is so particular about this event and it'll be crammed with churchy people. You know how scared I am of churchy people.'

'I didn't think you were scared of anything,' said Marianne, surprised.

'Only gatherings of churchy people. They're just so . . . strange.' Rita actually shuddered although whether it was from the cold – the usual sharp wind was whistling in from the sea – or because of the strange churchy people, Marianne couldn't tell.

'I thought Ethel went to that dinner-dance thing with, well, you know, Stanley,' said Marianne.

'Marnie, you do know that Stanley is dead, don't you?' said Rita, looking at Marianne with concern.

'Of course I do,' said Marianne. 'It's Ethel who seems to have difficulty with that fact.'

Rita sighed and shook her head. In her subdued outfit, she looked a little less than herself. She looked tired. 'She just . . . she misses him,' she said in a quiet voice. 'Every day.'

Marianne nodded. 'I know,' she said.

Rita straightened, gathered herself. 'Anyway, the thing is, Ethel is there, at the dinner-dance. But Stanley is a no-show.'

'There's a surprise.'

Rita ignored Marianne's sceptical tone. 'He usually sends his sign before the dinner is served. But they're already dishing out the baked Alaska and there's no sign of a sign, apparently.'

'What sort of sign?' Marianne asked, curious in spite of herself.

Rita shrugged. 'Different things. A song maybe. One year it was a smell. Marrows, I think. Stanley used to grow them. Or it could be something someone says or just, you know, Ethel gets a sense of him, nearby. It gives her great comfort.'

Marianne peeled off her gloves. 'I presume you'll want a lift.'

'Actually,' Rita said, 'Ethel wondered if you could come too.'

'Why?'

'She adores you.'

'Ethel adores everybody.'

'She says it will cheer her up.'

'I don't see how.'

'I'm just telling you what she said.'

Marianne sighed. 'How long do I have to stay?'

Rita shook her head. 'She didn't specify.'

'Bloody hell,' said Marianne, picking up the bucket and emptying it down the drain beside the glasshouse.

'So you'll come?' said Rita brightly.

'Fine,' said Marianne, gruffly. 'I just need to wash my hands.'

'And maybe brush your hair?' said Rita. 'The churchy people . . .'

'Nobody's going to notice my hair.'

'And could you put a dress on?' went on Rita. 'It's just . . .'

'I know, I know, the churchy people.'

Marianne tossed the gardening gloves inside the glasshouse. 'I'll meet you in the Jeep in five minutes.'

'How about ten?' said Rita. 'That'll give you time to put a bit of lipstick on.'

Marianne owned one dress. It was black. She wasn't sure what fabric it was made of; some synthetic mix that meant she could throw it in the machine and didn't have to bother with the iron afterwards. She'd had it for years. She'd worn it to every work Christmas party she had been unable to wriggle her way out of, and the few ICA events she'd had to endure. Brian had said it was 'nice' the few times she'd had occasion to wear it. She hunted through her suitcase for the black strapless bra she had to wear with it, since the dress was a halterneck, tying at the back of her neck with a piece of black satin ribbon. She wrestled her way into the dress, which stopped just south of her knees. Her bare legs were a blueish white. George, sitting on the rug, looked at her, his cocked head giving him a sort of concerned expression.

'Okay, fine, I'll put tights on,' she told him crossly. She found a tangle of tights in the zip section of her suitcase and managed to extract a pair with no obvious snags or ladders. They felt strange against her skin and she was reminded of Hugh and his aversion to trousers, and his kilts, and his hairy legs, which were also long and sturdy and . . .

She pushed her feet into the only pair of shoes she had that weren't runners. They were black sandals, a little higher than she remembered, the heels skinny as knitting needles and a slender strap that fastened around her ankle and didn't promise much in the way of support. She practised walking down the length of the room with George's curious amber eyes following her progress, like one of Rita's self-portraits. When she managed two consecutive lengths without stumbling, she put her hair up, using the biggest scrunchie she could find, brushed mascara onto her eyelashes, used her finger to dab a bit of grey eyeshadow across her lids and smeared some lipstick – a copper sort of brown – across her mouth, smacked her lips together as she had seen Rita do on many occasions.

She checked her watch. She had managed it in exactly five minutes.

'No,' she said to George, who had stood up and was now waiting patiently beside the bedroom door. 'You can't come. Not this time. The churchy people wouldn't like it.' Marianne pulled his ears gently between her fingers, just the way he liked and he took the opportunity to lick the inside of her arm, which she rubbed on the side of her dress.

Rita stood at the bottom of the stairs as Marianne inched her way down, clutching the banisters.

'I like your rig-out,' she said.

'It's not too much, is it?' said Marianne, looking down at herself.

'You look very elegant.'

Marianne shrugged. 'Well, you know, best to make an effort for the churchy people.'

Rita nodded grimly.

They set off.

The dinner-dance was taking place in the hall

behind the Church of Ireland. It was a fairly rudimentary building, which the committee had prettied up with fairy lights, dangling from the eaves, and an enormous red ribbon wrapped around the front door with an oversized bow stuck in the middle, making it look like a Christmas present somebody forgot to open. As they approached, Marianne could hear an amplified voice calling out raffle numbers. When they reached the door, another car pulled up and when Marianne looked, she saw it was Hugh's bottle-green Jaguar. The doors flung open.

'Bartholomew!' Rita called out. 'And Freddy! Shirley! Hugh! Oh, you darlings! What are you all doing here?'

'Got a damsel-in-distress call from Ethel,' said Bartholomew, looking very dapper in a top hat and tails. 'She left a message on your phone but was worried you mightn't listen to it until later, so she phoned me, and I phoned them, and Shirley plucked Mrs Hegarty's eyebrows so she'd look after the boys, and Hugh said he'd drive us.'

Hugh poked his head out of the car and grinned at everyone. He was in his usual kilt and shirt but had added a black tuxedo jacket to his ensemble, which gave a little gravitas to his appearance. With Freddy in a white *Cats* T-shirt under a faded but otherwise presentable black corduroy jacket, and Shirley, toned down in a khaki print, nearly knee-length dress and freshly polished Doc Martens, Marianne felt the churchy people could not deny them access on the grounds of their appearance, at least. She felt nearly proud of them.

'You all look beautiful,' Rita declared.

'No one's ever called me beautiful before,' said Hugh,

and through the shadowy darkness of the night, Marianne could hear the grin in his tone.

'Well, they should,' said Bartholomew, taking the opportunity to clasp Hugh's arm. 'Look at you, you're a magnificent specimen.'

Freddy's face curdled. He pushed his glasses up his nose with a long, bony finger. 'When you've quite finished,' he said pointedly to Bartholomew, 'we have Ethel to attend to.'

'Okay, okay, keep what's left of your hair on, Frederick,' grumbled Bartholomew, releasing Hugh. 'Now, follow me,' he told them, marching towards the door in a thick cloud of Paco Rabanne. Rita, Shirley, and Freddy followed in single file, like foot soldiers marching to the front line.

'I'll park the car,' said Hugh. Marianne nodded and hurried towards the building.

The Get-Well-Sooners crammed through the front door into a poky little foyer, a trestle table standing stoutly between them and the door into the main hall. The table was covered in crepe paper, raffle tickets, and a petty-cash box. A pair of old but well-maintained red velvet curtains were pulled tight across the door into the hall.

Behind the table, sitting on a plastic chair, was a solidly built woman with a tight, grey perm, pearl earrings embedded in a pair of long, loose ear lobes and enormous, thick-framed glasses, the same beige as her face, shielding magnified, unimpressed eyes with which she sized them up.

Rita's nostrils flared. Marianne made her way to the front.

'Good evening,' she said in her best audit voice.

'If you don't have tickets, I'm afraid I can't let you in,' the woman said in a voice high with self-righteous authority. 'The event is fully subscribed.'

'Really?' said Rita, her eyes bulging in disbelief.

'We are here to see Ethel Abelforth,' said Marianne, briskly.

'Why?' The woman narrowed her eyes, looked at Marianne with blatant suspicion.

'I am not at liberty to divulge that information,' said Marianne.

'Are you her . . . next of kin?' asked the woman.

'She's not dead,' piped up Bartholomew.

'We're her friends,' said Marianne. The others, flanking her, nodded enthusiastically.

'Why do all of you need to go in?' the woman asked. It was a reasonable question, Marianne felt.

There was a sudden draught behind them and the woman shifted in her chair, craned her neck. 'Ah, Hugh, I didn't know you were coming tonight?' She patted her rigid curls.

'Olwen, lovely to see you,' said Hugh, closing the door behind him. He swept his eyes around the foyer and Marianne could see him sizing up the situation. 'I'm loving the navy twinset,' he said, advancing on the woman behind the table. 'It's very elegant.'

'Oh, this old rag,' said Olwen, her face cracking into a smile. 'I've had it years.'

Marianne could see Bartholomew nodding, although he managed to stay quiet.

'I was just telling Olwen here,' Marianne smiled at the woman, 'that we need to get inside to check on Ethel.'

Olwen drew herself up as high as she could manage. 'And I was just saying . . .'

Hugh spread his hands on the table, leaned towards Olwen, lowered his voice. 'You know, I think I am free to do that haircare workshop at your next Ladies Who Lunch committee meeting after all,' he said. 'So long as you promise to be my guinea pig,' he added, with a wink.

'I prefer to think of myself as your muse, Hugh,' said Olwen, in an outrageously coquettish tone.

Marianne cleared her throat so hard, it hurt. Hugh looked up, as if he had only just noticed that there were other people in the foyer.

'Oh, yes,' said Hugh, frowning now. 'Olwen, is there any chance . . .?'

Olwen stood up, put her hand on Hugh's arm. 'Leave it with me, Hugh,' she said in a throaty, conspiratorial voice. She dragged her eyes away from his face and disappeared behind the curtains, into the hall.

'I feel filthy after that,' said Bartholomew.

'I thought you were magnificent,' breathed Freddy, beaming up at Hugh.

'You're like a sex toy for the aged,' said Shirley, shuddering.

'Olwen isn't that old,' said Rita, tartly. 'She's only about my age.'

'We haven't actually gotten in yet,' Marianne reminded them, just as the curtains parted and Olwen reappeared, looking triumphant. 'I got them to set up a table for you beside Ethel's,' she said, gazing at Hugh as if he was the only other person in the room. 'You're too late for dinner but I'll see if I can rustle up some dessert.' She beamed at him. 'Even though you're sweet enough.' She tittered at her joke. Shirley made a dry-retching sound, which Marianne covered up with a loud cough. Olwen snatched her head towards them but Bartholomew distracted her with a peck on the cheek and Rita pulled the curtain back. 'Once more, unto the breach,' she roared as she ushered them into the hall. Olwen looked at her, stricken. 'You will . . . behave with the decorum the event warrants, I assume?' she said. There was a plaintive note in her voice.

'Where would be the fun in that?' Rita said, with an enormous wink. She stepped into the hall and yanked the curtains across the gap, leaving Olwen and her worried face on the other side.

The Committee had done their best to cheer up the damp and draughty hall, with streamers, balloons, and banners sellotaped to walls and windows, and handfuls of glitter strewn across each table. The venue was further enhanced by the significant number of people inside, the heat of their bodies giving the room a warm, if slightly meaty, aroma. The stage area at the top of the room was edged with candles, which, Marianne felt sure, would be counter to health and safety regulations. Two musicians – a pianist and violinist – stood on the stage playing a waltz, the violinist swaying as she played so that the full skirt of her black acrylic dress billowed alarmingly close to the line of candles. Marianne couldn't look. Instead, she scanned the crowd for Ethel.

'There she is,' said Bartholomew, pointing through the sea of tables.

'Ethel! Darling!' shouted Rita, charging across the dance

floor so that the couples waltzing around the floor had to one-two-three out of her way.

Ethel was sitting alone at a table for two. Her baked Alaska was untouched and slumped, melting, in the bowl in front of her. They reached her and formed a perimeter around her. She looked even smaller and frailer than usual. Marianne put it down to her dress. It was a pale pink taffeta affair, all ruffles and bows. But the bodice was baggy on her now, her arms poking out of the puff sleeves, skinny as reeds.

'You all came,' she said in a choked voice.

'Of course we came,' said Rita, sitting in the chair opposite Ethel.

Ethel shook her head. 'I shouldn't have bothered you. I should have just gone home when Stanley didn't show up.'

'You could never bother us, Ethel,' Rita said, picking up one of Ethel's delicate hands. 'Right, everyone?' She looked around at Bartholomew, Freddy, Shirley, Hugh, and Marianne. They all nodded and said, 'Right,' like a chorus line.

Ethel squeezed Rita's hand. 'You must think me a foolish old woman,' she said.

'We would never think that,' said Rita, while the rest of them shook their heads in unison. 'We love you. And so does Stanley.'

'But why hasn't he sent me a sign?' said Ethel. 'And, believe me, I know I sound like a mentally retarded person and . . .' She stopped then, looked at Shirley. 'Oh dear, am I allowed say mentally retarded?' she asked.

Shirley shook her head. 'No,' she said. 'And don't say crazy, mad, demented or insane either.'

Ethel took a breath. 'I know I sound . . . like I'm losing my mental faculties . . .' She paused and looked sideways at Shirley who nodded. 'But that doesn't change the fact that Stanley sends me a sign. Every single year, without fail. Why not this year?' Her eyes became glassy with tears and she looked so alone and lost, in her oversized dress, her thin hand still clasped in Rita's and her tiny feet in a pair of sparkly red shoes with a kitten heel.

Marianne was horrified to feel a lump at the back of her throat. If Ethel cried, here, in this shabby hall masquerading as a ballroom, there was every chance that Marainne would too. She would wail like a baby.

Two babies.

Twins.

'The night is but a wean,' said Hugh, hunkering down beside Ethel and placing his hand gently on her boisterous purple curls so that her head seemed to suddenly shrink.

'He means the night is young,' said Freddy, glancing around at everyone.

'We managed to work that out for ourselves,' said Bartholomew.

'But he always sends me a sign before dessert,' said Ethel. 'Last year, it was the starters themselves. Prawn cocktail. That was Stanley's favourite starter even though prawns tend to repeat on him.'

The musicians began to play 'Chanson de Matin' and couples surged onto the dance floor. Ethel watched them with melancholic eyes. 'There's no one like Elgar for romance,' she said, in a sort of long-ago and faraway voice.

Hugh stood up and held out his hand to Ethel. 'Would you do me the honour of dancing this dance with me?' he said.

Ethel shook her head. 'I'm much too old for dancing now, Hugh.'

'Well, I'm not too old for dancing and I'm older than you, Ethel,' declared Rita, who had never, as far as Marianne knew, owned to being older than anyone.

'What?' said Rita, looking around at the Get-Well-Sooners, all of whom seemed to be in the same state of disbelief as Marianne.

'Very well then, Hugh,' said Ethel, getting unsteadily to her feet. 'I shall do you the honour of dancing this dance with you.' She took his hand. 'I hope you'll be able to keep up with me.'

'I'll do my best,' said Hugh, grinning so broadly that his eyes did their disappearing act. He led her away.

The others took their seats at the table beside Ethel's. There were paper hats at each place setting and Rita insisted they put them on, to get them in the mood.

Bartholomew looked longingly at Ethel's table. 'Do you think Ethel is going to eat that Baked Alaska?'

'You need some distraction, Bartholomew,' said Rita, standing up and stretching out her hand. 'Dance with me.'

'Certainly, my lady love,' said Bartholomew, standing up and performing a flamboyant bow. 'But be warned, my dance moves are, I'm going to say, advanced.' He swivelled, fast, on his heel, doing a complete 360-degree turn, then lunged forward and lowered himself to the floor on one bended knee. 'See?'

'That is impressive, darling,' Rita told him. 'Now, come on. Get up.'

'I will,' said Bartholomew. 'It's just . . . I seem to be ever so slightly stuck.'

'Oh for Pete's sake,' said Freddy, gripping Bartholomew's hands and hauling him to his feet so fast that Bartholomew ended up in the circle of Freddy's arms. After a moment, Freddy stepped backwards. 'Sorry, I . . .'

'Not at all,' said Bartholomew, two high spots of colour blooming on his face. 'I didn't realise you were quite so . . . strong.'

Now it was Freddy's turn to flush. Marianne could see him doing his best to look away but he couldn't quite manage it.

'Are you coming, Bartholomew?' called Rita from the edge of the dance floor.

'Oh,' said Bartholomew, dragging his eyes away from Freddy's and waving at Rita. 'Yes, my love, I'll be right there.'

Freddy slumped back into his seat.

'I'm glad I'm not in love,' Shirley said, patting Freddy's hand. 'It looks way too much like hard work.'

'I wouldn't know,' Freddy said primly.

'I'm bored,' declared Shirley. 'Do you want to dance with me?' She glared at Freddy, who sighed a defeated sort of sigh.

'Fine then,' he said.

'Correct answer,' Shirley told him, standing up.

They set off.

Now it was just Marianne at the table. She was glad of some alone time. From her vantage point, she watched Hugh dance with Ethel. He was oddly graceful for such a big man. He danced like someone who had taken a ball-room dancing class. It would be just like him. All that making up for lost time business that he was so keen on. He swept Ethel around the floor, the two of them turning and turning. Marianne could see Ethel mouthing the rhythm – one, two, one, two – over and over. Hugh said something then and Ethel laughed her girlish giggle. It was infectious and Marianne couldn't help laughing too. The people at a nearby table turned to look at her. Marianne stopped laughing and smiled at them. They smiled back. That was the great thing about churchy people, Marianne thought. They were polite. They couldn't help themselves.

The tune ended and Hugh and Ethel arrived back, Ethel a little out of breath and her face flushed pink.

'He's nearly as good as Stanley,' she told Marianne as she sat down. 'You'll have to have a go.'

'Oh, no,' said Marianne, shaking her head. 'I can't dance.'

'Everybody can dance,' said Hugh, shaking his hips to the music so that his kilt swung around his knees.

'And you look so beautiful tonight, my dear,' said Ethel. 'It would be a shame to waste it.'

'I really can't, Ethel,' said Marianne. 'I never have.'

Ethel cupped her ear with her hand. 'I'm sorry, dear, it's terribly noisy. What did you say?'

'She said she'd love to dance,' said Hugh, stepping forward and reaching for Marianne's hand.

Ethel clapped her hands together. 'Oh, how lovely,' she said, her eyes shining. 'I think you two make such a dashing couple. Don't they?' She looked past Marianne at Rita and Bartholomew, who had returned from the dance floor, Bartholomew massaging his shoulder, which he claimed to have sprained when Rita insisted that he lower her to the floor in his arms at the end of the dance.

Marianne felt the tug of Hugh's hand in hers and she felt herself shift from the chair and trail along after him towards the dance floor, as if she were somebody else. Someone who would casually approach a dance floor with a man in a kilt. Someone who had every intention of dancing with abandon.

She had no intention of dancing and certainly not with abandon. She would tell him so when he stopped walking, which he eventually did, right in the middle of the floor where there was a circle of empty space, as if he had ordered it especially for them. He turned and smiled at her and, before she could say a word, he placed her left hand on his shoulder, slipped his right hand behind her, rested it on her shoulder blade, then picked up her free hand and held it in his so delicately, as if it were something precious and breakable, that Marianne forgot to voice her objections before they began to move and then it was too late. They were moving.

Dancing.

It wasn't as difficult as Marianne had envisaged. Maybe because the musicians were playing 'Moon River' now and it was such a beautiful piece of music. So familiar. Like she'd danced to its soft strains before.

Which she had not.

One-two-three, one-two-three.

It was maths really.

'You dance well for someone who can't dance,' said Hugh.

'It's just walking, really,' she said. 'In circles.'

What was difficult was Hugh himself. There was no

getting away from him. He had a solid, undeniable presence that Marianne found difficult to negotiate past. She had never been more keenly aware of anyone. It was an uncomfortable sensation. The feel of his fingers along her hand and the heat of his hand against her back, his leg taut against hers as they stepped forward, back, to the side.

One-two-three, one-two-three.

After a while, she stopped looking at her feet. Instead she looked straight ahead. Now her eyes were level with the top button of Hugh's silver-grey cotton shirt. The button was a small silver one, tethered to the fabric with pale grey thread, which was not something Marianne would ordinarily notice. She decided she liked this small attention to detail. It reminded her of the tiny flowers that grew in the crevices of the limestone of the Burren, ones you could only see if you stopped and looked in the gaps between the rock. The hair sprouting from the top of the shirt was thick and gold. It looked like it would be soft to touch.

'You're very serious there, Marianne,' said Hugh as they turned once more. Now they were near the stage. The yellow flame from the dangerous candles blurred on the edge of Marianne's peripheral vision.

One-two-three, one-two-three.

'I'm concentrating,' said Marianne.

They danced on.

Hugh cleared his throat and Marianne looked up. This close, she could see his eyes were a paler green than she'd thought, darkening to sage around the black pools of his pupils in which she could see her pale, worried face. Marianne concentrated on her feet. One-two, three, one-two-three.

'I . . .' Hugh looked uncomfortable now, as if he too was counting in his head. 'I was . . . there's a classics literary festival at the theatre in Rush next month.'

'Oh,' said Marianne.

One-two-three, one-two-three.

'And I wondered . . . I thought you might be interested.'

'In going?'

'Yes.'

'With you?'

'That was the idea, yeah.'

'Would it be a date?'

'Well . . . I suppose it would be.'

Marianne shook her head. 'I don't go on dates. I never have.'

'Well, you said you never dance and here you are,' said Hugh, and she could hear the grin, back in his voice.

The song ended then. Marianne stilled and lifted her hand from his shoulder, from his hand. In her chest she could feel her heart beating faster and louder than it probably should and she felt hot. Sort of feverish. She did not like it. It was uncomfortable. Hugh was looking at her, waiting for her to say something. She drew herself up to her highest height and nodded at him briskly. 'Thank you for dancing with me,' she said, 'but the truth is, I meant it when I said that I don't dance. And I don't go on dates. I'm . . . better on my own and that's . . . that's it, really. But, thanks. For the dance.'

'It was my pleasure,' he told her, with a small nod of his head.

They walked back to the others and Marianne was relieved that they'd had that conversation. There could be no misunderstanding, no miscommunication, no crossing of lines. She had drawn the line along her boundaries as surely as the line she had drawn all those years ago down the middle of the bedroom at Ancaire. And Hugh had understood. She was sure he had. He had seen the line she had drawn and he would not cross it.

Back at the table, there was still no sign of a sign. Ethel was rallying well, mostly because she wasn't given much time to dwell on it. Everybody danced with her, even Shirley ('You're sprightly enough for an old dear. No offence').

Bartholomew continued to eye up Ethel's now almost completely melted dessert and was enormously cheered when Olwen arrived bearing a tray of Baked Alaskas for all of them. Marianne noticed she saved the biggest slice for Hugh, but neither Bartholomew nor Freddy noticed as they sat beside each other and discussed the best way to tackle it.

'I like to eat all the meringue first,' said Freddy, poking at it with his spoon.

'I thought I was the only one who liked to eat it that way,' said Bartholomew. They regarded each other with wary curiosity, then began to eat in perfect synchronicity.

Patrick arrived with Agnes, both of them removing matching bicycle helmets as they walked into the hall. Olwen gestured them towards the table. 'Sorry I didn't get here earlier, Ethel,' Patrick said, bending down to give her a swift peck on the cheek. 'Rita messaged me but I didn't see it until now.'

'My dear boy,' said Ethel, struggling out of her chair to

hug him gently. 'There was no need to come. I'm making a fuss over nothing, really.'

Agnes stood beside Patrick. She was tiny and pretty and delicate with short blond hair and brown eyes behind an enormous pair of glasses. When she spoke – which she did once, only to politely refuse a bowl of Baked Alaska – she had a strong Polish accent. She poked Patrick's arm and pointed at the dance floor. He hung their helmets from the back of Ethel's chair and took the hand Agnes offered. She led him to the floor and they began to dance with great familiarity as if they danced that dance every day.

Everybody smiled at them, like they couldn't help it.

'I must say,' said Ethel later, as the evening drew to a close, 'you've made this foolish old lady very happy.'

'You're not one bit foolish,' Rita told her, flushed and breathing hard from dancing the tango with Hugh. 'You're just a human being, looking for a sign. Something to provide some meaning in this ridiculous world. Isn't that what we're all doing, at the end of the day?'

'Why, yes,' said Ethel, 'I suppose you're right.'

'And we've all had a lovely time,' said Hugh, sitting down beside Ethel.

'We have,' shouted Bartholomew and Freddy in tandem.

Hugh picked up two glasses of the pink lemonade Olwen had sent over to the table earlier. He handed Ethel one of them. 'I think we should drink a toast,' he suggested.

Everybody raised their glasses, stretching their arms into the middle of the table.

'To Ethel and Stanley,' said Hugh. 'Happy anniversary.'

'Happy anniversary,' everybody roared, clinking and

drinking. Rita refilled their glasses and stood up. 'And to love,' she declared. 'It's not always easy but it's always worth it.' Everybody stood up, and roared, 'To love,' and they clinked again and drank again, and Marianne could feel the bubbles rush up her nose.

It was a most pleasant sensation.

'And I'm sure there's a good reason why Stanley didn't send me a sign this year,' said Ethel, taking a sip of her pink lemonade. She lowered her glass and was about to set it on the table when she stopped, all of a sudden, like she was frozen in place. Marianne followed her stare. There, on the table, unmissable against the bright red crepe paper, was a single, white feather. Small and delicate and so perfectly intact that it sort of took Marianne's breath away. Ethel lifted it carefully, placed it gently on her palm, which she held out so they could all see. So there could be no doubt.

'It's a sign,' bellowed Rita.

Bartholomew held his hand up for a high five and instead of leaving him hanging, Freddy obliged, smacking Bartholomew's hand with the flat of his own so that they both laughed as they rubbed their reddened palms along the legs of their trousers to soothe the sting of them. Agnes gave a small thumbs up and Patrick smiled, and Shirley stood up on a chair and belted out their 'Get Well Soon' song, her voice high and pure and sweet.

They all joined in, even Marianne. In the car park, as they bid each other goodnight and Marianne rummaged in her handbag for the keys of the Jeep, Hugh, standing by his car, called over to her. 'Marianne, I found this on the beach the other day,' he said, holding up a waterlogged woolly hat with a sodden bobble on the top. 'I think it might be yours?'

She walked towards him. 'Oh, yes, George made off with it the other morning.'

'Did you think it was a sign?' said Hugh. 'The universe telling you to stop hiding your hair under a bushel? Or a hat?'

'I don't believe in signs,' said Marianne. She looked at him, lowered her voice. 'Was that you, by the way?'

'What?' Hugh looked suspiciously innocent.

'The feather,' said Marianne. 'That was you, wasn't it?'

'So cynical for one so young,' said Hugh, shaking his head.

Marianne wrung the hat between her hands, squeezing the water out of it, held it up. 'Good as new,' she said.

'You look just like Rita when you smile,' said Hugh, studying her face.

'That's why I do it as seldom as possible,' said Marianne.

'Goodnight,' he said, bending towards her, kissing her cheek. His mouth was soft against her skin and she could smell him, this close. Something warm and spicy and sweet. Like cinnamon and cloves baked in a pie.

'Time, ladies and gentlemen, please,' roared Shirley, appearing beside them. 'Have yiz no homes to go to?'

Marianne smiled at her. 'Goodnight then,' she said to Hugh, who nodded and folded himself into his car.

'Did you correct the maths exam I did the other day?' said Shirley, as they walked towards the Jeep.

'Yes,' said Marianne.

'And?'

'I'll give you the results tomorrow.'

'I want them now,' demanded Shirley. 'And a gold star. If I get over eighty per cent.'

'You'll get a gold star,' said Marianne.

'So I got over eighty per cent?'

'You'll have to wait till tomorrow.'

'But you said . . .'

'You got a hundred per cent.'

'Fuck off,' screeched Shirley, grabbing Marianne by the hands and twirling her around the car park. Marianne shrieked and Shirley whooped and Marianne laughed then. She couldn't help it. There was something so joyful about Shirley's whooping. And the hundred per cent itself. The gold star. She felt a part of it somehow, like she had played a part, however small.

Chapter 24

When Marianne awoke in the morning – prompted by George licking her face – she felt . . . okay.

No. It was more than that.

She felt . . . sort of content.

Although perhaps she was overstating it.

Suffice to say, Marianne woke feeling not as dreadful as she usually did. In fact, there was a curiously optimistic bent to her world view.

For starters, at breakfast Pearl slid the *Northside People* over to Marianne's side of the table, pointing to an article she had circled with her ballpoint pen.

It wasn't quite an article. It was a paragraph really. Accompanied by a photograph of the Get-Well-Sooners, outside Shirley's house with their placards and banners, their mouths open as if they were in mid-chant. Marianne, who disliked looking at herself in photographs and never posed for them, had to own that they all looked great. Something vital about them all, with their hands clenched into fists and their arms raised high. The headline read, 'Mother of Two Takes a Stand Against Eviction Order'. Shirley was front and centre. She looked fierce and beautiful, her long, navy eyes glaring out of the photograph like a challenge.

Later, Bartholomew was tap-dancing outside his house when Marianne pulled up to collect him.

He ran to the Jeep, flung open Marianne's door, then jumped up and down on the spot several times.

'You are not going to believe it,' he panted. 'Guess,' he said. 'Go on, you'll never guess.'

'You got the job at the theatre?' piped up Ethel from the back seat.

Bartholomew's face fell. 'How did you guess?' he demanded.

'Because I knew you'd get it,' said Ethel, looking perplexed.

'Free theatre tickets for life,' shouted Shirley, reaching out to punch Bartholomew's arm.

Even Freddy offered his congratulations, leaning forward to shake Bartholomew's hand. 'I knew you'd get it too,' he said in a quiet voice.

'Did you?' Bartholomew bent to study Freddy's face for traces of mockery but all Freddy did was nod solemnly.

'The theatre is getting a bit of a facelift so I'm not starting til May which gives me plenty of time to assemble a new wardrobe,' said Bartholomew, beaming. 'And it's all thanks to this beautiful woman right here,' he went on, straightening and turning to Marianne, who looked startled.

'No, I only . . .' she began, but Bartholomew shook his head and waved her words away with his hands.

'I am going to have to insist that you get out of that death-trap and hug me.'

'Really, Bartholomew, there's no need for . . .' But Bartholomew released Marianne's seat belt, lifted her hands off the steering wheel and pulled so she had no choice but to clamber out of the Jeep. Bartholomew held his arms wide open and Marianne, who now knew that he would remain in that position until she succumbed, stepped into the circle of his arms and patted his shoulder, then screamed as Bartholomew picked her up and swung her around. Not just once but several times. She shrieked all the while, as if there was nobody else about, which was most certainly not the case. When he finally put her down, the others cheered and the world rushed towards her at a tilt as Marianne staggered across the path, gripping Bartholomew's arm to steady herself.

Then there was the incident with Freddy, in the kitchen at Ancaire, where Marianne was making tea.

Not an incident as such. Just a conversation, really. Freddy joined her, sat heavily on a chair and sighed deeply.

'You okay?' asked Marianne.

'I'm fine,' said Freddy, expelling another sigh from the depths of his body.

Marianne sat beside him. After a while, Freddy shrugged. 'It's just . . . I'm happy for Bartholomew, don't get me wrong. He's changing his life and he knows what he wants and he knows who he is. I suppose . . . it's hard not to feel a bit, well, a bit left behind.'

'Your turn will come,' Marianne told him, handing Freddy the last slice of Rita's butterscotch tart, left over from yesterday.

'You don't know that,' said Freddy, absently picking at the crust. 'Not for sure. Mother says—'

'You need to tell her,' said Marianne.

'Tell her what?' said Freddy, but his voice was small and there was no real conviction in it.

'What's the worst that can happen?' asked Marianne.

'If I tell her I have . . . only occasionally, mind . . . found men . . . not many, hardly any in fact . . . more, well, attractive than, say, ladies?' Freddy glanced at Marianne over the rim of his glasses to see how she was taking that. She nodded.

Freddy slumped in his seat. 'She'll disinherit me. Fire me from Razzle Dazzle. Kick me out of the house.'

'And you'll find a new place to live. And you'll get a new job. It could be the best thing that ever happened to you, in the end,' said Marianne.

'I don't know,' said Freddy, shaking his head nervously. 'I'm not good at being brave.'

'Neither am I,' said Marianne, and for some reason that made Freddy smile.

Rita appeared then to take the Victory Cake she had made for Bartholomew out of the range. Marianne rummaged in the cupboard for the appropriate cups and mugs and arranged them on trays. Freddy pushed the last of the butterscotch tart into his mouth and excused himself.

'They like having you around,' said Rita, taking plates out of the cupboard.

'Who?'

'The Get-Well-Sooners,' said Rita.

Marianne shrugged. 'They're easy to be around,' she said. A slice of – unevenly cut – cake fell off the blade of the knife as Rita was using. Marianne supposed she couldn't blame her. She didn't think she'd ever said that before. About anyone. She stood up and took the knife off her mother. 'I've developed a system,' she said, rearranging the cake back onto the plate and cutting it lengthways, then widthways. 'This way, the slices are of equal proportion and everybody gets one of the chocolate icing fist bumps you've made, see?'

'Oh, that's clever,' said Rita, collecting herself.

'Self-preservation,' said Marianne shrugging.

'We're writing letters to Shirley's local councillors today. We could use your help?' Rita licked the pad of her finger and used it to collect crumbs that had fallen onto the counter, put her finger in her mouth, sucked noisily. Marianne used to give out to Flo for doing that. 'It's un-hygienic,' she told her. The narrow delicacy of Flo's finger hovering over the toast crumbs. The tiny bed of nail, pale pink, the shape of a teardrop.

'Marianne?' Rita dried her finger on the skirt of her red satin dress.

'Fine,' said Marianne, putting the plates of Victory Cake on a tray and moving towards the kitchen door. 'I'll help.' It sounded plausible too, the way she said it. As if she would be able to help. As if perhaps she had been wrong when she told Hugh she was better off alone.

As if she might, after all, turn out to be the sort of person who manages to rub along adequately, when it came to other people.

With these and other foolish thoughts, Marianne managed to convince herself that all was well. Maybe not well, exactly. Or even ordinary. But okay. Everything was ticking along somehow. Marianne seemed to have stumbled upon a routine that wasn't awful. That was sort of all right. Even though it was not what she would have wished for herself. Even though it was unfamiliar and unpredictable.

Later, she would berate herself for being lulled in that way. When she should have been making plans to extricate herself from Ancaire and all its attendant memories and peculiarities. That had been her plan. She had allowed herself to become distracted. As if a spell had been cast upon her. Perhaps by the sea itself. The ebb and flow of it. The pull and push of it. There was something hypnotic about it.

* * *

February had been a freezing month for the most part, dark and wet, the days so short it sometimes seemed to Marianne like they were over before they'd properly begun.

But then, at the end of the month, the weather changed. The rain stopped and the low, heavy cloud that had plagued the coast since Marianne's arrival thinned and loosened, came away to reveal a touch of blue around their edges, the blue becoming brighter as the clouds got smaller and fainter until one day, when Marianne arrived at Ancaire after dropping the Get-Well-Sooners home, Rita was in the garden, twirling with her arms spread and her face lifted towards the sun, declaring it spring.

Aunt Pearl shook her head through the kitchen window at this wanton display of seasonal joy before marching up the stairs, holding a pair of nail clippers aloft like she was going into battle. Marianne did not know how Pearl had been persuaded to clip George's nails. She did, however, know how George felt about it. When he heard the clip of Pearl's court shoes along the landing, he bolted into Marianne's room, hid under the bed.

For all the good that did him.

Rita stopped twirling and rummaged in her swim bag on the grass. 'I got you a swimsuit yesterday,' she said, holding out a pair of pale pink togs for inspection. 'Do you like them?'

'I can't swim,' said Marianne. 'You know that.' Marianne pre-empted Rita's response with a swift, 'Please don't say there's no such thing as can't.'

'I should have taught you,' said Rita instead.

'You offered,' said Marianne, to give her mother her due. It was just that Marianne had never believed Rita when she told her that she wouldn't let her go.

'You could paddle,' said Rita, irrepressible as always.

'The water is too cold,' said Marianne.

'Not today it isn't,' said Rita.

Marianne had to agree that the day was unseasonably mild. The sunshine spilled through the windows, spinning golden light through the house, camouflaging the ancient ache of the place and lending it an air of spring clean.

'So?' said Rita. 'What do you say?'

'No,' said Marianne. Then added a brief, 'Thank you.'

'Suit yourself,' said Rita, turning and heading for the steps down to the beach.

'Where's Patrick?' Marianne asked then.

'It's not high tide yet,' said Rita, pausing at the top of the steps.

'So why are you going now?'

'I can't wait.' Rita grinned.

'You shouldn't swim alone,' Marianne called after her. But Rita had already started down the steps, taking them two at a time as if they weren't steep and treacherous and slick with moss.

'Oh, for Christ's sake,' Marianne mumbled under her breath. She snatched a hoodie from the coat stand in the back kitchen and pulled it over her head. It must have been Patrick's since it was black, with the words, *Welcome to Hell* written across it, which Marianne assumed must be the name of some death metal album. Still, the cotton was marshmallow soft and Marianne did not have to struggle too hard to get her head and its oversized cargo of hair out the other side.

When Marianne reached the beach, Rita was already in the water, her clothes lying in careless mounds at random intervals, as if she had taken them off while running towards the water, hurling them so that they lay where they fell, retaining the shape of her.

Marianne held her hand over her eyes like an awning, to protect them from the light of the sun, glinting against the edges of the slate-grey waves that rose and fell as if in time to music.

She was easy to spot, Rita, in her yellow swimsuit the colour of buttercups.

'Do I like butter, Marnie?'

Marianne closed her eyes, shook her head to dislodge the voice and the image it dragged up, like a wreck from the ocean floor.

When she opened them, Rita was floating on her back, arms and legs splayed like a starfish, bobbing up and down on the waves and squealing every now and again when the water splashed over her face.

She righted herself then, treading water. 'You should come in, Marnie,' she called out. 'You'd love it.'

'How do you know?' Marianne called back, suddenly curious.

'It'll make you feel alive,' Rita screeched.

'I already feel alive,' Marianne told her, cupping her hands about her mouth so her words weren't whipped away by the sea breeze, which was, as she had suspected, sharper here.

'Not like this,' said Rita, and she dived under the waves, the water closing over the place where she had been, so that it looked, for a moment, like Rita had never been there.

Marianne kept her eyes trained on the place where her mother had been. It was only when she spotted Rita's head again, wrapped in a rubber swimming cap covered in canary-yellow flower petals, that she realised she had been holding her breath. She remembered a party Rita and William had thrown once. It hadn't been a party exactly. Marianne remembered only a handful of people. Maybe six. They had ended up in the sea, in their clothes. Marianne knew because she had seen them from her bedroom window. She had held her breath then, too. Waited for them all to return to shore before she allowed herself breathe normally. As if that might save them from harm. And why had she been bothered anyway? She didn't know any of them. Why had she cared?

She didn't think she had cared. She only knew that she had felt responsible.

Rita got out of the water and ran up the beach, her arms flailing like windmills.

'What are you doing?' Marianne shouted after her.

'Drying off,' Rita shouted back, not stopping.

'Your towel's here,' shouted Marianne, but Rita was already halfway up the beach, flailing.

Marianne stuffed the towel back inside Rita's carpet bag. Sticking out of the inside pocket, a bottle full of pills, a sticker on the side with Rita's name on it. One to be taken three times a day. Marianne did not recognise the name of the tablets. Something long and Latin. They were probably for bone density. Lots of older people had to take tablets for bone density.

Marianne looked up. Her mother had stopped running. Now she was bent in two, her hands on her knees. She was probably out of breath after all the running. She was probably just resting there for a moment, getting her breath back.

Marianne watched and waited. For Rita to straighten. To turn round and run back towards her. Or just walk, since she seemed to be out of breath still. Marianne could see the heave along the curve of her back as Rita breathed in and out, in and out. She walked, slowly at first, up the beach, towards her mother. Rita's legs bent at the knee and now she was kneeling in the sand like she was getting ready to do the Downward-Facing Dog. Which she might very well have been getting ready to do, Marianne reasoned. It was Rita, after all.

Marianne picked up her pace. 'Rita,' she called. Her mother did not turn, did not look up.

Marianne was jogging now.

Rita fell forward, a bright yellow line in the sand now. She lay there, unmoving.

Marianne ran. When she reached her mother, she kneeled, rolled her onto her back. Rita's eyes were closed. Her lips were blue and her face was a sheet of white.

'Rita.' Marianne's voice was sharp, like a reprimand. She gripped her mother's shoulders, shook her.

Nothing.

She pressed her ear against her mother's chest. Listened. It was hard to hear anything over the pound of the sea and the pitiful cries of the gulls, wheeling overhead.

She wrestled herself out of Patrick's hoodie and threw it over Rita, tucked it around her. She eased the swimming hat off her mother's head. It left a bright red line along her forehead. She lifted Rita's head onto her lap. Without the benefit of her turban or the swim hat, Marianne noticed how fine her mother's hair had become. In places, the fleshy pale pink of her scalp was visible.

Marianne fished her phone out of her pocket, rang Patrick. In hindsight, she probably should have rung the emergency services first. Got them to dispatch an ambulance. But it was Patrick she rang instead.

'Is she breathing?' he asked. Marianne squeezed her eyes shut, shook her head. 'I don't know,' she said. 'I can't hear anything.'

'Do you know how to do CPR?' he asked.

'I don't know.'

'You do. Thirty chest compressions followed by two rescue breaths, okay?'

'I don't know.'

'You do,' said Patrick. 'Do the chest compressions to the rhythm of "Staying Alive", okay?'

'I don't know.'

'You do.'

He hung up so he could ring for an ambulance.

Marianne dropped the phone on the sand, looked at her mother. Her whole face had a blue hue to it now, the skin of her eyelids fragile, almost transparent.

She had seen a demonstration of CPR at the back of a St John Ambulance vehicle once. In the park one Saturday. She had been on her way home from her annual visit to her dental hygienist.

Marianne placed her hand on her mother's chest. Rita had grown thin. She put the heel of her other hand on top, pushed down. She shuddered at the feel of it. Like she was crushing bone. She tried to get into a rhythm. 'Ha, ha, ha, ha, stayin' alive, stayin' alive,' she whispered, pushing her hands against the bony plate of her mother's chest. Her mother lay there, unresponsive. Marianne increased the pressure of her hands against her chest. 'Ha, ha, ha, ha, stayin' alive, stayin' alive.' She said it louder this time. She kept doing it, out of breath now. She lost count of how many times. What had Patrick said? Thirty compressions? Had she done thirty? She didn't know. She stopped and bent down, towards Rita's face, tilted her head back. Was she supposed to pinch the bridge of Rita's nose with her fingers? She couldn't remember. She did it lightly, covered Rita's mouth with hers. It felt soft. Slack. She breathed gently. Out of the corner of her eye, she could see her mother's chest, rising slowly. She lifted her head, took another breath, breathed it into Rita's mouth again, saw the rise of her chest. Marianne straightened, arranged her hands against Rita's chest again. 'Ha, ha, ha, ha, stayin' alive, stayin' alive.' She was nearly shouting it now. Perhaps she thought Rita might be able to hear her. The insistence in her voice. 'Stayin' alive, stayin' alive.'

Beneath her hands, Rita never moved.

Chapter 25

When Patrick arrived, he had warm, thick blankets with him. He covered Rita with one and draped another across Marianne's shoulders. She hadn't known she was cold until he did that, her teeth banging against each other and her fingers, bloodless and rigid.

Patrick put his hands on Marianne's hands, still pushing against Rita's chest. 'It's okay, Marianne,' he said. 'You can stop now.'

'What do you mean,' shouted Marianne, her voice hoarse and breathless.

Patrick gestured towards two men coming up the beach, carrying a stretcher between them. Marianne stood up, her legs cramping hard from kneeling on the sand for so long. She stood beside Patrick and they watched as the paramedics lifted Rita onto the stretcher, covered her with a foil blanket.

Marianne could not bring herself to ask any questions. She nodded when one of the paramedics suggested one of them travel in the ambulance with Rita while the other followed in a car so they could get themselves home later.

By the time Marianne had run up the treacherous, moss-slick steps, across the garden and into the house through the back door, she was breathing hard, her heart hammering against the walls of her chest like a trapped animal. She threw open the door into the kitchen and the handle banged against the wall, startling Gladys the cat, who leaped off the windowsill where she had been sitting in a puddle of sunshine.

'More haste, less speed, Marianne.' It was Aunt Pearl who inspected her watch as she lowered an egg on a tablespoon into a saucepan of boiling water.

'Rita,' Marianne managed.

Pearl looked up, her hand suspended above the pot, steam coiling around it.

'What happened?' she said.

'I need to go to the hospital,' panted Marianne, her chest burning with effort.

Pearl nodded, moved the pot off the hob, turned off the flame. 'I'll drive us,' she said to Marianne, walking into the hall. She lifted her car keys from a hook over the hall table and pulled on her gaberdine coat.

'Come along,' she said, marching to the front door and holding it open.

Marianne hesitated. 'I'm . . . afraid,' she said. 'That she'll be dead. When we get there.'

'Well, us being there or not being there won't have any impact on that,' said Aunt Pearl briskly. 'Now, chop chop, my girl, I don't have all day.'

In the car on the way to the hospital, Marianne leaned her head against the window and closed her eyes. She was glad that Pearl was driving. She was also glad that Pearl did not say much. Just the odd comment about traffic or the best way to get to the hospital. She did not seem to require a response, and for this, Marianne was grateful. She kept her hand on her phone in her pocket and took solace from the fact that it didn't ring.

Patrick would ring if anything happened.

Pearl pulled up outside the front door of the hospital. 'You get out here,' she said. 'I'll go and park.'

Marianne fumbled her way out of her seat belt and reached for the door handle. Aunt Pearl's car was pristine. And it smelled unlikely. Like candy floss. It was quiet inside the car. Everything was in order. Marianne's fingers tightened around the door handle.

'Go on now, there's a good girl,' said Aunt Pearl. The sharp edge of her voice was softer here, inside the car.

Marianne opened the door. Immediately, the noise of the world rushed at her, as did the wind, which had picked up now and went straight for her hair, lifting it and tying it in knots, to match those in her stomach.

She asked a woman behind the information desk where she could find Rita. The woman didn't look at Marianne but began tap-tap-tapping on her keyboard, glaring into her computer screen.

'St Luke's ward,' she said, briskly. 'Lift is down that corridor on your left-hand side. Take it to the second floor, turn left. She's in the room at the end of corridor, on the right-hand side.'

'Do you know if . . .?' Marianne began, but the woman

had turned away, smiling now as a man approached the counter. 'Hello, sir, how may I help you today?'

Marianne pressed the button for the lift. Nothing happened. She pressed it again. Jabbed at it. A man glared at her. She glared back and he jerked his head away.

It was quieter on the second floor. There was a hum of machinery and the shuffle of patients' slippers on tiles, the rustle of starch across a nurse's uniform and the cheerful whistle of a porter pushing a bed down the corridor. Marianne turned left and walked towards the end of the corridor. She could hear Rita before she saw her.

'What are you doing with that needle?'

'Don't you dare stick it . . . Ouch, that hurt.'

'Such a lot of fuss about nothing.'

Then a woman's voice, exasperated, affectionate. 'You're the worst patient I've ever had. And I had to lance a boil on a Progressive Democrat's arse once.'

Rita's laugh then. Like a cartoon in a comic.

Hee hee hee.

Marianne put her head round the door. Her mother was propped up on pillows while the doctor, in a white coat, a headscarf, and high heels, perched on the edge of the bed, pressing one end of a stethoscope against Rita's chest.

'That's freezing,' said Rita.

'I warmed it between my hands,' the doctor said. 'You're such a whinge-bag.'

'Are you even a real doctor?'

'There could be a spot of colonic irrigation in your immediate future, if you're not careful.'

Marianne coughed. One of those discreet coughs – ahem

– to alert attention to one's presence. Rita and the doctor looked up.

'You seem . . . better,' said Marianne.

'You must be Marianne,' said the doctor, smiling. She was one of those women who looked healthy everywhere; the bloom of her skin, the whites of her eyes, the pink of her nails, the shine of her teeth. 'You're the image of your mother.'

She lifted the stethoscope from Rita's chest, wrapped it round her neck and stood up. 'I'll leave you two to talk,' she said. She touched Rita's hand, squeezed it briefly. Rita nodded.

When she left, the room seemed very quiet.

'I thought you were . . .' Marianne began. 'Aunt Pearl drove through an amber light, driving here.' She could hear the sharp edge of accusation in her tone.

'Aunt Pearl is here?' Rita said, sitting up.

'You were unconscious,' said Marianne. 'We didn't know what . . .'

'I just . . . felt a little weak,' said Rita, shrugging. 'I forgot to have breakfast this morning. And maybe you're right about the water. It's pretty cold, this time of the year. Especially for an old bag of bones like me.'

'You've never admitted to being old before,' said Marianne.

'It's probably the shock,' said Rita, grinning. Marianne shook her head and sat down, her legs shaking now as the adrenalin drained away.

'I thought you'd be on a trolley in A&E,' she said.

'I must have got lucky,' Rita said, brightly.

'Nobody gets that lucky in an Irish hospital,' said Marianne.

'Maybe they thought I'd set Patrick on them if they didn't prioritise me,' said Rita, grinning.

'Where is Patrick?' asked Marianne.

'He said he'd be back after Fadela finished examining me,' said Rita.

'Is Fadela the doctor?'

'Yes.'

'You seem to know her very well.'

'You know me,' said Rita, shrugging. 'I'm over-familiar.'

Patrick arrived then, carrying three paper cups of tea and a carrier bag full to the brim of fruit, biscuits, chocolate, and a teddy bear at the top, wearing a blue T-shirt, proclaiming, 'It's a boy.'

'It was the only teddy they had left,' explained Patrick, lowering the teas onto Rita's bedside locker and tucking the teddy in the bed beside her.

'It's not even a maternity hospital,' said Marianne, looking at the bear in confusion.

'Delivery mix-up,' explained Patrick. 'Holles Street got the Get Well Soon bears.' He handed Marianne a cup.

'Thank you.' Marianne took the tea, savouring the warmth that seeped into her cupped hands.

'I suppose nobody thought to wonder if I had a mouth on me.' Aunt Pearl stood in the doorway with her arms folded tight across her chest.

'You can have this one,' said Patrick, holding his cup out, but Marianne stepped between them. 'Have mine. It's the way you like it, black with no sugar.'

Pearl accepted the cup and allowed Marianne to steer her into the only available chair in the room, which was an armchair by the window and deemed acceptable by

Pearl once she had sprayed it with the anti-bacterial spray she kept in her handbag and wiped it down with a square piece of muslin she also kept in her handbag.

'Well,' she said to Rita, when she eventually sat down and had taken a sip of tea that produced a grimace of distaste across her face, 'have you quite finished putting the heart across us?'

'See?' said Rita. 'I knew you cared. Deep down.'

'I'll be back in a minute,' Marianne said. She needed to be on her own. Get her bearings. Regroup a bit. She walked up the corridor, breathing in as deeply as she could, in spite of the stagnant heat of the ward.

She glanced into bedrooms as she walked past them. There was a young woman, bald and pale, playing solitaire on her iPad. There was a man, maybe thirty, sitting in an armchair attached to a drip, reading *Talk to the Headscarf*. What remained of his hair had a frail, wispy look about it and he had no eyebrows to speak of. There was an elderly couple, sitting on either side of a bed with a woman, maybe forty, in it. They were laughing at something the woman had said. A colourful scarf covered the woman's head.

Marianne reached the nurse's station. She stopped there.

'Are you all right, Marianne?' It was the doctor. Fadela. She was checking a computer behind the desk.

Marianne scanned the name badge on the lapel of Fadela's white coat. 'Prof. Fadela Rahaman'.

'You're a consultant,' said Marianne.

Fadela nodded. 'Yes.'

'An oncologist,' said Marianne. Her voice sounded louder here. Everything sounded louder. The shrill ring of a phone. The rustle of paperwork on a clipboard. The metal rings of a curtain, jangling along a rail. Marianne stepped back as if she was trying to distance herself from the noise. From the facts that were coming at her now, bearing down on her, the truth rising to the surface like air bubbles, bursting into sharp focus.

'I'm glad Rita told you,' Fadela was saying. 'I told her she should, when she was in for her radiotherapy last week. It'll give her great comfort, having your support.'

'Last week?' said Marianne. She lifted her hands, gripped the edge of a windowsill. The movement was laden with effort, like she was walking underwater.

'Yes,' said Fadela, looking curiously at Marianne now. 'She is so happy that you're helping out with the Get-Well-Sooners.' She smiled. 'She says you're great with them.'

'It's lung cancer,' said Marianne, and it sounded like a statement rather than a question, with the monotone of her voice.

Professor Rahaman nodded slowly. 'Which we were very positive about before it spread to the bones.' Fadela looked closer at Marianne. 'Rita has spoken to you, hasn't she?'

'Why isn't she having chemotherapy?'

'Well, it would have compromised her quality of life and she didn't want to put you all through that, for the sake of a few extra months. You know what your mother's like,' said Fadela, gently.

'No,' said Marianne, and her voice was brittle. 'I don't know what my mother is like. I have no idea what my mother is like.'

'I'm very sorry, Marianne,' said Fadela. She put her hand on Marianne's arm but Marianne shook it off. This time she glared at Fadela. 'Why is she bothering to have radiotherapy at all then?' She knew she was speaking much too loudly in the close confines of this suffocating corridor. She might even be shouting. But she didn't care. She didn't care about anything.

About anyone.

'Marianne?' It was Patrick, approaching her like she was a wild horse he was trying to slip a bridle on.

She spun round. 'I suppose you knew,' she said.

'I—'

'Of course you did. You're her golden boy. The only one she didn't manage to wreck.'

'Marianne, please, you—'

'How long does she have?'

'I think you sho—'

'How. Long.'

Patrick took a breath and his body seemed to sag all of a sudden. 'Maybe three months.'

Marianne glared at Fadela. 'Is that right?' she said.

Fadela nodded slowly. 'I'm so sorry, Marianne.'

Chapter 26

Marianne did not return to Rita's room to collect her anorak or her handbag. She did not wait for the lift to arrive. She took the stairs, two at a time, pounding down them like she pounded down the treacherous, moss-slick steps to the beach at Ancaire.

On the ground floor she marched down the corridor towards the front door but then, on her left, she saw the gift shop. She tried to urge herself past it but could feel herself slow as she approached it, her feet nearly too heavy to lift now, like they were tethered to the ground. Through the window, she saw the racks of glossy magazines. The boxes of Milk Tray. Black Magic. The bars of Lindt. Green and Black. She saw the cards. Get Well Soon. The baskets of grapes. The books of crosswords. Suduko. Word searches.

She did not need any of those things. She did not want any of those things.

She stepped inside.

Behind the counter was a jaded man with thick glasses and one of those faces that seemed colourless, as if it had faded, like a photograph left on a windowsill for years. He did not appear to notice Marianne's arrival. She glanced around. There were no other customers in the shop. She moved to the back of the shop, stood beside a shelf of toiletries, her fingers reaching for a Lynx deodorant.

She twisted off the lid. Held the nozzle to her nostrils. Sniffed it. The smell was overpowering. Saccharine and dense. She thought she might throw up. She slipped the bottle into the pocket of her tracksuit bottoms. Into the other pocket, she shoved a bottle of Johnson's Baby Shampoo. No More Tears. Guaranteed.

She moved to the magazine rack. She picked one up, leafed through it. How to shed eight pounds in two weeks. Ten ways to spice up your sex life. Get brow ready. Photographs of an actor, smelling a melon in a supermarket. Agony aunt. *I think my husband is having an affair with my brother.* Horoscopes. *A change of plan is imminent. Embrace it.* Ads for collagen injections. Nips and tucks. Botox. How to make your mother-in-law like you. How to look good naked. How to look good with your clothes on. How to look good in a bikini. How to look good pregnant.

Marianne rolled the magazine up tight and pushed it down the waistband of her tracksuit bottoms. She walked towards the door of the shop. Behind the counter, the man shifted his weight from one foot to the other and then slowly, slowly, looked up. His eyes settled on Marianne, blinking as he processed her.

'Can I help you?' he asked eventually.

Marianne could feel the magazine slip from the grasp

of her waistband, which had lost some of its elasticity from overuse. It slipped down her leg, the gloss of the cover cold against her skin. Marianne shivered. The magazine got all the way to the bottom before it stopped, held in place by the elasticated ankle, which Shirley had taken exception to.

'No. Thank you,' Marianne managed.

The shopkeeper continued to examine Marianne. 'Are you buying something?' he said, after an interminable pause during which Marianne could smell nothing but the sickening sweetness of the deodorant.

'I'm just . . . browsing,' she said.

'Hmm,' he said, his eyes fixed on the bulge of the shampoo bottle in Marianne's tracksuit bottoms. Why did she have to take such a big bottle?

Why did she have to take anything at all?

What was she going to do with No More Tears baby shampoo? Give it to bloody Brian for the twins?

'Have you got a magazine down the leg of your trousers?' the man said then, his tone more curious than confrontational. Marianne looked at him mutely.

'If you do, I'm going to have to call the police,' he said, shaking his head. 'It's my policy now. Because they're all at it. Patients, visitors, nurses. Even one of the fecking consultants tried it. Like what am I running here? A charity?' His look to Marianne was imploring, willing her to understand, hoping perhaps that she might pull up the leg of her trousers and reveal something other than contraband. A sticky-out bit of a prosthetic leg perhaps? They were in a hospital, after all.

Marianne felt the fight go out of her all at once, like a tyre punctured by a long shard of glass. She almost heard the hiss of it. She lowered her head and pulled up the leg of her tracksuit. The magazine fell onto the floor with a dull slap. A beautiful woman on the cover in a sequined dress, wrapped snugly around her pregnant belly. It was true, Marianne supposed. Some women could indeed have it all. Career, babies, startling good lucks. Marianne hadn't wanted any of that. She'd been happy with her lot, hadn't she? And now it felt like everything was just sort of falling down around her. Like she was standing in the middle of a derelict house in a storm, tiles flying off the roof and water gushing out of pipes. She felt cold. And alone. It had never bothered her before. Being alone. She didn't know why it felt so raw now.

'And you needn't bother turning on the waterworks,' said the shopkeeper, hanging up the phone. Had he already called the police? 'You should have thought about the consequences before you went on the rob.'

Marianne picked up the magazine and placed it on the counter, then removed the deodorant and shampoo from her pockets, set them in front of the man, who looked at the items, shook his head. 'I just don't know at all at all at all,' he said, his voice weary. 'What goes on in your head, like?' He looked at Marianne as if he really wanted to know but she had no answers to give him. She walked to the far end of the shop and sat on the floor, her back against the wall. She closed her eyes. She thought she could sleep, right here, at the back of this tiny gift shop, on the cold, stained floor.

'Get up outta that,' the shopkeeper snapped at her. 'I have customers to think about, you know. Paying ones, some of them.'

Marianne ignored him and tried to think about nothing at all, which was much more difficult than it used to be.

She thought about Flo.

She had tried so hard not to think about Flo.

She taught Flo how to ride her bicycle. Flo was five. It was September. Flo's voice, high and shaking, as she pedalled furiously, Marianne running alongside her, trying not to trip over Bruno, who insisted on running alongside Flo too.

'Are you holding onto me, Marianne?' Flo shouted at her big sister. 'Are you still holding on?' And Marianne, running alongside her, lifted her hand from the back of the saddle and shouted, 'Yes,' and Flo, cycling on, her small feet a blur of pedals, her face flushed with the possibility of success.

Marianne slowed and slowed and eventually stopped. Flo kept going, still shouting, 'Are you still holding on, Marianne?' but she didn't seem to notice that there was no response. She was cycling now. Cycling on her own.

Marianne's abiding memory of that moment, watching Flo cycling on her own, was one of acute anxiety. That she might fall. That she might hurt herself. That she might blame Marianne, who had, after all, told her she would never let her go.

Chapter 27

'What time was I actually born?' Flo asked that morning. Marianne was making her bed, folding her pyjamas under the pillow. Flo sat cross-legged on her bed, Bruno's head in her lap, the dog succumbing to Flo's efforts to tie a pink ribbon around his neck.

'Caroline Cassidy knows the exact time she was born. Her mother wrote it in a book.' Flo looked a little put out.

'Why does it matter, what time you were born?' said Marianne, reaching across the line she had drawn down the middle of their bedroom to pick up Flo's denim jacket. She arranged it on a hanger, put it into the wardrobe.

'So I'll know exactly when I'll be ten,' said Flo, her small, heart-shaped face serious. 'Do you think Mum will know?' Flo's big blue eyes settled on Marianne's face as if Marianne knew everything. As if Marianne had all the answers.

'You were born at eleven o'clock,' Marianne said, closing the wardrobe door.

'How do you know?'

'Aunt Pearl told me.'

Flo nodded. If Aunt Pearl said it, it must be true.

'Now come on,' said Marianne, 'shift yourself so I can make your bed.'

'Eleven in the morning or in the night-time?' asked Flo.

'Night-time,' said Marianne.

Flo held a hand mirror in front of Bruno's face so he could admire the bow she had fashioned for him.

'Get your brush and I'll do your hair,' said Marianne.

'French plaits?'

'Ah, Flo, that takes ages.'

'It's my birthday.'

'Okay, fine. But you have to promise not to moan when I brush your knots out.'

'I promise.'

Rita and William were celebrating their daughter's tenth birthday by throwing one of their lavish parties. It was April but the house looked like Christmas, fairy lights strewn across mantelpieces and windowsills, and candles glowing in every window. A band was setting up in the drawing room, playing jazz. Caterers arrived in vans, carrying platters of smoked salmon, quiche Lorraine, beef wellington, jacket potatoes, salads, apple tarts and cream. By noon, the guests began to arrive and they kept arriving until it seemed to Marianne as if the house might burst at the seams.

She and Flo and Bruno arranged themselves on the wide windowsill beneath the long, narrow window on the first floor, watching the antics like it was a film reel.

That was the version of her sister that Marianne remembered most vividly. Flo, in the midnight-blue party dress that had been Marianne's, when Marianne was ten. They both adored it because of the tulle, beneath the silk, that made the skirt spool like a ballerina's tutu.

Flo, small and slight, sitting in a cloud of blue silk on the window sill, her arm around Bruno's neck, watching Rita and William as they danced on the lawn, holding onto each other. Holding each other up.

Marianne remembered hearing the grandfather clock in the hall chime and she counted the chimes as was her habit, then went downstairs to get a plate of food for her and Flo. 'I'll be back in five minutes, okay?' she said to her sister.

'How long before I'm ten?' asked Flo, yawning.

'One more hour,' Marianne told her before she left.

In the dining room, the buffet. Rita, pouring a bottle of gin into an enormous bowl of punch with pieces of fruit floating at the top. She picked up a ladle and stirred the punch so that it swirled around the sides of the bowl, the liquid breaching the top and spilling onto the table, down onto the floor. A man exclaimed as drops stained the front of his linen trousers and Rita clamped her hand across her mouth. Marianne could see her face creasing in laughter and, after a while, the man laughed too.

On the other side of the room, William bent towards a young woman in a sequined dress, her back pressed against the wall. He whispered in her ear and a tendril of her hair escaped from a complicated up-do and swayed gently against her long, pale neck. William wound this fallen piece of hair around his finger and the woman giggled as if he had tickled her.

There was a chance that Marianne could make it to the buffet and smuggle some food into the pockets of her dungarees but she didn't want to run the risk of Rita spotting her. Rita might remember then. She might insist that Marianne bring Flo downstairs. Roar at everyone to, 'Shut up, shut up,' and insist they sing 'Happy Birthday'. Stick candles in the remains of a side of salmon because no one had remembered to pick up the birthday cake she'd ordered from the bakery. Or put her on a man's shoulders like she had done last year. Flo hadn't cried when the man stumbled. When he fell. She hadn't hurt herself but she'd been frightened. Marianne could tell from the way she'd wrapped her thin arms around Marianne's neck afterwards, when she carried her up the stairs.

Marianne ducked out of sight and crept into the kitchen, which was crowded enough so she could pick her way through the thicket of adults without being noticed. A woman stood in front of the fridge, crying. She grabbed Marianne's arm and told her that she must never, ever fall in love because men did nothing but break women's hearts. 'Do you hear me?' the woman said. Marianne nodded and the woman tightened her grip and asked again, louder this time. 'Do you hear me?'

Marianne nodded. In her experience, it was easier to agree with adults. You got away quicker if you agreed. She tried not to wince at the sour, stale smell of the woman's breath.

'Do you think I'm old?' the woman said, clamping her hands on Marianne's shoulders now. Marianne shook her head.

'Don't you speak?' the woman said, her hands tightening like a vice.

'Come along, Bea darling, let's get you a little something

to eat, shall we?' A man in a beret and a cravat put an arm around the woman's waist and winked at Marianne.

When they were gone, Marianne opened the fridge and stood on her tiptoes to reach two mini quiches and half an apple tart. She clamped a carton of orange juice under her arm and crept back up the stairs, glancing at the clock as she went.

It was twenty past ten.

Another forty minutes and Flo would be ten.

Flo and Bruno weren't on the windowsill when Marianne returned. Nor were they in the bathroom. Or the studio where Flo sometimes liked to make a fort out of Rita's self-portraits.

Marianne looked in all the bedrooms. Apart from Aunt Pearl's, obviously. She even opened the door that led to the attic. She stood at the bottom of the stairs and called up.

'Flo?'

There was no answer.

Downstairs, Rita was dancing with a woman. A tall, stately woman with black nail polish and a diamond in her nose. They were swaying with their eyes closed and their arms above their heads. Marianne tapped her mother on the back. When Rita didn't respond, Marianne grabbed a handful of Rita's dress and tugged it.

'What is it, darling?' Rita didn't stop dancing but her eyes were open now as she did her best to focus on Marianne.

'I can't find Flo.'

'What do you mean?'

'She was upstairs with Bruno. But now she's not.'

'You just haven't looked properly,' said Rita.

'I have.'

'Have you asked Daddy? He probably knows.' Rita lifted the strap of her black velvet dress, which had fallen down her arm, rearranged it onto her shoulder. She was wearing the pearl ring William had bought her that Christmas and her nails were long and bright red. Marianne remembered thinking that her mother looked beautiful at that moment, with her dark brown hair, glossy and wild, pouring like a waterfall over one shoulder and down towards her waist, clashing gloriously with the chilly blue of her eyes, grown up and sophisticated in the small, pale circle of her face.

Marianne tugged again at her mother's dress. 'Daddy won't know,' she said.

'Stop it, you'll tear my dress,' snapped Rita, pulling the material out of Marianne's grip. Marianne didn't move. She looked at her mother.

'Sorry about this,' Rita said to the tall, stately woman, who shrugged and lit a cigarette.

Everybody looked for Flo in the end. Marianne remembered shadowy outlines of people in the garden, calling, 'Flo? Flo? Where are you?'

She remembered one woman asking another what Flo was short for.

'I don't know. Florence, I imagine.'

Marianne had never known that Flo was short for something.

When Rita started panicking, racing about the garden with a flashlight, shrieking, 'FLO!' over and over again at the top of her voice, Marianne still thought everything would be all right. Flo must have fallen asleep somewhere. Maybe in Bruno's basket. Marianne had found her there one time, curled between the dog's front paws as he sat up tall, as if he was standing sentry over her. But when she went to look, Bruno's basket was empty, the blanket lining the bottom cold to the touch.

Memory became ragged after that. The sound of sirens in the distance. It didn't occur to Marianne that they had anything to do with Flo. She kept searching, looking in increasingly unlikely places. Behind the dresser in the drawing room. The cupboard in the back kitchen where the mop and sweeping brush was kept. The coal shed. The poky room at the end of the hall that didn't have a name and was stuffed full of old books and suitcases and a box of rusting keys and black and white photographs of people nobody remembered any more.

The sirens, closer now. Marianne remembered sitting on the first step of the stairs. The flashing of lights – blue and red – through the fanlight. Somebody opened the front door. She remembered the light pouring into the hall, across the floor, a disco ball of lights with no music and no dancing.

She remembered the policeman getting out of the car, opening the back door and then Bruno jumping out. The relief then. Marianne remembered that. Relief. The solidity of it. Like algebra. Undeniable.

Flo had taken Bruno outside to do his business and he had caught the scent of a hare on the wind and ran off. He sometimes did that.

And Flo had followed him.

And maybe, because it was so dark, Bruno had run further than he usually did.

And Flo had followed him.

That was all.

Marianne waited for Flo to jump out of the police car.

She remembered the policeman – a big slab of a man with a soft, pained face – approaching Rita, talking, saying something.

'The driver swerved to avoid the dog,' he said.

And then, 'He didn't see her until it was too late.'

Marianne remembered her mother's face, the features frozen in place, her hands held in front of her as if she was warding the policeman off, her head shaking from side to side like she was saying, 'No.' Like she was shouting it. Over and over again.

She remembered being in the back of a car. Her face pressed against the window as they drove away, watching Bruno do his best to follow them, straining at his leash held in the hands of some glamorous man Marianne never saw again.

She never saw Bruno again either. And she never asked where he'd gone.

The hospital. Long corridors lit by tubes of fluorescent lights, doors swinging open, doors swinging shut, walking, walking, down those endless corridors that were all the same shade of porridge grey with the same swinging doors.

Marianne remembered a blue uniform. A nurse. Kind. Narrow wrists. A smell of antiseptic. Her mother wailing. Her father standing behind her, his hands covering his ears so he couldn't hear what it was the nurse was telling them.

She remembered the nurse's voice. Low and gentle. The voice of a woman who has to say things that nobody wants to hear.

Marianne heard her. She remembered what she said.

'She wouldn't have felt a thing.'

Chapter 28

The room at the back of the police station wasn't exactly a cell. More of a waiting room, although not one that had been designed with any notion of comfort. The only furniture it contained was a table that wobbled any time Marianne leaned on it, and a hard wooden chair that had already leached any feeling Marianne's buttocks might have previously enjoyed. A small window was set too high in the wall to offer much in the way of natural light. Overhead, a bright fluorescent tube, flickering in a perverse, methodical way. Marianne felt positive that, had she a baseball bat to hand, she would smash it to bits.

She was appalled at the strength of her feelings towards it.

Marianne had no idea how long she'd been in the room. She had answered all the questions the short, stocky, mildly exasperated policeman had asked her, signed the brief statement she had made, flushed as he read out the items she had attempted to steal, neatly typed on an adjoining page, in a bold, oversized font, then refused the offer of tea in a haughty, decisive manner. The guard shrugged, gathered his paperwork and left, the door banging behind him, the key turning in the lock with a deadening thunk, and then the sound of his shoes against the floor, a smart tap-tap-tapping, fading away to nothing. And then silence. Just the sound of Marianne's breath, harsh and hot and abundant. She wanted to shout. To roar. To expel all the breath that was inside her, keep shouting, keep roaring, until it was all spent. Until she was spent.

She thought about pacing. To use up some of the ferocious energy she was burdened with. But the room would allow only two of her long strides before she encountered the wall, another two to the other side of the room, two more to reach the back of the room, two to the door. And then what?

In the end, she neither shouted nor paced. She merely sat where she was and breathed her harsh, hot breaths.

When the door finally opened, Marianne came to with a start, banging the jutting bone of her ankle against the leg of the table. The pain was sudden and shrill and dragged her mind from wherever it had been to the present moment in a way that was both effective and vivid.

Rita stood in the doorway, framed by the architrave, so that she seemed, for a moment, like one of her self-portraits. Her face was freshly made up and her turban – a violent shade of purple – clashed with the bright green of her cocktail dress in a way that Marianne was certain Rita would describe as 'magnificent'.

'What are you doing here?' said Marianne. Despite the

abundance of breath that rampaged about her body, her voice sounded high and reed-thin.

'I've come to bail you out, darling,' said Rita, glancing around the room, her nose wrinkling in distaste. 'You'd think they could put a few home comforts into the place, wouldn't you? An armchair, at least. With a bright, soft wool throw. That would make all the difference, wouldn't it?'

'I don't need you to bail me out,' said Marianne. She was sure that, if she looked down, her fists would be clenched. She felt coiled, like she was about to spring.

'Nonsense, Marnie,' said Rita, rummaging in her bag for her vape pen. 'Everybody needs to be bailed out, now and again. Goodness knows, I have.'

'I'm nothing like you,' said Marianne, her voice louder now. Rita stopped rummaging and looked up. 'I can sort out my own affairs. I don't need someone like you – a do-gooder like you – to bail me out. I'm not one of your Get-Well-Soon adoring fans.'

'Come on,' said Rita, zipping up her bag. 'Let's get you out of here, Marnie.'

'Stop calling me that,' snapped Marianne.

'Sorry, darling, old habits and all that.'

'There's nothing habitual about our relationship,' said Marianne. 'We never had a relationship. It didn't suit you, remember? It cramped your style.'

'Well, it's been lovely having you home this past while,' said Rita brightly.

'Shouldn't you be in the hospital?' said Marianne, cutting across her mother. 'Since you're dying?' The last word – dying – spurted from her mouth, lava from a volcano.

Rita smiled her jaunty smile. 'We're all dying, Marnie.'

'Yes, but you're dying soon,' said Marianne. She couldn't seem to stop herself. She was both appalled and curious at the extent of her viciousness. She didn't know she could feel so vicious. 'Three months. Isn't that what the doctors reckon?'

Rita found her vape pen and hoisted herself onto the table, her legs swinging girlishly. 'You know what those doctors are like, Marnie, they abhor a vacuum. They'd rather say something than nothing.'

'Why aren't you having chemotherapy?'

'It'll just make me feel sick. And it won't change anything, it'll just prolong the inevitable. I don't want to be a burden. On anyone. Especially not you.'

'That never stopped you before,' said Marianne. That hit a nerve. She didn't care. She rushed on. 'Why didn't you tell me?'

Rita recovered herself, wrinkled her nose and brushed at the air with her fingers as if there was a nasty smell in the room. 'It's such a tedious subject. I didn't want to bore you with it.'

'So you thought you'd do your usual and act like nothing's happened? Just reinvent yourself again? Now, you're a person who's not sick. Now you're a person who doesn't have a terminal illness. Now you're a person whose daughter never died?' Marianne's voice was a crescendo, rising and rising, louder and louder, so that it seemed like a chorus of voices, dissonant and shrill. Rita stopped swinging her legs. She put her vape pen on the skirt of her dress, placed her hands on the table on either side of her body, palms spread as though to steady herself. She took a deep breath in, released it slowly through the bright orange lipsticked O of her mouth. 'My daughter did die,' she said, not looking at Marianne, her voice low and deliberate.

'It's like she never existed,' spat Marianne. 'There's nothing of her at Ancaire. Her wardrobe is cleared out. There's not even a photograph. It's like she was never there.'

'I think about her every day,' said Rita.

'But what good is that now?' stormed Marianne. 'She's dead now. And instead of blaming yourself, you just re-invented yourself, didn't you?' Marianne was filled with a sort of savagery. Her hands shook with it. Her whole body. She was afraid of what she was capable of, but also ener-gised by the possibilities. What she could do, with this savage fury. 'You thought, oh, I'll just stop drinking. That will make everything all right. That will wipe the slate clean. That will absolve me of any blame. Well, it doesn't.'

Rita shook her head. 'Marianne, I'm sorry, I know you—'

'Don't you dare,' shouted Marianne. 'Don't you dare apologise. Don't think for a moment that I'll forgive you just because you're dying. I don't care that you're dying.'

Rita looked at her. 'You don't mean that.'

'You have no idea what I mean and what I don't mean. You know nothing about me.'

'I know that I love you.'

'No you don't. You just feel guilty that your daughter – the one who somehow managed to survive you – turned out to be a petty thief.'

'That's not tr—'

'Look at me, for Christ's sake. I'm in a police station. I steal things. I keep stealing things.'

'You're stressed, you just need—'

'I need you to leave,' said Marianne. Her voice was hoarse. Her throat hurt. She felt wrung out, like an old, stained dishcloth.

Now the room was silent but it was a pounding sort of silence, like the sound of a headache forming at the base of your skull. Rita used her hands to lower herself to the floor, then brushed the fabric of her dress as if for crumbs. Or creases. She hooked her handbag onto her wrist and dropped her vape pen inside. 'Your bail's paid so you are free to go whenever you like,' she said, concentrating on the clasp of her bag, not looking at Marianne.

Marianne bent down, put her hands on her knees, closed her eyes. Her breath was coming in fast bursts.

At the door, Rita paused.

'Marianne?'

'Don't,' said Marianne, straightening. 'I'm not one of your clients that you can just talk at and fix.'

'I know that, I . . .'

'Thank you for paying my bail. I'll pay you back as soon as I can. And I'm grateful. You didn't have to let me stay at Ancaire.'

'Ancaire is your home,' said Rita. 'You're always welcome there.'

'I hate being there,' Marianne said, and it was like there was a full stop after each word and each word had been dipped in bitterness and the bitterness hardening like a crust around them. Marianne's jaw ached with the effort of spitting them from her mouth. 'I'm only there because I have to be. Because there's nowhere else for me. I've lost my job. And I've lost my husband. And I've lost my home.

And I should have known that I was going to lose all those things. I deserve to lose all of those things.'

'Don't say that.'

'And so do you. You deserve awful things. Because of Flo.'

Rita looked at Marianne. 'I know.' She whispered it.

When she left, the room seemed smaller, too small to contain Marianne and her furious savagery. She wanted to place her hands on the walls, to push and push, expand it, make it big enough to contain her and the furious savagery stampeding about her body. She sat down – she hadn't remembered standing up – and pushed her head between her knees. Held it there. She didn't think she was going to faint. Instead she felt keenly conscious of every single thing. The static of electricity in the air, the hairs along her arms, lifting and stiffening, the breath erupting from her body, hot and humid and strained, like she'd run the length of the beach against a gale-force wind. She hadn't been running. There was nowhere to run to.

It was more accurate to say that she had been running away.

She was too old for running away. Too tired. But what was the alternative? In the static silence of the room that seemed much too small to contain her, she could find no answer.

Chapter 29

Outside the police station, rain came at Marianne in slanting lines, water streaming down her face, hanging off the end of her nose, the hard line of her jaw, collecting along the scoop of her eyelashes, reducing her hair to a thick pulp against her head. She didn't put her hood up. Instead, she stood in the middle of the path. People tutted when they encountered her, changed their course, circled around her and still she did not move. Her pale grey tracksuit bottoms were black with rain, clinging to her legs, making her aware of the cold now, made colder with the sharp edge of an easterly wind whipping around her.

Still, she stood there. She couldn't think of anything else to do.

'If you don't get in, pigeons are going to start nesting on you.'

Marianne looked towards the road and there was Hugh, illegally parked with his hazard lights on, leaning out of the window.

Marianne glanced towards the back seat but it was impossible to see through the windows with the deluge. Hugh shook his head. 'Rita's already gone. I called one of the other drivers. She asked me to wait for you.'

'There was no need,' said Marianne. Her voice sounded flat and worn.

'Come on,' said Hugh, reaching across the passenger seat and opening the door. 'Get in.'

'I'll get your seats all wet,' said Marianne.

'They'll dry,' said Hugh, shrugging. 'Now hurry up, I haven't got all day.'

'Don't bother putting yourself out, on my account,' said Marianne, folding her arms stiffly across her chest.

'Don't bother getting sniffy,' said Hugh, checking his rear-view mirror for traffic. 'Just get in.'

'I'm not sniffy, I'm merely saying . . .'

'I've driving away in five seconds,' said Hugh.

'I was only . . .'

'Four . . . three . . .'

'Okay, fine,' said Marianne, getting into the car and banging the door shut. An articulated lorry tore past them, leaning on his horn as he swerved around Hugh's illegally parked car.

'You really shouldn't be parked here,' said Marianne primly, pulling the seat belt across her body.

'And you really shouldn't nick stuff,' said Hugh, scorching down the road, pasting Marianne to the back of the seat with the force of the acceleration.

'Slow down, you'll get arrested,' said Marianne. She rolled her eyes. 'I suppose you're going to make a quip about me getting arrested now.'

Hugh shook his head and kept driving.

'I presume it was Rita who told you about me shop-lifting,' said Marianne.

'She didn't say a word, actually,' said Hugh, slowing to let a car out from a side road.

'How did you know then?'

'Well, I picked you – a seasoned shoplifter – up from outside a cop shop. I'm not just a pretty face, you know?'

'Do you mind if we don't talk?' said Marianne.

'Not in the least,' said Hugh, turning on the radio.

Marianne was torn between offence and relief. Hugh fiddled with the buttons until he found a country and western song. Some man singing about his woman who went off and left him, his voice forlorn as a foghorn and only slightly less grating. 'Mind if I turn it up?' said Hugh, already twisting the volume button so that Marianne's tart 'Yes' was lost in a cacophony of mournful harmonica, against a wail of minor chords.

It was only when they were nearing the turn-off for Loughshinny that Hugh spoke again. He turned down the radio – a woman this time, droning on about her no-good, two-timin' man – and glanced at Marianne. 'Where are you going?'

'Ha!' said Marianne. 'That's a good question.'

'I don't mean philosophically,' said Hugh.

'I can tell you where I don't want to go,' said Marianne.

'I'm going to go out on a limb and say that you're a fairly infrequent user of taxis,' said Hugh.

'I don't want to go to Ancaire,' Marianne went on, ignoring him.

'Okay, well, that narrows it down,' said Hugh, nodding encouragement. 'What else?'

'I want to go home,' said Marianne all of a sudden, her shoulders slumping. She knew she sounded like a child. An overtired child. But she had such a yearning just then, for her house. Her home on Carling Road. The neat square of garden at the front with the artificial grass that she never had to tend. The paved patio at the back. The gleaming, tidy rooms where there was a place for everything and everything was in its place. The smell of it. If she closed her eyes and imagined herself there, in the hallway, just inside the door, she could smell it still. Wood and polish and the dried lavender hanging on a hook beside the coat stand.

The coat stand itself. A beautiful piece of wood, heavy and curved with four hooks: two for her (winter anorak/summer mackintosh) and two for Brian (his all-year-round tweed jacket and a navy overcoat for when the weather was inclement).

Hugh stopped at a junction, looked at Marianne. 'I need an address,' he said gently.

'I don't have one.'

Hugh scanned the road for cars and, when the way was clear, he pulled away.

Marianne didn't ask him where they were going. She didn't care, so long as they weren't going anywhere near Ancaire. Or Rita.

When Hugh stopped the car, pulled on the handbrake, Marianne looked up. They were parked outside his cottage in Rush.

'What are we doing here?' asked Marianne.

'I made tomato soup earlier,' said Hugh. 'It's a cure-all.'

'Did you know about Rita?'

The question produced the type of silence that told Marianne everything she needed to know. Of course Hugh knew. And Patrick and Pearl. Shirley, Ethel, Freddy, Bartholomew. All of them. Sheldon and Harrison probably knew, too.

Everybody except Marianne. She was in her usual position, on the outside looking in. She was hot all of a sudden, like the anger inside her was on fire, raging through her blood and her bones, scorching everything.

'I'm sorry, Marianne,' said Hugh. He got out, walked round the car and opened the door. 'Come on inside,' he said.

'I'm too angry. I'll damage something.'

'I have insurance,' he said.

She got out of the car. The rain had stopped but she felt the weight of it in her hair, her clothes. Hugh opened the front door, ushered her inside

'I'll make tea,' he said.

'I don't want tea,' said Marianne.

'I'll make some anyway.' He disappeared into the kitchen.

Marianne paced around the room. It felt too confined. Too small to contain her and her emotions, which seemed to have come undone inside her, spilling everywhere, pouring out of her.

She glared around the room. Perched on top of the bookcase, she saw a copy of *How to Go Around the World in 80 Days*. There was no getting away from Ancaire, it seemed. The fire inside her spread and raged. Through the kitchen door, Marianne heard the ordinary sounds of the tap running, the kettle being switched on, the rattle of the cups on their saucers. She put her hands against her ears but she could still hear them. The ordinary sounds, when everything felt so alien and nothing was ordinary. Despite her best efforts to pursue a quiet, ordinary life.

'Are you okay?'

Marianne looked up and saw Hugh, watching her with concern from the kitchen door.

'Stop feeling sorry for me,' she said. Her voice was loud and harsh. 'You're always feeling sorry for me.' He shook his head, crossed the room towards her. She put her arms out, warding him off. 'When you danced with me that night at the dinner-dance. You felt sorry for me. Poor, lonesome Marianne. Awkward, gawky Marianne. I'll put her out of her misery.'

'That's not why I danced with you,' said Hugh, and his voice, in sharp contrast to her own, was soft and low. It was like a match to Marianne's short fuse. She wanted to grab her hair and pull it. Yank it.

'I danced with you because I . . . like you,' said Hugh.

Marianne stared at him. 'Nobody likes me,' she said. 'Why would they? I don't like them. I just want to be left alone.'

'Nobody wants that,' said Hugh, gently. 'You don't want that.'

'What do I want, then?' snapped Marianne. 'Since you're such an expert.' She was breathing hard. It was difficult to keep a grip on herself.

The kettle whistled. A loud, shrill sound that filled the room, filled Marianne's head until she felt it might split. Hugh was saying something. She could see his mouth moving but she couldn't make out the words. His mouth. She was focusing on it now, still not hearing what it was he was saying. His lips were the colour of a ripe peach. She felt herself think of the word 'luscious'. What a peculiar word. Luscious. Did she even know how to spell it? A tricky arrangement of s's and a c somewhere in the middle, she thought. The clash of the peach with the orange of his hair. And his eyes. As vibrant as her anger. Fixed on her face with such sympathy.

'Stop,' she shouted. His mouth stopped moving. The kettle, still whistling, collided with the thump of her heart and the beat of her blood. She moved into the space between them, glared up at him. And then she kissed him.

As she had suspected, she had to stand on her toes to reach him.

As she had suspected, his mouth was delicious, like biting into a peach, sweet and, yes, there was that word again, luscious. She wasn't thinking about how many s's there were in that word any more. Or where the c went. She didn't think she was thinking about anything at all. There were no thoughts, only sensations. The hard length of his body against hers. The soft fall of his hair against her face. The slide of his hands down her neck. The slick dance of their mouths. The noises she made. Like she was tasting him. Like she hadn't eaten in days. In weeks. She couldn't get enough of him. She grabbed fistfuls of his hair, pulled him closer. He hoisted her onto his hips and she clasped her legs around him and even then, she wasn't aware of any thoughts. Like how heavy she must be. How cumbersome. How she never did anything like this.

Ever.

But she was only sensations. A glut of sensations. All she could feel was her pulse and it was everywhere. Along her neck, down her arms, between her legs. Even her ankles, crossed behind his back, seemed to be throbbing.

There was movement, too. Hugh, staggering around the room like a drunk, trying to gain purchase. She couldn't see. She didn't care. She clung on. She heard sounds. The ragged catch of her breath. The suck and gush of her mouth against his. The moan that issued from her when they glanced against a wall and the groan of the couch when they finally reached it and he lay her there, pinned her there with his body, the weight of him against her so sudden and so exquisite, she came in a series of what felt like explosions inside her body. Sharp and intense. Almost painful. She cried out. She couldn't help it. She didn't think it was a word. It was a sound. A guttural sound. Hugh lifted his head, looked at her. 'Are you okay?' She nodded. Her breath was coming hard and fast, the orgasm pounding through her body like a herd of wild horses.

She couldn't remember the last time she'd had such a sensation. Brian prided himself on his ability to keep going until she'd climaxed, on the occasions when they'd got round to having sex. She often told him she had and he had believed her.

She grabbed Hugh's hair again and pulled him towards her. He looked at her, sort of dazed, his eyes black with pupil, then pulled away from her and sat up.

'What?' she said.

He shook his head, ran his hand down his face. 'We need to stop.'

'Stop?' said Marianne, sitting up.

Hugh looked at her, reached over to push the hair out of her eyes. She slapped his hand away. 'I don't want you to be gentle with me,' she said. 'I want you to have sex with me.'

'No,' he said, standing up and rearranging his kilt, which had ridden around on his waist and was back to front. 'You're upset. You're not yourself. I feel like I'm taking advantage of you.'

'I don't mind,' said Marianne. 'I want you to take advantage of me.'

Hugh shook his head again. 'I can't,' he said. 'It's not fair. On either of us.'

'What's fair got to do with anything?' shouted Marianne. 'I just want to bloody well feel something. I should feel something. My mother is dying and I feel nothing. I don't even feel numb, I feel nothing. I want to feel something.'

Hugh nodded. 'I understand,' he said.

'But that's it, you're not going to have sex with me?'

'No,' he said. 'But we can talk.'

'I don't want to talk. I want to feel something.'

'You will feel something,' said Hugh gently. 'You're just in shock. I should have—'

'Are you still talking?'

'I should have made you tea,' said Hugh. He bolted into the kitchen. Marianne struggled off the couch, stood up and looked down at herself. Her tracksuit bottoms had ridden up her legs but other than that, she looked the same as she always did. She even had her runners on, for Christ's sake.

She felt spent. Like she could lie on the floor and sleep. But also twitchy with energy.

Her body was still responding to recent events, the

blood charging around inside her, as if it was looking for a way out. Marianne looked around for her anorak, then remembered she hadn't taken it off.

No wonder Hugh hadn't wanted her. She'd never read any column where the agony aunt recommended leaving your anorak and runners on during sex.

They hadn't even had sex.

Hugh hadn't wanted to have sex with her.

A flavour of the humiliation she would later feel passed like a dry retch through her body.

'Marianne?' called Hugh from the kitchen. 'I've only got Earl Grey tea. That do you?'

Through the kitchen door, Marianne heard the rustle of a packet of biscuits opening, the press closing, the glug of milk into a jug, the rattle of the cutlery drawer opening.

This time she did not put her hands against her ears to drown out the sounds. The ordinary sounds.

She moved to the door, opened it and left, without making a sound.

Chapter 30

When Marianne woke up the next morning, she felt hungover. Or at least, how she imagined a hangover might feel. The remnants of the day before were coated on her insides, leaving her mouth dry and bitter to the taste.

The raw edge of the anger Marianne had felt yesterday had blunted, leaving a sodden sort of regret in its stead, like the driftwood she came across on the beach, misshapen and swollen and good for nothing.

Rita.

Rita was dying.

She pulled her legs out from under George, still asleep at the bottom of the bed, and struggled into a sitting position, looked at her watch. Six o'clock. She lifted the curtain. It didn't look anything like morning. It was middle-of-the-night dark, for starters. She could see nothing. She could hear the rain. The lash of it against the window. She forced her legs out of the bed, planted her feet squarely on the floor and waited for the shock of the cold floor to galvanise her.

It took longer than usual.

Flo's little porcelain owl sat on the bedside locker and seemed to reproach her with his enormous yellow eyes. Marianne reached out and touched him. She hated how hard and cold he was. Why had she given Flo something so hard and cold for her birthday? She should have given her a fabric owl. With soft feathers instead of cold, hard porcelain.

She felt a yearning build inside her. To fall back into bed. Bury herself in blankets. Shut her eyes. Succumb to the dark and the quiet. Stay there. People did that, didn't they? Every day. They opted out.

Now she remembered the incident at Hugh's house yesterday.

The incident.

That made it sound very formal. Official. As if it was something important. Something worthy of note. Instead of nothing more than the ungainly advances of a desperate woman, trying to gain purchase.

She pulled on a pair of socks and reached for her tracksuit bottoms, on the floor where she had discarded them last night. In the last few weeks, she had mastered the art of dressing in the dark although she felt that there were people – Bartholomew and Shirley, for example – who would disagree.

'Come on, George,' she said, lifting the dog's floppy ears and pulling them gently through her hands. 'Let's go to the beach.'

It seemed an unlikely sort of thing for Marianne to say.

Especially to a dog. In the middle-of-the-night winter light of morning. But that's what she said all the same.

She stopped outside Rita's bedroom door. Put her ear against the wood. Listened. She didn't know what she was expecting to hear. She could hear nothing.

She walked away.

She was a person who said cruel things. Had she known that about herself? Well, she did now. She had said cruel things to Rita. The fact that the things she had said were true gave her scant comfort.

She continued through the house, the soles of her runners making little sound against the bare boards. The kitchen was dark and cold and somehow cheerless in the murky light. It seemed emptier, without Rita in it, making potato cakes in the shape of love hearts, frying eggs and singing Doris Day's 'Everybody Loves a Lover'.

Of Patrick there was no sign. Marianne wondered when Rita had told him. She would have told him first. She told him everything. He probably told her everything. They told each other everything.

Because they liked each other.

They loved each other.

Marianne let herself out of the house, pulling the hood of her anorak over her head, trying to fit all her hair inside it. She walked to the bottom of the garden, opening the gate that Patrick had, of course, fixed.

This morning, she didn't fly down the steps two at a time, daring them to do their worst, as was her habit. She felt sluggish. Heavy, like her limbs were dragging her down. She thought it might have something to do with the hangover feeling. Her regret. It was an exhausting emotion.

Pretty useless, too. But difficult to dispel. Like the smell of George's fur after he'd rolled in wet seaweed.

Marianne walked down the steps, one at a time, until she reached the bottom.

The sea was loud and restless, always moving, always thumping waves against the hard sand, the white water rushing over the pebbles on the shoreline with a fizzing sound.

She threw stones for George without being asked. He chased them, returned them to her, dropped them at her feet and waited there with his head cocked.

She had an urge then, to tell him she loved him. To kneel in front of him, gather him in her arms and push her face into his coarse, scratchy fur as if he didn't reek. As if he smelled of rose petals and lavender. Whisper the words.

Imagine that.

Saying 'I love you.' For the first time in her life.

Saying it to a dog.

She and Brian had never said, 'I love you.' That kind of carry-on was for films and songs. It hadn't been a discussion as such. But it had been agreed between them none the less. Theirs had been a practical arrangement. Two people were better than one when it came to things like paying a mortgage, settling bills. Even going away for city breaks, which they occasionally had. Hotel rooms were geared towards two people. Rates were Per Person Sharing. That was standard-speak for couples. Conversations were easier when you were one of two. People relaxed when they knew that someone was coming back for you. 'My husband, Brian, has just gone to the bar.' Or maybe it was just Marianne who people felt uncomfortable around. She had never mastered the art of making people feel comfortable. She had never considered it her responsibility. Brian had called her a hedgehog. 'Because you're prickly,' he'd said, but with a smile so she'd thought he'd liked that.

Another mistake on her part.

She flung another stone for George. She threw it so far into the sea that George had no chance of retrieving it. Still, he plunged into the water, like he could.

In a rockpool, Marianne saw two minnows, which made her think of twins, which then made her think of Brian. And Helen. But the thought was only as darting as the minnows themselves, gone before she'd had time to get a good hold of it, to get stuck into it.

What did that mean? That she was over him? Or that she had never really loved him in the first place?

'I'm not the marrying kind,' she had told him, when he brought it up.

'Neither am I,' he said, his smile wide, as if this was an advantage. Perhaps it was, at first.

Both of them shared a deep, intrinsic distrust of relationships. It was what they had in common, like other people shared a love of theatre, say. Or badminton.

Perhaps they thought, by being in a relationship, they could protect each other from relationships. As a philosophy, Marianne knew it was not exactly romantic. And she was fine with that. She had not reneged on their deal. It was Brian who had done that.

George had found a crab, sidling back towards the sea, and was jumping around it, pushing his nose towards it, then leaping back when the crab lunged at him with its claws. Marianne held the dog's collar, drew him back and they watched the crab, wary at first, continue its journey towards the water, faster now until he was a blur of shell and claw, until he disappeared beneath the first foamy wave that reached him.

Marianne wished she could disappear too.

She looked up to the top of the cliff. Her eyes settled on Ancaire. Her rock bottom. As isolated and weather-beaten as Marianne felt.

She wanted more than anything to walk away from it. To walk away from Rita.

But it would be Rita who would walk away from her in the end.

Chapter 31

There was no sign of Rita back at the house. She must be in her bedroom. Having a lie-in perhaps.

Rita didn't have lie-ins any more.

But much had happened yesterday. It was enough to induce exhaustion into the hardiest of beings. Even Rita.

There was no sign of Patrick either. Marianne remembered it was Saturday then. Patrick was probably on his bicycle, delivering the fruit and vegetables he grew in the kitchen garden to some of the local restaurants and cafés.

All around her, the house was quiet. Still. It felt like an animal, hibernating through these endless winter days.

Although it was spring now. March. Marianne looked out the window. The sun was struggling up but made little impact behind a thick band of low-lying grey clouds that suggested rain.

A floorboard creaked overhead and Marianne heard Aunt Pearl's bedroom door open, the clip of her shoes along the landing, the low rasp of the bathroom door being persuaded open, then shut, the slide of the bolt in the lock.

Marianne looked at her watch. It was too early to collect the clients but she did not want to be in the kitchen when Aunt Pearl arrived with her newspaper. She would have questions and Marianne had no answers.

She grabbed the keys to the Jeep. George's ears shot into twin peaks on his head and he hauled himself from his warm spot in front of the range and followed Marianne out of the house.

Marianne belted him in and petted his head before she drove away.

Today, the flowers leaning against the small wooden cross were daffodils. Marianne tried not to look but the splash of bright yellow they made on the side of the road was impossible to miss. She drove on. If anyone saw her they might possibly assume that she was just some ordinary woman out for a Saturday morning drive with her dog. Perhaps taking him to be groomed. Or for a walk. They wouldn't know that Marianne was not a woman who drove for pleasure.

She did not do anything for pleasure. This thought washed up an image of yesterday, at Hugh's house. The way she had wound her body around his, like a parasite, feasting on him. And Hugh, disentangling himself from her. His face, when he looked at her. Like there wasn't enough sorrow in the world to express how sorry he felt for her.

Marianne wanted to clench her eyes shut so she wouldn't have to see his face, but she couldn't because she was driving and no matter how bad things got, she would never be a woman who drove with her eyes shut.

Things were bad.

The arresting officer thought it was likely she'd get community service. Since it would be her second conviction. His face when he said that. Not angry or disgusted but sort of sad. Not as sad as Hugh's. But there could be no mistaking his pity, all the same.

Marianne drove on. She was glad she was driving. Not for pleasure, obviously. She was simply driving in the absence of anything else to do. And not finding it as tedious or unsettling as she might have imagined. It might have something to do with the road she was on. The coast road to Skerries, the careless wend of it, the reassurance of the sea on her right and the fields on her left, running riot to the horizon, some wild and fallow, others brown with soil, neat lines of furrows waiting for tender, green shoots to emerge.

She refused to think about Rita. How she had collapsed on the beach. How she was going to die. The things Marianne had said to her. The unsayable things.

Instead, she thought about the Jeep and how it must still make all the sounds that it had made that first time. When she had driven it on her own. The near-death rattle, the crash of the gears, the groan of the engine when she accelerated. But she didn't seem to hear them any more.

She stopped at the deli in Skerries for a double espresso. The waitress smiled at Marianne when she walked in, as if she knew her, which she most certainly did not although it was true to say that Marianne had been in a few times since her exile to Ancaire. The waitress was a bright-eyed young woman with a perky high ponytail and a picture of a unicorn on her sweatshirt above the word 'Believe'.

'Good morning, Marianne,' the waitress said. Instead of asking how she knew her name, Marianne said, 'Good morning,' and took a seat.

On the draining board behind the counter, heads of lettuces with the muck still clinging to their stalks.

It was like a signature.

Patrick had been here.

She was early picking up the Get-Well-Sooners but they did not seem to notice or, if they did, they did not seem to mind. From the snatches of their conversation that Marianne overheard when she clambered out of her head and zoned back in, it seemed clear that they were unaware of the events of yesterday and expected nothing less than Rita, in her usual swashbuckling form, when they arrived at Ancaire.

If she wasn't going to be there, she would have let them know. Wouldn't she?

'You're looking a little flushed, sweetie,' said Bartholomew, peering at Marianne through the rear-view mirror. He leaned through the gap in the front seats and clamped one of his massive, fleshy hands across Marianne's forehead.

'I hope you're not coming down with something contagious,' said Freddy fearfully, pulling the neck of his jumper over his nose and pressing himself against the back seat. 'My immune system is lower than usual since I had the flu.'

Bartholomew glared at him. 'You had a sniffle. You couldn't even call it a cold.'

Bartholomew returned his attention to Marianne, now feeling her neck with the pads of his fingers. 'Your glands are not swollen and your temperature is within the normal range,' he told her authoritatively, releasing her from his careful ministrations. 'It's probably just the heartache. It's worse than glandular fever, the way it takes an age to clear up.'

'I'm fine,' said Marianne.

'You shouldn't bottle things up, dearie,' Ethel said in a rush of unsolicited advice. 'Those pent-up feelings are not going to do your innards any favours.'

'I don't have any pent-up feelings,' said Marianne.

'Feelings are over-rated,' said Shirley in a bored voice.

'You *do* have feelings,' said Bartholomew, patting Marianne's shoulder. He sounded so sure of himself that Marianne found herself curious. 'How do you know?' she asked.

Freddy unpeeled himself from the back seat and pushed his glasses up his nose. 'Did you cry at the end of *Toy Story 3*?' he asked Marianne.

'Yes,' she said.

'Well, then,' said Freddy, slapping the back of her seat. 'There you go. You do have feelings.'

'Can we please stop talking about feelings now?' said Shirley.

When Marianne drove through the gates of Ancaire, up the avenue, she scanned the front of the house but there was no sign of Rita, who, on the days she didn't accompany Marianne in the Jeep, positioned herself at the front door, waving wildly and calling, 'Coo-ee!' and 'Heidy-ho!' and other such exclamations.

Marianne herded the Get-Well-Sooners into the drawing room. 'I'll put the kettle on,' she told them. 'Rita will be with you in a minute.'

But the kitchen was as empty as it had been earlier. The kettle was warm and there was a plate scattered with toast crumbs in the sink. Also a cup with no lipstick on the rim. Aunt Pearl must have had her breakfast and then left for mass. Was there a chance that Rita had gone with her? No. Absolutely out of the question. No matter how bad things were, Rita would not darken the door of the local churches. Vultures, she called them. Picking at the bones of people's fears.

Marianne took the stairs two at a time and strode down the corridor to her mother's bedroom, stopped outside.

She tapped the door with the tips of her fingers. 'Rita?'

From behind the door, there was no sound. Marianne knocked again, with her knuckles this time. A sharp rap.

'Rita?' Her voice was loud this time. Clear.

There was no answer. Marianne wrapped her hand around the door handle. Gripped it. Her mouth was dry. She yanked the handle down and pushed open the door. The room was in darkness.

'Rita?'

Marianne snapped on the light, blinking in the sudden brightness. She couldn't remember the last time she had been in her mother's room. Not for years. It hadn't changed. The same wallpaper with its print of pink cabbage roses, faded now where the light had worn it away, swollen with damp around the window. The same square rug with its long tassels stretching across the floorboards, now more of a beige than the canary yellow Marianne remembered. She stepped inside. Rita's dresses were everywhere, draped over the backs of chairs, thrown over the top of the stand-alone mirror, pitched across the arm of the ancient chaise longue in the window. Those were the lucky ones. Other dresses lay where they had fallen, in crumpled heaps on the floor. The dressing table was strewn with make-up, bottles of nail polish, hairbrushes and combs and two jewellery boxes, both open and leaking beads and baubles. The room smelled of paint and perfume. Marianne could taste it.

The bed was on the other side of the room: an ancient four-poster, with moth-eaten damask draped across the posts, piled high with blankets and an eiderdown.

The wall behind the bed was covered in so many framed photographs, the wallpaper was no longer visible.

All of the photographs were of Flo and Marianne.

Marianne sitting solemnly on the couch in the sitting room, surrounded by cushions. In her arms, Flo. Brand-new Flo, barely visible through the cocoon of cotton swaddling her.

The two of them at the water's edge, jumping over the waves. Marianne could see how tightly she held Flo's hand, the white grip of it.

Gap-toothed Flo on a makeshift stage in the garden, tap-dancing and singing 'On the Good Ship Lollipop'. Her party piece.

Flo on Marianne's shoulders at the fairground, her arms outstretched in a sort of V for victory and her mouth open wide like she was shouting something. Cheering it. A candy floss in one hand, a wisp of it stuck to her face. Swing boats behind them. Marianne hadn't let her go on them. 'You might fall out,' she had said, and Flo had sulked but only for a minute. She was awful at sulking. She couldn't sustain it.

There were lots of other photographs. Every photograph that Marianne remembered being taken was here.

On the wall at the end of the bed was a painting. Marianne and Flo, sitting on the edge of the cliff at Ancaire, looking out to sea, with their arms around each other's shoulders.

Rita had painted it in bright pastels, so that it seemed like something out of a fairy tale. A fairy tale with a happy ending.

Even though she couldn't see their faces, Marianne knew that Flo's thumb was in her mouth. She could tell by the tired slump of Flo's head against Marianne's shoulder.

She sucked her thumb when she was tired. Marianne had forgotten that.

She pulled the eiderdown back, folded it neatly along the base of the bed. She picked the dresses up off the floor, lay them over the arm of the chair, then sat on the edge of the bed, the mattress dipping and sighing beneath her weight. Rita could do with a new mattress, Marianne thought before she remembered.

The tallboy was in her line of vision now, a great slab of solid wood, listing to one side where one of the feet had buckled, some of its brass handles missing. Rita's clothes – scarves and tights, in the main – gathered in the space where the drawers were supposed to close, spilled down the side, hung there like they were hanging on for dear life.

Marianne looked around the room again, as if there was a chance she might have missed Rita. That she might be here yet.

She pulled her mobile from her pocket, checked it for missed calls. There was none. She dialled Rita's number and listened to her phone ring and ring. Then Rita's voice. 'Hello, darlings, thanks for calling. Please don't leave a message because I always forget to check my voicemail. And it's not an age thing, I've always been absent-minded, you know that. Why don't you text me instead? Or even better, call in! We can have tea.'

Downstairs, in the drawing room, Marianne cleared her throat to get everyone's attention but they were arguing over the jam tarts. Both Bartholomew and Freddy wanted the raspberry one, which Shirley was holding on a plate over her head while Ethel tried to tempt them with the lemon curd ones, of which there were plenty.

'I just don't know why Rita insists on making so many lemon ones,' said Bartholomew, sulky as a teenager, when Ethel had finally persuaded them into their seats by promising to cut the raspberry one in half. But when Shirley lowered the plate, only crumbs remained and Shirley's cheeks were bulging.

'Okay listen, everybody, I need to tell you something,' said Marianne, moving to the top of the room.

'What about our tart?' said Bartholomew and Freddy in unison, which caused them to turn to each other and grin like schoolboys.

'I ate it,' Shirley told them, poking the last of it from her teeth with her finger, which she then sucked noisily.

Freddy shook his head. 'God grant me the serenity to accept the things I cannot change,' he said, closing his eyes.

'That's AA,' said Shirley snippily.

'So?' said Freddy, setting his hands on his hips. 'I can still say it. If I want to.' He took a step back so he was no longer within swiping distance of her.

'Are you all right, my dear?' said Ethel, peering at Marianne over the top of her spectacles. 'You're very quiet today.'

'She's usually quiet,' said Bartholomew. 'Aren't you, Marnie?'

'That's because she can't get a word in with you two spouting off,' said Shirley, pointing at Bartholemew and Freddy.

'It's rude to point,' said Freddy. 'But I do agree that it's difficult to make oneself heard with Mister Boombox over there.' Before Bartholomew could come up with a stinging retort, Ethel, taking her usual seat by the window through which the morning sun spilled, said, 'Where's Rita?'

'That's what I wanted to talk to you about,' said Marianne.

'What?' said Shirley, suspiciously.

'Rita,' said Marianne. 'I . . . I don't know where she is.' All of a sudden, she had their attention.

'What do you mean, you don't know?' said Bartholomew, as if Marianne did know. As if Marianne had hidden her somewhere.

'I just . . . I don't know.'

'But she always tells us if she's not going to be here for our meetings,' said Freddy, his eyes widening behind the small, round lenses of his glasses.

'What did she say before she left?' asked Bartholomew.

'I don't know,' said Marianne again. 'I mean, she didn't say anything. Not to me, anyway. I haven't seen her since yesterday.'

'But she must have said something,' said Freddy, his narrow face pinched with concern. 'To somebody. Patrick.

She would have told Patrick where she was going. Patrick will know.'

'Patrick's out,' said Marianne. 'And Pearl's gone to mass. Rita is . . . well, I don't know where Rita is.'

'This is most out of character,' said Ethel, worrying at her lip with her oversized dentures.

Marianne found herself rubbing Ethel's arm. 'I'm sure it's nothing to worry about,' she said. 'She probably just had an errand to run and forgot about the meeting.'

The others withered her with a look, then turned to each other, mumbling and shaking their heads.

'What?' said Marianne.

'You haven't got a clue,' said Shirley baldly. 'No offence.'

'It's just . . .' Ethel began, sitting up in her chair, 'what Shirley means is, that for non-alcoholics like you,' she gestured to Marianne with one of her tiny hands and her gentle smile, 'it's difficult to understand the importance of the meetings, you see?' She peered at Marianne through her bifocals.

Marianne nodded. Shirley was right. She didn't have a clue. About anything. Anything to do with other humans. With relationships. With interacting with the world. It was all too confusing, too much, too hard.

She started to cry.

Marianne rarely cried. For starters, she looked awful when she cried, her eyes red and her face streaked with tears.

Also, she was much too tall. Tall people looked awkward when they cried, like a bull trying to pick its way through a china shop. Crying was for children and small adults. Big adults could only get away with crying if they did it silently.

Marianne was a noisy crier. Mostly because she was a wet crier and had to blow her nose regularly, and it sounded like a foghorn when she blew her nose. Then there was the attention she attracted between her height and the red eyes and the swollen face and the foghorn noise. She was attracting attention now. She knew it even though her eyes were shut. She could feel it. The Get-Well-Sooners. They gathered around her, put their hands on her shoulders, her hands, her arms. She wanted to shout at them, to tell them to back off, to go away, to leave her alone. Instead, she stood in the centre of them with her eyes shut, which did nothing to stem the flow of her tears, which poured down her face and hung from the line of her jaw before dropping onto her T-shirt. They were a curiously comforting group of people to cry around. They didn't ask her questions – *What's wrong, Marianne? Are you all right, Marianne?* – and they didn't do the dreaded hug. They just stood around her, near enough so she could feel the warmth of their collective bodies but not so close that she could smell their breath or feel anything other than the slightest touch of their hands on her.

She stood like that for way longer than she would have estimated, had she been asked how long she could withstand such an encounter.

She didn't just cry, she sobbed. She thought she might have said things too. Random words, but these were mostly lost in the maelstrom of her cries. They didn't ask her to repeat, to explain, to clarify. They didn't ask her anything but stood, like first responders on a runway, waiting for a distressed plane to land.

Afterwards, they guided her to the nearest chair, which happened to be Shirley's, lowered her gently into it.

Shirley did not object.

'And I didn't even know she was sick,' Marianne said when she managed to quieten.

'She wanted to tell you,' said Bartholomew, rubbing her shoulder.

'She was waiting for the right moment,' said Freddy, squeezing her hand.

'I'd be the same with the boys,' said Shirley, nudging George aside before squatting in front of Marianne and lifting her fringe away from her tear-stained face. 'I wouldn't know how to tell them.'

Marianne squeezed her eyes shut, but still she could feel the fall of her tears down her face. Ethel rummaged in her handbag and handed Marianne a handkerchief with a tiny daisy embroidered in the corner and a monogram above it in elaborately cursive script. The initials S.A.

'I can't blow my nose with Stanley's handkerchief,' Marianne managed to say, in between shuddering gulps.

'Please do,' said Freddy, pointing at her nose. 'You have . . . residue.'

'It's snot,' Shirley told him.

'Stanley doesn't need it any more,' said Ethel, dabbing at Marianne's face with the enormous piece of linen.

'Maybe Rita's gone to the graveyard?' Marianne said when she had blown her nose for what she hoped was the last time.

She didn't say Flo's name out loud. She thought that might set her off again. Although anything might set her off. Shirley's nails, bitten down to the quick. Ethel's glasses

Ciara Geraghty

perched in her hair that she wouldn't be able to find later. Freddy picking one of Bartholomew's hairs off Marianne's shoulders. Bartholomew glaring at him and then smiling, a sudden smile, as unlikely as a warm breeze in November but all the more tender for it.

Marianne thought any of these things might set her off again. The Get-Well-Sooners shook their heads in tandem and with authority. 'She only ever goes to the graveyard in the afternoons,' said Bartholomew gently, not quite looking at Marianne.

'She'll have had to take a taxi to wherever she went,' said Freddy, striding towards the door. 'I'll ring Tried and Tested Taxis and see if Hugh might be able to throw some light on the situation.'

Marianne thought that was a sensible plan. Something she might have come up with ordinarily.

She blew her nose again. The noise made Ethel jump. 'Sorry, Ethel,' said Marianne. Her voice was watery with tears and when Ethel smiled her sweet, kind smile at her, Marianne thought she might start bawling again.

'Hello?' came Freddy's voice from the hall. 'Is Hugh there? . . . Well, yes, I hope you can. I'm looking for Rita. Did she phone for a taxi this morning? . . . Oh, I see, well, we're a little worried about her so I would appre— . . . What do you mean, who is this? It's Freddy. Frederick Mongomery. Oh, for goodness' sake.'

Freddy poked his head into the drawing room. 'The other guy is there today. The one who calls himself "the controller".' Freddy rolled his eyes. 'He says he can't divulge information relating to any of their clients' activities over the phone,' he said. 'He thinks he's the bloody secret service.'

Marianne walked into the hall, followed by Bartholomew, Shirley and Ethel. Freddy handed her the phone.

'You should talk to him,' he said.

'Where is Hugh?' Marianne whispered, pressing her hand across the receiver.

'He's on a day off,' said Freddy, also whispering.

Marianne felt weak with relief. She knew she'd have to talk to him sooner or later. She was glad it would be later. She put the receiver to her ear. 'Hello?'

The Get-Well-Sooners gathered around her, straining forward as if that might allow them to hear what the person on the other end of the line was saying. Marianne could hear their breathing all around her, in and out in unison, it seemed to her. She usually hated other people's breath. Too hot. Too pungent. Too personal.

Right now, she found it comforting. 'The Wind Beneath My Wings', Rita would probably start singing if she got wind of Marianne's train of thought.

Marianne tightened her grip on the phone. Where was Rita?

'Yes, this is Marianne. I'm her daughter . . . I see . . . Okay then . . . If she does ring, you'll tell her I'm . . .? Thank you. Goodbye then.'

She hung up.

'Well?' said Bartholomew in his booming voice.

'Rita didn't order a taxi from them today,' said Marianne.

'Do they know where Hugh is?' asked Shirley. 'Maybe Rita's with him?'

Marianne shook her head. 'I asked. They don't know.'

'We could try him on his mobile telephone?' said Ethel.

Freddy wrestled his phone out of the pocket of his

trousers. 'I'll ring him,' he said. After a while he shook his head and hung up. 'It's just ringing out.'

'Let's sit down and have a think, shall we?' suggested Ethel, when it became clear that nobody had any further suggestions to make.

'Good idea,' said Bartholomew. 'And, just as an aside, I think there are some rock buns left over from the other day. I spotted them in the biscuit tin. If anyone's hungry, that is.'

Nobody wanted to admit they were hungry in such circumstances but there was nothing any of them could do in the face of Rita's gigantic, misshapen rock buns. Marianne made tea.

Peppermint tea for Ethel, served in a china cup, with the tea bag left on the saucer so she could pop it back into the cup if she went for a refill, which she sometimes did and sometimes didn't.

A pot of tea made with PG Tips for Freddy and Bartholomew, which they shared today without their usual bickering over who should get the second cup, the second one being stronger.

Lyons tea for Shirley, who did not make her usual reference to 'Blueshirts' when Marianne made a mug of Barry's Classic Blend for herself.

It was good to have something to do.

Her worst fear was that Rita was drinking somewhere.

That she was drunk somewhere.

The others didn't seem to think this was likely.

As if Rita had never been a person who disappeared when she was supposed to be somewhere. Like a parent-teacher meeting. Or one of Flo's school plays.

'Where's Mum?' Flo would ask Marianne after the show.

'She had to rush off.'

'Did she see me?'

'She said she'd never seen a better Pinnocchio.'

Cadging a lift from one of the other mothers back to Ancaire.

'Was your mother feeling unwell again, dear?'

'Yes.'

Marianne struggled to remember where William had been. Why hadn't he been there? And how had he managed to escape scrutiny in these matters? She supposed it was his gender, expectation being so much less for fathers.

The woman alcoholic.

Or worse, the mother alcoholic. She was not somebody to be excused. Or even pitied.

And being the daughter of alcoholics, especially a mother alcoholic, that seemed inexcusable too. Something Marianne had done wrong. Or something she had failed to do right.

'What's going on?'

Marianne looked towards the door of the drawing room. Patrick stood in the hallway, holding an empty crate in his arms, peering at them through the open door.

'Rita's disappeared,' said Freddy, his grey eyes huge behind his glasses.

'We don't know that,' said Bartholomew, glaring at Freddy.

'Not for certain,' said Ethel, peering at the face of her Timex watch. 'But she never misses a class without letting us know.'

'That's true' said Freddy. 'Even when William had his

first stroke, Rita told us she conducted the meetings round his bed in the hospital.'

'How that poor fucker survived to have another stroke is beyond me,' said Shirley shaking her head.

Patrick set the crate on the hall table and walked into the room. He looked at Marianne. 'Rita left a note,' he said. 'On the kitchen table.'

Immediately, Marianne felt the usual flare of annoyance – Patrick knowing everything as usual – but also relief – Patrick knowing everything as usual.

'I didn't see any note,' said Marianne. She sounded peevish. Her usual self.

'It was there,' said Patrick. 'On the kitchen table.'

'Well, it's not there now,' said Marianne.

'Was Gerard in the kitchen earlier?' said Patrick.

'I shooed him out.' Marianne did her best to avoid the goat, whose horns seemed longer and sharper than goats horns were supposed to be.

'He must have eaten it,' said Patrick. 'He loves Bond notepaper.'

'Just tell us what the note said,' shouted Bartholomew, making everybody jump, including Patrick.

'It just said something like, "My apologies. I have to be elsewhere today. Please go ahead without me."'

'Where's elsewhere?' said Freddy.

'Clearly, she does not want us to know,' said Bartholomew.

'She wouldn't skip a session unless it was important,' said Ethel, glancing around the room and patting the pockets of her cardigan.

'Your glasses are on your head,' said Marianne.

'Oh, so they are, dear, thank you,' said Ethel.

'Do you think she'll be back before we leave?' asked Shirley, looking at Marianne. 'Sheldon got eight out of ten in his spelling test this week. He was hoping for one of Rita's gold stars.' When Shirley smiled, it was like the sun coming out after a nuclear winter. It was a thing of beauty, her smile, made all the more beautiful by its scarcity. Nobody could do anything in the face of it except smile back, which they did.

'Well?' said Shirley, her smile vanishing and impatience taking over.

'I know where she keeps the gold stars,' said Marianne, standing up. 'I'll go and get them.'

In the kitchen, Marianne took her phone out of her pocket and rang Happy Hair's landline. Perhaps Hugh was in the salon and had his mobile on silent?

He answered on the sixth ring.

'Happy Hair, good morning, Hugh McLeod speaking. How can I be of assistance?'

'Hugh?'

'At your service,' he said. Marianne could tell he was smiling. Also that he had put on a telephone voice.

'It's Marianne.'

'Oh. Hello,' he said, a little hesitant. Then rallied with a more cheerful, 'How'd you like my new and improved telephone technique?'

'It's very . . . professional,' Marianne had to admit.

'I thought you'd like it,' he said. 'Now, what can I do for you?' His tone was brisk now.

Marianne couldn't blame him.

'I can't find Rita,' she said.

'Oh.'

'I thought maybe she might have mentioned something to you?'

'No, I'm afraid not.' Marianne could hear the rasp of stubble and knew he was rubbing at the side of his face with his fingers, which was the thing he did when he was trying to work something out.

'She had quite a . . . busy day yesterday,' said Hugh after a while.

Marianne thought 'busy' was a kind word to use to describe the events of yesterday.

'Maybe she's just gone somewhere to have a rest?' he suggested.

'Yes, but where?' said Marianne.

Hugh blew into the phone and the sound tickled Marianne's ear. 'Well,' he began, hesitant, 'she mentioned recently Flo's anniversary. Marking it.'

'But that's not until the end of April.'

'Aye, I know, but she . . . she thought she'd do it a little earlier this year.'

'Oh,' said Marianne. 'I see.' She clenched every muscle in her body so she wouldn't cry again.

'I'm sorry, Marianne,' said Hugh. 'I know it's hard.'

'Please stop being nice to me,' she whispered. She was terrified she might cry again.

'Newbridge Farm,' said Hugh all of a sudden.

'What?'

'Rita mentioned it recently. Does that ring any bells? Something to do with Flo? Her anniversary?'

'Yes,' said Marianne. 'It does.'

Chapter 32

Flo was supposed to go to Newbridge Farm for her school tour.

Marianne remembered her contagious excitement when she came home from school that day. Announced the trip. 'We're going in a week and there are seven days in a week so that's seven sleeps.'

Marianne forged her mother's signature on the consent form. Their parents had gone somewhere – Marianne couldn't remember where, an arts festival, probably – for a few days. She took a ten-pound note from the milk jug in the kitchen cupboard, where Rita left cash for emergencies whenever they went away. She folded it carefully inside an envelope, sealed it shut with spit from her tongue. She remembered the sour taste of the paper, pressing the flap down, making sure it was sealed. Flo counting down the days.

'Three more sleeps,' she told Rita when she and William returned home, bouncing up and down on her feet like she had springs in her shoes.

The night before, an argument erupted between Rita and William. Nothing unusual but it had gone on for hours, the pair of them charging around the house, banging doors, throwing books, filling their glasses to the brim. The usual. But it had ended on the beach, and Marianne, terrified that they might decide to go swimming as they had before, couldn't sleep until she heard them returning home at dawn, holding hands and singing, stopping only to kiss each other. Or hug each other. Or hold each other up.

Maybe Marianne forgot to set her alarm. Or perhaps she slept through it. She didn't know. All she knew was that they were late.

Too late.

The school bus had left by the time she and Flo arrived. They were out of breath with the rushing and the running and Flo was doing her best not to cry but crying anyway.

'It's not fair,' she cried. 'It's not fair.' She said it over and over.

'I'll bring you some other time, darling,' Rita told Flo when she managed her way down to the kitchen that afternoon. 'I'm so thirsty,' she told them. 'It must be that cheese I ate yesterday.' She opened the fridge and drank deeply from a bottle of water which, Marianne had worked out years before, was gin.

Now, when Marianne got to Newbridge Farm, the man in the café was drying a cup in that distracted way people sometimes did when their minds were not on the job.

'Excuse me?' said Marianne, standing at the counter.

The man rubbed the cup with a tea towel and stared off into the middle distance.

'I think it's dry now,' she said in a very Shirley tone. It worked because the man said, 'Huh?' dragging his eyes from some distant point over Marianne's right shoulder and fastening them on her face.

'I'm looking for someone,' Marianne blurted.

'Aren't we all?' the man said, setting the cup on the counter and flinging the tea towel onto his shoulder. Marianne cleared her throat. 'I'm looking for my mother,' she said. 'She's . . . I think she might have gone to the animal farm. But she could have stopped here first?'

The waiter leaned on the counter. 'What does she look like?' he said.

This bit was easy. 'She looks like Rita Hayworth,' she said.

'In which film?' he asked, interested now.

Marianne shook her head. 'I don't know. I've never seen a Rita Hayworth film.'

The waiter widened his eyes, shook his head. 'You've never seen *Gilda*?' he asked.

This was one of Marianne's pet hates. Didn't she just say she hadn't seen any of Rita Hayworth's bloody films?

'She'll be wearing a dress. Like a deb's dress. You know the ones, in silk or satin, with sequins and complicated straps and a full skirt. High heels. Bright red lipstick. She wears a turban on her head. It could be any colour, apart from black, navy or grey.'

The waiter took a moment to digest the details. 'Sounds like Rita Hayworth in *You Were Never Lovelier*,' he said then. 'Great film. You should do yourself a favour and watch it.'

'Have you seen her?' asked Marianne.

The waiter shook his head and picked up the cup, began drying it with the tea towel all over again. 'Can't say as I have,' he said. 'It's been sluggish in here today, with the rain.'

'Okay,' said Marianne, backing away. 'I'll try the farm.'

The waiter shook his head. 'You have to go through the café to get into the farm and I'd remember somebody like your mother.'

Despite her naturally low reserves of trust, Marianne was inclined to believe the waiter. Perhaps it was the stead-fast and attentive way he dried crockery.

She cast about the café. A few pockets of people here and there; two couples; one woman feeding her baby. Marianne fished her phone out of her pocket, examined the screen. No missed calls, no messages from Rita. Or from any of the Get-Well-Sooners to let her know that Rita had returned.

She phoned Rita's number again. It began to ring. And as it did, she heard Rita's ringtone: Rita Hayworth's character in *Gilda* singing 'Amado Mio'. She snatched her head this way and that but still couldn't see Rita. She began to make her way towards the sound. Towards the back of the café, a woman sat alone with her back to Marianne. She had sparse, thin hair, dark with a good two inches of coarse grey at the roots. She sat hunched over a mug, both her hands wrapped around it, warming them. On the table beside her, a phone, shuddering every time it rang. The woman paid it no attention.

'Rita?'

The woman turned slowly and even when she looked up, it took Marianne a moment to recognise her mother. Without her false eyelashes, pan stick and lipstick, her face seemed faded. As if someone had pulled a plug and drained it of all colour and vitality.

She wore what looked like one of Marianne's tracksuits. On her feet a pair of thick socks and runners. Thrown over her shoulders, a woollen shawl, but even so, Rita looked frozen with the cold, her lips tainted a blueish-white. For the first time since Marianne had known her, Rita looked her age. That is to say, she looked old. Properly old. Elderly woman old, her face creased and lined like a page, loose and forgotten at the bottom of a handbag.

It was shocking.

Marianne pulled out a chair and sat down. 'Rita?' she said again. 'Why didn't you answer your phone? I've been phoning you. And looking for you. I've been . . . worried about you.'

At first, Rita just shook her head. Eventually she said, 'How did you know I'd be here?'

'Something Hugh said.'

For a while they sat there, the two women, not saying anything.

'Do you remember Flo's school tour?' asked Rita.

Marianne nodded.

'It took so little to make Flo happy,' Rita said then. She closed her eyes and two enormous tears swelled and rolled, slow and solemn, down the worn skin of her face.

Marianne nodded. That much was true.

'Let's go home,' said Marianne, putting her hand on her mother's arm.

Rita shook her head. 'I'm supposed to go around the farm,' she said. 'I always go around the farm when I come. There are owls. Flo loved owls, didn't she?' She looked at

Marianne then, with bloodshot, tired eyes, and there was a pleading in them, too. A request for confirmation.

Marianne nodded. 'Yes,' she said. 'Flo loved owls.'

Rita stood up, her face whiter now as the light caught it. She gripped the back of her chair.

'You're in no state to go around the farm today,' said Marianne, standing up too, putting her hand on Rita's arm to steady her.

Rita didn't argue. She didn't say anything. Just nodded.

'We'll come back another day,' Marianne said.

Rita shook her head. 'No,' she said, with quiet authority. She threaded her way past the tables and chairs like an old person. A properly old woman, worried about banging her hip, falling, breaking something.

Marianne followed her. Most of her was glad that she wouldn't have to come back another day. She'd be like Ethel looking for a sign. A sign of Flo. And there would be none.

Through a glass he held before him, inspecting it for flaws, the waiter watched Rita's careful walk to the door. He removed the cloth from his shoulder, wiped the rim of the glass with it and examined Marianne as she passed the counter. 'You didn't find her, then?' he asked.

'I did,' said Marianne.

'Oh,' said the waiter, confused.

'She's just . . . she's not herself,' Marianne explained.

It struck her that she had spent her whole life wishing that Rita was not herself. Wishing that she was somebody else. And now, it seemed, she was. The realisation gave Marianne no pleasure.

Chapter 33

Marianne slept in the next day.
So did George.

She put it down to yesterday, the strangeness of it. She was a creature of habit. Even here, at Ancaire, she had somehow found a routine. Had managed to grasp the hang of it, and even though she often felt like she was hanging onto it with the whitened tips of her fingers, she had gleaned some small comfort from it nonetheless.

She hated the way nothing ever stayed the same. Like yesterday, when they arrived home, Rita insisted on going in the back door so she wouldn't have to face them. The Get-Well-Sooners.

Her Get-Well-Sooners. Their faces pressed up against the window of the drawing room as Marianne drove up the driveway. Waiting for Rita.

She bypassed them and retreated up the stairs, to her bedroom. 'I'm tired,' she said when Marianne asked her why she was getting into bed.

'I'm not hungry,' she said later, when Marianne, having beaten the ancient biscuit tin with the wooden spoon to announce dinner, went up to her.

When Marianne woke the next morning, George was not leaning over her, licking her face and pawing her arm. He was asleep at the end of her bed. Marianne sat up and rubbed her eyes. The day was already lit by the sun, the light streaming through the gap in the Paddington Bear curtains. Marianne had long given up trying to get them to meet in the middle, like curtains should.

She blinked in the unfamiliar light, tried to get her bearings.

It felt like some line had been crossed and everything was different and nothing was the same.

She pulled her feet out from under George's dead-weight, struggled out of bed, threw on some clothes and brushed her teeth. When she returned to the bedroom, George had not stirred and she approached him cautiously, put her hand on his coarse fur. He was warm. She watched her hand lift and fall with his breathing.

She left him to sleep.

She thought briefly about going to the beach alone but then she thought about George.

George would smell the sea on her and would look at her with his head cocked to one side and such sadness in his amber eyes.

She didn't go to the beach.

She couldn't.

In the kitchen, only Patrick, making a pot of coffee, and Aunt Pearl, reading the newspaper. She lowered it when Marianne walked in, peered at her across the top of the page, her eyebrows arched like meringues, in stiff peaks.

'You look tired,' she said, her tone not as sharp as her usual nib.

Patrick appeared beside her with a mug of coffee, the steam rising from it in pungent swirls.

'Thanks,' said Marianne, taking it from him. He smiled his small smile at her.

'Is Rita still in bed?' she asked then, sitting down.

'Yes,' said Aunt Pearl, but beneath her disapproving tone there was a note of worry that Marianne could hear as clearly as Rita's dinner gong.

Patrick was worried too. Marianne could see it along the rigid line of his shoulders. She set her mug on the table and stood up.

'I'll go and get her,' she said.

'Rita?' Marianne knocked briefly on her mother's bedroom door and opened it. She stepped inside and the air that enveloped her was musty and stale. She waited for her eyes to adjust to the darkness, approached the bed.

'Rita?'

The covers shifted and Rita's head appeared. She shielded her eyes from the daylight streaming through the door with her hand.

'What's wrong?' she asked.

'Patrick is worried about you.'

'There's no need.'

'So is Aunt Pearl.'

'Now you're just being ridiculous,' said Rita, sitting up. It was a struggle, the movement, like an echo of her unmade-up face, gaunt and grey in the suggestion of pale light behind the curtains, the parched thinness of her mouth, the wispy hairs of her brows.

'I'm fine,' she said, reaching for a glass of water. 'I'm just tired.' Her hand shook with effort. Marianne picked up the glass, handed it to Rita. When she drank, the bones in her neck poked through her skin in a way that looked painful. When she looked up, Marianne saw that the whites of her eyes were shot through with red thread veins.

'It's time to get up,' said Marianne, taking the glass from her.

Rita shook her head. 'Not today,' she said.

'You have work to do.'

'They can manage without me today.'

Marianne shook her head stoutly. 'You have commitments,' she said.

Rita lay back against the pillows. Closed her eyes. She looked like a carbon copy of herself, faint and fragile.

'Did you hear me?' said Marianne, stepping closer, her voice louder.

'Give me a break,' said Rita. 'I'm dying.'

'You're not dying today,' said Marianne, grabbing a fistful of Rita's bedcovers, reefing them down.

'Stop,' said Rita, sitting up. 'It's freezing.'

'You're always saying how invigorating the cold is,' Marianne reminded her, moving the covers out of reach as Rita tried to snatch them out of her hands. 'Nothing like the cold to make you feel alive. That's your line, remember?'

'I can't believe you're quoting me back to me,' said Rita, petulant.

'It seems like the least you deserve,' said Marianne,

tossing the eiderdown behind her and facing her mother again with her arms tightly crossed. 'Now get up.'

'There,' said Rita, pushing her legs off the bed and perching on the edge.

'And get dressed.'

'Right now?'

'Yes.'

Rita signed and shook her head. Marianne did not budge. 'Oh, fine then,' said Rita after a while. 'Pass me those tracksuit bottoms.'

'You don't wear tracksuits,' said Marianne, kicking the bottoms under the bed.

'What are you . . .?'

'Here.' Marianne picked one of Rita's complicated dresses off the back of the chaise longue and held it towards her. 'This one is nice.'

'But you were right about tracksuits,' said Rita. 'They are very comfortable.'

'Don't make me wrestle this over your head,' said Marianne, taking a step towards Rita with the dress.

'I'll freeze in that rig-out,' said Rita.

'You can wear thermals underneath it,' said Marianne, dropping the dress on Rita's lap.

'Thermals?' said Rita, as if Marianne had said the word in Chinese. Marianne took succour from her tone. She sounded more like herself.

'A vest then,' said Marianne.

'Vests are for men,' said Rita, moodily.

'Shirley would not be impressed with such gender-normativity,' said Marianne, searching through Rita's chest of drawers. 'Here, this will do.' She took out a slip, a pair of hold-ups and the biggest, warmest pair of knickers she could find, which were silk and neither big nor warm.

'That's better,' said Marianne when Rita was dressed. 'Now, what colour turban are you wearing today?'

Rita shook her head. 'I'm not going to bother.'

'Orange, you say?' said Marianne, spying a snatch of bright orange silk hanging off the full-length mirror. 'Excellent choice.' She sat beside Rita on the bed and did her best to arrange the scarf around Rita's head in that nonchalant, jaunty way that Rita usually did. She leaned back to survey her work. 'Not bad,' she said. 'You look nearly civilised. You just need a bit of make-up and—'

'No,' said Rita. 'The smell of it makes me feel sick.'

'That's never stopped you before,' said Marianne, opening her mother's monstrous bag of cosmetics and peering inside. She found a foundation.

'I'm hardly going to blend in with that shade,' said Rita when Marianne picked it up.

'You're not supposed to blend in,' said Marianne, dabbing blobs on Rita's forehead, her cheeks, her nose, her chin. She used the pads of her fingers to rub them in, as gentle as she could, trying not to notice how worn out Rita's skin was, how threadbare.

She used a pencil to draw on Rita's eyebrows and even managed to stick lashes on without taking her eyes out, although they did water quite a bit.

'Eyedrops,' said Marianne. 'And lipstick. Then you're done.'

Afterwards, she marched Rita over to the mirror, stood her in front of it. 'There,' she said. 'What do you think?'

'I think I'm depressed,' said Rita.

'I meant, what do you think of your rig-out,' said Marianne.

Rita shrugged. 'I don't know why you've gone to all this—'

'Just tell me what you think.' said Marianne.

'It's fine,' said Rita, her shoulders slumping with resignation.

'That's the spirit,' said Marianne, smiling at her mother's reflection in the mirror. 'Now,' she went on quickly, steering Rita towards the door, making sure they gave the bed a wide berth. 'Time to eat.'

'I'm not hungry.'

'Hunger has nothing to do with it,' said Marianne. 'You need to eat something.'

Rita opened her mouth to say something else, to feebly throw another obstacle in Marianne's way, perhaps, then didn't. Instead, she followed Marianne down the stairs to the kitchen.

'Well,' said Pearl, folding her newspaper in two with a sharp snap. Marianne narrowed her eyes at her and shook her head. Pearl bristled. 'I was merely going to ask if Rita would like a cup of tea.'

'Oh,' said Marianne.

'Did you think I was going to make some snide comment about Rita finally deigning to join us for breakfast at this ungodly hour of the day?'

'Well,' Marianne began, flushing, 'I . . .'

'I'd love a cup of tea,' said Rita, sitting down. Marianne filled the kettle.

Patrick, who had been busy at the pan, now set a stack of pancakes on the table, along with a bowl of melted chocolate, a plate of raspberries, banana slices, and a jar of honey.

'What's the occasion?' asked Rita.

Patrick didn't answer but placed his hand on Rita's shoulder. She touched his hand with her own and the gesture was so quiet and tender, Marianne had to look away.

Aunt Pearl put a pancake on a plate, decorated it with two raspberries, a slice of banana and a semi-circle of melted chocolate. She set the plate in front of Rita.

'Is that a smiley face?' Marianne asked, looking at the pancake.

'What else would it be?' snapped Aunt Pearl.

'Thank you, Pearl,' said Rita, picking up her knife and fork. Pearl nodded stiffly and left the kitchen, trailing 4711 and carbolic soap.

Rita ate one of the raspberries, the slice of banana and two mouthfuls of pancake. She drank half a cup of the tea Marianne made her with the mucky weeds.

'Right,' said Marianne, picking up the keys of the Jeep. 'Come on.'

Rita looked at her in alarm. 'What do you mean?'

'We're going to pick up the Get-Well-Sooners, of course,' said Marianne, walking with purpose to the door. She turned round when she reached it. Rita had not moved.

'The doctor said I should rest,' Rita said.

'You can rest in the Jeep,' said Marianne. She knew she was being heavy-handed. She didn't know what else to do. The only thing she could think of was routine. Routine might tow them out of whatever lay-by they'd broken down in, give them a jump start.

It wasn't a brilliant idea but, in the absence of anything

else, it would have to do. She handed Rita her faux-fur jacket, her cashmere scarf, and was amazed when Rita, obedient as a child, stood up and put the jacket over her shoulders, wound the scarf around her neck. She looked up and nodded at Marianne. 'Okay,' she said. It wasn't a massive endorsement of Marianne's plan but it was a tentative lean in that direction.

'You look lovely,' said Marianne.

'So do you,' said Rita, which was worrying since Marianne was wearing her usual uniform of tracksuit bottoms, a fleece jumper over a T-shirt and her worn-out runners. She threw on her anorak and looked at Rita. They studied each other, perhaps noticing the small hollow in the middle of their chins, the gunmetal-blue of their eyes and the shape of their mouths, wide and full and a little too big in the small, pale circles of their faces.

Marianne opened the passenger door of the Jeep and waited for Rita to negotiate her way inside.

It took longer than usual.

The Jeep did its usual groaning protest when Marianne turned the key in the ignition but she had developed a knack by now; three short pumps on the accelerator followed by two long ones and the engine roared into life, although perhaps roar was overstating it. Still, it started. Ethel would consider that a sign. A good sign.

Today the flowers on the side of the road were tulips, in pinks, reds, yellows, and purple. Marianne did not hold her breath or accelerate as she passed them. Instead she looked at them. So did Rita.

'I always thought you put the flowers there every day,' said Marianne.

Rita shook her head. 'Pearl does,' she said.

'Oh,' said Marianne.

She drove on.

At the traffic lights on the way into Skerries, the Jeep cut out. The lights were red.

Marianne turned the key. Three short pumps on the accelerator, then two long ones.

Nothing happened.

She looked in her rear-view mirror. Three cars behind. She tried again.

The lights turned green.

Marianne put on her hazard lights.

She tried a different tack, this time applying gentle but persistent pressure on the accelerator.

A horn blared.

Marianne looked in her rear-view mirror again. The driver of the car – a burly man with a hipster beard and a tweed peaked cap – stabbed the air with his finger towards the green traffic light. With his other hand, he leaned on the horn.

Marianne looked at Rita, who seemed to be following her doctor's orders for the first time in her life and was resting, her head leaning against the worn leather of the seat and her eyes closed.

The car behind pulled out to overtake the Jeep but the traffic lights, already amber, turned red. Marianne could see the man mouthing a profanity. The F word. And the C word.

'That is well out of order,' said Marianne, glaring in the rear-view mirror.

When the lights turned green, Marianne floored the

accelerator. No response from the Jeep. Now the man pulled down his window, leaned out, shouting.

Marianne put on the handbrake and took off her seat belt. She rolled down her window. It stopped halfway so she had to push it with her hands to get it all the way down.

'What are you doing?' said Rita, opening her eyes.

'That man is being reprehensible,' said Marianne, kneeling on the seat.

'Does that mean he's being a dick?' said Rita, sitting up.

'Yes,' said Marianne.

'Well, why didn't you say so?' Rita unclipped her seat belt, rolled down her window, turned and kneeled on her seat. Then, like a pair of synchronised swimmers, Rita and Marianne leaned out of their windows at the same time, waited until they had the driver's full attention before extending their hands out as far as they would go with their middle fingers raised and rigid.

The man was purple with rage by the time he manoeuvred his car past them. He glared at the two women, hanging out of either side of the Jeep, and then spat at them, out his window as he drove by. But the wind was not in his favour. It caught the line of his spittle in mid-flight before flinging it back in his face. It landed in one of his furious eyes. Marianne and Rita cheered loudly.

The lights were red again.

Rita, her cheeks flushed pink, sat back in her seat and reached for the seat belt. Marianne did the same.

'You have to talk nice to it, remember?' Rita said.

Marianne leaned forward. 'Who's a lovely Jeep then?' she said, patting the dashboard. She turned the key in the ignition and stepped cautiously on the accelerator. The engine, old and tired and in need of a good deal of attention, wheezed and juddered but turned over. Eventually.

It felt triumphant and exhilarating. Like something extraordinary had happened. Marianne flung her hand out the window and gave a thumbs up sign to the unfortunate woman waiting patiently behind the Jeep, whose car was full to the brim with babies and toddlers, all of whom appeared to be crying. The woman had banana mashed into her fringe. In spite of that, she rewarded Marianne with an exhausted but warm smile.

The lights turned green.

Marianne drove on.

Chapter 34

Things kind of went back to normal after that. Not the normal that Marianne had once known. Long ago.

An Ancaire kind of normal.

The picking up and dropping off of the Get-Well-Sooners, for example. Freddy yelling, 'Go-go-go,' as he hurled himself into the Jeep ahead of his mother's steady but slow beeline towards them, with her mantilla of hair and her interminable air of injury. So far, Mrs Montgomery had made it as far as the driver's window only once, bending at the waist and peering inside at them like a drill sergeant carrying out a uniform inspection.

Carefully, Marianne lifted her hand from the steering wheel and waved and, from the back seat, Bartholomew and Ethel followed suit.

'Whatever you do, don't lower the window,' Freddy hissed at Marianne, without seeming to move his mouth. He was waving too. 'She'll invite you to tea and make you marry me.'

'What will I do?' hissed Marianne.

'Pull out slowly,' he instructed. Marianne did as she was bid, and in the rear-view mirror, she watched Mrs Montgomery straighten, her rigid eyes tracking the Jeep's ungainly progress up the road.

'She glared at everyone except me,' grumbled Bartholomew, when they were safely around the corner. 'She never so much as glanced at me.'

'Maybe she didn't see you, dear,' suggested Ethel.

'How could anyone not see Bartholomew?' said Freddy, pulling on his seat belt.

'That's offensive,' said Bartholomew.

'I just meant, you know, you're larger than life.'

'Do you think so?' said Bartholomew.

Freddy smiled shyly. 'I do.'

Then there were the meetings themselves, filled to bursting with all the ways Rita distracted them from themselves so that, when she presented Freddy with an '80 Today!' birthday badge to mark his 80th day of sobriety, everybody was surprised that so much time had passed.

'It's bad enough being fifty,' grumbled Freddy, reluctantly accepting the badge from Rita.

'You make fifty look fabulous,' said Bartholomew.

Freddy tensed, waiting for the punchline but none was forthcoming. He smiled and pinned the badge to his lapel.

Marianne made the various different types of tea, carefully divided the cakes and buns so that all pieces were of equal size and none was more equal than another.

Of Hugh, there was little sign. When he came to pick Rita up for one of her now twice-weekly hospital appointments, Marianne made herself scarce, usually behind the curtains in the drawing room.

'You can come out now,' Aunt Pearl said on one such occasion and Marianne had jumped so hard, she banged her elbow off the dado rail and it had throbbed for the rest of the afternoon.

'I . . . didn't see you there,' she said, emerging from behind the curtain, nursing her funny bone.

'Don't worry, he didn't see you there either,' said Aunt Pearl with a hint of amusement in her silvery-blue eyes.

'Who?' said Marianne, glancing about like a mime artist. She would never get past the first audition at Bartholomew's amateur dramatics society.

'He's a polite young man,' said Aunt Pearl. 'You could do worse.'

Marianne was stunned. Polite was the pinnacle of compliments, in the world according to Aunt Pearl.

And it was true. Hugh was polite. There was every chance he would never mention the . . . episode in his house. Marianne clenched every muscle in her body as she tried not to remember. But she mustn't have clenched hard enough because there it was, all laid out neatly for her, like numbers down the column of a spreadsheet.

'I don't want you to be gentle with me,' she'd said. 'I want you to have sex with me.'

She burned with shame. The bang of entitlement off that, Shirley would have said.

But it was nothing compared to Hugh's response. The way he looked at her. Disentangled himself from her. The way he pitied her. The way he said, 'No,' in his gentle voice, his attempt to take the sting of rejection out of it.

Marianne buried her face in whatever was to hand when she thought the thought: a cushion, a towel, the tea cosy and, that day, the heavy, unyielding curtains in the drawing room.

She tried to think the thought as seldom as possible. It wasn't as seldom as she would have liked.

She tried too not to think about Rita dying.

She never talked about Rita dying.

The Get-Well-Sooners did not talk about it either.

There were things to be done.

'Listen up, everyone,' said Rita, clapping her hands to get their attention at the end of tea-break one day. 'I have a Plan B for our eviction day protest.'

She had their attention. It seemed that Marianne was not the only one who appreciated a good Plan B.

'Not that we'll need it, of course,' said Rita airily. 'But just, you know, in case, I've come up with a plausible back-up plan.'

Even better than a Plan B was a plausible back-up plan. Marianne set the tray on the table and gave Rita her full attention.

Rita looked around, smiling her wicked smile at each of them in turn, which meant that her idea was either dangerous, ludicrous, illegal or all three.

'If all else fails,' she began, 'I intend to take my clothes off, climb onto Shirley's roof and protest from up there. Bartholomew, you can film me. You've got a really good camera on your phone, don't you?'

'Well, yes,' said Bartholomew, struggling to digest the news. 'But . . .'

'You can put it on the internet and I'll go . . . what do you call it when everyone likes and shares a video?'

'Oh, it's viral, dear,' said Ethel, delighted with herself.

Rita grinned. 'So it is, thank you, Ethel.'

Marianne said nothing. She was pretty sure she had heard correctly but there was a part of her – albeit small – that still harboured the hope that she had not.

'You haven't misheard me, by the way,' said Rita, looking at Marianne.

'Right,' said Marianne.

'Any questions?' asked Rita.

Nobody said anything.

'You probably want to know why I have to be naked,' said Rita in her helpful voice.

'To, eh, attract attention?' Freddy offered.

'Exactly, darling,' said Rita, with emphasis. 'I mean, one never sees images of women my age – seventy, let's face it – naked, does one?'

Nobody pointed out that Rita was seventy-eight.

'So that will garner a bit of attention, won't it?' she went on, smiling at them. 'And I'll refuse to come down. I'll chain myself to the chimney pot. I'll use one of the chains Patrick uses to lock his bicycle. They'd do, wouldn't they, Patrick?'

'I . . . I'd say so,' managed Patrick.

'That'll show them that we mean business, won't it?' Rita's cheeks were flushed with – premature and unlikely, Marianne felt – success. She did not look like someone who had cancer. Who was dying. Who would die.

'Yes,' said Marianne loudly. She was amazed at the

conviction in her voice. Perhaps she was wrong and she would be granted admission to Bartholomew's amateur dramatics society after all? 'It will indeed.'

'I knew you'd love that idea,' said Rita.

'Really?'

'Well, I knew you'd come round to it,' said Rita. 'Eventually.'

Marianne couldn't help smiling at her mother. She seemed like her old self again, buoyed up with enthusiasm that was as infectious as a tropical disease.

Chapter 35

It was nearly April and, while the mornings and nights remained cold and clear, the days were often bathed in bright, warm sunshine, lifting the temperature into unseasonal double digits.

'That's because of climate change,' said Sheldon in a disapproving tone, during the second week of good weather.

'Yipppeeee,' shrieked Harrison, doing a lap of the garden, with George trying his best to keep up.

Harrison and Sheldon took this meteorological improvement as an opportunity for Rita to make good on her promise to teach them to swim. They arrived at the Get Well Soon meeting the following Saturday with wetsuits under their football kit, and bright orange armbands, inflated fit to burst, clamped around their skinny arms.

'Ne'er cast a clout e're May is out,' Aunt Pearl intoned at them. The boys looked at her, confused, then attached themselves to either side of Rita like limpets.

'Please can you teach us today?' begged Sheldon, training his long, navy eyes on Rita and smiling his dimpled smile.

'Pretty please with fairy buns on top?' shouted Harrison, pumping his arms around his head like he was already in the water, attempting the butterfly stroke.

Rita looked at Shirley, who, right on cue, rolled her eyes and shook her head.

'I did promise them,' said Rita.

'They promised to put away their Lego yesterday and they still haven't done it,' said Shirley.

The boys got down on their muddy knees and pressed their palms together, raised them towards their mother. 'We promise we'll do it later,' said Sheldon.

'Or tomorrow,' added Harrison, with his adorable grin, which even Shirley couldn't resist.

'Oh, fine then,' she said. 'If it's okay with Rita.'

In the end, they all walked down to the beach. Bartholomew and Freddy headed the posse, which meant progress was slow as Freddy negotiated the treachery of the moss-slick steps. 'Oh, come on,' snapped Bartholomew, holding out his hand. 'I'll help you down.'

Freddy hesitated, then slipped his long, narrow hand into Bartholomew's short, fleshy one. 'Your hand is freezing,' Bartholomew huffed.

'Yours is lovely and warm,' said Freddy. Each of them seemed as surprised as the other by the admission.

'Hey! Mills and Boon,' Shirley shouted from behind them. 'Either get a room or get a move on.'

Bartholomew and Freddy managed to ignore her – a small triumph for both of them – and continued their careful way down the steps.

'Thank you, Bartholomew,' said Freddy when they reached the bottom. His voice was quieter than usual. Formal.

'My pleasure, Freddy,' said Bartholomew, in a similar tone.

Rita was herded down the steps by Harrison and Sheldon. Patrick placed himself in front of Rita and matched her pace without seeming to, ready to catch her if she fell.

Even Aunt Pearl came, wearing her usual high-collared blouse, A-line skirt, thick flesh-coloured tights, and sturdy brown leather lace-ups. To this she had added her outdoor apparel of a scarf around her head, tightly knotted beneath the point of her chin and her grey gaberdine coat that ended exactly one inch below the hem of her skirt.

'Do you really think you should be swimming in your condition?' Pearl said when she reached the bottom of the steps.

Rita laughed. 'Of course not,' she said.

Pearl nearly smiled.

Ethel put one tiny foot on the first step, hesitated, then managed to lift the other one on. She stood there, swaying in the gentle breeze. Marianne couldn't bear to watch. 'You should probably link somebody,' she said.

'Oh, thank you, my dear,' said Ethel, hooking her narrow arm around Marianne's. 'It would be such a nuisance if I broke my other hip.'

Marianne tightened her grip.

On the beach, the boys tore off their football shorts and jerseys, used their toes to push down the backs of their runners, then kicked them off their feet.

'I'll untie my laces later, Mam,' said Harrison before

Shirley had a chance to roar at them. They ran for the water's edge, their arms and legs pumping like pistons. They shrieked at the shock of the cold water, retreated, ran in again, jumped over the waves, Harrison making sure he jumped as high as his brother each time.

Rita was already in the water, in her polka-dot bikini with matching swim hat. She was floating on her back. Marianne tried hard not to think about what happened the last time.

She tried hard not to think about how sick Rita was. She had said little about it because, Rita insisted, there was little to say.

She was sick.

She would stay at Ancaire for as long as she could. She had one of those brilliant morphine dispensers, she said. Easy as pie, she said. 'And then,' she said, 'when I feel like it, I'll go to the hospice.'

When she felt like it. As if it was a matter of choosing the day.

She had already spoken to the nurses who would attend to her.

'There's something very special about hospice nurses,' she told Marianne after her visit. 'I'm nearly looking forward to it. Also, the food is to die for.'

She chuckled at her gallows humour.

Rita was using George to teach the boys how to swim.

'Look how George does the doggy paddle,' she told them.

'He's very good at it,' said Sheldon.

Marianne, dodging waves at the water's edge, agreed. She could feel the warmth of the sun on her shoulders, how it sparkled across the surface of the water, lighting the top of the waves, curling towards shore, to a brilliant white.

'Look, Marnie,' shouted Harrison, standing on his toes and waving his arms to attract her attention. 'I can swim underwater now.' He bent down and dipped his face in and out of the sea.

'Did you see me?' he shouted, his eyes still clenched shut.

'Yes,' Marianne shouted back. 'That's . . . good.'

'Good?' said Shirley, appearing at Marianne's side, her ferocious eyebrows knitting together, thick as one of Rita's homemade Aran jumpers.

'I mean . . . that's great, Harrison,' Marianne shouted again and Shirley whacked Marianne's arm, a thump of camaraderie Marianne now knew, even though it smarted quite a bit. She pushed Shirley away – another of Shirley's ways of communicating camaraderie – and Shirley stumbled backwards and fell over Ethel's fold-up stool, which she took everywhere now. 'I used it in the post office the other day,' Ethel told them last week. 'The queue was ever so long.'

Shirley face-planted into the sand.

'Shirley?' Marianne ran over, kneeled beside her. 'Sorry, I . . . I didn't mean to push you so hard.' Shirley's shoulders were shaking. Marianne put her hand on her shoulder. 'Shirley? Please don't cry, I'm really sor—'

'Did your mother never tell you to play nice?' said Shirley, laughing as she sat up and spat sand out of her mouth.

'There was never any need, to be honest,' said Marianne.

'I find that hard to believe.' Shirley held out her hand and Marianne took it, pulled her up, brushed sand off her face.

'Come in, Marnie,' shouted Rita, waving at her. 'The water is so clear today.'

'And freezing,' said Marianne.

'Exhilarating,' corrected Rita. 'And don't worry about not having togs, darling,' she added. 'I brought that pair I got for you. They're in my basket.'

Harrison and Sheldon appeared, dripping, on either side of Marianne. 'Marnie, come and see us doing the doggy paddle,' said Sheldon.

'We're even better than George now,' said Harrison, gazing up at her, his small head tipped back. 'Will you come into the water? Pretty please with chocolate milk on top?'

Marianne shook her head. 'Sorry, boys,' she said. 'I can't swim.'

They looked at her with shocked faces.

'But you're an adult,' Sheldon eventually said. 'Adults can do everything.'

'Not all of them,' Marianne felt duty-bound to explain, even though it felt like she was letting the boys down in some real way.

'My mam can do everything,' said Harrison.

'Well, maybe she can get in with you,' said Marianne.

'She's got her periods,' Sheldon said.

'I used to call them my *ladies*,' piped up Ethel. She picked off a piece of fluff that had attached to her lip from the woollen scarf, wound several times around her neck.

'Please, Marnie?' The boys looked at Marianne with their endless, pleading eyes. Marianne wanted to tell them that she had her period too, except she didn't, and also she couldn't bring herself to say 'period' out loud in public.

Instead, she said, 'I'm scared.'

That seemed to shock the boys even more than her admission that she couldn't swim.

Flo hadn't been scared of anything so Marianne had been scared enough for the both of them.

'Come in, Marianne,' Flo used to say. 'The water's lovely.'

'I prefer it here,' Marianne always said, standing at the edge.

It was easier to remain vigilant on dry land.

'I'm not scared of anything,' declared Harrison.

'You are so,' Sheldon told him. 'You're scared of the lollipop lady.'

Harrison looked worried. 'She has witch hands.'

Marianne looked out to sea. The water was calm today, the surface like a mirror, reflecting the innocent blue of the sky dotted with small white clouds, like drawings of nursery rhyme sheep. And Rita, beckoning her in.

'It's not cold,' she called, 'once you get used to it.'

The boys looked up at Marianne. One more 'No' would do it, Marianne thought. They were on the verge of giving up on her.

Instead, she said, 'Okay.'

The boys cheered and raced back into the sea to tell Rita.

'Those fellas would make great scientologists,' said Shirley, as Marianne rummaged in Rita's basket. 'They'd persuade anyone to do anything.'

Marianne changed into the pale pink togs Rita had brought for her.

'They're so pretty,' Ethel told her, pouring soup from a flask Rita had brought.

'You're a bit white and hairy,' said Shirley, looking Marianne up and down, 'but apart from that, you look . . . quite nice. For your age.'

'Careful Shirley-girl,' boomed Bartholomew from his vantage point up the beach where he and Freddy appeared to be collecting shells. 'You don't want to give her a big head.'

Freddy laughed.

'You want to come over here and say that?' said Shirley, and they stopped laughing and moved further up the beach.

Marianne inched into the sea. Rita had been wrong. The water was not exhilarating. It was freezing. The shock of it took her breath away. Not just took it away it but reefed it out of her mouth, pitched it into the air. She worried that she might hyperventilate. Or get hypothermia. She wondered if any of them would know what to do if that happened.

Further down the beach, she saw Patrick lifting a clump of seaweed, feeling it, smelling it.

She was somewhat reassured. Patrick would know what to do.

She looked down. The water was green. Clear. Marianne could see her feet, planted and solid, white against the dark sand.

A crab scuttled up to her and she curled her toes in case it attacked her foot with one of its long, lethal claws. But it moved past her, heading out to sea with a dogged type of enthusiasm.

Marianne stepped a little further out. The water was up to her knees now. She struggled to get her breathing under control.

'Go on, dear,' Ethel, wrapped up like a pass-the-parcel, called from the perch of her fold-up stool. 'You can do it.'

Marianne tried to smile, but her features were frozen in place. She waved instead. Ethel waved back.

Marianne steeled herself and took two long strides. The water was surging around her thighs now. Further out, she could see the boys and George, playing a complicated game of fetch, which George was winning. He really was an excellent swimmer.

Rita was watching her. 'Are you all right?' she yelled.

'Of course I'm not all right,' shouted Marianne.

'What's taking you so long, Marnie?' called Harrison, he and Sheldon bobbing on the surface like buoys.

'I'm coming,' she called back, taking another tentative step out. To her left, she could see the island, Rockabill, the sun glinting against the white of the lighthouse perched there. The water was swirling around her waist now and her blood pounded around her veins, thumped at the back of her throat. She swallowed hard. She bent her knees and let the water reach her shoulders, then shot up again, gasping with the shock of the water. 'It's baltic,' she shouted.

'It's like soup after a while,' said Rita, coming towards her, towing Harrison and Sheldon along by their shoulders as they lay on their backs.

'Look at us, Marnie,' shouted Sheldon.

'We're floating,' added Harrison so there could be no doubt.

'I'd say you could do it too,' said Sheldon, although there was an element of uncertainty in his tone that Marianne felt was warranted.

'Course she could,' said Rita, setting the boys on their feet and turning towards Marianne.

'I don't think I . . .'

'That's right,' said Rita, putting her arm around Marianne's back. 'You don't think it. You feel it.'

The boys cheered and clapped as Marianne leaned back. Beneath her, she felt Rita's arm under her knees, felt her legs lift through the water until she was horizontal, the water lapping around the circle of her face. 'Don't let go,' she gasped.

'I won't,' said Rita.

'Are you still scared, Marnie?' asked Harrison, clinging onto Rita's shoulder and staring down at Marianne.

'Yes,' said Marianne.

'Stretch your arms and legs out,' instructed Rita. 'Like a starfish.'

Marianne did as she was told. The boys laughed and beat the water with their hands. Their excitement was infectious. She wanted them to see that she could do it. Or that she was at least willing to try. 'What do I do now?'

'You float,' said Rita.

'How?'

'You'll see.'

'What do you mean?'

'I'll let go and . . .'

'No, wait,' shouted Marianne. 'I'm not ready.'

'You let me know when you are,' Rita said.

Marianne could still feel Rita's arms beneath her, keeping her up. She opened her eyes. She hadn't realised they'd been closed. Her mother's face came into focus. The gunmetal blue of her eyes, the concerned furrows along her forehead, her tongue trapped between her teeth.

'You look nervous,' said Marianne.

Rita shook her head. 'No,' she said. 'I was just . . . I wish I'd taught you this years ago.'

'You did try,' said Marianne.

'I should have tried harder.'

Marianne exhaled. 'I think I'm ready,' she said.

Rita let go.

Marianne held her breath and squeezed her eyes shut. She listened to the sounds. The boys shrieking and splashing. The lament of a curlew, moving out to sea. The soft lap of the water against her body.

She was floating. When a part of her body began to submit to the pull of the water, she gently moved it and there she was, floating again.

She opened her eyes a slit. Then wider. Everything was as before. Except now, she was floating. Rita smiled at her and lifted her arms out of the water. 'You're doing it, Marnie,' she said.

Marianne smiled back. 'I know,' she said. She was filled with a potent mix of feelings. Hope was one. The hope that, for her and Rita, there might be other days like this.

A resigned sort of sadness too.

The knowledge that, for her and Rita, there wouldn't be many.

Chapter 36

M arianne and Rita fell into the habit of sitting in the glasshouse most afternoons. Even on days when the sun was weak and faltering, ducking between clouds, it managed to penetrate through the glass and provide a warmth that felt personal, like a service laid on just for them.

The fine weather continued throughout April, and that afternoon, Marianne was persuaded to take off her anorak. She spotted herself in one of the panes of glass and, for a moment, was confused by her own reflection. That sensation of knowing someone from somewhere but being unable to put your finger on who. Or where.

She laughed.

'What's funny?' asked Rita.

'Nothing,' said Marianne. 'I was just noticing my rig-out.'

She was wearing one of Rita's silk skirts: the plainest one she could find, which wasn't as plain as she might have liked, being mostly pink with complicated swirls of orange, purple, and green. The skirt was too big so Marianne had tucked her T-shirt inside the waistband and borrowed one of Patrick's leather belts to keep everything in place. She slotted her bare feet into runners and left her hair down, tucking as much of it as she could manage behind her ears so she could see out.

'You look lovely,' Rita told her.

'I put my tracksuits in the twin-tub and forgot to turn it on yesterday,' said Marianne.

'You should do that more often,' said Rita.

Rita sat down on one of the two deck chairs Patrick had taken from the shed and cleaned, when Rita initially expressed a desire to sit inside the glasshouse and absorb the sun.

Marianne went to make afternoon tea.

Afternoon tea was another of the rituals that had developed. Today it was mint tea – made with mint from Patrick's kitchen garden – and a plate of Rita's lemon melts.

Of all the treats her mother made, lemon melts remained Marianne's favourite. There was a strict process in how she ate them that she was powerless to change. She began by manoeuvring the entire lemon melt into her mouth, placing it gently on her tongue. Then, she made herself wait until the pastry and the curd softened, dissolved on her tongue. She only allowed herself to chew when the entire concoction was in danger of melting away. She did the same with the second one. Washed them down with tea. When her tongue roamed the inside of her mouth for leftovers, she tasted the tartness of the lemon. The sweetness of the pastry.

She ate each one the same way, every time.

In the glasshouse, Rita watched Marianne's ritual with amusement. 'Here,' she said, rummaging in her handbag and handing Marianne a crumpled piece of paper. 'I've written down the recipe for you.'

It was an electricity bill. On the back, Rita's elaborate handwriting with instructions and even an illustration of how to rub the butter into the flour.

'Pastry should be handled as little as possible,' she said, pointing to the picture. 'So only use the tips of your fingers to do it.'

'They won't taste as good as yours,' said Marianne.

'They will,' said Rita, 'eventually.'

They leaned back in their deck chairs, closed their eyes and absorbed the sun like solar panels.

They never talked about death. About dying. Marianne sometimes forgot about it. She put that down to Rita herself, who seemed, in the main, her usual larger-than-life self, in her flamboyant rig-outs, talking in her rapid, clipped voice that was always louder than it needed to be.

It seemed impossible that she had cancer. That she was dying. That she would die.

'I spoke to the policewoman who . . . arrested me,' said Marianne then. 'On the phone yesterday.'

'Oh, yes,' said Rita. 'Karen, isn't it? A dote. How did her daughter get on in the mocks? She was a bag of nerves, apparently.'

'I . . . I don't know, she didn't say.'

'Well, what did she say?'

'She said there was a good chance I could do an addiction counselling course. That it could count as my community service.'

'Would you like that?' said Rita, sitting up and studying Marianne's face.

'I'm not talking about the Get Well Soon programme, obviously,' Marianne said in a rush. 'But just, you know, it could be an area I might be interested in getting involved with at some point in the—'

'I think you'd be brilliant, Marnie,' said Rita, setting her cup on the ground so she could clap her hands. 'When?'

'There's a course starting in September,' said Marianne.

'September is great for fresh starts,' said Rita.

Neither of them mentioned how unlikely this was, for Rita, at least.

Marianne stood up. 'Do you want some more tea?'

'I know you're just going to get another lemon melt,' said Rita.

'I am.'

Rita reclined on the deck chair and closed her eyes.

'Are you tired?' asked Marianne.

'I'm happy,' said Rita, smiling.

'Why?'

'I'm glad you came home,' said Rita.

'I didn't have much choice,' said Marianne.

'I know,' said Rita. 'But I'm glad all the same.'

Marianne made a great performance of gathering up their cups and plates and setting them on the tray. She walked with purpose to the door of the glasshouse, opened it, then stopped.

'I'm glad, too,' she said, before she opened the door and walked away.

In the kitchen, she washed the muck off the mint and put the leaves into the teapot, waited for the kettle to boil and put the last two lemon melts on the plate. Beside her, she could feel George's breath, warm against her leg. She trailed a hand down to his head, scratched him behind his ears the way he liked it. His tail thumped against the door of the press and it was such a happy sound, Marianne was compelled to squat down beside him, use both her hands to pull gently at his ears and whisper into his coarse fur, to tell him what a good dog he was. The rhythm of his tail, beating against the wood, quickened.

'You know he can't understand you, don't you?' Aunt Pearl said as she swept into the kitchen.

Marianne straightened and smiled. 'I used to agree with you but I'm not so sure any more,' she said. 'I think it's his eyebrows. They're so . . . expressive.'

Aunt Pearl shook her head and tutted. 'I thought you were the one person in this family who spoke a bit of sense, Marianne.'

'Me, too,' said Marianne, pouring water into the teapot. Behind her, she sensed Pearl eyeing up the lemon melts. Even she was powerless in their presence. She hated that about herself and only ate one when she knew nobody was watching.

Marianne picked up the tray, moved towards the back kitchen.

'If you and Rita are going to the graveyard this afternoon, make sure you take an umbrella,' Aunt Pearl called after her. 'It looks pleasant now but it's going to turn.'

'Thanks,' said Marianne, using her elbow to release the door handle.

That was another habit they had fallen into. The walk along the cliff to the graveyard, if Rita was feeling up to it. Marianne brought scissors so she could trim the grass if it needed a trim, and Rita sat on the blanket Marianne brought in her bag. They didn't speak about Flo and Marianne was glad about that. It was peaceful there, the only sounds the distant murmur of the sea far below and the soft coo of the wood pigeons, perched in pairs along the budding branches of the sycamore tree. And the tree itself, like a celebration of spring, a yearning for summer, with its pale green buds swelling along the branches, the shy tips of leaves, gold where the sun glanced against them, making their way out into the world.

Marianne walked into the garden, past the kitchen window. In her peripheral vision, she could see Aunt Pearl, reaching her hand towards the plate that Marianne had set on the counter with the last lemon melt placed irresistibly in the middle of it.

Aunt Pearl ate the biscuit the same way Marianne did, guiding all of it into her mouth, doing her best to wait before biting, savouring the sensation of the pastry and curd melting on her tongue.

She licked her lips when it was over.

Marianne smiled as she made her way towards the glasshouse, even though the plate on the tray now held only one solitary lemon melt. Still, Rita might agree to share it.

As soon as Marianne stepped inside the glasshouse, she knew.

Rita was where she had left her, lying along the soft curve of the deck chair. She looked peaceful, as if she was asleep. There were the remnants of her earlier smile about her face. A ghost of a smile.

Marianne set the tray on the floor and sat in the deck

chair beside Rita's. She took her hand, held it in her own. It was warm and soft. She closed her eyes. Listened. Through the glass, everything was muffled. Donal, braying for oats, and Declan, crowing his ragged crow as if it was the break of day and not the afternoon. Marianne thought she should know what time it was. Weren't people supposed to know? She lay there with her eyes closed, holding Rita's hand.

She wondered if Rita heard what she had said before she left. 'I'm glad, too.'

She hoped so.

She was glad. That she'd said it.

Out loud.

Chapter 37

R ita left strict instructions.

There was to be no crying.

Instead, there should be singing and dancing.

The wearing of black would not be tolerated. Colours, she wrote in her funeral instructions. Let there be colours. And there were.

The funeral was to take place at Ancaire. There were to be no eulogies and absolutely no open coffin. 'I might not be looking my best,' Rita had written on her list of instructions.

Ancaire felt colder than usual. Aunt Pearl had insisted on flinging open the windows to give the house a good airing before the funeral guests arrived.

Quieter, too. Marianne had never known the house to be so quiet. Even with the wind from the sea whistling through the windows, rattling the frames, Ancaire was quiet. Subdued. As if it were straining to hear the clatter of Rita's heels down the stairs. Or Patrick, hammering away at a rogue piece of wood somewhere in the house.

But Patrick had not stepped inside Ancaire since Marianne had told him. She couldn't remember what she had said exactly but she probably hadn't said it right. Used the wrong words. It was hard to know which words to use. Marianne had never known, when it came to Patrick. She had been too busy resenting him.

For being the perfect son.

And Rita, for being the perfect mother.

The Get-Well-Sooners were the first to arrive. They filed out of Hugh's taxi and gathered around Marianne. She closed her eyes and breathed them in. Even Bartholomew's Paco Rabanne was restrained. Ethel, in a lilac wool suit and pillbox hat, and a handbag dangling from the crook of her elbow that seemed slighter than ever today, dabbed at her eyes with the corner of a delicately embroidered handkerchief. 'My dear, brave girl,' she said, patting Marianne's arm. Marianne put her hand on Ethel's bony hand, squeezed gently.

'If you cry, Ethel, so will I,' said Bartholomew, already weeping into his pocket square. Marianne looked at him, almost blinded by his cerise-pink three-piece suit and rainbow-coloured dicky bow. 'You look magnificent,' she told him.

'It's not *de trop*?' said Bartholomew in a tear-sodden voice.

'Rita would have loved it,' said Marianne, hugging him.

Freddy, pale and gaunt in a *Les Misérables* T-shirt under a navy corduroy jacket with the obligatory leather patches at the elbows, did not rush to confirm that Bartholomew's outfit was indeed *de trop*. In fact, he did not say anything. Marianne straightened his glasses. 'Day one hundred and twelve,' she told him, smiling.

'Is it?' he said.

'It is,' insisted Marianne. 'Rita would be very proud of you.'

'You don't look as shabby as usual,' said Shirley, reefing herself out of a leather jacket to reveal a yellow and orange tie-dye T-shirt, which she wore as a dress, gathered at the waist with a school tie. Marianne waited for her to say, 'No offence' but she didn't.

It was true that Marianne had dressed up for the occasion. Another of Rita's instructions.

No leisurewear.

Marianne had taken that to mean tracksuits and had also taken it to mean, specifically, her.

'How many times did you wash it?' Shirley asked Marianne, nodding at the dress she had brought over yesterday. It was not something Marianne would have picked, being delicate in a pale yellow silk sort of way. Also short-sleeved and scoop-necked, the bodice fitted to her waist, the skirt falling just past her knees. It swished about her body when she twirled. Which she didn't do, since it was a funeral, although she had a feeling that Rita would have included twirling on her list of instructions if it had occurred to her.

'Twice,' admitted Marianne. Shirley rolled her eyes. 'I told you the charity shop washes all the clothes before they sell them.'

'I know, but . . .'

'And you owe me a tenner.'

'Right.'

'And it's shit, by the way. Rita being dead.' Shirley's voice seemed to teeter along the words. She clenched her eyes shut, her eyelashes long and spiky and laden down with mascara. She looked impossibly young then, like a child who was lost on an unfamiliar road. Marianne didn't think she could bear it if Shirley cried. She clenched her fist and punched Shirley's arm.

'That hurt,' said Shirley, opening her long navy eyes and glaring at Marianne.

'I'm really sorry, I—'

'Just fucking with you,' said Shirley, grinning and thumping Marianne back.

They moved inside the house and Marianne waited at the door for Hugh, who had parked his car round the back and was walking towards her now, flanked by Harrison and Sheldon, in matching black leather jackets over the Irish football strip. Their skin was pink from a recent and, Marianne guessed, vigorous scrubbing by their mother.

Harrison ran when he saw Marianne, stopped in front of her and looked up, his blond mohawk glinting gold in the sun. 'Mam told me to say I'm sorry but I haven't even done anything yet,' he said, his long, navy eyes intense with indignation.

Marianne crouched in front of him. 'Did you bring your football?' she asked.

Sheldon ran up the steps. 'It's in Hugh's car,' he said, 'But Mam said we shouldn't . . .'

'Rita left instructions,' Marianne told them. 'You have to play football after lunch.'

'Bagsy not goalie,' shouted Harrison, kicking off his

football boots before charging into the house. Sheldon rolled his eyes.

Marianne watched them skid down the hall in their football socks, glad of their energetic noise.

'You look lovely,' Hugh said, arriving on the doorstep. 'Not your usual uniform.'

'Rita's orders, I'm afraid,' said Marianne, turning towards him, conscious suddenly of the softness of the silk, glancing against her bare legs. 'You look . . . nice, too,' she said, nodding briskly at him.

He wore a suit jacket over his shirt and his tie was straight and arranged in a Windsor knot. His kilt was purple and green tartan today. Rita's favourite colours. Marianne assumed these facts were not unrelated and she felt a rush of warmth flood through her and she was grateful that Rita had such friends.

She put her hand out to shake his and he took it and held it, and it was so tender, the way he held it. She thought she might break in two with the tenderness of it. She was suddenly exhausted. She wondered what it might be like to lean against him. Just for a moment. She could breathe him in and feel somehow invigorated. Or maybe not invigorated. But able. Able for the rest of the day.

She hadn't intended to actually do it but there she was, all of a sudden, her forehead against his shoulder, leaning against him. She was mortified but not mortified enough to stop. Hugh put his arm around her and she stood still and closed her eyes and leaned. It was warm there, in the circle of his arm. Warm enough to sleep. Today, he smelled of the sea, a salty tang about him. She could feel the hard clench of her muscles stretch and yield.

'I'm so sorry for your loss, Marianne,' he whispered into her hair.

She nodded. 'I'm sorry for yours.'

Marianne stepped away from him then, tucked a strand of hair that had escaped from the gigantic bun at the back of her head behind her ear, cleared her throat. In his hand, a bunch of . . . she leaned closer. 'Are they thistles?' she asked.

'Aye,' he said, grinning. 'They're prickly but very beautiful. Rita loved them.' On top of each stiff spine was a tuft of dark pink petals and Marianne had to admit that the contrast was very pleasing to the eye.

'How are you managing?' he asked.

She shrugged. 'I've been mostly making sandwiches.'

'I make a mean cheese and pickle,' he said.

Marianne set him up in the kitchen with a wooden board, a pan of bread, a block of cheddar, and a jar of pickle.

'I do enjoy watching men do menial tasks,' said Aunt Pearl, admiring him from behind.

She had surprised Marianne by being helpful. 'Just because I don't cook doesn't mean I can't,' she remarked, stirring an enormous vat of soup. 'Roast butternut squash,' she proclaimed. 'It was Rita's favourite.' She stopped stirring for a moment and closed her eyes. Marianne thought perhaps it was her use of the past tense. Something so definitive about it. So unchangeable. Then she collected herself and nodded at Marianne. 'That bread is not going to butter itself, you know,' she said, nodding to a vast cake of wheaten bread she had baked earlier.

The house began to fill.

Marianne could not believe how many people managed to fit in the drawing room at Ancaire where Rita had requested the funeral take place. 'Spare me your man-made gods,' she had told the local parish priest and vicar whenever she came across them at various fêtes and fundraisers. 'I'll take my chances with Mother Nature.'

Both of them had come. Both of them had adored her.

So many people from so many places, all of them with their Rita stories. How she had touched them in her own, peculiar, insistent way.

When the drawing room had accommodated as many people as it could, Marianne opened the double doors into the dining room and they overflowed in there until that room, too, was full to bursting.

And still, they came.

Marianne was glad of them. They gave her something to do. She took their coats and made them tea and listened to their Rita stories, nodded when they told her how like her mother she was, buttered more bread, made more sandwiches, made more tea, put away more coats, listened to more stories.

Back in the kitchen, she met Shirley, who was taking Sheldon and Harrison to the beach in an effort to distract them from the coffin. 'I wish I hadn't told them that Rita was inside it,' she said to Marianne, grabbing their jackets off the hooks in the back kitchen. 'I caught them trying to open it. Sheldon was going to throw in a few fairy buns and Harrison had drawn a picture of hell with "Do not enter" in big, red letters. I should never have sent them to the national school.'

'I won't die, Mammy, won't I not?' asked Harrison,

skidding to a stop in front of Shirley and sticking his arms out so she could thread them through the sleeves of his jacket.

'Not if I don't fecken murder you first,' said Shirley, zipping him up before kissing the tip of his nose.

It wasn't until later, through the kitchen window that Marianne saw Patrick, sitting on a stool outside his workshop. He was so still, he might have been carved of wood.

'Can you manage here for a while?' she asked Aunt Pearl, who was rinsing the dregs of lemon meringue pie out of bowls at the sink.

'I've been managing here since before you were born, Marianne,' she said.

Marianne pulled on Rita's old Aran cardigan and headed out the back door. The grass was soggy underfoot with the recent rain and she had to run to prevent her runners sinking into the mud. George ran after her, and Donal and Gerard eyed her cautiously as she flew past them. She was out of breath when she arrived at the workshop.

'Patrick,' she said. 'There you are.' She stepped closer to him. 'I've been wondering where you'd gotten to. Everybody has. Agnes, too. She's at the house, you know.'

Patrick did not respond. He sat there, still, his eyes fixed on something beyond her.

'Patrick?'

He wore a pair of jeans and a thin T-shirt. Along his arms, goose bumps rose and his lips were tinged blue with the cold.

'Come on,' said Marianne. 'You're freezing. I'll make you some tea.'

Patrick shook his head. 'I'm not cold,' he said.

Marianne squatted down in front of him, took his hands in hers. They were like icicles. She rubbed them between hers. 'You are cold,' she said. 'You just can't feel it. You're in shock.' He shook his head again. Marianne could hear his teeth chattering in his mouth. 'We're going to the graveyard soon,' she said, as gently as she could.

Patrick stood up so suddenly, the stool tumbled back, rolled away. 'I'm not going there,' he said. There was a ragged edge to his voice. Marianne wished for Rita then. She would know what to say. How to say it. She had always known, when it came to Patrick.

'You don't have to,' said Marianne. 'I just thought . . . you might like to, you know? It's supposed to be good for . . . closure.' She couldn't believe she'd used that word. It was such a Rita word. Patrick shook his head.

In the end, Marianne took his arm and led him inside the workshop, up the stairs, into his apartment. She guided him into an armchair, took off her Aran cardigan and wrapped it around his shoulders. She turned on a lamp, switched on the heating, boiled the kettle. He sat there and let her do all those things without saying a word. He accepted the mug of tea she handed him. 'Wrap your fingers around that,' she said. 'It'll warm you.' He held the cup so that the steam rose and curled around his face. Marianne thought that was a good sign.

'If you change your mind . . .' she began.

'I won't change my mind,' he said.

Rita had always said Patrick was her brother but Marianne had been too angry feel that connection.

Perhaps it was too late to feel it now?

Back in the kitchen at Ancaire, Bartholomew was comfort

eating the last of the sandwiches, keeping a watchful eye out for Aunt Pearl, who often cited gluttony as the most heinous of the seven deadly sins.

'Have you seen Freddy?' Marianne asked him.

He pointed to his bulging mouth and she waited for him to swallow. 'I saw him in the drawing room earlier,' he said when he'd managed to empty his mouth. 'But that was ages ago. He's barely looked at me, let alone issued one of his caustic comments. I'm worried about him.' Bartholomew lifted another sandwich and pushed most of it into his mouth.

Marianne hurried out of the kitchen. She too had seen Freddy earlier, standing in a circle of people, looking dazed. Not even pretending to listen to their conversation. He seemed preoccupied, as if there was an argument going on inside his head and he was on the losing side.

She found him in Rita's studio, sitting on the floor by the window and in his hand was a full bottle of single malt whiskey. On the floor beside him, a crystal glass, empty. He looked up when she walked in, pushed his glasses up his nose and smiled as if he had been expecting her. He raised the bottle. 'Turns out you were all right about me,' he said. 'I am an alcoholic.'

Marianne approached him slowly, sat on the floor beside him, took his free hand and held it in hers.

Freddy shook the bottle so that the amber liquid swirled around inside it. 'I was trying to convince myself that I'll just drink today, you know? Because of the day that's in it. Nobody would blame me. It's what people do, isn't it? At funerals.' He sighed a long, shaky sigh, looked at Marianne. 'But then I realised that if I do, I'll drink tomorrow too, and the day after that and all the rest of the days. I won't be able to stop.'

'It's good that you know,' Marianne said. 'It's better to know.'

'I don't see why,' said Freddy. 'I feel exactly the same.'

'No you don't,' said Marianne, gently.

'What do you mean?' asked Freddy.

'You know what I mean,' said Marianne, and Freddy leaned against her and sighed.

'So now I'm an alcoholic and I'm gay,' he said. 'And Rita is gone. It's just . . . it's so unfair.'

Marianne put her arm around him.

'It's too hard,' said Freddy, his voice muffled against her arm. 'Why does it have to be so hard?'

'If it was easy, everybody would be doing it,' said Marianne.

Freddy lifted his head and smiled then. 'You sound just like your mother,' he said.

'Well, there's worse ways to sound, I suppose,' said Marianne.

They sat there like that for a while. Marianne could see her breath when she breathed out. She was glad of the warmth of Freddy's body, beside her.

'My bottom's gone numb,' said Freddy after a while.

Marianne scrambled up and hauled Freddy to his feet. 'Day one hundred and twelve,' he said, handing the bottle to Marianne. He pushed his shoulders back, did his best to swell his narrow chest.

'Day one hundred and twelve,' said Marianne, brushing specks of plaster that had drifted from the ceiling off the shoulders of his jacket.

It wasn't until they were at the graveyard that Marianne knew that her mother was gone.

She had known it before then – of course she had – but the knowledge had been theoretical in the main.

The graveyard brought everything into sharp focus.

She supposed it was because there was nothing else to do but watch Rita's wicker coffin being lowered into the ground. No sandwiches to make, no kettles to boil, no stories to listen to, no names to remember.

It was just Marianne, standing still and watching her mother being lowered into the ground, beside her sister. The deep, wide gash in the earth, the soil dark and glistening where it had been turned. She thought that some day, when the earth had been restored and the grass had returned, she might feel comforted by the idea that Flo and Rita and William were together. That they had each other.

But not today.

She shivered in the damp air, the sky overhead seeming to lower in the gloaming. Freddy and Bartholomew, on either side of her, put their arms around her shoulders. Ethel and Shirley, standing behind her, slipped their hands into her frozen ones. Sheldon and Harrison were playing chasing around the headstones and it was a mark of the day that Shirley did not admonish them in her loud, expletive-ridden way. It fell to Aunt Pearl – who disapproved of all children in general and of Sheldon and Harrison in particular – to reprimand them, which she did by hissing at them. This stopped them in their tracks as surely as if they'd been frozen in place.

Of Patrick, there was no sign.

Afterwards, the handshaking. Marianne was not a fan of handshaking. All those germs.

'You have to do it,' said Aunt Pearl. 'People want to pay their respects.' She snapped on a pair of black leather gloves. 'I'll assist.'

Marianne did what she was told. Every time she looked up, the line seemed longer than before. People didn't just want to pay their respects. They wanted to tell their Rita stories.

'Hello, Marianne.'

She looked up. Standing by the gate with his hands in the pockets of a black overcoat that seemed two sizes too big for him, was Brian.

'Can you manage on your own for a few minutes?' said Marianne to Aunt Pearl, who glared at Brian before nodding grimly. 'Two minutes,' she said.

Brian looked exhausted, his face wan and the skin dark and puffy beneath his eyes. They stood in front of each other for a moment and it was Marianne in the end who took charge of the situation. She put her arms around him and did her best to hug him. Had the frame of his body always been so slight? He felt like a bag of bones between her arms. She was pretty sure she could sling him over her shoulder and run the length of the beach with him without breaking a sweat.

'I'm so sorry, Marianne.'

'You're good to come.'

'Was she sick long?'

'It was quick in the end.'

It sounded like all the conversations that had gone before. Like lines learned off by heart.

Surely she and Brian should have a different script?

'You look . . . Are you okay?' said Marianne.

Brian shook his head and drew his hand down one side of his face. Marianne could hear the scratch of unattended stubble. 'Yeah, I'm fine, I'm just . . . I haven't had much sleep lately. The babies are colicky.'

'Colicky?' Marianne thought it sounded like a made-up word.

'Let's not talk about it,' said Brian. 'I'm so tired of talking about colic and nappy rash and cradle cap and wind and the texture of stools, I . . . Sorry, Marianne, it's just the tiredness. I'm like a bag of cats. Did you know that sleep deprivation is one of the most effective torture methods? I'd go a step further and say it's the most effective one. I mean, the twins are great, don't get me wrong, but sometimes, I honestly think I'd give one away in exchange for eight hours' sleep. But no, no, of course, I'm only joking. Well, not joking exactly, this is not a place to joke. I know that. This is a funeral. Your mother's funeral. I'm so sorry, Marianne. Did I say that already? Don't mind me. Just . . . you talk now. Tell me how you are. How are you? How are you doing?' Marianne had never heard Brian say so much in one go. His words tumbled out, one after the other with no pauses or intonation. A flatline of speech. His eyes were glassy and unfocused.

He had the eyes of a dead person. And his breath. Damp and gastric. Marianne took a step back. Brian looked at her. Really looked at her. She could not ever remember being so scrutinised by him. 'You look amazing,' he said, his dead eyes wider now, the better to see her. 'It's . . .' His dead eyes roved around her face, her person. 'It's your hair. And your face. You're glowing. You're not pregnant, are you?'

'Brian!'

'Sorry, sorry, sorry, I keep being inappropriate, my boss called me in the other day to tell me I had parked in the CFO's spot. Can you imagine?'

Marianne shook her head. Brian clenched his dead eyes shut. When he opened them again, they were watery as well as bloodshot and Marianne was terrified that he might cry. She had never seen him cry and suspected that he might be an ugly crier, too.

'I miss our old life, Marianne.' He whispered the words.

'Brian, I don't think you—'

'We had such an ordered, calm, comforting life. Didn't we?'

For a moment, Marianne allowed herself to remember. Their home. The white linen couch. A three-seater so they could sit at either end and stock their books and paperwork and the remote control in the middle. A Thai takeaway on Friday nights. A nature programme on the television. Walking down Howth pier. The throw cushions on their bed. Their pyjamas folded neatly under their pillows. The water in the tank always warm when you wanted to have a shower.

'The sale of our old house fell through,' said Brian then. 'Did you know that? It's back on the market. You could sell Ancaire and buy it back. I know how much you loved that place.'

The news came at her like a defibrillator against her chest, her heart leaping inside her. She had done her best to put the house on Carling Road behind her. 'Move on,' Rita had told her. 'It's time.' Maybe this was what she had meant? Selling Ancaire? Buying her old house back?

Her home.

'Marianne?' She turned and saw Hugh. 'I just came to let you know that Pearl says she's going to drag you back by your hair if you don't return immediately.'

'Oh, yes, fine,' said Marianne. The three of them stood there for a moment. Then Hugh extended his hand. 'Hugh McLeod,' he said in his enormous voice that carried around the entire graveyard.

'Inside voice,' shouted Shirley and he grinned, prompting his vivid green eyes to disappear into slits on his face.

Brian's body jerked up and down with the strength of Hugh's handshake. It was horrifying to watch. Brian gaped up at Hugh when Hugh released him. 'You're so enormous and vibrant,' he said helplessly.

'And you are?' enquired Hugh with a twitch of a smile.

'This is Brian,' said Marianne.

'We used to be together,' said Brian, 'and then I wrecked everything.' He bowed his head, ran his hands through his – thinning, Marianne couldn't help noticing – hair.

Hugh glanced at her with his eyebrows arched. She put her hand on Brian's arm. 'Take care, Brian,' she said.

Brian lifted a hand in a sort of exhausted goodbye. Marianne turned and made her way back to Aunt Pearl and the endless line of people and the germ-ridden hand-shaking.

As she resumed her position – 'Thanks for coming, yes, Rita would be delighted with your rig-out, no, just donations to Sister Stan at Focus Ireland. Rita would really appreciate that' – she saw Hugh lead Brian out through the gate and up the road towards the car park.

Chapter 38

Nobody was in form for the protest at Shirley's house the following week. After the suddenness of Rita's death, the flurry of arrangements and then the fanfare of the funeral, everything felt sluggish. A deep-seated lethargy settled into the cracks at Ancaire, infecting all who passed through. This was not helped by the weather, which had turned, just as Pearl had said it would. It was cold and wet, the wind whipping around the house, a wicked temper of a wind, everybody having to speak louder than usual to be heard over the battalions of rain that flung itself in slants against the worn-out windows.

Marianne was worried sick about Patrick, whom she had only glimpsed sporadically since the day of Rita's funeral.

In desperation, when a whole day had passed and she hadn't laid eyes on him, she phoned Agnes.

'Hello?' Agnes' voice was as quiet as Marianne had expected. Almost a whisper.

'I was . . . looking for Patrick?'

'He's not here.'

'Do you know where he is?'

'No.'

She never asked who Marianne was or why she wanted to know where Patrick was.

'Agnes is so weird,' she complained to Aunt Pearl in the kitchen after she hung up.

Aunt Pearl was not herself either. 'She's just shy,' she said, instead of using the golden opportunity to go for Agnes' jugular. To bitch about her to her heart's content. Marianne had handed the opportunity to her on a platter and all she could do was make a benign comment about shyness?

Things were bad.

In the absence of anything else, Marianne flung herself into her routine, grateful that there was a routine that she could fling herself into. She clung to it, insisting on collecting the Get-Well-Sooners every day, rain or shine.

Mostly rain, it seemed.

They complained roundly.

'What's the point?' moaned Bartholomew.

'You've got your new job next week to look forward to,' Marianne reminded him.

Bartholomew shrugged.

'I can't see any point either,' said Freddy.

'There is none,' declared Shirley.

Even Ethel, looking apologetically at Marianne, said, 'I'm sorry to say, I'm unconvinced of the point of anything myself.'

The Jeep cut out at a junction and Marianne sat there, waited for the driver of the car behind to blare his horn.

He didn't, just sat behind her and waited as she turned the key in the ignition, then stepped on the accelerator. One short pump followed by two long ones. The engine coughed, spluttered, then caught. She drove away and the driver in the car behind followed suit, slow as a funeral procession. If he had leaned out his window and mumbled, 'What's the point?' Marianne would not have been surprised.

Back at Ancaire, Marianne made tea, glad of something to do. She no longer had to think about who wanted what type of tea, in what cup, with what kind of milk, if any. It was ingrained in her muscle memory now. A muslin bag of peppermint tea in a delicate china cup for Ethel. Marianne was careful to leave the string hanging from the top of the cup so Ethel could fish the bag out when the tea was strong enough. Pop it back in if she decided on a refill.

PG Tips for Bartholomew and Freddy, in the Chippendales mug and Mr Neat cup respectively.

Marianne nearly gave Shirley a cup of Barry's in her #mefuckingtoo mug, just to hear her roar, 'Blueshirts' but she decided against it because . . . what if Shirley didn't roar, 'Blueshirts'? What would be the point then? Of anything?

She made a tray of shortbread. She thought shortbread might be an easy one to begin with.

It was dry. It didn't crumble when Marianne cut it but rather snapped, and the pieces, when she arranged them on a plate, were of wildly contrasting shapes and sizes.

When Bartholomew and Freddy didn't argue over whose slice was bigger, Marianne felt her spirits, already flagging, sink lower.

'We should talk about the protest,' she said, in an artificially bright voice when she cleared away the cups and plates and returned from the kitchen.

'Well, I'm all set,' said Shirley.

'Are you?' said Marianne, astonished but relieved.

'Yeah, I've got all our stuff packed up,' said Shirley. 'Three suitcases. One for me, one for the boys and one for *Star Wars* merchandise. The amount of lightsabers those fellas have. If we're ever invaded by the Dark Side, we'll be grand.'

'Where are you going to go?' said Ethel, fearfully, with no mention of Shirley's fighting spirit or its whereabouts.

Shirley shrugged. 'I asked Mam if I could move into her flat for a while.'

'Rita said you could stay here,' said Marianne. 'At Ancaire.'

Shirley shook her head. 'But Ancaire is yours now, isn't it? You'll be selling up.'

Everybody looked at Marianne and she felt the weight of their stares. 'Developers would pay a pretty penny for the land, I dare say,' said Bartholomew with authority.

'All good things must come to an end,' said Ethel, lifting her chin and doing her best stiff upper lip.

'Will you?' asked Freddy gently. 'Sell up?'

Marianne shook her head. 'I . . . don't know,' she said. 'I . . . haven't really had time to think about . . . anything.'

Everybody nodded. They understood that much.

They discussed the protest. There was a local councillor who had promised to come. A Green. But he had promised to come to the last one and then had made his excuses, late in the day. Still, he was the only politician who had responded to the blanket invitation Patrick had emailed a few weeks ago, so that was something, Marianne supposed.

'I emailed everyone who signed our petition at the first protest,' said Freddy proudly.

'Did you get any responses?' asked Bartholomew.

'None,' admitted Freddy.

The man behind the counter of the local Chinese take-away said he'd come. 'Who's going to eat my chicken balls and curry chips if you move away?' he'd said to Shirley.

Bartholomew's troupe at the amateur dramatic society said they would definitely come. 'But they're actors,' said Bartholomew shaking his head. 'So they probably won't.'

'Hugh is cutting hair at the nursing home in Lusk tomorrow,' said Ethel. 'He said he'd make it to Shirley's if he could but . . .' She trailed away. Everybody nodded grimly. They'd seen the amount of blue rinse Hugh went through when he went to the nursing homes. He'd be there for the day and possibly much of the night.

Marianne felt equal measures of relief and disappointment. She wouldn't have to feel that feeling in the pit of her stomach when she saw him. It was an uncomfortable feeling. Like indigestion. She wished she could just put a bottle of Gaviscon on her head and be done with it.

But Hugh would be good at a protest, Marianne felt. The size of him, for starters. He could not be ignored. The timbre of his voice. It sounded like the voice of someone who could bellow a chant.

'Don't forget Patrick,' declared Freddy. 'He'll be there for sure.'

Marianne didn't share Freddy's certainty but, in a room filled with such toxic amounts of pessimism and, yes, hopelessness, Freddy's declaration was like a pinprick of light in the dark. Marianne reached for it, smiled so widely at Freddy that he took a physical step back and tripped over George.

George seemed to be the only one left that Marianne could rely on, stopping only briefly outside Rita's bedroom to paw at the door and sniff at the air, before following Marianne along the landing towards the stairs.

At night, the kitchen seemed unbearably quiet and tidy without the clatter of Rita's heels against the floor, preparing food for the following day, the bubble of one of her concoctions simmering on the hob, the collection of wooden spoons she used, spooling their wares in puddles along the counter. 'Try this one, Marnie,' she'd say. 'I've used basil instead of rosemary. I think you'll like it.'

Marianne had tried them all in the end.

Now, all she could hear was the creak of Aunt Pearl's bed as she tossed and turned, trying to find a position she could sleep in, the fumbling tick and tock of the grand-father clock in the hall, and the wind. Always the wind, wailing around the house like a lament.

She could leave. The thought presented itself at odd times. Especially on nights like these with the wind and the clock and the dark, empty kitchen.

She could leave.

Sell Ancaire.

But what about Aunt Pearl? She had her savings and Rita had bequeathed her the *How to . . .* books. She could rent an apartment in Skerries, maybe? Or even buy one, with the surplus left over from the sale of Ancaire and the purchase of the house on Carling Road. But Marianne couldn't imagine Aunt Pearl accepting what she would deem to be 'charity'.

And Marianne couldn't imagine Aunt Pearl anywhere that wasn't Ancaire.

Then there was Patrick. Technically, he was fine. He had his home and his business. Perhaps he would be glad if Marianne sold the house. It seemed clear that he was not interested in Ancaire. Not without Rita.

Marianne bristled. She could scarcely remember her old life, when she didn't have anybody to worry about other than herself.

Marianne looked up the house on Carling Road online. It was being sold furnished. There it was, exactly as she had left it, all her possessions still there, in the same place as she had left them, as if they were waiting for her to return. As if it was just a matter of time.

She clicked through the rooms, all of which were painted a uniform magnolia. Everything looked smaller than she remembered. She zoomed in on the venetian blinds that guarded each window, inspected them. The slats always managed to collect layers of dust at an exponential rate. Marianne had calculated the perfect downward angle for the blinds early on, which had the joint benefit of protecting the furniture from sun damage and compromising the view of passers-by. Now, they were open much too wide and Marianne winced at the clash of the white daylight against the magnolia paint. It made the place seem sort of . . . unlovable. Marianne shook herself. All she had to do was pull the cord and reposition the blinds and the house would look the way it always had when she had lived there. A haven. A place where she didn't have to consider anybody else.

Or listen to the melancholic shuddering of the wind about the house. After Brian left her, there were nights when Marianne sat in the dark and listened and listened, but all she could hear was the machinations of her own body.

It had been her haven for so long.

Maybe it could be again.

Chapter 39

Marianne held her placard high over her head, just like Bartholomew had shown her, that first time. It read, 'There's no place like home.'

She stood in the middle of a ragged line, made up of Ethel, Bartholomew, Freddy and Shirley. Also George, who leaned against Marianne's legs.

Marianne roared, 'Power to the people.' A magpie, ripping a discarded chip bag apart on the path, squawked and fixed her with its cold, black eyes.

One for sorrow. Marianne tried not to see it.

'Do we have to sing that one again?' said Freddy, moving his placard from one hand to the other.

''Cos the people got the power,' Marianne sang, louder this time.

'My throat is sore,' said Bartholomew, pawing at his neck.

'Tell me can you hear it,' shouted Marianne.

'I'm afraid my arms are aching,' said Ethel, apologetically

lowering her placard. 'And my feet.' She had forgotten her little fold-up stool.

'Getting louder by the hour,' said Marianne.

'This is hopeless,' said Shirley, pitching her placard on the ground and sitting on it.

Marianne lowered her arms. It was true that the situation did appear to be devoid of hope. The absence of Rita was proving an obstacle that nobody seemed willing or able to overcome.

Without her, they were falling apart like their placards earlier, during a brief but intense deluge of rain.

No journalists, no photographers, no bloggers.

No politicians. Not even a lowly councillor. Or the man from the Chinese takeaway.

Of Patrick, there was no sign either. Marianne had called to his house, rang his phone. She had been sure he would step up for them today. But he had gone to ground.

Very few motorists or pedestrians passing by offered a beep of a horn or a wave of a hand to cheer them.

The landlord was due at two o'clock.

Shirley was due to hand over the keys to him.

The boys were due home from school at half two.

Bartholomew's stomach rumbled like thunder.

'Will we have lunch?' said Marianne, thinking food might cheer them. Although probably not, as she had been in a hurry earlier and hadn't had time to go to Rita-style lengths. Inside the bag she had brought were a few cheese sandwiches, a bag of apples and a packet of Hobnobs. These meagre offerings would serve only as a stark reminder of what they were doing without.

Who they were doing without.

They ate the cheese sandwiches in the garden, grateful for any distraction from the hopelessness of their situation.

And it was fairly hopeless, Marianne had to concede. She checked her watch. Ten to two. She looked at the house, across which hung a banner – a bed sheet that Pearl had agreed to stitch – that read, 'Homes are for life, not for profit.'

She looked at the Get-Well-Sooners. Even if they managed to rouse themselves back into a line with their placards held aloft, what difference would it make?

The lure of these dismal thoughts was strong. Wouldn't it be so much easier to admit defeat and throw in the towel? Be done with it?

Marianne threw the remains of her cheese sandwich towards the magpie, now strutting around a drain. He grasped it in his beak and flew away.

'One in flight is worth two in sight,' said Ethel, absently.

'Is that true?' Marianne asked.

Ethel nodded.

'Two for joy,' said Marianne. 'Isn't that right?'

Ethel smiled. 'Yes, dear,' she said.

'It's a sign.' Marianne jumped up from the picnic blanket Ethel had insisted they sit on, to ward off all ills but most especially, colds in the kidneys. She ran to the Jeep, opened the back and yanked her handbag out. Her phone was at the bottom of it. She rang Patrick's number again. This time she left a message. 'Patrick, it's Marianne. This is urgent. I need the chain you use to lock your bike. I'm at Shirley's. Thank you. This is urgent. Did I say that already? Okay, bye.'

She hung up and threw her phone back inside her bag,

slammed the Jeep door. She steeled herself. The Get-Well-Sooners eyed her cautiously.

'Are you all right, Marianne?' asked Bartholomew, eating the crusts that Freddy had peeled off his sandwich.

'Do you have your phone with the fancy camera?' Marianne asked him.

'Yes,' said Bartholomew slowly. 'Why?'

'Can you get it?'

'Surely you're not thinking of . . .'

'Start filming.' Marianne bent down and reefed off one of her runners, threw it into the garden. Peeled off her sock. The ground was soggy and cold against her bare foot. She pulled off her other runner, yanked off her other sock, reached for the waistband of her trackpants, pushed them down her legs.

'You wouldn't,' said Freddy, alarmed.

'You'll catch your death, my dear,' said Ethel, as the trackpants went sailing past Bartholomew's head, snagging on the edge of the splintered, wooden awning over the front door.

'This is a respectable neighbourhood,' said Shirley, smirking as Marianne wrestled herself out of her anorak, her fleece, Brian's ancient T-shirt with the Rubik Cube on the front, its colours dull and faded now. She tossed it in the air.

Now she was standing in Shirley's front garden in a white bra and a black pair of knickers.

She would have worn matching ones. If she'd been thinking straight. Which she clearly wasn't. And anyway, what difference did it make, since she was taking them off anyway.

She was taking them off.

Was she?

Was she really going to do this?

She clenched her eyes tight shut. Someone tapped her arm. 'Excuse me, love?' She opened her eyes. It was the postman, handing her an envelope. He looked wary. 'Number three, yeah?' he said, nodding towards Shirley's front door.

'Eh, yes,' said Marianne, clamping one arm across her bra and accepting the envelope with her free hand. 'Thank you.'

He mounted his bicycle and rode away.

The Get-Well-Sooners cheered as Marianne tossed the envelope at Shirley and grappled with the catch of her bra. 'Do you need some help with that, Marianne?' said Freddy, taking a brave step forward. 'I've had a lot of experience in that department.'

'Yeah, right,' screeched Bartholomew.

'I'm talking about my job,' said Freddy crossly. 'Costume hire, remember?' He shook his head. 'I've obviously never undressed a woman in a . . . a romantic way since I . . . I'm a . . . gay man.' He seemed as shocked as everybody else by the declaration. He said it again, louder this time, as if he were making sure. 'Actually,' he said then, 'for the purposes of full disclosure, I should say that I am a gay alcoholic.'

'My dear boy,' said Bartholomew, shaking his head in something like wonder. 'I commend you for your honesty.'

They all swarmed around Freddy, taking turns to hug and kiss him. 'We're so proud of you, Freddy dear,' said Ethel, beaming at him.

Shirley thumped his arm. 'I think you'll make a great gay, Freddy,' she said. 'No offence.'

'None taken,' said Freddy, beaming.

'Eh, hello?' Marianne shouted over at them. 'I'm naked over here.'

They all looked at her. She had taken the balloons that Sheldon and Harrison had affixed to the front door and was using them and her placard to cover as much of herself as she could manage.

Which wasn't much.

'You got your bra off,' said Bartholomew. 'Well done, Marianne.'

'I'm definitely gay,' said Freddy, studying Marianne's breasts. 'Because I feel nothing.'

'Way to make a lady feel special,' said Marianne.

'What about your hat?' Shirley asked.

Marianne grinned as she pulled it off and flung it in the air. It skidded onto the roof of the Jeep.

It was too late to feel embarrassed.

Much too late.

Marianne turned round, moving the placard behind her now so that it shielded her bottom from the world in general and the Get-Well-Sooners in particular. She marched to the front door, opened it. 'Stand in a line in front of the door,' she told the others. 'I'll lock it from the inside.'

'There's a Velux window in the boys' room,' Shirley told her. 'You can get out to the roof through that.'

'What am I doing?' said Marianne, hesitating.

'You're doing great,' said Freddy.

'And the camera loves you darling,' shouted Bartholomew from behind his phone.

Upstairs, Marianne stood on a chair and poked her placard out through the skylight. She tied the strings attached to the balloons around her wrists and hoisted herself through the narrow opening, panting hard from the exertion.

The pitch of the roof was steeper than Marianne had imagined. Also higher than it had looked from the safety of the ground. Maybe fifteen metres. With terminal velocity an average of 200km/h, it would take her . . . she worked out the answer swiftly, although perhaps not as swiftly as she would hit the ground, were she to slip. The mathematical distraction did her no good whatever.

From below, George's frantic barking as he sprang up and down on his hind legs, as if trying to reach her. The others looked smaller from up here, all of them peering anxiously at her, issuing warnings and encouragement.

The chimney stack seemed very far away.

'You can do it, Marianne,' called Ethel, cupping her hands around her mouth to amplify her voice.

Marianne held the handle of the placard between her teeth and used the roof tiles for purchase as she crawled on her hands and knees to the ridge. When she got there, she clung to it and closed her eyes, pieced herself together.

She arranged herself so that her bottom was balanced on the ridge with her legs dangling down either side.

It was not a comfortable position.

Marianne used her hands and feet to inch her way along, the handle of the placard now tucked under her arm. The relief that flooded her when she reached the chimney was like a spring tide, deep and vast, and she wrapped her arms tight around the stack, closed her eyes and concentrated on quietening her breath.

From below, the sound of singing.

Power to the people.

The Get-Well-Sooners were singing. Together. Their voices loud and strong and getting louder and stronger as the song progressed. It cheered Marianne enormously to hear them. She thought she might whoop if there was any breath in her body. Soon she was able to open her eyes although she could not bring herself to stand up. Not yet.

The landlord arrived promptly at two, as he had specified, in a black Range Rover with tinted windows. He emerged from his car with a degree of wariness. He was younger than Marianne had expected. Somewhere in his thirties, carrying an attaché case and wearing a tight black suit. The back doors of the Range Rover opened simultaneously and two enormous men emerged, in matching black suits and white shirts.

The landlord had brought hired goons.

Marianne stood up, clung on to the chimney stack with one hand as she raised the placard with the other, the balloons bobbing and swaying around her.

'Power to the People,' she began and from below, the Get-Well-Sooners took up the refrain.

'What is going on here?' demanded the landlord.

'I should think it's perfectly obvious, you brute,' said Ethel, before bellowing, 'The people got the power,' straight into his face.

'I don't want any trouble,' said the landlord, taking a step back.

'Leave me and my family alone and there won't be any,' said Shirley.

'This is my property,' said the landlord. 'I'm entitled to do whatever I like with it.'

'This eviction is illegal and you know it,' said Bartholomew, now training his phone camera at the man's face. 'You refused to give Shirley a lease, you've raised the rent several times without any notice and you're not registered with the Private Residential Tenancies Board. We checked, so don't bother denying it.'

'You better not be recording me,' the landlord shouted, making a lunge for Bartholomew's phone. Bartholomew performed a slick side-step. 'And may I add,' Bartholomew went on, 'the wallpaper in the front room is an absolute disgrace. It positively screeches at that hideous green carpet.'

George jumped around the hired goons, making dives at their ankles as if he was going to bite them, which of course he would never do. But the goons were not to know that. They shouted as they twitched this way and that, and it was amusing to watch, Marianne had to admit, from her elevated position on the roof.

A car drove down the road and stopped outside the house. It was Aunt Pearl, looking mutinous, although Marianne hoped that was because she always looked mutinous and not because she had caught sight of Marianne. Not yet. The passenger door opened and Patrick emerged with the chain he used to lock his bicycle against lampposts. Marianne hoped it was long enough to secure her to the chimney stack. She felt precarious. And cold.

Aunt Pearl drove further up the road to park.

'Patrick,' Marianne shouted, waving at him. 'Up here.'

Patrick didn't react, adversely or otherwise, when he worked out where Marianne was situated. 'I'll come up to you,' he said, doing his best to make his voice heard above the chanting and the barking and the shouting.

'I've locked the door,' she shouted.

'I'll get the spare key from Shirley.'

'Be careful of the landlord. That's him there, in the cheap suit.'

This attracted the landlord's attention and he looked up, his eyes widening as he saw her. 'I'm calling the police unless you get down from there,' he said. 'And, for your information, this suit cost a thousand euros.'

'You were robbed,' said Shirley.

'Go ahead and call the police,' said Freddy, sheltering behind Bartholomew's bulk. 'We'll film you while you do it,' he added.

'Get that camera out of my face,' the landlord shouted at Bartholomew.

Patrick's head poked through the skylight. He lifted himself effortlessly through the window, walked along the roof towards her.

'Please be careful,' said Marianne. 'Rita would haunt me for ever if anything happened to you.'

Carefully, he reached around her and secured her to the chimney stack with the chain. 'Is that comfortable?' he asked when he was finished and Marianne couldn't help laughing at the absurdity of the question. After a while, Patrick laughed too.

It was good to hear it.

A warm feeling expanded in Marianne's chest. Which was strange, given how cold she was.

'Do you want my jacket?' asked Patrick.

Marianne shook her head, her teeth chattering. Patrick leaned over and rubbed her arms vigorously with his hands. His hands were warm. 'Rita would be proud of you,' he said softly.

'She'd be proud of you, too,' said Marianne.

'Marianne Gwendoline Cross, what on earth do you think you're doing?' Aunt Pearl, walking into Shirley's garden, had clocked Marianne's position and state of undress.

'I'm protesting this illegal eviction,' shouted down Marianne.

'I fail to see why you can't do it with your clothes on,' snapped Aunt Pearl.

'I'm trying to go viral.'

'Go where?'

'Bartholomew, you explain,' Marianne roared. She turned to Patrick. 'You should get down,' she said.

He shook his head. 'I'm staying,' he said, settling himself along the ridge in a more permanent position.

'I wish I could hug you but I'm too afraid to let go of the chimney,' said Marianne.

'You can hug me later,' said Patrick.

They started singing 'We Shall Not Be Moved'.

People stopped and stared. After a while there was quite a crowd, gathered outside the house, along the footpath, spilling out onto the road, coming up the driveway. Marianne's voice was hoarse from the slogan-shouting and singing, but she kept it up, buoyed along by Patrick beside her and the others below, with George barking intermittently.

'Marianne? Is that you?' A familiar voice reached her. Marianne looked down, into the crowd but couldn't see the source of the voice. Then she saw the buggy. The double buggy. With the babies inside.

The twins.

'What on earth are you doing?' Brian could not have looked more incredulous. Marianne couldn't blame him.

'Hi,' she called, waving down at him. 'How are you?'

'Eh, fine,' he said.

'And the babies? Still colicky?'

'Ah, yes, although not as bad as before.'

'That's good,' said Marianne.

One of the twins started to cry and Brian reached down and picked up a soother, which had popped out of the baby's mouth, put it in his own mouth, sucked vigorously on it, then stuck it back into the child's mouth. Marianne was certain that this did not conform to the surely exacting hygiene requirements of brand-new human beings.

The baby kept crying. Brian jiggled the buggy up and down.

'Brian,' she roared down at him, 'remember what you said? The other day? About me, selling Ancaire? Buying back our old house?'

'Eh,' said Brian. 'Vaguely.'

'Well, I'm not going to do that.'

'Right.'

'And I want you to know something else too.'

'Okay.' Brian looked nervous.

'Don't worry, it's nothing bad.'

Brian did not look convinced.

'I just want you to know that you were right,' said

Marianne. 'When you left me. Our relationship was just
. . . it was wrong. I was with you for all the wrong reasons.
I was just . . . I was scared of everything and I thought you
were a safe bet.'

'Oh,' said Brian, slowly. 'Right.'

'And I think you'll be fine, you know,' Marianne went
on. 'With Helen. When the babies stop being colickly.'

'Do you really think so?' Brian looked suddenly hopeful.

Marianne nodded. 'Yes,' she said. 'I do.'

Brian was saying something else but Marianne could
only see his mouth working. His words were swallowed in
a wail of sirens as two police cars scorched down the road,
skidding to a halt outside Shirley's house.

Both of the babies were crying now.

'I'd better go,' Brian mouthed, jiggling the buggy harder.
She smiled as he turned and walked away, pushing the
enormous buggy with his back bent, the babies shrieking.

The policewomen had loudspeakers and ordered the
crowd to get off the road, move away from Shirley's
house. They spoke to the landlord and he pointed at the
roof and they looked up and saw Marianne and Patrick.
They turned back to the landlord, who was gesticulating
wildly. One of the policewomen pointed to his attaché case
and he lifted it, used his leg, bent at the knee, as a table
on which to place it, open it. He took out a sheaf of papers,
rifled through them, his mouth working furiously.

After a while, he looked up, with a practised and
charming smile. The policewoman did not return his smile
but spoke briskly, shaking her head as she did. Marianne
could see her mouth the words, 'I'm sorry,' but she didn't
look sorry.

A cheer from the Get-Well-Sooners in the garden. Marianne craned her neck. 'What's going on?' she called down.

More cheering. They couldn't hear her. She looked at Patrick. 'Can you make out what's happening?'

'I'll go and check,' he said, moving along the ridge towards the skylight.

'Be careful,' Marianne said, tightening her grip on the chimney.

Patrick nodded. 'I'll be back.'

It was maybe the most comforting thing in the world, Marianne thought. To know that he would be back.

To know that he had her back.

And she had his.

They were family, after all.

'Is it yourself, Marianne Cross?' A roar from below. She swiped the balloons out of her way and peered down. Oh good Christ, it was Hugh, towering over the crowd, which seemed to part for him.

'I hardly recognised you without your hat,' he shouted.

She rolled her eyes like Shirley. 'Funny,' she said. 'What's going on down there?'

Hugh shrugged. 'The landlord can't find the lease agreement.'

'That's because there isn't one.'

'Aye, I know,' said Hugh, with his huge grin.

'Does that mean Shirley can stay?'

'For the moment, I think, yes.'

'For the moment?'

'Yes. For the moment.'

Marianne whooped. A loud whoop that attracted even more

attention. In the street, people were pointing and staring.

She didn't care. She raised the placard high and whooped instead.

For the moment. That wasn't bad. It was actually pretty all right. In Rita's world, that was all anyone ever had. The moment. The one happening right now.

The placard slipped out of her grip and fell off the roof. Hugh caught it in his hand.

'Thank you,' she shouted at him.

'I've to go back. There's more blue rinsing to be done at the nursing home,' he said. 'Will you be all right?'

Marianne nodded. 'I'll be fine.' She was pretty sure she would.

She watched him hug all the Get-Well-Sooners and Patrick and even Aunt Pearl. She watched as he walked out of the garden, headed up the road towards his car, his thick, red hair streaming behind him like a mane.

She took an almighty breath and shouted, as loud as she could, 'Hugh.'

He stopped and turned. 'Yes?'

'Do you still want to go on a date?' she roared.

'With you?' he shouted.

'Eh, yes.'

'Okay,' he roared back.

'Just okay?' yelled Marianne.

'Better than okay,' he said. He smiled at her before he got into his car.

From below, the Get-Well-Sooners cheered and, from the rooftop, Marianne joined in.

The landlord and his hired goons returned to the Range Rover and roared off in it. The policewomen asked Marianne if she needed assistance getting down and she told them no. She felt they'd done enough. They waved at her and left. The crowd, bored now, dispersed and the Get-Well-Sooners formed an orderly line across the garden and peered up at Marianne.

Bartholomew and Freddy were holding hands.

'Are you coming down from there?' asked Shirley.

'I'm not sure I can.'

'I'm on my way,' said Patrick, moving towards the house.

'Aren't you cold?' said Ethel, shivering in her thick wool coat.

Marianne grinned. 'It's like Rita says,' she said. 'Nothing like the cold to make you feel alive.'

And she did.

Read on for a taste of Rita's recipes, a Q&A with Ciara, and reading group questions.

Rita's Recipes

Patrick's Flourless Brownies with Orange and Cardamom

It may not surprise you to know that I was a reluctant student but every Saturday after my arrival at Ancaire, Rita insisted on teaching me how to bake. She said there wasn't a problem in the world that couldn't be eased by stirring a pot of melting chocolate and butter. Turns out she was right.

Ingredients
    250g dark chocolate (at least 70% cacao)
    250g butter
    50g cocoa powder
    2tsp orange essence
    200g caster sugar
    3 large free-range eggs, beaten
    120g ground almonds
    8–10 cardamom pods, seeds removed and crushed in a
pestle and mortar

Method
Preheat the oven to 160°C.

Use a butter paper to grease an 8" by 8" square tin. Then, line it with parchment paper.

Melt the chocolate and butter in a heavy-bottomed saucepan slowly.

Remove from the heat and mix in the orange essence, sugar and cardamom.

Leave to cool, then add the eggs and ground almonds.

Transfer the mix to the prepared tin and bake in the oven for 30–35 minutes.

Allow to cool completely before dividing into squares.

Aunt Pearl's Spicy Roast Butternut Squash Soup

Just because I do not cook does not mean I cannot. Follow these instructions to the letter.

Ingredients
    1 butternut squash (do not discard the seeds)
    2 leeks
    2 carrots
    2 sticks of celery
    2tbsp butter
    1 red chilli
    1 clove of garlic
    1tsp cumin
    3tbsp of good quality olive oil
    1l hot chicken stock

To garnish:
    Crème fraîche
    Roasted squash seeds
    Chopped flat-leaf parsley

Method
Firstly, prepare your *mise en place* and if I have to explain

what that is, may I suggest you remove yourself from the kitchen before you do yourself an injury.

Preheat your oven to 200°C.

Wash, peel, and remove the pith and seeds from the butternut squash, place on a roasting dish with the olive oil, cumin and sea salt, ensuring that each chunk gets a good coating. Roast in the oven for exactly 25 minutes.

Meanwhile chop the celery, carrots, and leeks, *mirepoix* style.

Heat a large, heavy-bottomed saucepan and add the remaining tbsp of olive oil and butter.

Add the vegetables and sweat slowly, covering them with parchment paper. Secure a lid on the pot. Leave for precisely 30 minutes.

Add the chilli, garlic and roasted squash to the pan.

Pour in the chicken stock.

Bring to the boil and permit to simmer for 10 minutes.

If you insist on blending the soup, you could use one of those noisy, new-fangled electric blenders. I like it lumpy.

To serve, swirl a teaspoon of crème fraîche on top and sprinkle with the roasted seeds and some chopped flat-leaf parsley.

Rita's Socialist Squares

What do we want? Socialist Squares for all! When do we want them? Now!

Darlings! I do realise that all confectionery is equal but, in this instance, I have to agree with and paraphrase Orwell. Some confectionary is simply more equal than others and the Socialist Square is one such sweetmeat. These delicious little squares of soft buttery shortbread, gooey caramel, topped off with lashings of chocolate is my mother's recipe and can be found in her book 'How to . . . Care for Your Sweet Tooth'. She made these delights once a year for our birthday teas and I loved them almost as much as the party itself.

Ingredients
Shortbread base:
  60g icing sugar
  300g plain flour
  175g of unsalted butter (melted)
  Pinch of salt

Caramel:
  1 can of that store cupboard faithful, Carnation condensed milk

180g unsalted butter
40g caster sugar
3—4 tbsp golden syrup

For the top:
100g of cooking milk chocolate

Method
Heat your oven to 150°C.

Make the melt-in-the-mouth shortbread by adding all the ingredients to your mixer and mix until it becomes a dough.

Press the dough into a lined swiss roll tin, I find your hands are best for this job. You should probably wash them first.

Pop in the oven for about 20 minutes but do keep an eye on them as ovens invariably differ. Take them out when your kitchen is filled with the most delicious buttery smell. The shortbread will delight you with its pale golden-brown look.

Next, in a large saucepan (heavy-bottomed is best) add all the caramel ingredients and heat gently until the sugar has dissolved.

Turn up the heat full blast and let this golden concoction boil furiously. Don't neglect it! You must keep stirring, even when you lower the heat and wait for the mixture to cool and thicken. I promise it will be worth it.

Pour the caramel over the shortbread base and allow to cool.

Last bit is to melt the chocolate. I realise that there is an array of high-quality chocolate available and by all means use one if you wish, but cooking choc brings me right back to my childhood at Ancaire. Swirl the chocolate over the caramel and leave to set, if you can.

Enjoy my darlings, preferably with a cup of my wild herbal tea.

Rita's brown soda bread

My grandmother tried to teach me how to make this bread when I was a girl but I'm sorry to say I wasn't all that interested back then. Luckily, she wrote the recipe down. It's a traditional Irish recipe and can require a few attempts before it's just right. Even if, like me, you get it wrong at first, the very act of kneading dough is like meditating. But in a good way. You'll see.

Ingredients
  4 cups (I use Ethel's china cup) of plain flour
  2 cups wholemeal flour
  1 cup of bran
  1tsp of breadsoda
  Pinch of salt
  I cup or so of buttermilk
  Handful of mixed seeds plus extra to scatter on top

Method
Preheat the oven to 200°C.

Sieve the flour into a large baking bowl.

Add in the wholemeal, bran, breadsoda, salt, and seeds. Mix it like you mean it.

Add a splash of buttermilk, a bit at a time. You need the mixture to be not too soggy, not too dry. Add extra flour if it's too soggy, a drop more buttermilk if it's too dry. Don't worry! It's all trial and error, just like life.

Plop out onto a floured service and knead gently.
See? You meditated, didn't you?

Shape the dough into a circular loaf on your lightly buttered baking tray and use the handle of a dessert spoon to draw a cross on the surface of the loaf.

Sprinkle with the remaining seeds.

Pop into oven for 30 minutes, after which turn the oven down to 160°C and bake for another 50 minutes or so.

Remove from the oven, inhale that heavenly aroma and wrap the loaf in a slightly damp tea-towel. Try and leave it to cool awhile. It will be worth it.

Rita's Lemon Melts

This is the very first recipe I perfected when I got sober. It took me a few goes to get it right so don't be disheartened if you don't succeed at first. No matter what happens, there's always the pot to lick.

Ingredients
Shortbread base:
  60g icing sugar
  300g plain flour
  175g of unsalted butter (melted)
  Pinch of salt
  1 tsp fresh grated ginger (optional)
  Zest of 1 lemon (optional)

Lemon Curd:
  Juice and zest of 2 lemons
  50g butter
  100g caster sugar
  5 egg yolks

Method
Heat your oven to 150°C.

Firstly, make the buttery shortbread by adding all the ingredients to your mixer and mix until it becomes a dough as per the Socialist Slices.

Put the dough into a lined swiss roll tin. Use your fingers. They really are the best tools. Also, you can lick them afterwards.

While it's in the oven, you have 20 minutes to make the lemon curd. Here's how:

Slowly heat the butter, sugar, lemon zest, and juice in a heavy-bottomed pot until it's a warm puddle of lemony loveliness.

Separate your eggs. Don't waste the egg whites mind! They will be delicious in a meringue. Or an egg white omelette for a light supper with a fennel and beetroot salad. Sorry darlings, I digress!

Add the egg yolks to the pot and whisk away, taking the pot on and off the heat to ensure the eggs don't do anything awful, like curdle.

Increase the heat slowly until the curd begins to thicken. Once you can coat the back of a spoon with it, give yourself a pat on the back, turn the heat off and allow it to cool completely.

I like to make circular melts, but you could use any shape your heart desires. I use a small cutter about the size of the brass buttons on my faux-mink coat (Aunt Pearl tells me they're 3cm in diameter). I fill up a piping bag with the cooled curd and use a star shaped nozzle to pipe a swirl of lemon curd on each base. Serve straight away and store any leftovers in an airtight tin. Only joking, of course. There won't be any leftovers.

Q&A with Ciara Geraghty

What was the inspiration behind *Make Yourself at Home*?

I've always been interested in the idea of the provident child of improvident parents. What kind of person do two benignly neglectful parents raise? The answer, in this case, is Marianne Cross. In the novel, I centre the action around Marianne and her mother, Rita. The mother/daughter relationship is one that fascinates me. I suppose I have skin in the game, being both. The 'bad mother' is someone who is harshly judged. Society holds these women to a much higher standard than the fathers, who seem to get away with it more often than not. Can people change? Marianne Cross certainly doesn't think so. On behalf of mothers everywhere, I wanted to see if I could persuade her — and perhaps myself — otherwise.

You write about the Irish coastline so beautifully, is it a setting that resonates with you personally?

I moved to a coastal village in north County Dublin when I was eight. From my bedroom window, I could see what my eight-year-old self thought was the sea. It was actually an estuary, but we hadn't done that chapter in geography class yet. Eight is an impressionable age and I was very impressed with my sea-view. The sound of the water, the colours it could assume, the constant movement of it. Even on boring days when there was nothing to do and no-one to play with, there was always the sea to look at through my window. When I grew up and left home, I lived in lots of places and some of them were more inland than I would have liked. I used weekends and bank holidays and annual leave to make my way to the coast. I was like a compass, my needles always pointing seaward. Now that I'm – mostly – grown up, I have settled in a coastal village in north County Dublin about two miles north of where I grew up, as the crow – and the kittiwake and the heron – flies. Life has changed a lot since my impressionable eight-year-old days. Everything, really. Except the sea. Is that why I love it? It is one of the reasons.

What does the writing process look like for you? Has this changed throughout your career?

Well, I'd love to get all 'writery' and say that I repair to a tall tower where I wander around in a kaftan and smoke cigarettes from long, slender cigarette holders and wait for the muse to arrive . . . Now, wouldn't that be grand!

But, no.

Instead, I write at home. In the early days, I wrote at the kitchen table when everyone else had gone to bed. Now, I write in the attic, at a desk, with a laptop, in the daytime. How pedestrian is that? I will say that, for me, the most important part of the process is getting my butt into the seat at the desk. The chair is an all-singing, all-dancing display of ergonomic engineering (it's got wheels!) and this is important because one thing is for sure; I'm going to be sitting on it for a long time. Kaftan and cigarette holders are optional (and rarely employed), but the rule I absolutely insist on is never, under any circumstances, wait for the muse to arrive. I just steel myself and start writing. Even when I don't want to. Especially when I don't want to. Otherwise, I'll convince myself that the words have all dried up and the cupboard is bare.

Have you always wanted to be a writer?

No. When I left school, all I really wanted was to travel and have a flat. Then, when I was thirty-four, I realised that I didn't know what I wanted to be when I grew up. This felt bad, given that I was, technically, grown up. I was an insurance loss adjuster at the time. I had never planned to become one. It just happened. All of a sudden, as I stood on the train platform in the throng, I realised I was in a rut. The realisation settled on me like a dark cloud and followed me around for months. My husband noticed. He said, 'What ails you?' I said, 'I don't know what I want to be when I grow up.' He said, 'But you are — technically — grown up.' I said, 'I know, it's worrying.'

Then, a man fell off a roof in Plunkett College, Whitehall. Don't worry; he sustained only minor injuries. On the plus side, I — as the college's insurance company's loss adjuster at the time — was dispatched to the scene. In the course of my investigation, I spoke to the principal who told me about the college's adult education programme. He gave me a syllabus. I signed up for a creative writing course the following week. Which is when I realised I wanted to be a writer. Immediately.

Who are the three writers who have inspired you throughout your life?

1. Maeve Binchy. They say you should never meet your heroes, but I met Maeve once. She was in a wheelchair by then. I crouched beside her for a photograph and accidentally pressed a button on the arm of the chair, nearly tipping her out. She smiled in the photograph all the same. I still miss her.

2. Margaret Atwood. I am a staunch feminist and it's all Margaret Atwood's fault. I was 15 when I read *The Handmaid's Tale*. As a fairly self-absorbed teen, I would not have recognised the text as the feminist manifesto it is. I read it for the sheer enjoyment of it. It was compelling, terrifying, fascinating. I consumed it like a piece of pop culture but something inside my brain was unfurling. It was small back then but noticeable all the same. Like a tiny splinter sticking out of your skin.

3. Nuala O'Faolain. Being a strict fiction-only-reader, I had to be persuaded to read Nuala O'Faolain's memoir *Are You Somebody?* The book had a powerful effect on me. What drew me in and kept me reading well past my bedtime was the searing honesty of the writing. And then there was the writing itself — clear and accessible — that helped me to

understand the power of words on a page. Reading *Are you Somebody?* was like a call to arms to my thirty-year old self. The one who hadn't started writing yet. The one who was gathering her nerve.

What have you read recently that you enjoyed?

Voices which is an Open Door publication, edited by Patricia Scanlan. It is a book of short stories from a variety of writers, including Christine Dwyer-Hickey, one of my favourites. I am a fan of the short story; the way they can haul you into another world, through a window left ajar. And this collection features twenty-seven of them. What's even better is that all royalties from the sale of the book go to NALA, our National Adult Literacy Agency, who work to support adult literacy and numeracy. The agency is forty years old this year and *Voices* is a lovely way of saying thank you.

Reading Group Questions

- Marianne left Ancaire, her childhood home, when she was fifteen, following a traumatic and tragic incident. She planned never to return. What struck you most about Ancaire? Can you understand why it was difficult for Marianne to come back after so many years?

- Which character in the novel did you relate the most to, and what was it about them that you connected with?

- Marianne is a socially awkward accountant who needs to be in control of every situation, and her mother, Rita, a flamboyant artist and recovering alcoholic who lives by her own rules. How do you feel their differences affected their relationship throughout the novel?

- How did you feel about the ending of the novel? Is it what you expected?

- What would you say about *Make Yourself at Home* when pressing it into the hands of a friend?

- Which of Rita's recipes are you most excited to make and why?

If you enjoyed *Make Yourself at Home*, you'll love *Rules of the Road*, a gripping, emotional, and uplifting novel about the true power of friendship.

The simple fact of the matter is that Iris loves life. Maybe she's forgotten that. Sometimes that happens, doesn't it? To the best of us? All Terry has to do is remind her of that one simple fact.